Also by Alisha Rai

MODERN LOVE
The Right Swipe • *Girl Gone Viral*

THE FORBIDDEN HEARTS SERIES
Hate to Want You • *Wrong to Need You*
Hurts to Love You

THE PLEASURE SERIES
Glutton for Pleasure • *Serving Pleasure*

THE CAMPBELL SIBLINGS SERIES
A Gentleman in the Street
The Right Man for the Job

THE BEDROOM GAMES SERIES
Play with Me • *Risk & Reward*
Bet on Me

THE KARIMI SIBLINGS
Falling for Him • *Waiting for Her*

THE FANTASY SERIES
Be My Fantasy • *Stay My Fantasy*

SINGLE TITLES
Hot as Hades • *Cabin Fever*
Night Whispers • *Never Have I Ever*

First Comes Like

A NOVEL

ALISHA RAI

AVON
An Imprint of HarperCollinsPublishers

P.S.™ is a trademark of HarperCollins Publishers.

HarperCollins books may be purchased for educational, business, or sales promotional use. For information, please email the Special Markets Department at SPsales@harpercollins.com.

FIRST EDITION

Designed by Diahann Sturge

Library of Congress Cataloging-in-Publication Data has been applied for.

ISBN 978-0-06-287815-1 (paperback)
ISBN 978-0-06-305943-6 (hardcover library edition)

21 22 23 24 25 LSC 10 9 8 7 6 5 4 3 2 1

For the girls who are "too much."
(Actually, we're just right.)

Chapter One

Jia Ahmed knew how to make herself look good. Angles, lighting, makeup, clothes, poses, postproduction editing. She could manipulate eternal factors to the point where cameras caught only the best parts of her, the funny, charming, clever, beautiful parts.

They didn't catch the parts like now, when she was so anxious and insecure she was hiding in a bar's bathroom and applying and reapplying her lipstick ten times.

She carefully traced her lips with the pink liquid. *It's perfect.*

Except for the bow of her upper lip, which was blobby. Blast it. Her hands were getting more shaky, not less.

Leave the blob. Leave it!

Like she wasn't a perfectionist when she wasn't meeting a potential love interest. She pulled out yet another makeup wipe and swiped the pink off.

She needed to chill. No need to be nervous, couples met on apps and then in real life all the time. True, this was a little different, given that she was crashing a party to get face time with the man who had slid into her DMs.

What was a girl supposed to do! It had made sense to only talk via text when they'd first started chatting over a year ago, given he lived so far, and they were rarely awake at the same time. Though she'd been smitten, without physical interaction, the conversation had fizzled out after six weeks.

She'd been so busy with everything going on in her life and exploding career, she hadn't really spared him much thought until she got sick a couple months ago. She was recovering, he was across the world; she'd accepted that he wanted to see her face for the first time in person.

But he'd been in America for a week now, within driving distance of her. She'd pressed to see him, but there was always some reason he couldn't.

Do you want to get dinner?

How's life in America treating you? Want to get a drink?

Do you like bowling?

And his responses:

I'd love to, but am tied up with work this week.

We can meet once I get adjusted.

Jet-lagged right now. Rain check?

So she'd done what any normal red-blooded woman would do. She'd used her frightening Google skills to track down where the cast for his new show was having a little party, scored an invitation through her various influencer connections, et voilà. Here she was.

Jia leaned closer to the mirror and applied the lippie again, going slow and steady. Finally, no blobby blobs. She critically inspected the rest of her face for any other possible flaws. She'd gone with a smoky eye for the evening and paired it with a light bronzer and nude lip. Her God-given cheekbones didn't require much contouring, but she'd done a heavy beat tonight regardless. One of her sisters had once accused Jia of using makeup as a shield, but it wasn't that deep. Art had always been her favorite class.

The bathroom door opened and a beautiful redhead walked in. She came to stand next to Jia at the sink, her own compact in hand. Jia gave her a smile and dropped her lipstick in her purse. She washed her hands again, though she'd already done it. One could never wash their hands enough. Plus, it would delay her having to leave the bathroom and put on her big-girl pants. Metaphorically speaking, since she was wearing a dress.

Jia caught the sideways glance the woman gave her, and then the double take. "Hey, do I know you from somewhere?"

A little thrill ran through her, the same thrill she always felt when she was recognized in L.A., a city where half the population was vaguely familiar. Internet famous was a weird thing, one where it was easy to forget that people might recognize her. She spent most of her time filming on her own or with a single cameraperson. There were modeling gigs and sponsorships, but those had dried up lately.

Part of her wished she could feel weary about attention— that was how humble people reacted to that sort of thing, right? But she loved attention, especially now. It was a nice reassurance that her recent mandatory illness-induced social media absence hadn't totally tanked her career.

"You might." Jia used a napkin from the classy stack on

the counter to wipe her hands. "Are you plugged into the beauty side of social media?"

The woman brightened. "You do makeup tutorials! You're that model!"

That model, which was better than *oh you!* or *is that a real job?* "That's me."

"So cool. You're not as tall as I thought you'd be."

Jia resisted the urge to straighten up. When one was five foot nothing in an industry where height was a conventional beauty standard, one grew accustomed to such comments. "Uh, thanks."

"I love meeting influencers. I'm an entertainment reporter." She named an outlet, but Jia had never heard of it. "Can we take a selfie, and can I tag you?"

Something else to delay her crashing a party? "Sure!"

"Oh my gosh, thank you!"

"No problem!" One of the big benefits of this industry was that she got to indulge her love of speaking in exclamation points. "Wait, move like this." Jia scooted so the toilet stalls weren't behind them, but a more flattering red wall.

"Ha, I forgot we were in a bathroom. Do you want to step outside?" the woman asked.

No, Jia did not want to step out of the protective force field that this bathroom was providing. If she stepped out, she might explode from anticipation and anxiety. "Fun fact. Bathrooms often have the best selfie light." Jia feared her smile might be more strained than not, but the woman seemed satisfied with their pic.

"Thanks again," the redhead enthused. "Are you going to the party? I'm covering it. Hoping to snag a pic with Richard Reese."

"I am going to the party." Jia hesitated. If she said the words out loud, maybe she could manifest it. "I'm hoping to meet Dev Dixit."

The woman gave her a blank look. "I don't know him."

"He and his family are kind of legendary in Bollywood. Vivek Dixit? Shweta Dixit? Arjun or Rohan?"

"Nope, nope, nope, nope. Sorry, I bet he's more popular for Indians."

Jia could explain that she was Pakistani American and had known about the Dixit clan despite being not very familiar with Hindi cinema, but she had too much on her mind tonight to sweetly explain geography and the popularity of a foreign film industry to outsiders. "You'll get to know him. Anyway, *Hope Street* is his U.S. debut."

"Ooh cool." The redhead glanced at her phone, her interest exhausted. "See you up there?"

"Yup." She just had to . . . leave the bathroom and take the elevator up. Her new bathroom selfie friend made it look easy.

"You got this," Jia whispered to her reflection, then bounced on her feet and lip-synched a few bars of Destiny's Child. Surely if anything could get her motivated, it was Beyoncé telling her she was a survivor. She was gonna make it. She was a survivor. Keep on surviving.

No, that didn't help. She had never felt like this before,

terrified and excited and nervous. All those feelings separately, yes, she'd had them, but never all together.

Was this what infatuation felt like? Was this what she'd missed all those years when she'd been studiously avoiding distractions?

Jia pulled a wireless earpiece from the hidden pocket of her dress and stuck it in her ear. Then she navigated to her audio files and hit play on the latest one.

"Hi, Future Jia!" came her own cheerful voice in her ear.

If anyone knew that she taped affirmations for herself, she would die. Which was why it was a closely guarded secret, shared only with her twin.

Jia glanced around warily, but the bathroom was empty now. "You're nervous," said Past Jia, "and that's okay. You're meeting Dev face-to-face for the first time tonight, and that's weird."

It was weird, to feel like she'd connected so deeply with someone she'd never even been in the same room with.

"Are you scared you won't feel the same connection when you're physically in the same place?"

Yes.

"Are you scared you're going to hate the sound of his voice? Or he'll hate yours?"

Yes.

"Are you scared he's not even real and this has all been fake?"

"No," she whispered, with a conviction that she knew would cause her older, more cynical roommates to exchange a glance.

One of her many talents was stalking people on the internet, but there hadn't been any stalking necessary here. Dev had messaged her from his official account. She wouldn't have even responded to him if that blue checkmark hadn't declared his authenticity.

You want him to be real so badly, it may be clouding your judgment. That was possible. He'd been kind to her for the weeks she'd been sick and the weeks after, when she'd been too fatigued to get out of bed. His words had given her something to look forward to while she'd been quarantined from her roommates, on the opposite coast from her family.

"It's weird he's being so hesitant about seeing you right now, which is why it's even more important you bite the bullet and get in there. Things don't happen, you have to make them happen."

Yes, that was her mantra.

"Whatever your fears are right now, remember how sweet he is, and the beautiful romantic stuff he's sent you. *Time is nothing but a way to mark the beat of your heart.*"

She straightened and smiled, as she had when he'd said the romantic words. Yes, her roommates could keep their cynicism. She liked him.

Hopefully, he liked her! Liked her for who she was, unconventional and goofy and successful and not humble and an attention seeker. The pretty parts and the not-always-pretty parts. The parts he'd only get to see in real life.

A burst of confidence had her popping her headphone out of her ear. She did one last mirror check for any pesky wrinkles or blobs. She'd decided on a simple gold scarf for her hair today. The material caught the bronzer on her cheeks and matched the gold threads in her black-and-gold dress, and the matching dupatta she'd draped and pinned over her shoulders as a shawl.

She'd worn this dress for a party over a year ago, and it was the reason he'd messaged her that first time. *You look like you were dipped in gold.*

Her smile now was genuine. Of course this would work. He would be excited by this surprise, happy she'd taken matters into her own hands. That was one of the things he'd liked about her, he said. Her assertiveness.

It was time.

Jia took the elevator to the rooftop bar. She got why this was an It Place, with its greenery and flowers wrapped around the chandeliers and dripping off the ceiling. At any other time, she'd be joining the people over at the balcony, taking photos and selfies with all the concentration of an accountant doing taxes. Because for most of them, this was probably their job.

Not tonight. She wanted to speak with him before the party grew too crowded. That way, if it was wonderful, they could talk the night away. If it was terrible, she could escape.

The hostess's gaze flicked over Jia as she approached, and Jia knew what the woman was doing: calculating the cost of her clothes and shoes and cross-referencing it with her de-meanor. There were plenty of important people in L.A. who dressed down. "Hello, I'm here for the *Hope Street* party."

"Lovely. Your name, miss?"

"Jia Ahmed." She surveyed the restaurant. It was still

cool for March, and the windows that surrounded the room were all open, bringing in a nice breeze. Some people were wearing jackets, but Jia was fine in her long-sleeved dress. She'd grown up in the frigid Northeast; she could handle sixty degrees when it was salt-tinged ocean air.

She recognized more than a few faces. This wasn't her first Hollywood party. She got invites fairly regularly since she'd signed her last spokesmodel contract a couple years ago. The guest lists were usually a combination of influencers, young actors, models, sports stars, and Twitterati. Her roommate Katrina had been a model, and she'd told Jia she'd hated these soirees. Jia loved them, every single glittery, slightly fake part of them, from the laughably pretentious people to the gift bags. Ooooh, the gift bags. Dumping those adult goody bags out on her bed after the party and pawing through the loot was a delight, though she usually just gave away most of the stuff to her followers.

Tonight, the gift bag was the second-best attraction, though.

The hostess found her name on her tablet and her demeanor changed, becoming less haughty. "Welcome, Ms. Ahmed."

She'd known she'd be on the list, but impostor syndrome was a struggle. Jia inclined her head in what she imagined a classy gesture to be and tried to glide nonchalantly through the indoor spring wonderland of flowers and lush greenery like she belonged.

The bathroom selfie redhead was here, ordering a drink at the bar. Jia recognized a few of the actors, including the salt-and-pepper Richard Reese, the star of the show, who was animatedly talking to a rapt audience.

She stood up on her tiptoes, though the extra half inch of height wasn't enough to be effective. The crowd around Richard parted, and there he was.

A single spotlight falls on the hero, and the rest of the crowd ceases to exist.

Tall and dark and handsome, he wore a black suit with a stark white shirt and a skinny blue tie. No contouring needed for his face. It was too sharp and angular to be conventionally handsome like the rest of the famous men in his family, but the others could keep their handsome. Stern had its own thing going for it.

His lean lanky body wore that designer suit with casual elegance, like he'd been born to couture, which he had, as the eldest Dixit grandson.

He's far too sophisticated for little old you.

No, he wasn't. He was older than her, yes, thirty-two to her twenty-nine. She didn't have much experience with men, between school and med school and quitting med school and her internet side hustle becoming her main hustle. In her sleuthing, though, she'd discovered little in the way of an excessive or extravagant life for him.

All she wanted to do was gallop toward him eagerly, but she settled on a sedate walk. When she was a couple of feet away, Dev turned his head. Their eyes met, and Jia swallowed the lump of excitement in her throat. "Hello." Her voice was breathier than she'd ever heard it. Almost sexy. Not her usual vibe.

Dev's gaze dipped over her, and a flush worked its way to her cheeks. She could put to rest her worry about the physical attraction, on her end, at least.

Since she'd decided to crash this party, she'd played this scenario out in a dozen different ways. He'd be shocked, delighted, annoyed, angry, panicked.

Not one of those expressions was on his face right now. Which made sense! He was an actor and good at controlling his emotions. Of course he wasn't going to rear back in surprise or wrap her up in an embrace here in public.

"Hello," he said, his voice low, and that was all she needed to nearly swoon. He had such a clipped and sexy accent.

"Hi," she nearly responded, then mentally kicked herself. She'd already said that.

He held out his hand, and she accepted it automatically. His skin was a darker brown than hers, and a scar ran across his thumb. She almost jumped from the spark that leapt between them as flesh met flesh.

"I'm Dev Dixit. And you are . . . ?"

The spark extinguished at the splash of cold reality, and her hand slipped from his. He wasn't possibly going to . . . pretend he didn't know her?

Nobody. Didn't. Know. Her.

Lots of people don't know you.

She hushed her tiny voice of logic. That wasn't what he meant. *He has a reason for this. It's a joke. It's an act, for . . . reasons.*

Her heart supplied excuse after excuse, even though her rapidly growing logic shot them all down. He'd offered her a casual handshake, then asked who she was. If it was an act, he was committed.

She had to know. "Are you serious?"

His hair brushed his high cheekbones. It was longish, carefully cut to frame his face. "I . . . yes. I'm sorry. Have we met?"

She breathed deep, her brain racing. "You— We've been conversing."

"I converse with any number of people, I'm afraid." His smile was painfully polite, showed no teeth. "Apologies. Could I trouble you to give me a reminder?"

What on earth? He'd done this to multiple women? Found them on the internet, sent them messages? Wormed his way into their hearts? Why? Why do that?

"You're really saying you don't know who I am?" Her voice was hoarse.

His smile faded, and wariness replaced the charm in his eyes. He placed his glass of wine on the high-top table between them. "Uh. No. I don't think I do."

The cold ball of anger and panic that shot into her belly was welcome. It was a sharp distraction from the crack of her heart. After he'd written her long blocks of texts about how much he liked and admired her? He was going to do this? She took a step closer, and then another one, until they were only a few inches apart. She'd ignore his tall body and how much bigger he was to focus on this hurdle. "Where's your phone?"

His thick eyebrows rocked up. "I beg your pardon?"

"Give me your phone."

"I think you have me mistaken for someone else, Ms. . . . ?"

Her hands curled into fists. If her mom or sisters had been here, they would have seen the warning signs of her surge of emotions and immediately removed her from the situation, lest her impulsiveness take over her common sense. "I can't believe this," she whispered and was horrified at the pinprick of tears at the corners of her eyes.

Not as horrified as he was, though. He swayed forward, brow creased. "Are you okay?"

No, she was *not*. The kind, occasionally cheesy man who had talked to her during a lonely and vulnerable time in her life was now telling her he had no idea who she was.

"I'm fine." She had to leave. She pivoted on her heel—why had she wasted heels on this man!—but he stopped her.

"Wait, Miss—" He placed his hand on her shoulder, and she was too upset to appreciate this featherlight touch from one of the most famous faces on a subcontinent. She shrugged it off with a sharp jerk and was hauled to a stop by a ripping sound and a tug on her neck.

"Hang on," he said sharply. "I'm stuck on you."

She turned around, her face burning as he raised his arm, his smart watch band caught on the gauzy fabric of her shawl. She instantly took a step back as he took a step closer. "I'm sorry. I don't mean to . . . It'll rip. Let me . . ." He took another step, and she inhaled.

That was a mistake. He smelled exactly how she'd thought he might, clean and fresh. His head lowered as he focused. He had incredibly long lashes. "Almost got it."

"Rip it." *Before I start counting your lashes. Or ripping them out.*

She was feeling a lot of feelings right now, darn it.

"It's a beautiful fabric. I'd rather not."

It was a beautiful piece, one her grandma had brought her from Pakistan, but she didn't care. Humiliation and rejection burned her face. She couldn't resist her heartbreak coming out in her next words, though she hated herself for it. "You told me you'd searched the universe for a woman like me," she said, her voice breaking. "Why are you pretending you don't know me?"

Dev stiffened, but the pocket of silence around them snapped Jia from her turmoil faster than a siren could. She glanced around and found that the people at the bar were watching them, eyebrows raised. *A circle of people observe the heroine's embarrassment while the band plays on.*

The audience included the redheaded reporter—and the phone the woman held in her hands. Oh no. Jia shook her head, the sting of tears frightening her. She hadn't cried in years, and she definitely didn't cry in public. It would ruin her makeup and was extremely off-brand. "Are you done yet?"

He raised his wrist, free of her. "Yes."

"Goodbye."

"Wait—"

She spun around, her wide skirt flaring around her ankles as she half jogged away. She only paused at the table at the exit. "Where's the gift bag?"

She was going to have something to show for this night, damn it, even if it wasn't love.

Jia grabbed the fabric bag the bored employee held out and continued her dash.

The tears started falling by the time she got to the elevator. She jabbed the lobby button and collapsed against the back wall.

Jia, you are being extremely melodramatic right now.

She clutched the goody bag to her chest and let out a small sob. Yeah she was. She was the little piggy who was going to be melodramatic all the way home, too melodramatic to even care that strangers may have observed her embarrassment.

By the time she got to the lobby, she'd at least controlled the more vocal sobs, though the valet still looked at her askance when she handed him her ticket. She pulled out her phone while she waited for her car and scrolled through her voice notes. Why hadn't she thought to record an affirmation for herself in case this didn't work out? Silly optimistic Past Jia.

Either the person she'd been talking to all this time wasn't the man she'd met upstairs, or he was a cold-blooded internet seducer. Which reality was more palatable? Was she a naïve fool or was she a naïve fool?

Or, third option, you're too difficult to be lovable, and he realized that once he saw you.

Jia shook the insecurity out of her head, but it was deep-rooted, waiting for any hint of weakness.

She navigated to her messaging app and clicked on Dev's name. She'd put a heart next to it, during a mushy moment.

She scrolled through the last few messages she'd sent, then typed into the message box. Who the fuck are you???

Three dots immediately popped up, and she waited with bated breath, but the dots went away, and there was nothing.

"Ma'am?"

She swiped her tears and took her keys from the valet, putting a crumpled mound of cash in his hand for a tip. Judging by his effusive thanks, she assumed it was enough.

Her car was as silent as her phone. She cranked the volume of her radio up, until the bass vibrated, and then peeled away from the curb. There were so many thoughts flying around in her head, but right now, the only thing she could stomach deciding was whether she should pick up two or three pints of ice cream on her way home.

Chapter Two

DEV HAD only visited America three times. Once for a wedding, once for a graduation, once for an awards show. He liked the country, but found it a strange place, what with its citizens openly carrying large guns and holding events like pie-eating contests. He hadn't seen them do both those things together yet, though he supposed such a joint event would not be absurd here.

He never thought he'd end up leaving his home in Mumbai to come work in this country, but here he was. He also never thought he'd become utterly preoccupied with a strange woman within the space of time it took for her to walk up to him, but there she'd been.

You told me you'd searched the universe for a woman like me.

Dev quietly closed the door of his flat. He threw his keys in the dish on the foyer table, and winced as the metal met glass. He fished them out immediately and placed the keys on the table runner. The place had come furnished, the owners vacationing somewhere in Barbados. Given his tight finances and his teenage niece, he'd wanted to opt for a less expensive flat without thousand-dollar glass dishes, but his agent had pointed out that a decent address would be beneficial. His main attraction to these Hollywood hotshots was his famous family. He needed to keep the illusion of wealth intact until he was established here. Luckily, they'd gotten the home for a steal.

The muted sounds of the television led him to the living room. Loud snores from the man on the couch punctuated the forgotten Hindi movie on the screen. Dev picked up the remote and clicked it off.

His uncle sat straight up, coming from sleep to waking in a second. Dev didn't jump. The man had been a cab driver in New York for over thirty years, and was quick to wake up from his snoozes.

"Dev?"

"Yes. Sorry Uncle, did I wake you?"

"Not at all." Adil scrubbed his hands over his face. His uncle had just started to get a stoop to his shoulders and silver in his thinning hair. "I was waiting up for you."

Dev perched on the arm of the chair next to the couch. "You didn't have to do that."

"I wanted to."

It had taken some time for Dev to get used to having such a carelessly affectionate paternal figure in his life after so long. His uncle had been so busy scraping together here in America, Dev had only met Adil Khan a handful of times. Retired and newly widowed, his late mother's brother had traveled back to India last year to live with him when Rohan had died and had quickly become an invaluable part of his small household.

"How was the party?"

"Tiring." He'd never been the life of the party, even when he was young. His desire to make small talk and court the other guests was declining in inverse proportion to his age. The rest of his family loved socializing. Rohan had lived for parties.

As usual, he shoved his brother's name out of his head as quickly as it had popped in.

Adil settled into the couch. "Any pretty girls your age?"

"No." He could tell by Adil's eyebrow that he'd answered a little too quickly.

It wasn't a total lie. The girl had been a woman, and she'd been gorgeous, not merely pretty.

He'd noticed her immediately when she'd walked into the room. There weren't many South Asians in the Hollywood crowd, but that wasn't the reason she'd stood out. Though she was petite, she'd carried her shoulders with a bold confidence he'd wished to absorb. From her cheekbones to her dress to her hair covering to her shoes, she'd glinted and glowed like the gold foil that was sprinkled on his favorite desserts.

Another man might have immediately approached her, but he'd never been good at that. He'd averted his eyes, hoping his courage would build if he didn't look at her.

In the end, she'd approached him. A million things had raced through his head, but he'd only been able to fall deep into her warm light brown eyes and stutter out a hello.

Then her warmth had transformed into inexplicable wounded anger. What on earth had he done to inspire a reaction like that? He'd gone over his words a hundred times since she'd stalked away from him, and he couldn't find a single explanation.

You told me you'd searched the universe for a woman like me.

Dev rubbed his thumb against his palm, where her soft dress had imprinted on him as he'd untangled himself from her.

"Dev?"

He clenched his hand. "Yes?"

Adil gave him an assessing look. "Are you okay?"

"Yes, thank you." Dev cleared his throat. "I'm going to head to bed."

"There's a plate in the fridge for you."

He was tempted, but then he remembered the wardrobe fitting he had this week. "I ate at the party." It had only been a few carrot sticks. His stomach was still pretty empty, but Adil's food was delicious and high calorie.

Dev might have been the romantic lead on his show back home, but he hadn't had to stay in tip-top shape. Things were different here, where the pressure to conform to certain beauty standards was more intense.

Adil tsked, like he knew exactly how much food Dev had consumed. "I placed one of those garbage granola bars at your bedside."

Dev smiled, touched. He wouldn't eat the bar, but it was a nice thought. "Thank you. Is Luna . . . ?"

"Asleep? Yes. Or at least, she's in her room."

That twist to Adil's mouth didn't bode well. The last year

had been a long settlement period for all of them. "What happened?"

"I cooked a good healthy dinner for her, and she insisted on Bagel Bites."

Dev had only the vaguest idea of what those were, but he could guess they weren't fresh vegetables and protein cooked by his uncle's loving hands.

"Only, I don't buy such things, so she ordered someone to go to the grocery store and have them delivered. Did you know you can do that from your phone?"

"Yes. Though she shouldn't be doing it."

Adil grunted. "In any case, she made her disgusting food and took it to eat in her room even though I told her we'd eat at the table."

Dev frowned. Luna's most negative moods were characterized by depression or withdrawal, rarely open defiance. She'd been sweet lately, too, growing more comfortable expressing herself with both of her elders.

"She *stomped* away from me." Adil clicked his tongue. "If I had done the same to my uncle, I would have been thrashed."

Dev's lips twitched, despite the seriousness of the situation. Adil's blustering was just that, blustering. The man had fallen in love with his grandniece at first sight. The only person less likely to raise their hand to Luna was Dev.

He checked his watch. He'd gotten home later than he'd hoped. In Mumbai, he had the clout to leave a party whenever he wanted, but he couldn't insult the executives here. "I'll check in on her. You get some rest."

Adil gestured to the television. "I have to finish my show first, but good night."

His uncle would be asleep three minutes after Dev left. "Yes, good night."

He paused outside his niece's room, but all he could hear was the humidifier running. He cracked the door. The light glowing under the blanket winked out. He opened the door wider. There was plenty of light in the room from the moon streaming in and the nightlight he'd installed near the door for him to see.

"Luna," he whispered. "I see you're awake. Can I please speak with you?"

The cover shifted, and out popped a curly dark head. Luna's hair had been much longer, but right before they'd moved, he'd come home to find her standing in the bathroom, black strands all around her feet, scissors in her hand, and a blank expression on her small face. He'd hidden his concern by helping her clean up the bathroom and trim parts of the back she hadn't been able to reach. Once he'd been alone, he'd reached for one of the many books he'd bought on children and grief to assure himself that he hadn't somehow screwed something up.

Luna plopped her phone on the bed and leaned against the headboard. She looked much younger than thirteen, with her tiny heart-shaped face and short bob. She muttered something in Spanish. One thing his brother had done was engage good tutors for Luna. She spoke five languages fairly fluently and could slip in and out of them with ease.

She chose Spanish and French when she wanted to keep

something from him. Joke was on her, however. He'd down-loaded an app for that.

Knock was the only word he could make out, but that was enough. He took a step in. "I should have knocked. I'm sorry."

Even after a year, she still looked bemused when he agreed with her or treated her as an adult, which made him wonder exactly how his brother had treated his daughter. Probably with the same casual distracted affection Rohan had given to most things that weren't acting or women or drugs.

Perhaps if Dev had been around more, had paid attention to her before his brother had died a year ago, he would know more about how Luna'd been raised. A stab of guilt ran through him, a feeling he was so familiar with, it was almost second nature now.

She switched to English. "Thank you." Her manner was stiff and formal.

Internally, he heaved a tired sigh. He hadn't thought getting sudden guardianship of his niece after her father's death left her an orphan would be easy, but he'd been lulled into a false sense of calm over the last month or so.

"You know the rules, though. No phone this late." Monitoring and enforcing cell phone usage was something he did reluctantly. He hated playing the disciplinarian, but he also didn't want his ward to have unlimited screen time. All the experts seemed to agree that wasn't good for developing brains.

"Sorry. The book got good."

He tossed the screen time rule out the window. He couldn't see how limiting reading could ever be good. "What are you reading?"

"Stephen King."

"At night?" He wouldn't police age appropriateness in reading either, though he did wonder if scary tales at night were good for her.

"It's the best time to read it. Did you just get home?"

"Yes." He came to sit on the edge of the bed. "What did you do tonight?" He kept his tone mild and not accusatory.

A muscle ticked in her jaw. That tick had made Vivek Dixit famous back in the golden screen days. "Uncle's mad at me, I guess."

"Why would you think that?"

"Because we had a fight about dinner."

Dev nodded. "I understand you had a disagreement over something called a Bagel Bites."

"It's pizza on a bagel."

"That does sound . . . " American. "Intriguing. But perhaps not as healthy as a home-cooked meal."

"I'm tired of Indian food all the time. Junk food's the best part about coming to America."

He adjusted the teddy bear next to her. In many ways, Luna was becoming a young woman, but she still slept with this ratty blue bear. "That's the only reason you grew upset? You were fed up with the same style of food every night?"

She looked away. "Yeah."

"It wasn't kind of you to snap at Adil Uncle. He loves you very much and he deserves your respect."

Her eyes grew wet, but the tears didn't overflow. "I know. I'm sorry."

"You'll have to tell him that tomorrow." His uncle had the same soft heart as Dev's mother. The man would immediately forgive Luna.

Her throat moved. "I will."

Dev hunched his shoulders, trying to make himself smaller. The last thing he wanted to do was make his niece feel cowed or scared. "Where did you get the money for ordering the food you wanted?"

"Aji gave me a credit card to use for emergencies."

Now it was time for him to control the tic in his cheek. His grandmother. "I don't want you using that card for anything but emergencies," he said quietly. "Real emergencies."

"Okay."

"Perhaps we could go out to dinner, the three of us, when I get home tomorrow. Try some American cuisine. Get out a little and give your uncle a break from cooking. We can do so weekly."

Luna shifted. "That might be nice."

She didn't look especially enthused, which told him the issue wasn't really about the food. Or at least, not entirely about the food. "Sometimes when I'm acting and I have to act sad or angry, I have to think about something that made me sad or angry, and transfer my emotions from there to the scene."

"That's cool."

It wasn't, but he was trying to make a point. "Did something else make you frustrated today? Something other than Bagel Bites?"

She fiddled with her collar. "Maybe."

She had moved on to speaking Hindi now, and he followed her there. "Tell me."

"I want to go to school."

He raised an eyebrow. "You go to school." Her tutor in India had been one of the best, and Dev had kept the woman on, despite the hefty salary she commanded. She taught Luna virtually, willing to accommodate their new time zone.

He opened his mouth, but Luna held up a finger, her words coming fast, like she'd rehearsed them. "I have no real educational structure right now, except for the one my tutor makes up."

"You're two grade levels ahead of your age. Your structure is the four hours you work with your tutor in the mornings, plus any homework she assigns. Is it that you feel as though you don't have a dedicated workspace? I'll buy you a desk." Actually, he quite liked the idea of that, both of them working side by side in his office in the apartment when he wasn't on set.

"Please hold comments until the end."

Not for the first time, he wondered if Luna was actually a too-serious forty-five-year-old businessperson in a child's body. He mimed zipping his lips.

She held up a second finger. "While I do get to participate in many activities, group sports and social events are not possible. I want to join a football team, or play cricket—or baseball, whatever—or be on a fancy dress party committee."

She had a point there. He had no doubt Luna had gotten to do many things her friends didn't, by virtue of being a Dixit, but team sports and the like hadn't been one of them.

He noticed she didn't say theater. She'd demonstrated no interest in the art, and he wasn't about to push her into it. There had been enough unnecessary pushing in this family.

A third finger. "Currently, I have no friends except you and Adil Uncle. I am thirteen years old and require more friends my own age in close contact. Studies show this is when our brains develop to learn how to have relationships."

That, he couldn't argue with. He forever felt guilty that Luna wasn't around kids her own age. It was the reason she was even allowed to have social media, so she could keep in contact with her friends.

"What if we leave here in six months?" he asked. Hollywood was fickle.

"I don't care. I want to go to a real school." She swiped her hand at a curl over her eye. "I know how to work Uber or whatever other service they have here. I can take a car to school and back. You wouldn't have to come to any events. It wouldn't take any more of your time."

He raised his hand to stop the flood of words that mildly broke his heart. "I am not too busy to drive you to school," he said gruffly. "My concern is that you've never gone to school before."

She lifted one shoulder. "Only because Baba said tutors were easier for him."

Rohan.

"I know you think an American school will be like 90210, but it's not that glamorous," he warned.

She gave him a blank look. "What's that?"

"It's not like the TV shows, I mean."

"I don't want to go because we're in America. I've wanted to go forever."

"Why didn't you say something?"

"Because I needed time to think of reasons to give to you for me to go."

"You are a great debater," he conceded.

"Aji said I could play a great lawyer."

"Or you could *be* a lawyer." He might not pressure her, but their elder relative was a different story. "Why don't we discuss this in the morning."

Her shoulders slumped. "That means no."

"It means yes. However, it's too late to determine which school you should attend."

Her eyes brightened. "Really?"

He smiled, relieved that the dark clouds in her eyes had vanished. "Really."

"I don't want it to be a fancy school."

"If you're going to school, it will be the best school."

"I've heard the best private schools are quite the party places. Rich kids."

He narrowed his eyes. His schools had been decidedly

middle class until sixteen, and he could concede she was right. "You will go to the second-best school."

"I'd like to go to a public school."

He reared back. "Luna, that is too much."

"Don't be classist. A public school will allow me to meet different kinds of people."

"I'm not . . . fine." He gritted his teeth. He supposed his instant dislike of a public school for his niece was classist. Besides, it wasn't like he had the money to justify this particular ism right now. "We will investigate both options."

A smile spread across her face. "Thank you, Kaka."

He wanted to hug her, but he kept the space between them. Physical affection had never been something he craved, but he'd never before been faced with a young curly-haired orphan with his brother's chin and a polite smile and haunted eyes. "You will study at home independently, though. I want you ahead of your class, so you won't face any trouble if we return to India and you're back in a more rigorous curriculum."

"I'm okay with that. School doesn't take me much time."

She always had been a quick student, and Dev had told her tutors to advance her where necessary. "Perhaps they'll let you skip a grade—"

"No. The goal here is to be around people who are my age."

He tugged on a curl. "Very well."

"Can I call Aji to tell her?"

"Certainly. Tomorrow." He was perpetually surprised

by how close Luna and his grandmother were. Lord knew, Shweta Dixit, Legend of the Silver Screen, hadn't done much but toss cash at her grandchildren, especially the two she hadn't met until their teenage years.

Dev might harbor some rejection and resentment over that, but he took those emotions and dealt with them the way he dealt with all emotions: bundled them up into a ball and stuffed them deep deep down. Like all healthy people did.

"How was the party?"

It glowed for a few minutes. "Fine. Like any other party," he said, with a twist to his mouth Luna probably wouldn't catch.

"Did you meet anyone?"

Those fierce eyes popped into his mind. *Yes.* "No."

"Oh."

"Why do you ask?"

Luna crossed her arms over her chest. She wore an old Coca-Cola T-shirt of his. Vintage, she'd called it, when she'd politely asked if she could take it from his donation pile during the move. "Adil Uncle said you needed to find a woman, or you'd lose all your money, and since all you do is work, these parties are your only chance."

Adil. Why. "He said that to *you?*"

"No. I heard him on the phone."

"He's incorrect." *No, he's not.* "I'm quite content as I am." *No, you're not.*

Luna nodded slowly. "If you say so, Kaka."

"I do." He busied himself pulling her blanket up higher so she wouldn't see the frown on his face. Her mother had never been in the picture, and the therapist he'd obtained for Luna had stressed the need for consistency and calm since her father had died. His brother had been neither consistent nor calm, so Dev figured it was extra important he give her a stable home, and a stable home didn't include talk of shaky finances or an asshole of a grandfather essentially cutting his grandson and great-granddaughter out of his will. "Time for bed now. You have lessons early tomorrow. No more phone for the night."

Luna groaned, and it was music to his ears. He'd much rather she play the role of a conventional teen as opposed to the withdrawn, too-mature child he'd taken custody of. "Fine."

He took her phone and placed it in the dock on her nightstand. "Good night."

"Night."

He quickly undressed once he was in his room, and neatly hung his suit up, next to about a dozen suits like it. Every year or so, he had his stylist replenish his closet with clothes he could easily put together. He was hardly the fashion plate his cousin was. Dressing in neutral clothes didn't speak to his soul, but it ensured he didn't embarrass himself.

When he took his watch off, something glinted in the light coming from the bathroom. He brought the watch closer to his face. The thread was tiny, an itty-bitty souvenir from the night stuck between the links. He pulled it out and blew at it gently. It fluttered to the floor.

His version of a face routine consisted of removing his

contacts, a quick wash with a cleanser, and a pat down. He eyed his shower but decided to tackle that in the morning.

He opened the bedroom windows and listened. Santa Monica wasn't Mumbai. It was a different ocean and different sand, but if he closed his eyes he could imagine the clock had turned back. That his brother hadn't gotten drunk on a boat and died, leaving Luna and his astronomical debts to Dev. That he hadn't had to uproot his whole life because he couldn't stand to remain in the same country of his loss. That the fate of his small family wasn't resting on his shoulders, in a place where he couldn't simply glide on his family name.

Dev closed the windows. He'd love to fall asleep to the noise of the ocean, but when he slept, his brain couldn't tell the difference between what was real and fake. He didn't want to wake up homesick.

You told me you'd searched the universe for a woman like me.

He climbed into bed naked but for his boxers. Dev removed his glasses and placed them on the nightstand, then rubbed the bridge of his nose. He was tired, but he couldn't shut away her memory. Why couldn't he? He was usually so good at compartmentalizing.

He held his hand up and studied it. It was blurry without his glasses on.

Who was she? It made no logical sense, her reaction. Was she a fan? A stalker? He shuddered at the latter. He'd already had a couple of those, and he'd rather not repeat the experience, no matter how much of an instantaneous connection he'd felt with her.

If she was a stalker, though . . . he should know who she was, right? For his own purposes, for protection?

Yes, you most definitely need protection from that little scrap of a woman.

He hesitated, then rolled over and grabbed his phone. His agent had arranged for an assistant for him here. He'd met the boy, John, earlier in the week, and found him to be eager and bright.

Dev typed out a quick text. Can you get me a guest list for tonight's party? Tomorrow is fine. He'd surely be able to narrow the hundred or so women down before he googled the more likely names.

Though it was late, John immediately replied. Sure. I'll email it to you right now.

Of course he would. Dev typed a thanks, then went over to his email. One refresh, and there it was.

He opened the attachment and quickly scrolled the names. He'd try the more familiar ones first.

There were only three possibilities. He tried the first two, but came up with actresses he didn't recognize. The third one, though. There he hit gold.

Dev didn't really like social media, was reluctant to even have the apps on his phone. His agency handled those things, adding periodic photos of him, updating his appearances, if any, posting things like tributes to his brother and grandfather.

Jia Ahmed, though, *really* liked social media, judging by the links that popped up from a name search.

He clicked over to YouTube. She wore a green dress in her

profile photo, her eyes popping from the green eyeliner she wore. She was as stunning in emerald as she was in gold.

He ripped his gaze away. She had a ton of videos under her name, and even more followers. He raised his eyebrows at the number of subscribers she had. Literally millions.

He clicked on one video at random. Music blared through his speaker and he fumbled the phone, nearly dropping it.

He toggled the volume down to a more manageable level in time for Jia to layer over the melody. Her voice was pitched slightly different, professional, peppy. When she'd walked up to him at that party, it had been lower, more tentative.

Her face was shiny and makeup free, but it didn't matter. She was beautiful with the makeup and without it, and so confident it honestly wouldn't matter what she put on her face.

He'd seen that kind of innate confidence in his cousin and brother and grandparents. As the only seminormal person born into a family of exceptional artists, it was fascinating to him.

Dev wanted to click away and learn more about her, about who she was, what her story was, but she'd mesmerized him. There was an irrepressible gleam in her eyes, like she held a secret he needed to discover.

"Start with eyeliner, at the corner of your eye. Follow the line of your lower lid, you're going to draw a triangle, and then connect it to the line over your lid . . . Great, you did one beautiful wing. You're half flying! Now we copy it on the other. Remember, they can be sisters, not twins."

He checked the date. This video was almost four years old. She had been doing this quite some time. He scrolled up. Her more recent videos had millions more views, plus better production quality.

Dev rolled to his side and clicked on another video at random. Tomorrow, he'd ask his assistant to discreetly check to see if she had any kind of history with other actors or famous people. If Jia was an obsessed fan, he'd protect himself and Luna from her.

What if she's not?

Well, then, in that case, his path was a little more complicated. He tucked the hand that had touched her dupatta under his head and closed his eyes, her voice wrapping around him. And when he finally did sleep, she wrapped around his dreams.

Chapter Three

USUALLY ONCE Jia woke up for morning prayers, she started her day. Today, she'd groggily crawled right back into bed. Sleep was nice. Sleep meant she didn't have to face herself.

Unfortunately, she had an internal alarm that didn't quit, even when she wanted it to. Jia blinked open one crusty eye, then the other. She loved this room, with its cotton candy pink walls and feminine white furniture. It was the first place she'd lived on her own, outside her parents' home, and had been free to decorate to her taste.

It was far too bright for her mood this morning, though. She'd forgotten to close the shades the night before when she'd crept in, and the Southern California sun was blinding, reflecting off all that white furniture.

She groped for her phone on the bed next to her but came up with a spoon instead. Her therapeutic ice cream binge had clearly exhausted her. Thank goodness she'd tossed the empty ice cream container before falling asleep clutching her utensil like a security blanket, or she'd have a real sticky morning today.

Jia swallowed and made a face. Blech. That's what she got

for not brushing her teeth before falling into her ice cream and depression coma.

She peeked under the covers and the pillow for her phone. She always woke up with her phone under her or beside her, the result of falling asleep while scrolling.

Except last night, when she'd thrown her purse—with the phone inside—on her bureau and dug face first into her dessert.

She eyed her purse, the strap innocently hanging over the side. Her fingers itched, but she knew what she'd do as soon as she had it. She'd click on Dev's texts, read them incessantly, and obsess over what the hell had happened. Maybe even text him more. Something subtle, like *what the fuck* or *who the fuck* or *why the fuck*, though years of being hyperconscious of playing role model to her young fan base had knocked most of her swearing tendencies out of her.

Jia shoved back the comforter and rubbed her exhausted eyes as she rose. Her golden shot dress was draped over her armchair in a crumpled heap. She normally took good care of her clothes, but that particular dress could stay crumpled. Like her romantic dreams.

Jia yelped when she entered the bathroom and saw her own reflection. Yikes, this was not pretty. Raccoon eyes, smeared lipstick, one fake eyelash clinging to her cheek. Her bun had slipped loose at some point while she slept, and her hair was a tangled mess.

Luckily, her counter was filled to bursting with skin products and hair supplies—another perk of having her own space—and she cleaned herself up as best as she could. Once her face was scrubbed and her hair was relatively knot-free and in a low ponytail, she left the bathroom.

She got dressed quickly in tie-dyed sweatpants and a sweatshirt. "Sienna, where are Jas, Katrina, and Rhiannon?" she asked out loud.

There was a beat, and then a red pad next to her door lit up. "Jas has left the house. Rhiannon and Katrina are in the kitchen," came the pleasant robot lady voice overhead.

It was a little past breakfast time, but Katrina had gotten more flexible since her boyfriend had started a master's program. "Thank you." She always thanked the AI, on the off chance the robot came to life one day and went on a murderous rampage. Sienna was the brainchild of one of the start-ups Katrina invested in, and she seemed to know more than Siri and Alexa put together.

"You're welcome, Jia. May I say, you sound lovely today."

Her lips twitched. Katrina had programmed Sienna to give compliments, and Jia was not above liking them. "You, too, Sienna."

She had two options: avoid her roommates, or go right to them and blurt out all the deets on what had happened last night. Discretion wasn't her strong suit.

She made her way downstairs to the kitchen. Jia had lived here for almost a year and a half now, and she still hadn't lost her awe for the airy mansion. She'd grown up firmly middle to upper class, and though her work had left her with a solid savings account, there'd be no way she'd be able to afford a home like this on her own yet. She glanced out a floor-to-ceiling window at the view of Santa Barbara nestled below, the ocean a slice of blue in the distance.

Wealth disparity aside, Jia had wondered in the beginning if she'd be able to carve out a home here. This was Katrina's house, and she and Rhiannon shared a history, a deep friendship going back years and a business partnership. Rhiannon might have grown up in Jia's hometown, but she was closer in age to Jia's older sisters than her.

It had taken Jia about two minutes to slip into a groove here, though. She had so many sisters she hadn't thought she'd ever want more, but here she was, with two bonuses. Which was why she was dreading disappointing them. Sisterly disappointment was the worst.

She found her roommates in the kitchen, heads bent together at the counter. "Hey," she said, then stopped when they turned. Whoa: "What's that?"

Rhiannon raised a perfectly arched eyebrow. She was dressed in jeans and her signature hoodie, bright red today. The clothes were snug on her athletic frame. "Clearly it's a hologram."

"Not a hologram, exactly," Katrina corrected. She hadn't been a model in a long time, but she was still drop-dead gorgeous with her perfect skin and curves. She was also a shark when it came to pinpointing the next big thing or person to invest in. "Just a new kind of interface I wanted Rhiannon to see." She made a swiping gesture and images of people started flashing across the transparent blue screen hovering in the air.

Jia walked closer, then around the screen. She could see her roommates through it. "Katrina, are you Iron Man?"

Katrina gave a delicate, tinkling laugh. "I wish. I think we can bring this into the fold and integrate it with Crush."

Rhiannon folded her arms over her chest. "It's too flashy. Nothing wrong with good old-fashioned finger-to-screen swiping."

"Is that old-fashioned now?" Jia had spent too much time lately worrying about what was current and what was old. She walked back around the screen to stand next to her roommates. She stuck her hand into the apparition. "This is like VR without those ugly goggles."

Katrina pushed a button on the remote in her hand, and the screen disappeared. "I'm telling you, we need to innovate. Before one of our competitors does."

Rhiannon sneered, ostensibly at Crush's competitors. "I don't need tricks to beat them."

"They can't hurt."

"They can if we shell out tons of money for an upgrade that bombs. More focus on keeping people in love and happy and safe, less on tech."

Katrina shrugged, but there was a determined gleam in her eye that told Jia she wasn't done. Katrina was soft in the heart, not in her instincts.

"We'll see. Come on, let's eat breakfast so you can get a move on to work." Katrina pressed her palm on Jia's shoulder and squeezed. "Hungry? I made eggs and toast."

Jia leaned into the touch. Katrina was empathetic enough

to understand when someone loved being touched. "I'd like that, thank you."

Rhiannon tugged on Jia's sweatshirt hood as they gathered plates and flatware. At first glance, she didn't seem as squishy as Katrina, but Jia had come to realize she was possibly even more in tune with people around her. "Did you tie-dye this yourself?"

"Yup. Saw a thing online. You use bleach—"

Rhiannon held up a hand. "Please, I watched enough of those videos when I was working from home. Don't need any more tutorials or hacks from the youths."

"The youths are geniuses." Jia bumped the drawer closed with her hip. It had been the right decision, getting breakfast. Her spirits were rising just being here with her friends. "I like any generation that's, like, bleach, but make it fashion."

Rhiannon snorted as they sat down. Katrina served them eggs and hash browns. Jia helped herself to a perfectly toasted piece of bread. She'd tried to take over cooking breakfasts in the beginning, partially because she'd been so grateful that these women had given her a home away from home, but Katrina loved making them food and had firmly declined her assistance. Which was good—Jia's food wouldn't taste nearly so good.

"FYI, I'm staying with Samson this week," Rhiannon told them. Samson, Rhiannon's gentle giant boyfriend, lived in Los Angeles. "We have a fancy gala he's making me go to." She sneered, though her words had been tender.

"You're a nonprofit director's girlfriend now. Get used to galas." Katrina waved her knife at her friend, and the sunlight flashed off the diamond ring on her finger. It wasn't an engagement ring, she'd informed them both a few months ago. Simply a gift from her boyfriend.

Jia was privately skeptical, but she was willing to let her friend come to grips with the fact that Jas may have sneakily put a ring on it.

"I'm Samson's partner. Girlfriend sounds like we're in high school. Partner is responsible sounding enough to stop people from asking when we're getting married." Rhiannon made a face, like the word *married* had left a bad taste in her mouth.

"I like galas," Jia contributed. "Any excuse to dress up. You should wear that lime-green dress."

"Is it too much?"

"Nope." Rhiannon's skin was a dark brown, darker than Jia's, and the color would pop, while the sleeveless silhouette would bare her toned arms. "Put your hair up, do a light makeup."

Rhiannon touched her curls. She'd cut her hair recently, and they barely brushed her shoulders. "I'll think about it. Lakshmi will do my makeup, so I'm not worried about that."

Now Jia resisted the urge to sneer. There was no love lost between her and Rhiannon's assistant.

The woman had assumed Jia was frivolous and silly on sight. That wasn't uncommon. People didn't respect influencers nearly as much as they respected med students. Jia had responded as she always did to disdain, with an air-headed affectation guaranteed to annoy even more. "Sounds good."

"How was the party you went to last night, Jia?" Katrina asked.

Jia took a sip of orange juice, mostly to clear the sudden lump in her throat. "Fine."

"Uh-oh." Rhiannon glanced up from her plate, a sharp look in her eyes. "That doesn't sound good."

"I got a goody bag."

Katrina perked up. She liked the goody reveals too. "Ooh. Have you gone through it yet? Any new brands?"

"No, I didn't get a chance." Jia took another bite, though she didn't much want to eat any longer. "Something happened, and it upset me."

Rhiannon stilled. "Something or someone?"

"Someone."

Her roommate's dark eyes narrowed. "A man?"

"Yeah."

"Do you want me to take care of him?"

It was funny, Rhiannon sounded vaguely like she was threatening to put a hit on someone.

"Like, I can kill them," Rhiannon explained.

Or not so vaguely. Jia huffed out a soft laugh. "No need for an assassin. It was a stupid thing." She let the back of the chair mold to her spine.

"What happened?" Katrina asked.

Jia hadn't really rehearsed what she was going to say,

which was probably why she went with "I think I may have been catfished by someone pretending to be a famous Indian actor."

There was a beat of silence, and then Rhiannon spoke. "I feel like we need something harder than orange juice for this conversation."

Jia didn't drink, but she couldn't disagree. "Do you . . . do you guys remember that guy I was talking to like a year ago?"

Katrina and Rhiannon exchanged a look. "Yes," Katrina said gently. "You said you stopped talking to him after the holidays."

"I did. There was so much going on then, in the world, and with my family." She had two parents, three sisters, and two brothers-in-law who were doctors, and times had been tough in the medical field around then. "I got tired of us being so far apart, and him not wanting to chat on video, and it started to feel like a lot of his messages were rehearsed. I told him we could maybe talk in the future, when we were in the same place in the world."

"Sounds like you were listening well to your instincts."

She had been, damn it. If only she'd continued to do so. "Except for a message when his brother died, I cut off contact." He hadn't responded to that, but she hadn't expected him to. "A couple of months ago, though, when I was sick, I reached out again."

Rhiannon let out a breath, and Jia tried not to cringe. Her friend was clearly disappointed in her. She didn't blame Rhi. Jia soldiered through. Best to explain what a fool she was all at once. "I was in bed for so long, and I was bored, and it was like he gave me company? Especially at night, because of the time zones. He was awake across the world when everyone here was asleep." *Don't justify your silliness.*

Rhiannon put down her fork. "Oh honey."

Jia hated the sympathy in her friend's voice. She lowered her gaze to her plate. So much dismay and disappointment in those two words. "I was excited, because he said he was filming a show here soon. I thought we'd finally meet, but once he got to town, he kept putting off seeing me."

"Oh *honey.*"

"I know." Jia shook her head. "Looking back now, I can see it's all from the catfisher's handbook. I think that's why I just decided to go to him. It didn't take much to get invited to his cast party." Jia dejectedly cut off a piece of potato. "I walked right up to him, and he pretended not to recognize me."

Rhiannon drained her orange juice like it was something stronger. "Girl—"

"Please don't tell me you told me so." Jia's voice was sharper than she'd intended. Rhiannon deserved to be disappointed in her, but she'd spent her whole life with people who were perpetually poised to say exactly those words, and it was exhausting.

"I would never," Rhiannon declared, surprising her. "I understand why you did what you did."

"You do?"

"Of course." Katrina's gaze was soft and understanding. "You were sick! Worried and lonely. It's no surprise he snuck in under your guard. People who do this stuff, they know how to target vulnerable people."

"I'm sorry it turned out like this," Rhiannon added.

Jia let out a breath she hadn't realized she was holding. "Thank you for not gloating."

Katrina nodded. "We'd never gloat, love. We are very sorry."

Some of the weight fell off Jia's shoulders at their instant kindness. Still, she tried to absolve herself. "Before we moved to the texting app, the first messages came from his official account. He said he was shy, that's why he didn't want to video chat. He was so nice to me, said such beautiful things when I was sick and alone. I was so convinced that he was legit."

"Eight people have access to Crush's account," Rhiannon said quietly. "If this guy is famous at all, he has assistants who have access to his social media, even if it looks like he's the only one posting. Hell, someone may have even hacked him solely to catfish a bunch of girls."

Jia took a shaky breath. "I suppose it doesn't matter. Whether he pretended not to know me or whether he was someone else all along." Foolishness on her part either way.

"Has he—or whoever he is—messaged you today?"

"I don't know. I haven't checked my phone today."

Rhiannon pressed her fingers to her lips. "You must really be upset."

"I am."

Rhiannon pulled out her own phone. "You want to give

me his name? I won't kill him. I can maybe dig around a little."

"Or you can not dig at all." Katrina reached across the table and held Jia's hand. "I think you should let this go. Delete his number and his messages, block him everywhere."

"You're saying this?" Rhiannon snorted. "You're the queen of closure."

Katrina rubbed her thumb over Jia's. "I'm the queen of solid mental health. And as you said, there are two possibilities here. Either you were talking to someone who was using a famous man's face, or that famous man led you on for over a year for God knows what reason and then pretended he didn't know you last night. Neither of those things will be helped by ever seeing him or talking to him again."

Something cracked in Jia, like a boat set loose from a dock. It was . . . loss? That was so silly. She'd never had anything to begin with, in either of those scenarios. "I feel so dumb."

"Naïve, not dumb."

Jia cocked her head at Rhiannon. "That's not much better."

Rhiannon waved her hand. "We were all naïve at one time. You haven't had much experience with dating or love. With experience comes cynicism."

Katrina shifted. "Not necessarily cynicism. With experience comes experience. No one has a perfect track record. Life is about making mistakes."

"It was cynicism for me," Rhiannon said flatly. "I do run a

dating app, after all. You wouldn't believe the trash we deal with."

A thump came from under the table, and Katrina gave Rhiannon a warning look. "We also have tons of success stories, and lovely users, though. Jia, you're going to find a sweet guy who spoils you, and you're going to walk right into love, and it's not going to feel hard, you know?"

Jia nodded, tears burning her eyes. She let them fall now, because she didn't mind if these two saw them.

Rhiannon cleared her throat. "I have to ask, did you text this person any nudes? If so, I know a guy who—"

"No!"

"Don't sound so scandalized." Rhiannon shrugged. "Nothing wrong with a nude here or there."

"I know. I'm not judging anyone. I didn't send any nudes." Jia's face was turning red. She might talk to her audience rather frankly about adult matters, but it was different when she was the subject of those matters. "We never even discussed sex."

"And you didn't send any money or anything?" Katrina asked.

Jia shook her head.

"If you're trying to figure out what this person got out of this, Katrina, don't bother. Catfishers make no sense," Rhiannon remarked. "There are sickos out there. Who knows."

"I suppose you're right," Katrina murmured. "In any case, and I cannot stress this enough, love, don't text him. This is your first big hurt, yes? Don't drag it out any more than you have to."

"I'm going to be hurt more than this?" Jia's voice rose to a squeak.

Katrina winced, and Jia didn't know if it was because of her words, or Rhiannon's obvious return kick under the table. "Uh, of course not. I was—"

"Stop hitting each other. I get it." Jia did her best to give them her brightest, best smile. "Don't worry. I'm not going to call him. In fact, the first thing I'm going to do before work is erase his messages from my phone."

Rhiannon patted her back. "Atta girl. Are you sure you don't want me to . . . ?" She sliced her finger over her throat.

Jia smiled despite her blue mood. "Nah. We are going to banish this man from all our memories. He's never going to be a part of my life again."

And for a moment there, surrounded by sunshine and girl power, Jia actually believed those words might be true.

Chapter Four

OKAY, LET'S take a look at today's mask. It's a blueberry acai concoction, and it's meant to be particularly good for acne and oily skin. I used to have a ton of acne when I was in my teens, but once I started a regular skin care regimen, it cleared right up." Jia's laugh tinkled through Dev's speakers. In this video, she was in a blindingly white bathroom, perched on a small stool. Her hair was wrapped up simply, and she wore an oversize pajama shirt. Her face was shiny and clean. "Just kidding. I lucked out when my sister went into dermatology and I got buried in samples. Ten steps can't cure everything, some of us need prescription intervention. I'll link to some of those videos below."

She spread the blue mud over her forehead, her expression focused, as she continued to patter about cleanser and serum and exfoliation. This was a series she called *Unmasked Masks*, where she tried out a new face mask and answered viewer questions. Dev knew it was a regular feature, because he'd been watching far too many of her videos over the last fourteen hours or so. In fact, the only time he hadn't been watching one of her videos was when he was sleeping or on his way to the set or getting in costume. It was research! That was all. Until his super-assistant John got back to him on what her deal was.

He glanced around the bustling set. He was sitting at one of the makeup stations, waiting by himself. He'd done nothing but wait on set so far.

It was a far cry from his previous job. Twenty-five hundred episodes in over ten years meant he'd always been constantly filming something. When he hadn't been filming, he'd been writing or talking to the director or speaking with the other actors.

This is different.

It was. Their first season, an eighteen-episode run, and he was one of six lead characters. Not to mention, this was their first real week of work. He shouldn't compare.

Anyway, it meant more time for Jia.

"I was trying to figure out which question to answer during this video, and I'll be honest, I got stalled on one. It started with *you shouldn't*. Like, I don't even remember what the rest of the comment was, it started with those words, and I got so . . . annoyed. And I think it's because I'm so sick of strangers on the internet telling me what I should and shouldn't do, you know?"

Dev cupped his chin in his hand. This, he did know. The only time the public had left him alone was during his childhood in Dubai. As soon as he'd become Vivek and Shweta's grandson, his privacy had vanished. It was one of the many reasons he stayed off the internet.

Jia squinted as she carefully drew the blue mask over the

bridge of her elegant nose, and down to her upper lip. "I get it. When you make your life public, you open yourself up to criticism. But I feel like sometimes I get so much more of it than anyone else, and it's not fair. *You shouldn't wear that, you shouldn't go there, you shouldn't be so vain, you shouldn't talk like that.*"

Dev frowned. What rude creatures dared to say such things? He would fight them.

A tiny matching scowl emerged on her blue forehead. She looked like an indignant, cute Smurf. "Who made user89384 the police, I ask you? No one. I decide what I do and how I do it. Not you, user89384. Okay, the instructions say the mask should be on for ten minutes." She adjusted a timer next to her. "The other kind of question I get asked a lot starts with *should I,* and that also worries me. Honestly, I don't need anyone's approval or opinion, and in return, I don't want to force my approval on anyone else. That's so much pressure on me. What if I tell you the wrong thing! Everyone should be able to do whatever they want with their bodies and their lives." She wrinkled her nose, the mud creasing. "I think this mask is making my skin dry out, ew. I don't think I'm a fan, but let's wash—"

"Dev?"

Dev looked up and turned off his phone with all the speed of someone watching a far more illicit video than a modestly clad woman wearing a face mask. "Yes?" He cleared his throat. "Yes. Hello."

The man standing in front of him beamed at him. Hudson Rivers—his real name, he'd assured Dev—was a rising star with a chiseled jawline and sun-kissed brown hair. He was the star of the show, the beleaguered single father trying to raise a daughter on his own. Dev played his sidekick friend, and not a very good one at that. His character had cheated with the man's wife.

Dev had never done an infidelity arc. A romantic lead hero was supposed to be just that—a hero, and heroes didn't cheat.

He'd like to think that the writers were trying to create a layered, nuanced character, but he was starting to think he'd been slightly misled, and he wasn't one of the heroes of the show at all.

It is fine. Close your eyes and think of the money.

Hope Street had offered more than anyone else, and it did have some big American names in it. Like Hudson.

"Sorry to bother you. We haven't gotten to talk much. I was hoping to have time to chat with you at the party yesterday, but Richard monopolized me for most of the night." Hudson's good-natured shrug complemented the humble-brag.

Richard Reese played Hudson's father in the show and was the top-billed actor. He didn't seem to care much about anyone on the show, especially Dev, whom he'd dismissed on sight at their first table read.

Dev had wanted to politely explain to the older man that he'd had richer and more famous actors at his seventeenth birthday party, but his mother hadn't raised an asshole. "Not an issue," he said to Hudson. "How are you doing?"

"Well, thanks. Glad we're getting this show on the road

finally." Hudson leaned against the chair next to his. "I've been traveling a lot for features lately."

Another humblebrag.

"It's nice to work close to home sometimes. My kids are still young, I'd like to see them more. You got kids?"

"I'm raising my niece, Luna." Dev braced himself, but Hunter didn't change expression at all. It was kind of refreshing to meet people who didn't know the tragic circumstances that had led to his taking care of his niece. "She's thirteen."

"Nice. My eldest is around her age. Where does she go to school?"

"We're still looking."

"Ah, well, Marymount is the best. It's where my kid goes."

Dev had slowly warmed to the thought of public school. If part of coming here had been to get away from his privileged name and the baggage it entailed, Luna was right. He had to take apart his own classism.

Hudson dropped into the chair next to his and examined his face in the brightly lit mirror. "This makeup job was terrible, huh? And they didn't even do yours." He raised his voice and called out to no one in particular. "We need makeup over here!"

Dev rubbed his chin. A smear of brown makeup came off. "I already had mine done, actually—" he began, but a young South Asian woman had already materialized, her brown cheeks flushed.

She looked at Dev. "I'm so sorry, sir. Can I help you?"

Dev hooked his thumb at Hudson. "I didn't call for you, sorry."

Her face fell. "Oh." She turned to Hudson. "Yes, Mr. Rivers?"

"Mr. Rivers is my father," Hudson drawled, his smile blinding. "Call me Hudson. And what's your name?"

"Kalpana."

"Well, Kalpana, this other little girl did my makeup in my trailer and I don't think she got the blend right on my hairline here."

The woman snapped to attention and grabbed a brush off the vanity. "Oh yes. She's new, I'm training her."

"Would have been a shame if we'd gone on camera like this, yes?" Hudson gave her a meaningful look and she nodded furiously.

"I'll talk to her, I promise."

Dev shifted. In the early years of his show, they hadn't even had a makeup team, just a single woman with a brush and an attitude. "I don't think it would have been that big a deal," he said quietly. "They could have fixed it in post if necessary."

Kalpana shrugged her thick braid over her shoulder and shot him an inscrutable look.

Hudson's smile tightened. "Well, you gotta have something to fix. Kalpana, get some makeup on our friend here, eh?"

Kalpana came closer and peered at him. "Mr. Dixit's skin

is simply so good he doesn't require much." She pulled out a few pots and tubes.

Dev resisted the urge to examine his skin in the mirror. He knew it was too soon to credit Jia, but he had stopped on the way to work and picked up the drugstore cleanser she swore by.

"I wanted to tell you what an honor it is to work with you, Mr. Dixit." Kalpana ran the brush over his face with brisk strokes.

Oh no. She was going to tell him how much she loved his family and give him her tearful condolences. Was it wrong to hate sympathy as much as he did? "You can call me Dev."

"Dev. My grandmother nearly died when I told her you'd be here. She's been watching *Kyunki Mere Sanam Ke Liye Kuch Bhi* since the very first episode. I used to watch it as a kid with her."

Dev's shoulders relaxed. Easier to deal with someone who loved his show rather than someone expressing sympathy for his brother and grandfather. "Thank you."

"What's that?" Hudson broke in.

"My old show."

"It was on the air for eleven years," Kalpana told Hudson. Then to Dev, "My grandmother was heartbroken when it ended. We're so excited to have you back on our TV, even if I'll have to translate *Hope Street* for her."

"Thank you. I hope you both enoy it."

She gave him a slightly adoring look. "I'm sure anything you do will be wonderful."

A page popped up behind her, forestalling Hudson's response. "Mr. Rivers, they're ready for you. Mr. Dixit, we'll call you in about half an hour."

Hudson saluted him and stood. "Talk soon, Dev. Thanks, Kalpana, for the touch-up."

"I appreciate it as well," Dev murmured to Kalpana, as soon as the other man left.

She beamed at him. "No worries." She cleared her throat. "Listen, since you're new here, if you ever want to go grab a drink, I can show you around town. Open invite whenever."

He stared at her blankly. He'd never been good with romantic cues. Was she flirting with him?

After telling him that she'd started watching his show when she was a literal child? "Ah." His phone rang, and he snatched it up off his lap, grateful for being saved by the bell. "I have to get this."

"Oh sure." She looked disappointed, but she left while he answered.

"Devanand."

He sat up a little straighter. That was what he got for not checking the caller ID before taking an exit to an awkward conversation.

No one used his full first name except for his grandmother, and the way she drawled it always made him feel like his shoelaces were untied or his hair messy. "Aji. How are you? Why are you calling so late?" It was late in the evening in Mumbai.

"I don't sleep much." Back in her glory days, his grandmother's voice had been throaty on purpose, for sex appeal.

Now it was raspy from years of cigarettes and cigars. "Why is Luna not answering my call?"

"She has certain times when she can't use the phone, like during her studies."

"That is cruel."

He looked around, hoping the PA would pop up and tell him he was needed earlier. "It's the kind of parenting her therapist recommended."

"If she has no phone, she cannot talk to me. That is unacceptable. I shall send her a second phone."

"You will do nothing of the sort." He made his tone as firm as he could. When he and Rohan had been orphaned and sent to live with their grandparents at sixteen and thirteen, their elders had left them mostly to their own devices.

Dev would have much rather had some maternal softness or kind words. Rohan hadn't minded, or at least not outwardly. He'd taken the credit cards the couple had tossed at them and followed their cousin, Arjun, down scandal's path.

Luna was a different story. Aji wasn't exactly maternal with the girl, but as far as he could tell, they had an easy relationship where they both sought each other out. Though he didn't understand it, Dev was willing to respect their bond. But he certainly wasn't going to let Luna be spoiled without any checks like Rohan had been, and a second phone he couldn't monitor came under that category.

His grandmother ignored him, which wasn't unusual. "Luna tells me you are renting? You should buy a nice house."

"Real estate is rather expensive here." He didn't have the money for a hefty down payment.

"You know you could afford whatever you like."

Oh, it was going to be a call about *this*.

A shot of frustrated anger ran through him, as it did every time he thought of his too-controlling late grandfather. The man had died mere weeks after Rohan. Dev hadn't really counted on an inheritance, but his grandfather's final wishes, showing exactly how he felt about his wayward son's unwanted descendants, had still hurt. "Seeing as how I only have a few months left to meet the condition, I very much doubt I'm going to be able to make it."

"The will only said marriage by thirty-three, no specifics. Don't tell me you can't find a single suitable woman?"

"You'd be happy if I married any woman, eh?" He gave a humorless laugh.

"What is that supposed to mean?"

It means your husband disowned your eldest son for marrying a woman of a lower class and different religion. Dev couldn't say that, though.

He didn't actually think his grandmother had driven his parents away. She just hadn't stopped her husband from doing it. He lowered his voice, though no one was near enough to hear him. "It means I'm not picking up some woman off the street so I can inherit money." He had no issue with marriage—privately, he agreed that it was high time he settled down with someone. But that had nothing to do with this. He might be up to his ears in Rohan's debts, but he wasn't about to drag some poor strange woman into his family's mess.

Plus, honestly . . . it pained his pride to let his grandfather win. He could well imagine the old man in hell, cackling because he'd forced Dev to jump into a loveless marriage for money.

"A marriage in a couple months is not absurd. I knew your grandfather for two weeks before we got married. Your parents ran away after a month."

His grandmother must be extremely desperate, if she was going to mention his parents. They usually tiptoed around that subject. "It's not the time issue."

"I have told you, I have a number of friends' daughters who would make you very happy. You're being so stubborn. You should—"

You should. He thought of Jia's wise words on the subject of *you should.* "No," he said firmly.

"Then you pick a girl."

His face grew hot. The only girl who had captured his attention recently had nothing to do with any will.

"I will accept anyone, I promise, into our family. Think of Luna. You could turn right around and give it all to her."

That was the only tempting part of this charade. His grandfather had left nothing to his only great-grandchild.

Perhaps he was being overly stubborn. An inheritance could solve a lot of his problems and give him and Luna freedom.

No. He made good money. It might take some time, but he'd crawl out of this debt his brother had left him and take care of Luna by himself. "I have to go, I'm at work. I'll have Luna call you when I get home tonight."

His grandmother sighed. "Very well. Think about what I've said. Goodbye."

"Goodbye, Aji." He hung up and nearly rubbed his forehead before he remembered that his makeup would smear. *Then you pick a girl.*

He tapped his phone against his palm, and then opened Instagram. He'd taken the app off his phone years ago, since Chandu's agency handled most of his social media. He'd only downloaded it again a month or so ago when he'd realized Luna had an account. She mostly posted memes and odd-angled selfies, but he supposed it was a good idea to keep tabs on her. He had some time before he had to worry about bikini photos. Not that he knew what he'd do if she started posting those. Her body, her choice? But he was also her guardian and she was underage. Whose choice was it then?

Raising a little human was a real mind twister.

He typed Jia's name into the search bar now. He clicked on her avatar and was rewarded with a selfie. It was from last night, but perhaps before he'd done whatever he'd done to bring unshed tears to her eyes. The photo couldn't capture the metallic threads in her scarf or dress, or the high velocity sheen that had been on her cheeks.

He rubbed his thumb over her cheek but told himself it was just to pause it to read the caption. *If I meet Mr. Right tonight, I won't be mad.*

His heart did an odd double thump. He placed his hand over his chest.

His phone buzzed. John, with a phone number, and a note. I didn't find anything criminal on this woman. Here's her number, tho. Should I keep digging?

Dev replied immediately. No, thank you.

He had the information that she wasn't, for example, wanted in three countries for stalking actors. Which was, admittedly, a low bar.

He checked his watch. He still had some time.

What would be the point in using that phone number? He scrolled through the photos of Jia, faster and faster, until they became a blur of gold and brown and red and every other color of the rainbow. No unshed tears here.

Something had upset her yesterday before she'd darted away from him, right? He could check in on her. Make sure she was okay.

Yes. It would be entirely altruistic.

Chapter Five

THIS SON of a bitch.

Jia hadn't realized she'd sworn out loud, until her driver cleared his throat. "I beg your pardon?"

She glanced up, embarrassed. She always drove herself to her studio in Los Angeles, but today she'd accepted Katrina's offer to have her housekeeper, Gerald, chauffeur her to and from the city. While it was nice to not have to concentrate on driving, talking to herself was a lot harder when she wasn't alone in her car.

"I'm sorry. It's nothing."

Gerald hummed and turned his attention pointedly back to the road.

She looked down at her phone and tried not to swear again, but there it was, in her analytics. Dev Dixit had peeped her photo from last night.

She regulated her breathing as her thoughts raced. Why, this meant . . .

Absolutely nothing.

He could have still lied about knowing her. Someone else could still be in charge of his account. It didn't matter.

Katrina and Rhiannon had told her it didn't matter. If her twin ever responded to her—Ayesha was on some annoying camping retreat with her fellow residents, and not answering her texts—she would tell her it didn't matter.

Jia grimly navigated to her contacts and erased Dev's name, and that damn heart she'd put after it. She typed *Catfishing Asshole* in and nodded. There. That would remind her, if he ever did contact her again.

She was going to move on with her life, damn it. She was like if Destiny's Child's "Survivor" and Kelly Clarkson's "Stronger" were a person. She was a stronger survivor.

"We're here, Miss."

Here at *work*, which was what *adult women* who didn't need no *man* did. Jia grabbed her bag. "Thanks, Gerald."

"Not a problem. I shall pick you up at seven. Ring me if anything changes."

"Will do. Sorry you got dragged into Los Angeles for the day."

The older man met her eyes in the rearview mirror and cracked a grin. "There's at least three restaurants I've been meaning to try. A day wandering around the city is quite a treat."

She gave him a smile in return. "Good. See you soon."

She got out of the car and shut the door with perhaps more strength than necessary. Jia had started her empire—that's what she called it, her empire—in her messy childhood bedroom, with her kinda crappy phone and terrible lighting.

Look at her now. This wasn't the most glamorous building, what with the Trader Joe's on the ground floor, but 1600 Williams was well known to every internet-famous celebrity in the world. Many of them lived and worked here, but she'd only needed a place to film that wasn't her own bedroom. She split costs on a staged apartment with another woman who came in once or twice a week to use the pool.

A couple got into the elevator with her and ignored her, which was fine with Jia, and on par with what she knew about this particular duo. Young and fit and blond, they made a lot of nauseating fifteen-second videos about how in love they were with each other.

Jia had once seen the woman chuck her phone at her dear hubby's head in the hot tub because he was scoping out another woman, so how much of their on-screen presence was genuine was up for debate.

"Have you met the new guy down the hall?" Ken asked his wife. "I heard he's barely got ten thousand followers."

Barbie sighed. "They'll let anyone in here." She cast a sideways, malicious glance at Jia.

She was getting too old for this, but Jia wasn't so preoccupied that she couldn't react. She straightened and gave Barbie a sweet smile. "Sorry, have we met?"

The blonde surveyed Jia from head to toe and then smirked and tossed her hair. "I think so. You've been around for a loooong time, haven't you?"

In internet entertainment years, Jia was a grandma, but she didn't like other people pointing that out.

Bitchiness activated. The elevator dinged, arriving at her floor. "I have. You have that collaboration with frozen pizza, right?"

She walked out of the elevator while Barbie sputtered. "It was that one time!"

Forcing someone who underestimated her to eat dirt was quite nice.

Jia, nice *isn't the word I'd use.*

Jia wrinkled her nose at her mother's chiding tone in her head. That's what she got for going more than a few days without talking to her family; they invaded her subconscious.

Pettiness was one of her prime character flaws. She whipped out her phone and made a note as she walked. *Pray on how to not be so bitchy.* She hesitated, then deleted *bitchy.* She didn't think higher powers were reading her notes app, but to be on the safe side, she replaced it with *cranky.*

Once inside the apartment, Jia kicked off her shoes and placed her bag on the granite counter in her kitchen. The place was pristine and cold. Lots of sunshine came through the windows, but she flipped on the recessed lighting anyway. Sometimes she had a little crew, but since she'd been a little light on content lately, she hadn't called in her assistant or cameraperson.

She pulled the blinds higher, to let in as much natural light as possible, and also to procrastinate. She had a million things she could do. For one, she needed to start brainstorming ways to get her metrics back on track. Her emails were probably overflowing already today. She had that goody bag she'd brought with her; she could unbox that. Perhaps she could rehearse another at-home hair cutting tutorial with her long-haired friend Man E. Quinn.

Yes, she had a lot to do. A billion million things that had nothing to do with brooding over the fact that the sun had already gone down and up once since she'd first met Dev and he'd stared at her blankly.

The heroine stands in an empty, soulless apartment, her thoughts more melodramatic than a fifteen-year-old's.

Her phone rang and she was disappointed to see it wasn't her twin, but an unknown Los Angeles number. She answered it, already planning to yell at the scammer pretending to be from the IRS on the other end of the line. "Hello?"

"Ms. Ahmed."

She flopped onto the couch, putting her feet up on the cushions. She'd fluff everything back up before she left. "No, I don't want to buy any pills, I don't believe you're from the IRS, and I'm not giving you my Social Security number."

The man paused. "I don't want to sell you pills, I'm not from the IRS, and I don't care to know your Social Security number. Is this Jia Ahmed?"

His musically accented voice pinged a memory in Jia's brain and she sat up straight. "It is."

"My name is Dev Dixit."

Jia ran hot, then cold.

She was going to move on. Which was why she was going to hang up.

No, you are not.

She lowered her feet off the cushions. "Yes," she bit off. "This is Jia. How can I help you, Mr. Dixit?"

There was a brief pause, probably because he was trying to reconcile her testy tone with her cool words. "We met briefly last night. I was the one who got stuck on your, ahem . . ."

"Shawl," she supplied. Even the anonymous viewers who chided her if her skin was visible wouldn't find that word scandalous, she didn't think. "I know who you are. How can I help you."

"I was calling because . . . well, I got the sense that I had upset you somehow? And I wanted to ensure you were okay."

Her lips parted, and she had no capability for speech for a second. Maybe longer than a second.

Two new options: someone else had truly been messaging her under his name and he was oblivious, or he was the sickest of sickos. "Mr. Dixit," she finally managed. "Where and how did you get my number, to call me right now?"

"Ah, that's a bit embarrassing."

If he was going to say *from messaging you for months over the span of a year*, then she didn't think *embarrassing* was the word she'd use. "Tell me." The forcefulness of her words surprised her a little. She usually got her way through jokes and sneakiness, not blunt demands.

"Well, I found your name through the party's guest list and then had my assistant get your number. I apologize, I am well aware that it's a breach of privacy. I told myself checking up on you outweighed that, but now that I say it out loud, I see how odd this must be."

Oh honey. Odd didn't begin to cover any part of this situation. She rubbed her fingers over her lips, glad she'd used her long-lasting lipstick today. "So you didn't get my number from your own phone?"

He paused. "I beg your pardon?"

"It wasn't in your contacts already?"

"How would it be in my contacts already?"

"Because you've been texting me for quite a while."

The pause was longer now. "I beg your pardon," he repeated.

Jia didn't need to repeat herself, but she did. "Someone has been messaging me for the last couple months. Sending me poetry, telling me how beautiful I am, how special I am." It had been the second part that had truly won her over. She heard she was beautiful a lot. Rarely did anyone tell her she was remarkable in any other way. "It came from your account. You're saying it wasn't you?" She clenched her hand into a fist to stop the shaking.

Despite her nerves, this felt right. Listening to Rhiannon and Katrina was good, but her gut's first instinct was usually what she needed. She didn't want to leave this alone. She wanted this confrontation. She deserved it, damn it.

Confirmation. Closure.

"I assure you, no. It was not me. Since my brother's death, I've been busy wrapping up his estate and focusing on my niece and our move to America. I have had no time to be texting anyone, let alone someone I've never met."

She swallowed. She wanted to keep believing that he was lying, that he had been a malicious cruel prankster, and that she hadn't been catfished. For some reason, the latter was so much worse.

Yet . . . his bewilderment rang too true, even over the phone, and this was one of the two plausible scenarios she'd considered.

"Wait a minute," he murmured. "That's why you looked so sad."

Her cheeks flushed, but she was too tongue-tied to confirm it or deny it.

"You thought I was rejecting you. I was not."

She nodded, though he couldn't see her. Her throat was too clogged up to speak. So who had it been? "Are you sure it wasn't you?" She was dismayed at how plaintive she sounded, a far cry from the forceful demands she'd made a few moments ago.

If it wasn't him, that left a whole world of suspects who could have taken advantage of her. And if she never knew who it was, then how would she ever trust anyone again?

Dev's voice gentled. "It was not. Do you have the messages? Can I see them?"

Her first instinct was to say no, but this wasn't some sacred relationship to be preserved now, was it? Jia put her phone on speaker, opened the app, and scrolled back through her DMs. "I do. This is the first one you sent, from what appears to be your official account." Hello. I'm sorry to bother you, but I merely wanted to tell you that dress is gorgeous. You look like you were dipped in gold.

She took a screenshot and texted it. "There."

His long silence made her squirm. "Hello?"

He cleared his throat. "I'm sorry. I'm in a bit of shock. I'm trying to think who . . . others handle my social media, you see. I didn't even have any of these apps on my phone until recently."

It was exactly what Rhiannon had suggested then. Jia hugged her knees to her chest. Her outrage was leaving her in slow waves, and grief was setting in. It was harder to maintain anger when she couldn't visualize a clear target for it. "Oh." She should have known she wasn't talking to the real Dev. In the span of a few minutes, he'd already mentioned his niece. Fake Dev had never talked about her.

You should have thought that was weird then. You knew his brother and grandfather had passed away. Of course he would talk about his family.

"The date on this . . . it's over a year ago."

"We chatted for a while then, but it fizzled out. We reconnected a couple months ago."

"May I see the more recent texts as well?"

Jia was a little more hesitant to send those over. They felt vaguely personal, on her part, at least. She had been sick, and tired, and vulnerable.

When she didn't respond, he filled the silence. "I only want to see if I can recognize anything in the language that would explain who did this."

Didn't she want to know? "I can send you a few screenshots." She cherry-picked a couple that felt the least vulnerable and sent them over. Unable to think of him reading the beautiful words Fake Dev had sent her, she stared out the window, the sight of the city calming her. She'd shot footage up on the rooftop here more than once.

She didn't know how long he quietly read, but she knew it was a while. That made sense. Dev—or whoever—really had sent her mininovels.

Dev drew in a deep breath, and she shifted. "So?"

"If you don't mind, I need to speak with some people." His voice was hoarse. "I'm being called right now, I'm sorry, I have to go. I'm on set. Do you think we could have dinner tonight, Jia?"

Something warm exploded in her belly. To counteract the good feeling, she dug her nails into her palm. No. They could not have dinner. They could settle this formally, without ever having to see each other again.

Closure. Don't you want it? "We can have drinks," she found herself saying. Drinks was an acceptable compromise. Dinner was too intimate for what was essentially a . . . well, she didn't even know what this was.

"Very well. You can pick the place. I'm happy to travel anywhere."

As far as offers went, that was princely behavior in L.A., actually. *He's not your prince.* Of course he wasn't. She barely knew who he was.

Another fresh wave of grief went through her. "I'll text you a spot."

"Excellent, you can use this number." Another voice came from behind him, more urgent, and he said something muffled, then came back to her. "I look forward to seeing you, Jia."

A burst of warmth shot through her. She was so startled, she slapped her hand over her lower belly and hung up without saying goodbye.

It was her name that was the culprit. He'd switched from using a Ms. without warning. She repeated her name in her head, in his voice, as she stood and moved to her camera gear in a daze.

Yup, there was that heat. It was such a simple, utilitarian name, easy for her viewers to remember. Jia. Two syllables. How did he twist those two syllables into something so damn sexy with that accent?

Doesn't matter. Get over it. Tonight's about solving a mystery, not a romance.

Chapter Six

D<small>EV HAD</small> never liked suspense or betrayal arcs, but he liked them less when he was living them.

He was always a careful driver when he had to sit on the wrong side of the car—it would always be the wrong side, foolish to have a steering wheel on the left—but this time he was extra careful as he drove his rental back to his family's flat from the studio lot. He allowed others ample time to merge and he triple-checked every traffic signal before he hit the accelerator, didn't even make a face when someone cut him off.

When I hear your laugh, it's like a thousand angels. I can't wait to hear it in person.

My life has been nothing but a cycle of despair and joy, but no joy quite like the moment I saw your face.

I cannot wait to be in your arms. I'm dying to hold your hand and living to see you.

Dev slammed his hand on the steering wheel. Bloody *fucking* bastard.

He'd gone into his phone conversation with Jia vaguely optimistic that he'd misread the signs of her upset last night. A tiny part of his brain, the part that held his softest feelings, had even fantasized of her being happy to hear from him.

He had not anticipated there being baggage between them from the start. Baggage he hadn't even been a part of!

Thank God none of his scenes had been difficult today. While he'd smiled and recited his lines, his brain had been millions of miles away.

He'd left messages for his agent in India. As far as he knew, only his agency had access to his social media accounts, and until this very minute, he would have said he trusted Chandu and his employees with his life.

Jia had seemed reluctant to send him the additional texts, or he would have requested their whole chat transcript. Had this person plagiarized every text they sent Jia?

All those flowery words? He'd said all of them in another life, in another language.

Dev pulled into the garage and removed his phone from the mount. It was when a nice older lady in the lift gave him a strange look that Dev realized his breathing was fast and rough. He cleared his throat and inhaled deeply, trying to strangle some of his emotions back. *Into the box.*

Only they weren't in the box anymore.

The anger in her gaze made sense now. She should be angry at him. Hell, he was enraged, and he wasn't the young woman who had been toyed with. *Who could have done this?*

"Kaka?" Luna called out from the kitchen when he opened the door.

Drat. Normally he would have been filled with warmth at

her seeking him out the second he entered, but he'd hoped not to see anyone before he strangled—er, confronted—his agent. He took a deep breath, made sure his face was wiped clean of emotion, and then strode to the kitchen. He found his niece sitting at the kitchen counter, a plate of chocolate chip cookies in front of her, and Adil stirring a pot at the stove. Adil gave him a nod. Luna smiled at him, and his lips curved up automatically, though he didn't much feel like smiling.

"Hi, beti. Uncle." He stopped a foot away and rested his hand on the counter so he wouldn't be tempted to hug her. He could really use a hug now.

"How was your first day?" His uncle wiped his hands on the towel tucked into his waist.

"Relatively easy."

"That's what happens when you're not in every other scene. Enjoy this break. Once you hit the big-time here, you're going to be busier than you can imagine."

Dev gave a half smile. Adil was a cheerleader to his core. "Right."

Luna offered Dev the plate. "Want a cookie? Uncle made them."

"I didn't know you baked, Adil Uncle."

His uncle's smile in profile was sad. "Your aunt liked anything chocolate. I learned. Eat, eat. You're getting so skinny."

He wanted nothing more than to stress stuff eight of them in his mouth, so Dev settled for one. He took a bite and let the sweet chocolate raise the serotonin in his brain. "These are good. Did you have one, Luna?"

"I haven't had any yet."

He finished his cookie in two bites. "What are you waiting for?" He nudged the plate closer, and she picked up one.

She nibbled it. "Did you find out anything about the schools around here?"

The schools, right. "I spoke to one of my coworkers, but his children go to a private school."

"It's okay. I requested a copy of my birth certificate, since I didn't know if you have that."

This time his smile was real. "I think there's a copy somewhere, but it's probably in storage." Rohan hadn't been great about paperwork, but luckily, Luna's documentation had been in their mutual agent's possession. "We can go tour the local school tomorrow."

Luna's eyes brightened and she sat up straighter. "Really?"

"Yes, really."

She made an aborted motion and he wondered if she was going to launch herself at him, but instead, she folded her hands in her lap. "Thank you."

"Have you called Aji today? She said she's been ringing you."

"Not yet. I wanted to make sure it was okay."

"Of course. You don't have to ask." He tilted his head at the doorway. "Go call."

Adil waited for her to leave before turning around. He waved his spoon. "That girl is far too obedient. She sat here with a whole plate of cookies in front of her, waiting for you to come home to ask if she could have one."

"Weren't you complaining about her being disobedient yesterday?"

His uncle sniffed. "She apologized to me for that, and even I know such moods are normal for teenagers. It's not natural, this kind of obedience."

"Not natural for any child or for Rohan's child?"

"Both. Neither of you were like this at her age."

His uncle had only seen them a handful of times as children, but Dev trusted his judgment. "Her therapist said she's doing well, all things considered. It's entirely possible my brother's wild genes skipped a generation."

"Hmph." Adil turned the flame on the stove down. "If you think so."

He absentmindedly grabbed another cookie and sat in Luna's vacated seat. He didn't really know if he was right or not, but he couldn't stress over whether he was doing a decent job as a guardian tonight. Not when he had so many other things on his mind. "I will talk to her therapist again."

"Good." Adil tasted the curry he was making. "Hungry yet?"

"I'm actually going out soon." The scent of garam masala and chili powder teased Dev's nose. He took a third cookie. He'd have to spend a few extra minutes working out in the morning.

"Another party?"

"No, I'm meeting someone."

Adil turned the stove off and fetched two sodas from the

fridge and handed him one, popping another for himself. "You look a little pale."

Dev rubbed his forehead. "Something's come up."

"What?"

"You won't believe it."

His uncle leaned on his elbows. "Tell me."

Dev hadn't really intended to tell his family any of this, but the words spilled out of him, like someone had taken that box of stuffed emotions and turned it upside down. Dev quickly recapped what he knew of the situation, withholding some details, like how the texts he'd ostensibly sent to Jia were eerily familiar. Adil's eyes grew wider as he spoke, until they took up half his face. "Uhh," he finally said. "Who would go to that much trouble to set you up with a girl?"

"Set me up? This wasn't matchmaking."

"Then what was it?"

"I don't know." His phone rang, and he released a gusty sigh when he saw who it was. "Thank God." He answered. "Chandu."

"Hello, Mr. Dixit. Chandu isn't in yet, but since you said this was a social media issue, I thought I'd return your calls." Chandu's assistant had a posh and very fake British accent.

"Nandini. I need to know who has access to my accounts?" He turned slightly away from his uncle's inquisitive and scandalized face.

Nandini made a thoughtful noise. "Chandu and I, though I do all the posting and management of your content. Why? Is there a problem?"

"That's it? No one else?"

"No one."

"No one else has ever had access to my accounts?" he persisted. "No intern or employee?"

"No, sir. Me, Chandu, you." Nandini paused. "Oh, I suppose your brother, that time you were sick."

Dev stiffened. "What? My brother?"

Her voice turned wary. "You sent me an email, remember? You had the flu, and I was off, so you asked me to give your brother your credentials so he could post some things for you."

What? "I never did that, Nandini."

She was silent for a second. "I'm sure I still have the email, sir. I called Rohan myself to give it to him. I remember him telling me how sick you were." Her accent slipped, some of her native Delhi coming through.

There was no need to send the girl into a panic. "I have no doubt you do. But I didn't send it. I have actually not been sick in years."

Adil inched into his line of vision, clearly trying to eavesdrop.

"I'm so sorry, sir. I can assure you, if it hadn't been your own brother, I would never give your information—"

He cut her off. "It's okay." How was she supposed to know that he and Rohan weren't that close, that they'd regularly gone a year or two without seeing each other? "When did this happen? Do you remember the date?"

The date she gave him was a couple months before Rohan's death and matched up with the date on the first message Jia had sent him.

Dev tapped his fingers on his chin. There was something else about that date, though . . .

"Next time, I will be sure to verify with you over the phone before I give your information to anyone, family or not," she finished.

"Thank you," he said woodenly. "Don't worry about this. And don't tell Chandu."

"Yes, sir." She sounded relieved, like she'd expected him to fly into a rage. The rage was there, for sure, but it was directed where it belonged. At his late brother.

He hung up and looked at Adil. "It must have been Rohan. They gave him my password, and the dates match up."

"Why would he do this?"

Dev closed his eyes, remembering. "I saw him the night before." It had been at an awards show. Dev didn't go to many of those, but his friend had been honored that night.

The main times he did see Rohan were at industry events. That night, his brother had been holding court at his table, dressed in a bright peacock-blue sherwani.

Rohan had noticed him and waved him over. Dev had reluctantly gone.

His parents had raised them with love. They'd had a good relationship for thirteen years, him and his pesky little brother. But after their parents were gone, the industry and their grandfather's favoritism and distance had driven them apart. Dev hated that he couldn't be close with Rohan, and every time he saw him, it was like that icy longing pierced his heart anew.

He didn't think he was a particularly haughty person, but his brother's devil-may-care attitude and playboy lifestyle had never failed to prick his temper and annoyance. The louder his brother had gotten, the colder Dev had gotten. "We fought," Dev murmured. Rohan had asked if he'd wanted to come to an after-party, and he'd told him that he needed to get up early for work.

You must live a little, Bhai. God, you're boring.

You live too much. Don't you have your own responsibilities?

Rohan had stomped off. Later, Dev had felt bad, holding Luna over Rohan's head when he barely knew the child.

"So he did this as a prank?"

"Possibly."

"But you said this woman's been getting messages as of a week ago," Adil said slowly. "Reincarnation doesn't work that fast."

"Right."

"So what? Someone took over for him?"

Dev scratched his head. "They'd need Rohan's phone, at least, right? Or access to his information. Luna has it, I believe. She wanted the photos off it." Dev had scrolled through the photos first before giving it to her. He'd had to delete two folders full of nudes. At least Rohan had been organized in his porn collecting.

They locked eyes. Dev could tell the second the realization crashed into Adil because it hit him at the same time. "No," Dev said, his voice low. "It couldn't be."

"She's better with phones than we are."

"You cannot possibly be saying our thirteen-year-old niece picked up the catfishing torch for her father."

"If she did, Rohan should have named her Anjali," Adil mused, referring to the famous Bollywood movie plot moppet who had matchmaked her widowed father and his childhood friend.

"Implausible."

"But not impossible. You should speak to her."

Dev did not want to do that. "Perhaps I should speak to her therapist first."

The lines around Adil's eyes crinkled. "You must learn to trust your own gut sometimes when it comes to parenting." The man clapped his hand on Dev's shoulder. "Your parents didn't have therapists on speed dial when you were young. And look how you turned out."

Right. He'd been kicked from his modest middle-class loving family to a too-rich famous extended family without any therapy and he'd turned out fine. If one could call an emotionally repressed and lonely man fine.

He was not a ringing endorsement for no therapy, that was for sure.

"Go talk to her, Dev. Or you're going to be left with more questions than answers. Luna?" Adil yelled.

"Yes?" The faint voice came from the living room.

Adil gestured with his chin. "Go."

Dev sighed. He found Luna ensconced in front of the TV, her ever-present phone in her hands. "What are you doing?"

Luna shrugged but didn't look up. "Playing on my phone."

He stiffened. "Mmm. Talking to your friends?" *Or talking to strangers, pretending to be me?*

Her short curls bobbed as she nodded.

Dev sat down on the coffee table in front of her. The therapist had told him it would help for him to get down to her level whenever possible. "Can we talk for a minute?"

She glanced up. "Okay. About school?"

"No." He hesitated. "Luna, do you remember when I gave you your father's phone?"

Now she looked wary, and Dev hoped it wasn't for the reason he suspected. "Yeah. I thought it might have photos of me and him on it. Or maybe him and my mom." She fiddled with her sweatshirt. "It didn't."

Damn it, Rohan. Dev didn't know who Luna's mother even was. Rohan had simply shown up with a baby one day and announced that he was a father and that he'd paid off the mother.

That was how the Dixit family handled things. When in doubt, pay them off. "And that's all you did with the phone? Went through the photos?"

"Yes."

"Do you know where the phone is now? Do you still have it?"

"Arjun Kaka said he wanted to look through the photos, too, so I gave it to him."

Dev's eyes slowly closed. Oh no.

Arjun was his first cousin. He was successful in his career, but he had nowhere near the star power of his late father, his grandparents . . . or Rohan.

Dev didn't disbelieve that Arjun might have wanted to have a memento of Rohan's. The two had been around the same age and close, partners in debauchery. It had been Arjun who had taught Rohan how to drink and do drugs and sneak women in.

Dev was about as close to his cousin as he'd been to his brother, which was to say, not very. They had nothing in common and tended to butt heads as soon as they were in each other's vicinity.

He could very well imagine the man being delighted to find a way to mess with Dev from afar.

"I-I'm sorry. Was I not supposed to?" Luna's hands clenched in her lap. "Am I in trouble? I don't know what I did."

"No, you're not in trouble," Dev said, hurrying to reassure her. "I'm having a problem, and I'm trying to figure out who could be behind it."

"What's the problem?"

"Don't worry about it." But the lines on her face told him she would worry. "It's truly nothing. I merely wanted to get a phone number off of it."

"Oh." Luna's shoulder's relaxed. "Arjun Kaka should be able to help you with that."

He rose to his feet. "I'm sure he will. I'll go call him right now. I have to go meet a friend"—*friend* wasn't the right word, but *your father and/or uncle's victim* didn't sound right— "tonight, why don't you get cleaned up for dinner soon."

"Okay."

He stopped at the door. Her head was already bent over

her phone again. "Eat as many cookies as you want tonight, okay?"

She looked up and a flash of humor crossed her face. He took it and tucked it away in his heart. "I will."

Dev scrolled through his contacts for Arjun's number as he walked to his room. He should have put his cousin's full name as Arjun the Asshole.

The phone rang and rang without going to voice mail. Dev hung up and called again. Just when Dev thought Arjun may not pick up, a sleepy voice came over the phone.

It didn't matter that it was daytime in Mumbai right now. Arjun slept about fourteen hours a day, snug in his lavish, too-ornate bedroom in their grandparent's mansion. "Hello?"

"Arjun."

"Yes?"

Dev walked into his bedroom and closed the door. It was a testament to his restraint that he didn't slam it. "Tell me something . . . why did you do it? What pleasure did you get out of lying to this poor woman?"

Arjun yawned. "What are you talking about?" Sheets rustled. "You're becoming rude living in America, Dev. No how are you doing, no—"

"Shut up, Arjun."

Arjun actually shut up, probably shocked. Dev was too. He'd never uttered that kind of snarl. Even at his angriest, he kept a cool head. "It had to be you. You must have seen the messages in Rohan's phone. Or perhaps he even told you about this little prank. What possessed you to use my old scripts? You couldn't even be original?"

I'd cross the ocean for you.

Season seven, he'd said that to his wife on the show, when she was going abroad for a cooking show competition . . . the actress had actually been pregnant and too big to hide her belly behind large pots any longer. He remembered it vividly, because he'd written the dialogue.

He'd never wanted writing credit. The show runners had been more than happy to defer to him, at first for his name, and later because the audience liked what he came up with. He'd written or ad-libbed most of his own dialogue, and shaped a good number of the arcs as well.

Which was why he could spot the lines, even in another language. "Answer me."

"I don't know what—"

He almost beat his phone against the dresser. "This was a real person you lied to and misled. She is hurt. I cannot bear to think my own family could do this to anyone."

Arjun went silent for a second. "You met her?"

Confirmation. It didn't taste as sweet as he'd hoped it would. A yawning pit of guilt opened in his belly. "I did."

"What did you think of her?"

"I— What the hell does that matter?"

Another long beat. "Rohan never meant to hurt anyone, ever. Sometimes he just didn't think."

More confirmation. Another avalanche of guilt. He rubbed his temples. "I'm sure he meant to hurt me," he said thickly.

It was an admission he wouldn't have normally made to his cousin.

"Um, I have to go. The connection is terrible."

"It's fine."

Arjun made a scratching, yowling noise, clearly from his own mouth. "I cannot hear you." More hissing. The man wasn't exactly their family's best actor.

"Arjun, don't you—" But Dev was talking to dead air. He fruitlessly tried calling back twice more. "Damn it." He sat on his bed, stymied. Arjun may as well have confessed, but what was he supposed to do with that? He couldn't go running to their grandmother. She'd probably tell them to stop squabbling like they were children and avert her eyes from her youngest grandson's atrocious behavior.

Dev was a fixer, and he had no idea how to fix this.

He considered the various possibilities. He could lie, tell Jia he had no idea who had done this to her, and they could both move on.

He could tell her everything and humbly apologize and beg her forgiveness.

He could stare into her beautiful eyes in person again.

He shook his head, getting rid of that last thought. And the first one. There was no way his conscience would allow him to ignore a situation his blood had created. No, he had no choice but to fling himself on her mercy.

And then find a way to spend the rest of his time in Hollywood *not* obsessed with her.

Chapter Seven

Jia HAD spent the day vacillating between loss and anger, ricocheting so much that she was firmly in numb territory by the time she pulled up to the bar seven minutes late.

Dev had texted her at eight on the dot with an I am seated at a table in the back right corner. So she could add punctuality to his list of sins.

"Thank you," Jia said to her Ryde driver. Gerald would pick her up at the restaurant in a couple hours. She hadn't wanted him to chauffeur her all over town.

Her stomach was in a mess from nerves, and deep under that was an unhealthy amount of excitement, the same excitement she'd felt last night at the thought of seeing Dev for the first time. She had to remind herself that this wasn't the man she'd been speaking to.

Jia glanced around when she entered. She'd been to this bar on Melrose before. The lighting was dim and soft. Gauzy fabric draped over the chandeliers. It was romantic, which wasn't good, but it was also private, which was. She stopped at the hostess stand and forced a smile. "My—" *Companion?*

Date? Face of my catfisher? She began again. "I'm meeting someone here. He's already seated."

"Ms. Ahmed?" The hostess nodded and smiled. "Come with me."

Jia followed the hostess to the table in the back. Candles flickered everywhere, and the lighting was otherwise dim. She spotted more than a couple of celebrities, on lists from A through F, along the way. It wasn't too crowded, and the tables were set far apart from one another, the better to gossip and conduct secret assignations.

She would have spotted Dev even if there had been a million people in the room. He had an air of utter stillness about him. It was a calm that was foreign to her and her often frenetic mind.

Their eyes met, and he grew even more still before unfolding himself from the chair he'd been sitting in. Wow, he was . . . long. Tall. Had he been this tall at the party? Yes, of course, the venue had been bigger, and she'd been too busy drinking him in to notice any particular feature.

Very tall, and lanky. He wore a suit, a well-fitted, expensive one. Black-rimmed glasses sat on his nose, framing his dark eyes. His beard was neat and trimmed.

Dev held out his hand. "Ms. Ahmed."

Disappointment ran through her. Her last name was fine on his lips, but it was no . . . "Please, call me Jia."

"Jia."

That was better. She hoisted her bag up higher on her shoulder. "Sorry I'm late. I needed to make a detour to grab a shot of espresso before I came here. I didn't sleep much last night." She'd also bought a new pair of shoes at the mall, but he didn't need to know how she coped with her stress.

"Not a problem at all. I am accustomed to being too early to things."

She sat down opposite him. Though the tables were far apart, the one they were sitting at was rather small. Too small.

A cheerful waiter popped over. His eyes widened slightly when he took in Dev, but otherwise he gave no outward sign that he recognized either of them. "Can I get you two anything to drink?"

She nodded. "Iced tea, please, unsweetened."

"I'll have a glass of Malbec, thank you."

"Do you need a minute with the menu?"

"No, thank you." Ordering food would make this more intimate, and she needed to keep Real Dev and Fantasy Dev separate in her mind.

Dev handed both their menus to the waiter. "How was your day?" he asked politely when the man left.

Utterly unproductive. She'd shot a video for the goody bag unboxing, dodged one of her older sister's calls because she feared her foolishness would seep through the phone line, lain on the couch for an hour feeling bad for herself, fallen asleep, and then accidentally deleted the goody bag video. "Good. How about yours?" Small talk was fine, if that was where he wanted to start. She could make small talk in her sleep, and it delayed them having to discuss the mortifying events that had led to this evening out.

"Good. It was my first day filming the new show."

"That's cool. Did you like it?"

"It's different from what I've done before. But I shouldn't expect an evening American drama to be like a Hindi serial I suppose."

He had never talked about his work in his texts. Another red flag she'd ignored. "Different in a bad way?"

"I'm not sure yet. Just different."

She nodded. "I liked your soap."

"You watched it?"

"I'd watch it occasionally, yes, over the past year. I don't speak Hindi, so I had to hunt down subtitled episodes."

He rested his arms on the table. The candlelight on the table reflected against his eyeglasses. "What did you think?"

"They were entertaining. I don't know how you kept a straight face for some of those story lines."

He angled his face, and within a blink, he became Raj, his character, complete with haughty sniff. "I think my evil twin trapping me in a cave for two months so he can take over my life is quite serious actually."

She chuckled.

He dropped the act and his eyes warmed. "You look lovely tonight, by the way."

His voice was low and intimate and it sent goose bumps across her arms. "Thanks." Mentally, she slapped herself. What was she doing here, chatting with him like everything was fine? Those goose bumps were far too unnerving. Enough small talk. "Can we . . . can we talk about the incident?"

Dev nodded, but paused while their drinks arrived. He

twirled the stem of the wineglass between his fingers. "I don't quite know how to say this, Jia, except to note that I am deeply sorry. I have never contacted you, not from my social media, not via text."

"You already said that." And it hurt just as much, hearing it now, as it had then. "So who was it?"

"I believe . . . my brother and my cousin may have worked in concert to send the messages."

Who knew it was possible to choke on air? She inhaled so sharply her lungs contracted and she started coughing. It took her a second to get over her fit.

"Are you okay?"

"Yes," she wheezed. "I'm sorry, did you say . . . your brother?"

"Yes."

"Do you have another brother who is alive?"

"No."

That was a tasteless way to remind him of his brother's death, Jia, her inner mom scolded. "I mean . . . what?"

"There is some strong evidence my brother may have contacted you, a year ago, before he passed away. My cousin has his phone. I believe he started messaging you a couple months ago when you reached out again."

She cradled her head in her hands. "This is some bananas level stuff."

"I am aware."

"And your cousin confessed all this to you?"

"Not in so many words, but I could read between the lines. He won't answer my calls now."

"What did I do to make them hate me?"

Dev's fingers tightened around his glass. "I don't think they hate you. I think it was a prank aimed at me. You simply were the vehicle for the prank."

"Oh cool. That makes me feel great." She jabbed her finger against her chest. "I'm the one who got hurt here."

"I agree. I'm sorry you were placed in the middle of this."

His immediate apology doused some of her ire. Some of it, not all of it. "What kind of messed-up family do you have?"

Dev's sigh was so weary, she might have felt bad for him if she hadn't been very much caught up in this. He replied, "A more messed-up one than I previously imagined."

"How old is your cousin? Is he a child?"

"Only in maturity. He's thirty."

She racked her memory. Why hadn't she cared more about Bollywood movies? "It's . . . Arjun. Right?"

"Correct. You've seen his movies?"

"No, I don't care for college sex romps."

His laugh was strained. "I shall make sure to remember that phrase when I speak with him next. It will make him extremely angry."

Thank God she hadn't said anything particularly intimate or sexy in those texts. Blech. "This was a terrible thing to do."

"I agree." Dev's tone hardened. "I will figure out some way to ensure Arjun never does something like this again. He will not get out of this without consequence. In the meantime, Ms. Ahmed . . ." He reached into the inside of his jacket pocket and pulled out a check and a pen. He leaned forward, placed it on the coffee table, and wrote on it. He slid it over to her, across the table. "Please take this as a token of my family's regrets."

Jia looked at the zeroes, and a deep, inescapable anger flared to life in her belly. *The heroine is aghast, that the villain's cousin thinks she can be bought off.* "This is in dollars?"

"Yes."

She crossed her arms over her chest and sat back. She was actually pretty proud of herself. A year ago, she would have jumped on him and ripped his hair out by the roots for this insulting offer. "What are the conditions on this check?"

"No conditions."

"So I can take this money, deposit the check, and then go tell a tabloid about what your brother and cousin did to me?"

He blinked. "I trust you'll be discreet about this."

So it was hush money. "I want a million."

His fingers rested lightly on the check. "Dollars?"

"Yes."

"Impossible. I do not have that kind of money. I barely have— This is all I can afford right now."

She scoffed. A part of her was really loving this cold rage. It was a nice change from her usual flailing anger. "Your family is obscenely wealthy."

"I no longer share in my family's wealth. Everything I own is from my own sources."

She might have found that admirable, if it weren't for the

fact that he wouldn't have any of those sources without his family name to begin with. "Too bad. Everyone has their price, and a million is mine."

"A million is an outrageous sum for—"

"For hush money?"

"It is not anything as sordid as that. The money is merely my way of apologizing on behalf of my family," he said coolly.

"And in return I don't do anything, like, say . . . leak the texts, right?"

"If that was my concern, I wouldn't need money for that. Leaking the texts would hurt you as well."

Her temper fired hotter, partially because he was right. If any of this ever came to light, she'd get made fun of mercilessly. It took a second for the internet to turn against someone. Not to mention how her family would react when they found out she'd been catfished. *Shamed and cowed, the heroine returns to her family's home, because she cannot be trusted to be on her own.* "That sounds like a threat."

"It's not." He leaned forward and spoke, and every calm word only made her madder. "I am trying to be as nice as possible. Please accept the gesture."

Be reasonable, Jia.

Stop being so emotional.

Why do you cry so much? It's not rational.

Don't be hasty, Jia.

It hurt her a little to do this, given what she knew of her declining revenue, but Jia picked up the check and ripped it in two, and then two again and then again. "I don't want your bribe."

"It's not a bribe." He stared at the confetti she'd made. "Do you know how long I had to hunt for a paper check in my moving boxes? Everything is electronic now."

"Thanks for hunting. To be honest, I never thought I'd get to rip up a check in indignation in this day and age."

Dev closed his eyes and pinched the bridge of his nose. "Jia . . ."

Do not *get all flutter tummied over your damn name.* "I think I should leave."

"Please," he said, his voice low. "I understand how much this must have hurt. Please, let me make it up to you somehow. What can I do for you?"

She shook her head and shoved her chair back. "There's nothing you can do that can make up for this."

His eyes darkened. "I can't accept that. I must make amends. I—" A small commotion near the front of the bar caught their attention, along with that of others in the bar.

"What's going on?" He craned his neck to look around her.

"It's paparazzi. Someone superfamous must be coming or going." A few people around them were hastily donning their jackets, eager to capitalize on the free publicity outside.

Internet-famous celebrities didn't appeal to most paps, but for once she didn't want any attention. She waved the waiter over. "Is there a back way out of here?" Jia asked the waiter.

"Yes, of course," the man said calmly, used to sneaking people out.

"Wait for me, please," Dev said.

Jia cursed the innate politeness that froze her feet at Dev's request. Dev was a bigger fish than her for sure, and as annoyed as she was at him—and his family—he'd personally done nothing to her to justify throwing him to the publicity wolves.

Dev handed over his credit card, and the waiter pulled out a handheld machine and swiped it right there, while she texted Gerald where to pick her up.

She and Dev followed the waiter through the kitchen and to a back door. "Goes into the side alley," the waiter said.

"Got it, thanks," Jia murmured. The cooler air hit her face as they stepped out.

"What is that smell?"

Jia sniffed. "Pot," she said curtly. She'd gotten used to the scent of it here.

"Oh."

"It's legal, don't sound so scandalized."

"I'm not scandalized." He was silent as they walked through the alleyway. "Jia—"

They stepped out onto the sidewalk. "I don't want to hear anything—" She gasped when he placed his hand on her arm, whirled her around, and stepped in front of her. The smooth move crowded her back against the building. His arm slipped between her and the brick, though it didn't touch her. His other hand came to rest on the wall next to her face, locking her in the cage of his body. If she took a step back, she'd hit his strong arm. If she took a step forward, she'd hit his strong chest.

"What the hell are you doing?" she whispered furiously. Or she tried to sound furious. Yes, it was definitely fury that had sent her heartbeat racing and her breath into her throat.

His chest moved quicker, like maybe his heart was racing too. His forehead almost rested against hers. "I'm sorry to startle you. Give it one moment," he said softly. "There's a man running up the street. He has a camera. He'll be past us in a second. You seemed eager to avoid the press, I'm trying to keep him from seeing you."

Oh. If she listened carefully, over the pulse in her ears, she could make out a pounding on the pavement coming from the other direction. "I see."

His head dipped low, silky black strands of hair falling into his eyes. "If you're uncomfortable, I can create a distraction, and you can run."

"No. It's fine."

His hand fisted on the wall next to her head, and her breathing grew deeper, to match his. With the way his body was positioned, it probably did look like they were just a couple kissing or intimately embracing. Only they knew they weren't touching at all.

Except for where their breath intermingled. He smelled so good. Expensive and woodsy. Like a fancy forest.

The cage grew warm, and so did she.

She moved slightly. Not to force a touch! That would be wrong. As wrong as the little tingles that raced over her skin. They stood there like that for a few seconds, or maybe minutes, she didn't know, until Dev risked a glance to the side. "I think they're gone."

Who? "Oh. Good."

His breath puffed against her skin. "Do you have a ride home?"

"Yes." She looked up at him. "He'll pick me up on Almont. What about you?"

"I'll call a car. I don't care if I get photographed by myself."

She nodded, unable to think clearly. He smelled so good, expensive and soothing. "Okay." Her phone vibrated. Gerald. "My ride's here."

He looked around more carefully, his dark eyebrows meeting over his eyes. Big and protective. Like a sexy bodyguard.

No! Her body wasn't being anything-ed by this famous virtual stranger, let alone guarded. "Coast seems clear."

He took a large step back, and she immediately had to bury the yearning she felt for his warmth. They stared at each other for a moment. It wasn't often that she felt shy. "Okay. Goodbye." That's right. It was a goodbye, not a see you later.

He nodded, but didn't say the word back to her. "I wish there was something I could do to make this all up to you."

"I don't think there is." Which was too bad.

His lips turned down. "Please let me know if you change your mind."

Jia turned on her heel and walked away, the back of her

neck hot. She tried to resist glancing over her shoulder, she really did. But when she reached the road where Gerald had pulled up, she couldn't restrain herself.

Dev stood right where she'd left him. He raised a hand, and she did the same, then got into her car. The door closing was a metaphor for his exit from her life.

That's what she'd tell herself.

"Is everything okay?" Gerald asked.

"Yup." Her voice sounded higher than normal, though. Everything was cool. She'd been catfished as some kind of family prank, and the man whose face they'd used had tried to buy her silence and then she'd smelled him and it had made her tummy drop. A totally normal night.

She covered her hot face with her hands. *Should have taken the check.* Then she might have gotten something out of this whole debacle.

Chapter Eight

JIA SIPPED her latte and pretended not to stare at the girl dancing on the other side of the pool. She knew of her, Harley, a teenager who had moved into an apartment in the building a few months ago. Jia tried not to be the fuddy-duddy grandma who wondered where the kid's parents were, but seriously, the girl was definitely under eighteen, where were her parents?

Off enjoying the girl's money, most likely, in their new Hollywood Hills home. Word on the street was that Harley gained about a hundred thousand followers a day on her platform of choice and easily made five or six figures on a fifteen-second post.

Don't be bitter. You cannot compare success.

Jia returned to the legal pad she'd balanced on her knees, filled with scribbled ideas for new content. She couldn't dance, she was shit at lip-synching, and her expertise was in long-form original videos, not fifteen-second clips borrowing someone else's music. She doodled a heart in the corner. Maybe at twenty-nine, she was a grandma.

Harley finished her dance and downed a water bottle before packing up her ring light and tripod. Their eyes met across the pool, and Jia tried to pretend she was still working and not spying on the girl.

It must not have worked, because the lithe brunette crossed the distance, her gear in tow. Her face was flushed. "Hey!"

Jia glanced over her shoulder, but Harley was definitely talking to her. "Hi."

"What did you think?"

"Of your dance? It was great. I wish I could do that."

"Oh please. You have actual talent." Harley dropped into the chaise next to her. "I'm a big fan. I've been watching you since middle school."

Grandma. She tried not to grimace. "Aw. Thank you. I'm a fan of yours as well. You're a great dancer."

"I know we're not supposed to be filming at the pool, but I figured if no one was here, the management wouldn't know."

"I won't tell." Jia had filmed in her share of no-trespassing places in her day. When the light was right, it was right.

"I didn't know you lived here." A sweet smile lit up Harley's face. "I just moved in."

"By yourself?" Jia couldn't help but ask.

The girl's smile dimmed. "Yeah. My parents gave permission. It's better this way."

Jia made a mental note to check in on Harley from time to time. "It's good to do what's best for us," Jia said gently. "And no, I don't live here, I rent it as a set, basically."

"Oh. If you're ever around at night, let me know. I'd love

to have a movie night or something. I haven't met many people here yet."

Jia wasn't usually here in the evenings, but she could make an exception for a new young friend who might otherwise easily fall into a more predatory crowd. "Absolutely. Here, take my number."

"Cool," Harley enthused, after she'd entered Jia's number into her phone. "I'd love to talk to you about doing a collaboration or something."

Hundreds of thousands of new followers a day.

Jia smiled and swallowed her envy. "I'd like that. I can't dance." She had zero rhythm, much to her family's amusement.

"That's cool, we can come up with something else, sometimes I do nondancing videos. Maybe you could give me, like, makeup tips or something."

"Your makeup is already fantastic." A touch of mascara, eyeliner, and lip gloss, plus what looked like a BB cream.

"That's because my parents made me learn how to do it on my own when I was thirteen. They said my skin was so bad I wouldn't get an acting gig if I couldn't hide it."

Jia blinked. Sometimes she wished she'd had more involved parents when it came to her career, but not if they'd be involved like that. "Oh. Um."

A beeping noise filled the air, and Harley looked around. "What's that?"

"Just my timer." Jia tapped the plastic box on the table. "I get distracted by my phone, so I put it away while I'm working."

Harley clutched her phone to her chest. "My nightmare, not having my phone."

"It used to be mine, until I realized how hard it was to focus on work with it in my hand."

Harley looked at her blankly, and Jia realized the younger woman wasn't there yet, the point where content creation felt like an uphill climb because she'd used up all her best ideas. Hopefully she never experienced it. She was probably pulling in way more income than Jia had after a year of working in entertainment. "Anyway, it means I should head up for lunch."

Harley tucked her pin-straight hair behind her ear. "I'll be in touch!"

"Looking forward to it."

They said their goodbyes and Jia gathered up her stuff to head to her staged apartment.

Her lunch consisted of a sandwich she'd slapped together at the crack of dawn this morning. She'd gotten up extra early so she could beat traffic. And avoid Katrina, whom she'd have to tell about Dev.

Remember how you told me I should delete him and never see him again? I had drinks with him and smelled him instead.

She chewed the PB&J and grimaced. She was doing her best to not think about him. Because it wasn't her shame or wounded pride that was foremost when she did think about him. It was the heat, when he'd spun her around and placed his body between her and danger.

Between you and a photographer. Girl, please, he wasn't taking a bullet for you.

She took a swig of her milk and grabbed her phone out of the kitchen drawer she kept it tucked in when she wasn't working.

Her first clue that something was wrong was all the notifications on her lock screen. Her second was that they were all from family members. Her mother and two eldest sisters, to be exact.

Uh-oh. That wasn't good at all.

Her phone rang before she could navigate to her texts, her mother's sweetly smiling contact photo popping up. She answered it with some trepidation. What had she done now? "Hello?"

"Jianna."

Well. This was already bad, if they were at the name that was on her birth certificate. "Hi, Mommy," she tried again, though she didn't know what she was wheedling for.

"Where have you been? I have been trying to call you for *hours*."

"I was working." The joy of her parents not viewing her work as actual work. Her mom would never assume any of her sisters would be glued to their phone at noon on a weekday.

"Video call me. I need to speak to you face-to-face." Her mother hung up, and Jia flinched.

She steeled herself as she sat on the couch and opened her laptop. Her worry grew as she found not one, but three pairs of dark eyes looking back at her with various degrees of concern and doubt and annoyance. "Oh good," she said, with as much enthusiasm as she could muster, which wasn't very much. "Salam. Everyone's here." Or at least, her two oldest sisters and her mother. "Where's Sadia?" Her middle sister was one of her staunchest allies. If Ayesha had to be off the grid communing with nature somewhere, Sadia would be a good stand-in advocate for her.

"We're trying to limit what disturbs her."

Sadia was pregnant with her second child, and she was having miserable morning sickness, so that made sense, but the sentence ratcheted her anxiety higher. "What's going on?" Jia shoved a cushion behind her back. Best to make herself comfortable while she got yelled at for whatever she'd done—or not done—now.

What did I do or not do now?

It wasn't easy to be the black sheep of a successful family. When she was younger, Sadia had occupied the role, for running off to elope with a boy her parents didn't approve of. Jia had seen the example her parents made of her sister— not talking to or about her for years, until their precious first grandson was born—so Jia had tried to toe the line. Until she couldn't take it anymore and quit med school.

"Jianna."

Again with the full name, yikes.

"Why did I leave surgery to find no less than two Whats-App messages featuring a photo of you wrapped around some man like a vine?"

"The messages were from us," her oldest sister, Noor, interjected.

Jia was so preoccupied by how her mother said *man*, the same way she might say *serial killer*, that it took her a second to process the rest of that sentence. "Uh. What." *How.*

Noor crossed her arms over her chest. She was a mini-version of their mom, though her recent illness had taken some of her healthy plumpness away. "We are very worried about you," Noor said severely. Noor was always severe. The eldest of the five sisters, she felt the weight of being the future matriarch very heavily.

"You didn't answer our calls." Zara, her second-eldest sister, tipped her head and gave Jia a concerned look, the same one she probably gave to her psychiatric patients.

"What kind of shenanigans are you getting up to in that city?" Her mother closed her eyes. "I knew you'd fall prey to the evils of Hollywood. Didn't I tell you girls that?"

Jia held up her palms. "I haven't fallen prey to anything. I don't know what you guys are talking about." *Don't you?* A pit opened up in her stomach, and it widened when Zara held her phone up to the camera. It took a second to focus, and then Jia had to swallow.

There she was, she and Dev, against the brick wall of that bar. His face was slightly turned toward the camera while hers was away. It looked like they were hugging, perhaps seconds away from kissing.

While they'd been avoiding one photographer, another had caught them with a nice wide angle lens. And, apparently, he or she or they had known who they were photographing.

"Legend's Grandson Romancing His Way Through America," the headline read. Jia squinted, trying to make out the text of the article, but it was too blurry. "Ahhh . . ."

"It doesn't name you, thank God." Zara put the phone down. "Of course, I recognized your scarf right away, I gave it to you last Eid, and then I looked closer at the profile. This is definitely you, isn't it, Jia?"

Her shoulders sagged in relief. She hadn't been named in the press. That was something. At least her extended family wasn't blowing up her mom's phone about why her youngest unmarried daughter was going around doing something as scandalous as smelling a man. "It's me, but this isn't what it looks like." She paused. "By the way, what do you think it looks like?" Just so they were all on the same page.

"It looks like you are *kissing* a man at a *bar*!"

Her mother said it with all the scandal of someone else saying, *"It looks like you are murdering a man at a murder house."*

"That's not what kissing looks like, Mama."

"Don't get fresh with me."

"I'm not being fresh!"

"You are nuzzling, at the very least." Zara tossed her hair.

"Nuzzling is worse than kissing," her mother announced.

"How . . . ?" Jia rolled her shoulders. It was no surprise how tight they were. "We were both avoiding photographers. Clearly not well enough."

"Avoiding photographers? Is that what they're calling it nowadays. Convenient," Noor said dryly. She readjusted the nasal cannula under her nose. Jia felt a stab of worry, as she always did when she saw the device. While she'd been sick in California, Noor had been battling the same illness in their hometown in Western New York. Jia had recovered without long-term side effects, but Noor hadn't been so lucky. She didn't need supplemental oxygen all the time—she could do her rounds at the hospital as an ER doc without it—but she still depended on it when she was home.

Nothing had made Jia feel more homesick or helpless than being sick all the way across the country, except for knowing her sister was sick and she couldn't help out. Her sisters might be annoying as hell, but that didn't mean she didn't love them fiercely. "Look . . ."

Zara sighed. She was always stylish and glowed with health, and today was no different, though she wore a sweater instead of a suit. "Jia, I'm sorry, but the jig is up. I told Mom and Noor."

"Told them what?"

"I overheard you speaking with Ayesha weeks ago. I know you've been talking to this man."

Oh, for fuck's sake.

The rare swear could be forgiven right now. Jia had told Ayesha about Dev, but only because she told Ayesha everything. Of all the conversations for Zara to overhear . . .

"Imagine my surprise to find out my youngest daughter is going around with a boy and I know nothing about it," Farzana announced, hurt dripping off her words.

"I'm not going around with him."

Her eldest sister snorted. "You are clearly talking to him."

Talking to was the euphemism all her sisters had used for dating until they got engaged or married. Their mother got scowly at the thought of her daughters engaging in American dating, what with its premarital sex and all.

Except Jia had literally only been *talking to* the Person Formally Known as Dev. She opened her mouth, but her mother continued. "I would not have been opposed to this, Jianna. It is time for you and Ayesha to settle down. And obviously, Devanand Dixit, well . . . he is not the star his grandfather was, but clearly he is from a good family and well-off. You did not have to hide him." Farzana's mouth turned down in a frown. "Am I so scary you could not tell me?"

Yes.

Jia rubbed her hand over her forehead. But that wasn't the issue right now. She hadn't told her mom because there had been nothing to tell. "It's not about that . . ."

"Despite his wealth and family, he's still an actor," Noor said, but it wasn't with the same level of accusation as when the call had started. She liked to be on the same page as their mother. Noor's eyes turned calculating. "I bet the wedding would be bonkers fun, though. The Dixits probably know how to throw a party."

Wedding! "I'm not marrying Dev Dixit," Jia blurted out.

Zara rolled her eyes. "Yeah, sure you're not. Then why were you squealing over how sweet he was with Ayesha?"

Did her sister have bat ears? "We did talk about Dev, but I'm not dating him."

"So you're just kissing him in public? Sorry, nuzzling. Full mouth to neck action." Noor's lips puckered up, like she'd eaten something nasty.

Jia's neck went pink at the attention. "He didn't have his mouth anywhere on me!"

Farzana gave a small growl, like she hadn't heard Jia at all, which wasn't unusual. "That, I will not tolerate, Jia. What would people say?"

"We weren't doing anything—" Jia was interrupted by Noor's coughing fit. She watched helplessly as her sister bent over almost double from the force of it.

"I'm coming over," Zara said to Noor, when she subsided.

"No, it's fine." Noor cleared her throat. "When I get too worked up or emotional, it's like my lungs can't quite keep up." She said it in a detached, almost clinical way. Her sister's job as an ER doc required she be clinical.

"There is nothing to get upset over," their mother said soothingly, her manner completely changing. "Everything is fine. It's okay, Jia." Her mom sniffed. "I will forgive you keeping this from me for who knows how long. Dev is an actual good prospect for you. I did not think you would find someone so eligible."

Well, ouch. She felt that backhanded compliment like a slap to the face.

Jia twisted her fingers together. She hadn't seen that beaming look of pride in her mother's eyes in a long time, and she hated that she had to ruin it now. She was going to tell them the truth—that she'd been catfished. That was exactly what she was going to do. She could anticipate their reaction.

Hollywood has ruined you.

You must come home.

Typical Jia.

It was the last one that was the worst. Typical Jia, flighty and unpredictable. Someone who had to be kept stuffed away, lest she embarrass the family. The disappointment.

She was going to tell them everything. Except then Noor gave another slight cough, and what came out of Jia's mouth was "Yes, he's a good guy."

Uh-oh. Whaaaaaat.

"Of course, we'll have to meet him to be sure of it," her mother mused.

"What?" *Whaaaaaat.*

"Oh yes." Farzana waved her hands. "I'll talk to your father about this. You know how protective he can get. We'll try to come out in a few weeks."

Her father was protective of his daughters, but he was a pussycat compared to her mom. "Wait, you probably won't get to meet . . . Look, this is all still new. I haven't been talking to him for long, nothing's determined. Imagine if things don't work out, you'll have made your trip for nothing."

"Not for nothing. We haven't seen you in over a year. I told you we'd visit as soon as we were able. Don't you want us to come there?"

"Of course I do, but not to meet some guy."

"This will kill two birds with one stone," Farzana said briskly. "We see you, we meet this prospective groom for you."

Was it her imagination, or was it hot in here? Jia unpinned and unwound her head scarf and dropped it next to her, taking her stretchy net underscarf off next. She didn't bother to fix her hair, which was sticking up everywhere. "He's not my prospective groom."

"Fine, fine, the boy you are talking to."

Jia's hands clenched in her lap. Oh dear. *Tell them the truth now.* They would be so much more disappointed when they got here and there was no Dev.

What if there was?

Wait, no. That was impossible.

Or is it?

It was.

Or, hear me out . . . is it?

To what end, though? Even if Dev was willing to play along, she'd have to tell her family eventually that she and Dev weren't dating.

"In the meantime, please be discreet. It won't do for your aunts and uncles to recognize you in any photos. No need for anyone to think you went off to California and started acting wild once you were away from us."

Jia raised an eyebrow. That was the first time she'd heard her mother speak of her career with any semblance of pride. Or look at her with that level of approval.

Actually, her sisters were looking at her with approval too. It was like a drug, making her feel heady and invincible. Is this how it felt, for people whose families believed in them?

"I am so proud of you, Jia."

She nearly whimpered at her mom's words. She could do this. She didn't have to tell them the truth right now, and she wouldn't have to do it when they came here. She could maybe even keep this charade going for a while, until she figured out a way to make them so proud of her in other ways that they didn't care that she wasn't marrying a Bollywood legend's grandson.

"You are finally getting your life together, MashAllah," Noor remarked.

She'd *had* her life together. Kind of.

"Keep this up, and we'll all worry about you less," Zara said cheerfully. She was holding her phone and moving through her house. Her daughter, Amal, was screaming something in the background. "I'm off. Noor, we'll be over in ten minutes."

"I don't need—" Noor began, but Zara winked out. That was the way in their family; state the intention and then disappear.

Noor sighed. "I have to tidy up. See you later." She hung up.

Her mom gave Jia a bright smile. "Wait until I tell your father. He'll be so happy."

Jia almost whimpered again. She was lying to her dad too? About this fake man they'd never meet? Oh God. Was she catfishing her parents? "Dev's very busy and . . ."

"I'm sure he'll make time for your family," Farzana said firmly. "He knows what's expected. I'm very excited. You don't know how much we'd all worry less about you if we knew you were settled with a good boy."

Jia licked her lips. "Cool."

Farzana glanced over her shoulder. "I have to go, love."

"Okay. Love you." Best to be superagreeable. She hung up

with her mom and stared at her wall. Then she sent a message to her twin. IF YOU GET THIS CALL ME ASAP PLS 911.

Slowly, she collapsed back onto her couch. Had she truly invented a fake boyfriend to impress her family? One who was an international star she'd had no intention of seeing again, let alone producing to her family in a few weeks' time?

Welp. Someday she'd learn not to dig herself into a deeper hole while getting out of one.

Wasn't she still furious with Dev? Or had her anger at his offer of money and his family been drowned out by needing him now? Or by the faux nuzzle?

Even if she could control her negative emotions, how was she going to get Dev on board?

I wish there was something I could do to make this all up to you.

Jia raised an eyebrow. Maybe that part wouldn't be an insurmountable challenge, actually.

Chapter Nine

Dev reclined on the sofa in his trailer. His script was in his hands, but his brain was a million miles away. Across the ocean, even.

Legend's Grandson. His inner ambitiousness was annoyed by that. He'd worked hard to make a name for himself. It was the main reason he'd chosen a completely different medium.

"It's actually excellent press," John had explained to him earnestly over the phone earlier. "Chandu was concerned it might be scandalous, given the obvious differences between you and the girl, but people are really loving it."

Dev didn't bother to explain that the differences weren't as large as they appeared. As much as his grandfather had wanted to erase their background when he'd taken Rohan, at least, under his mentorship, their mother had been Muslim and quite middle-class.

Dev wasn't surprised Chandu was happy. If they were talking about Dev's love life, they were talking about him. For the most part, Dev had never given people a reason to gossip, unlike the rest of his family. His father had run off with a woman, his uncle had died young, his grandfather had been a playboy. Arjun and Rohan had never met a drug, drink, or model they didn't want to try.

Meanwhile, Dev kept a low profile in his personal life. Wrongly, according to his team. *It softens you*, John had told him. *Makes you more human. Plus, they miss talking about your family. It's nice to get over the grief of your brother and grandfather's deaths.*

People were quite human with or without relationships, in his opinion, but Dev couldn't deny the public did feel an odd sort of possessiveness with his family. He remembered being bewildered when he'd come to live with his grandparents. Every morning, his grandfather and Arjun would go to the balcony and wave at the fans screaming outside. Rohan had joined them, a cute cherub-faced thirteen-year-old. Dev had been lanky and awkward and had never asked or been asked to engage in the morning greeting. As far as he could tell, the crowds had dispersed after his grandfather died.

All the public had needed was a tiny crumb to get similarly excited over Dev, it seemed. And Jia had been that crumb.

John had asked if he could leak the name of the girl in the photo, and Dev had heartily declined. If he didn't want to drag some woman into the spotlight to inherit millions and millions of rupees, he definitely wasn't going to do it to get some extra space in a newspaper.

Dev stared blindly at his script. He wanted to call Jia, to

see if she'd seen the photo, but she'd been pretty final about saying goodbye to him last night.

Jesus, had he only known her for a matter of days? Perhaps it was all the videos he'd watched of her that made him feel like he'd known her longer. His gaze strayed to his phone. He wasn't watching them any longer, though. Not since . . . well, since a few hours ago.

The knock at his trailer door had him sitting straight up. It wasn't his call time yet, but perhaps the writers wanted to speak to him about some of his notes. Unlikely, given how quickly they'd dismissed him, but one could dream. The script was fine but it was also incredibly . . . boring. And so was his character.

He opened the door and took a step back, he was so startled.

Was he a wizard? How had he conjured this? "Jia."

"Hi." She gave him a little wave.

He'd always thought American accents to be flat and boring, but her voice was anything but. She had a slightly different cadence when she spoke in person. Online, there were more peaks and valleys, and it felt like there was an inflated quality, like a bright and bubbly glass of champagne. Offline, it was more natural, throatier, but no less vibrant. No, he wasn't watching her videos any longer . . . but he may have fallen asleep to one last night.

Do not tell her that you fell asleep to a video of her explaining the differences between fake eyelashes. Actually, don't tell anyone that.

She stood with one foot on the step up to his trailer. He would be perpetually surprised at how small she was. Her personality made her seem bigger. She wore wide-legged black slacks and a cream sweater today, her hair covered by a light gray scarf. Her makeup was equally muted.

He wasn't a man who had ever understood or paid attention to makeup, but after watching so many of her videos, he wondered what had made her choose that coral lipstick and light blush. Online, at least, she seemed to choose each color and brand deliberately.

What on earth was she doing here? He glanced around, but no one seemed to be paying them attention. As he'd learned, though, one could never predict where a photographer was hiding or who on set may have seen the photo and gossip floating around today. "Would you like to come in?"

"Yes, please."

He backed up so she could come inside. Dev quickly checked himself out in the mirror hanging behind the door. Yes, tie straight, jacket lint-free, glasses clear.

She glanced around the trailer curiously, but it was a standard set trailer. He'd put nothing of himself in it. "Have a seat." He gestured at the table, since the couch had his script spread out all over it. "Would you like a drink?"

She sat down. "I don't want to put you through any trouble—"

"Not trouble. I was about to have some iced tea." He wasn't, but it was hot out and there was a tiny trickle of sweat at her temple.

"I'd like some as well, then."

He grabbed two bottles of iced tea from the stocked fridge he barely touched and brought them to the table, sitting across from her. This felt oddly intimate, but it shouldn't. People took business meetings in their trailers all the time. It's not like this was his bedroom or anything.

She took a long sip and set the bottle down. "I'm sorry to bother you here."

It wasn't only her makeup. There was something more subdued about her today, like her anger and indignation had been calmed, though he wasn't sure by what. "How did you get on the set?"

"Eh. It's easy enough to know somebody who knows somebody in this city."

"I . . . assume you saw the photo of us."

"I did."

"And you saw what they implied?" He tried to keep his tone matter-of-fact, but wasn't sure if he succeeded.

She nodded.

He winced. "I apologize. I truly was trying to shield us from a photographer. I didn't think there would be someone else."

"Who would?" She gave a halfhearted smile. "Everyone's paparazzi these days."

"Indeed."

She placed her purse on the table. "My family saw it."

He grimaced. "They recognized you? I'm sorry, I told myself the only good thing was that your face was obscured."

By my body. He took a sip of his iced tea to get the word out of his head. No need to go thinking about bodies around this woman. "Are they particularly conservative?"

"Not terribly conservative, but they worry."

"I'm sorry," he repeated. "I am usually careful about paparazzi. I became too relaxed here."

She nodded. "What's the reaction been like for you?"

"My agent is delighted. I have never been the one the media gossips about in my family."

"How do you feel about it?"

He lifted his shoulder. "I suppose I'm mostly worried about how it may affect you."

Her eyes softened. "That's kind of you."

"It's not kind. I owe you, as it is."

Her lip curled up in the corner. "Please don't offer me money again."

"I wouldn't, now that I know how you feel about it." He'd had to scrape his account to put that check together, so a part of him was glad she hadn't taken it. He still didn't see anything wrong with compensating her and soothing his guilty conscience, but he could see how it could be misconstrued as hush money.

She traced the water ring the iced tea bottle had left. "I don't need money."

"Understood."

"But there's something else you could do for me."

He leaned forward. "Anything."

She looked up, and he was so captured by her pretty light

eyes and the long lashes she'd artfully curled, that he almost missed her next words.

"I'd like you to date me."

Jia wondered if she'd shocked proper Dev into silence. He'd gone still and stared at her like she'd grown two heads.

He finally adjusted his glasses, as if to see her two heads better. "You want to date me?"

"Oh no." She didn't want him to get some foolish idea that she was still pining for him, because she was *not*. This was a business arrangement that would benefit them both. "I want to *pretend* to date you."

Dev leaned back in his seat and tapped his fingers on the table. It was hard to breathe in this little trailer, and that was most definitely because he was taking up far too much space. She'd seen him only in suits before, but this one was more relaxed, the tie pulled loose and slightly askew. She was going to assume that was for the role he was playing, and not of his own volition. His hair was ruffled up, and there was a trace of eyeliner on his eyes, which told her hair and makeup had prepped him already.

They'd done a bad job of blending, though. She ripped her gaze away from the line of foundation at his collarbone. It wasn't her problem, that foundation line.

"I do not think that sentence is as explanatory as you believe it is."

"Okay. Here's the deal." She steepled her fingers in front of her face. She'd rehearsed this on the drive over. She knew exactly what to say, and she wouldn't have her brain turned to mush because she was in front of an attractive man, damn it. "It sounds like this publicity helped you, right?" That was what she'd been banking on. The tabloid articles had been gleeful, not condemning, and she knew how much actors loved their attention.

He shrugged. "Sure."

"So now you owe me twofold?"

"Ah . . ."

"Because you could help me out. By meeting my parents in a few weeks and posing as my boyfriend. Did I mention that you owe me?"

Dev blinked at her, his glasses magnifying his eyes. "Uh."

Dev's shock wasn't entirely unexpected. This sounded like something out of a zany comedy. She backed up. "I may have allowed my family to believe that I was dating you."

"Why would you do that?" he asked slowly.

"They saw the picture," she reminded him.

"You could have explained it was a misunderstanding."

"I know. I tried to tell them that. But you see . . . one of them overheard me talking to my sister about you. Or the man I thought was you." She scrunched up her face. "You know what I mean. Anyway, this confirmed things for them, and I didn't know what to say. I either had to confess that I had lied about ever talking to you and knowing you, or I had to say that I was catfished, and I couldn't do that without them getting mad, and the next thing I knew I was saying that, yeah, we were totally dating, and then my mom said they'd come here and meet you and—"

She was shocked when he lightly placed his hand on her arm. "Hey, hey," he said, and his voice was so low and soothing it almost brought a tear to her eye. She hadn't realized how worked up she was. "It's okay. That makes sense."

"Does it?" She blinked rapidly to control potential leaking. Stupid emotions.

"Absolutely." He patted her arm and withdrew his touch, which made her slightly sad. "What will you do in the long-term? Your parents will be disappointed if it doesn't work out, yes?"

As disappointed as I was when you turned out to be fake. "They'd be more disappointed at the alternative explanations. You're authentic and a good guy. They'll approve."

"You want their approval?"

"Of course."

Dev rubbed his hand over his jaw. It was a nice jawline. She'd seen photos of him without the beard. The facial hair made him look older and slightly nefarious, though now she knew he would be careful to not touch her in an untoward manner even when they were hiding from discovery.

Which was good, she totally didn't want him to touch her. She discreetly brushed her fingers over the still warm spot where he'd patted her on her forearm. No touches wanted at all.

"How do you know I'm a good guy?"

She cocked her head. "You could have lied to me about your cousin being the one to send those messages. You didn't have to apologize."

"That is what any decent person would have done."

"Sadly, the bar is on the floor when it comes to decency these days."

"You know, my sister on *Kyunki Mere Sanam Ke Liye Kuch Bhi* had a similar storyline once. She pretended to have a fiancé from Canada, and hired an actor. The problem was when he met our parents on the show, the lie fell apart because they were clearly strangers to one another." He paused, and his tone gentled. "I am an actor, Jia, but your parents know you well, and I do not think they will be fooled by someone who does not. Or suppose they ask us simple questions, such as how we met, or what our first words to each other were?"

"We have time before they get here, like a month at least. We can learn everything we need to know about each other by then, and we can get our stories straight. We can even get together in advance. Have some study sessions."

"It wouldn't be proper for us to meet in private like this too much." He gestured around them at the otherwise empty trailer.

His concern over impropriety was an ingrained, earnest part of his personality, it seemed. "Can I ask you something? How are you like this? Not to stereotype, but I wouldn't think anyone raised in the movie industry would be so concerned about what's proper."

"I wasn't in the industry for my formative years." His small smile encouraged hers. "I don't judge anyone else for what they do, but I am conscious of my own behavior. It was how I was raised, but perhaps at some point it became a rebellion against the excesses of the industry. I understand if that seems boring."

"Not boring. Old-fashioned, maybe." But she didn't mind. It was kind of refreshing to be around a man her own age who cared about such things. "We can meet in public. It doesn't have to be in private."

He stilled. "Like . . . dates?"

Her heart sped up, an extra couple of beats per minute. "Um, sort of."

"Someone could see us together, though. It's one thing for me to be caught in an embrace with a woman, another thing for me to be seen with a specific woman. You will be scrutinized and criticized." He paused. "If we were actually dating, I would keep it so tight under wraps, no one would know."

If we were actually dating . . .

She steepled her hands under her chin and tried not to swoon at the protective declaration. "They might be mean to me, yes. But I'm in the public eye already. If you think those same people haven't already canceled or threatened or harassed me for other things I've said and done, you're mistaken." Her smile was faint. "They're not my audience. So long as we're not making out, I think the scandalized outrage will be kept to a minimum. "There would be no physical stuff," she added hastily.

"Of course. I'd never do anything a woman wasn't comfortable with."

"So, yeah. If we did happen to get photographed together,

it would be inconvenient as far as my extended family is concerned, maybe, but it wouldn't be the worst thing in the world. It might even be good for both of us. Publicity is always helpful."

His eyes sharpened. "Do you need the boost? I was under the impression that you were very successful."

She squinted at him. "You know what I do?"

"Of course. I googled you before I contacted you."

"Do not believe that Wikipedia article, it is off on my numbers."

"I didn't read Wikipedia."

"Good." She wouldn't ask what he had looked at, damn it, even though she was curious. "I am successful. But I'm getting old."

"You're under thirty."

"Old in internet years." She stretched her legs out, and her knee cracked, punctuating her claim. It was because of an old softball injury and not her age, but she liked the drama of her body concurring. "I lost momentum a while back."

"Sponsors?"

"Yes." That had hurt, though she'd understood how the game worked. Sponsors and brand partnerships went where numbers went. "My five-year plan was on track before. I need to get it back."

"What's your five-year plan?"

"I want to have my own makeup company."

"Ambitious."

"I suppose." She spun her bottle. "So. What do you think?"

He nodded once. "Okay."

"Okay?" She wanted to rub her ears and make sure she was actually hearing right, but that would ruin her confident approach.

"Let's do it. I can certainly charm your parents for a weekend."

Charm them? He was tall, handsome, rich, famous, and breathing. He didn't even have to talk to charm her mother.

He stuck out his hand. "Here's to a mutually beneficial, manufactured, and discreet romance."

Just what every girl dreams of for her first romance.

It wasn't a romance. It was a fauxmance at best. Jia hesitated for a second. It had been her idea—why was it spooking her now that it was coming to fruition? She forced herself to accept his shake. "Yay," she said.

A knock came on the trailer door. "Five minutes, Mr. Dixit."

She came to her feet and Dev immediately followed. "I'll let you get back to work."

"When will I see you again?"

Oh damn. She hadn't really planned that far ahead. "Um . . ."

"This Friday. We can have dinner somewhere."

"Somewhere private," she reminded him.

"That would be nice."

"Cool. You can pick me up at work. I'll text you the address."

She followed him to the door, and she kept her gaze studiously on his back. She was noticing nothing other than his back. She was not going to look—

Oh no, she looked. Her gaze shot back up to his head from his firm backside. Almost immediately, she averted her eyes. She wasn't going to look *anymore*.

She was surprised when Dev descended the stairs first—he seemed like he was all about manners and ladies first. But then he turned around and extended his hand to help her down the concrete.

Jia hesitated on the top step, where she was eye level with him. His makeup was going to haunt her if she drove away without fixing it. "Hang on a second." She popped open her purse and pulled out one of her emergency makeup sponge blenders. "Do you mind tilting your chin up? May I touch you to fix your makeup?"

"Sure." He slowly angled his face up to her.

She dabbed the sponge on his skin. Absent-mindedly, she lightly rested her fingertips on his shoulder to steady herself. "There we go," she half murmured. "This isn't quite the right shade for you, but that's no surprise. Ask them to blend this color and a lighter one next time to get you closer." When she had her company, she was going to make sure to offer more base colors. Mixing was such a pain.

Jia withdrew her touch and examined the work critically. It wasn't perfect, but at least it wasn't offensive. "There."

"Thank you," he said. "Apparently, there is a new makeup artist, this seems to be her weakness."

"You're welcome."

"If I may suggest something . . ."

"Yes?"

Something entered his gaze, and it took her a second to

identify what it was. "If you want to keep our arrangement discreet, probably best to leave my makeup snafus alone from now on."

He was *teasing* her. Uh-oh. Teasing Dev was probably the cutest form of Dev.

She had to be careful here. Finding her fake boyfriend cute might complicate things.

She would not be swayed from her goal! Jia descended the rest of the stairs and looked up at him. "Is makeup blending a girlfriend-ish act?"

"I'm not sure," he murmured. "I haven't had a lot of girlfriend experience. I assume we'll find out. I'll see you soon, Jia."

At some point while she was not being swayed, she'd get over the way he said her name, too.

Chapter Ten

D̶ᴇᴠ ʜᴀᴅɴ'ᴛ been on a date in years. *And you're still not going on one.*

He fixed his hair for the millionth time. That's right. He must not forget what this was. A mutually beneficial arrangement. He didn't even care if it benefited him, to be honest. He'd be happy enough to help her. And spend some more time basking in the warmth of Jia's smile.

Not a date. Just a chance to pretend he was on one.

"You look nice."

He stopped fussing with his hair and met his niece's gaze in the mirror. She stood in his bedroom doorway, clutching her tablet. "Thank you."

Luna drifted into his room. He'd taken her to get enrolled in school this morning, and to his eye, she already looked a little more grown up than she had when the day had started. It had pained him to leave her there. He imagined it was similar to the separation anxiety parents felt when they first took their children to school. Luna had seemed happy when he'd picked her up, though, so he'd swallowed his misgivings.

"Where are you going?"

He readjusted his tie, though he didn't need it. "I have a—" He hesitated. He didn't quite know how to explain Jia to Luna. So far, she hadn't said anything about the photo of him and Jia in the press, which led him to believe she hadn't seen it yet. Otherwise surely she would ask who the woman was, right?

He didn't want her to get her hopes up that Jia might become a permanent fixture. He imagined Rohan had paraded more than one woman in and out of her young life. Plus, he didn't know what to say. *You see, when a man and a woman are both in public positions and/or one of them has an overprotective family, they have to occasionally pretend to like each other.* "I have a work event, is all."

Luna ran her gaze critically over him. "Where are you going?"

"Someplace private." Jia had mentioned she had a place in mind.

"Is it trendy?"

"Probably."

"Hmm." She looked him up and down. "Are you sure you want to wear that?"

"You said I looked nice," he protested.

"You look nice if you're going to a business meeting."

Ouch.

"Do you own jeans?"

"Of course I own jeans." He half turned to his dresser. "I think."

"Okay, never mind. Lose the tie."

He loosened the tie, feeling vaguely naked as he shed it. "Good?"

"Better. I can pull up a couple looks tonight and you can purchase whatever you need tomorrow. Personally, I think you need slimmer cut pants."

He looked down at his legs self-consciously. All he'd wanted as a teenager was to wear baggy clothes to make his slender frame look bigger. It had taken him years not to feel odd in tighter-fitting clothing. "Thank you, Luna, I would appreciate that. Perhaps you could discuss this with my stylist. I am due for a refresh." He'd skipped it this year, thanks to their strained finances.

"Speaking of clothes . . ." she said, giving him a bright smile. "Can I get some new clothes to fit into the school here?"

Aha. That's why she was commenting on his clothes. "Of course." He went to his closet and pulled out his black shoes. "I can take you to the store—"

"I'll buy them online. I've gotten used to that."

He sat in the chair next to the closet and put his shoes on. Adil Uncle would fuss on him for walking to the front door in them, but maybe he could escape detection. "Very well. Are you also buying slimmer cut pants?" he teased.

"More like sweatpants and tank tops."

Dev nearly bit his tongue off to keep from sounding like a scandalized aunt. If the other children wore such casual clothes to learn in, his niece could as well. "Do you need a new backpack as well?"

She hesitated. "I feel bad spending so much."

Dev came to his feet and tugged on her hair. "Nonsense. You've never shopped for school, have you? We must make sure you're prepared. I should have thought of it last week."

She named a brand he'd never heard of. "That's what most of the girls use."

"Then pick one up for yourself. Black, I suppose."

"Actually, yellow seems to be the popular color." She wrinkled her nose. "Two people asked me if I was from New York City. I guess they wear more colorful stuff here."

"You should wear what you feel comfortable in." He didn't want his niece changing to please anyone.

"I feel comfortable not sticking out. Thanks, Kaka."

There was an odd tremble in her voice. He nudged her chin up. "Are you okay?"

"Yes." She hesitated. "Are you going on a date?"

He almost raked his hand through his hair before he remembered that it would muss it up. "Why would you think that?"

"Baba was always going on dates."

The careful way she said that, without inflection, made up his mind for him. There was no need to tell Luna about Jia yet. "It's not a date. Just a meeting with a friend."

"Oh. Okay."

"Try to go to bed before midnight or so?" He didn't bother enforcing a bedtime on the weekends. "And no—"

"No phone after ten, got it. Have fun."

With the woman he'd been obsessed with for the better part of a week?

No, not obsessed. He was impressed by her, he thought

her skin was luminous and perfect and she had the prettiest eyes he'd ever—

He cut himself off. "I'll try."

"HI, JIA!"

"Hi," she said to her own voice, coming out of her phone. Jia put her bare feet up on the sofa.

"Look, you are bound to be a little nervous tonight, so I'm going to keep this short and sweet. This is business. Think of it as a photo shoot or a sketch. You have no feelings for this guy. Forget whatever feelings you had for his photos and words before—they weren't him. He's an actor, and you're a professional too. Be cool."

"I will be cool," she whispered to herself and placed the phone in her lap. She would be cool! There was nothing to be not cool about. This was her plan, and it was a good, logical one. As logical as semimanipulating a man into fake dating her could be.

"And if all else fails, and you start to waver, or you feel attracted to him, think about your parents."

Yeah, the thought of Farzana and Mohammad Ahmed should kill any hesitation or arousal.

Jia jumped when her front door buzzed. She didn't know why she was startled. It was seven o'clock on the dot, and that was when she'd told Dev to meet her. He'd never be late.

She'd assumed, though, that he'd pull up outside and text her, the equivalent of honking his horn. But no, he'd come up, like a proper gentleman. If this was a real date, she'd be impressed. She was glad she'd already told the receptionist downstairs that he ought to be let in.

Jia caught her breath a little when she opened the door. Dev was adjusting his cuffs and glanced up, and it was like a picture-perfect *GQ* shot. He looked a little more casual today, but still as crisp as ever. "Hi," she said.

"Hello." He kept his eyes locked on hers. "You look lovely."

She resisted the urge to fidget. She didn't usually dither on her outfit choices, but it had taken her some time today to decide on the one-piece long-sleeved, wide-legged jumper. Her scarf matched it, and she'd tied a bow low at her nape, letting the fabric drape over her shoulder. "Thank you." She gestured. "I just need to grab my purse. Come on in."

He didn't move. "I thought this was your studio? It looks like an apartment. It wouldn't be proper for me to enter your home."

She might have laughed at his earnestness except it was cute. "No. I mean, yes, it's an apartment, but it's not used as my apartment, it's my office and photo studio. I live in Santa Barbara."

"That's far?"

"A little bit. I don't mind the drive. I get to live with my two closest friends in the area, so it's a pretty sweet deal." She also paid under market rent, because getting Katrina to accept any money had been a significant challenge, but she would have paid any amount to live in the beautiful ocean view house.

"I see." He glanced around as they entered the living room. "It looks like you—"

"Live here, I know." Jia tilted her head at the kitchen, which was sparkling clean. "But I really don't. There's no food in the fridge or anything, so I can't offer you any coffee or tea. Sorry."

"Not a problem." Dev walked farther into the living room. "So you maintain and stage an entire apartment to make it appear like it's your own?"

"Yup."

"Isn't that misleading?"

"Maybe," she admitted and smiled at his raised eyebrow. "Surprised at my candor? There's a lot on social media that isn't what it seems, but I have started to try to think about what I'm contributing. The truth is, I used to film in my own house and in my own bedroom, but the bigger I got, the more . . . protective I got, about what I was sharing with the world." She shrugged. "So this is all one giant green screen, but it's not meant to be a way to fool my viewers and make them think my life is so much better than theirs. It's more like a shield for me."

"I understand that."

"Also I like to eat in bed, and I didn't want to have to clean up crumbs before every single shoot."

He chuckled, and she plucked the noise out of the air, wrapped it in a bow, and tucked it away.

She fetched her purse from the couch as he picked up the framed picture on the side table. "Oh, that's my sister." Sometimes she deliberately brought a few photos and placed them around the place so it would look more lived in on camera.

"You have a twin?"

"Yeah. She's perfect." There was pride in her voice, not bitterness. Ayesha was as perfect a human as one could get, and Jia was in awe of her.

His smile was faint. "That's what some people think about siblings, I understand."

"No, she really is. Doctor, really kind, always knows the right thing to say, never does anything bad. The polar opposite of me."

"I can't believe you do bad things."

She busied herself with rummaging in her purse for nothing to avoid how she felt about the way he said *bad*. "I've been known to rebel a time or two." She zipped her purse closed and glanced at him. "Ready?"

Dev nodded, and gentleman that he was, he didn't point out that he'd been waiting for her to be ready as they walked out. "What kind of rebellion?"

She locked the door behind her and fell into step next to him. "It was honestly only a rebellion by my parents' standards. I think anyone else would have been fine with it."

"What did you do?"

"The big thing? Moved out here to do this gig."

"You seem quite successful at this gig."

Not successful enough. "I do okay."

"You're famous."

She shot him a sideways glance as they got in the elevator. "Internet famous is . . . bizarre. I mean a lot to a smaller, passionate group of people."

"Millions of people."

"It's not like your kind of famous, though."

"Apples and oranges." His mouth twisted. "I am known for a name."

She raised an eyebrow. It was rare to hear someone famous sound so resigned to yet bitter about the name that made them famous. "I can assure you, starting off from scratch, without any help, isn't fun."

"But you know you've earned it."

But what happens if I fail? She gave a slight shiver.

"Are you cold?" He held the elevator door open for her as they left.

Observant man. "No, I'm fine. You're pretty popular for your own career. What made you settle on soaps instead of big-budget films?"

"It was fun. And I knew it would piss my grandfather off."

She gave him a sideways glance. "So you're rebellious too."

Dev gave a half laugh. "I suppose so."

They exited into the parking garage. Their footfalls echoed. Jia fiddled with her purse strap. "Do you want to take your car or mine?"

"I got car service here. I wasn't sure about parking."

"You're learning about this city. Excellent, we can take mine."

He slowed when she pressed the key fob for her car and it chirped. "*That's* your vehicle?"

She smiled proudly at the yellow Beetle. "Yup."

"Ah, what are the things on its headlights?"

"Eyelashes!" She patted the hood fondly. "Isn't it cute? I always wanted one of these, but when I lived at home, my parents insisted I drive a sensible car. I love Buggy."

"Interesting." Jia was confused for a second when Dev slipped in front of her, but then she realized he was getting her door for her. Gosh. It had been a long time since she'd met a man who opened a door for her.

Charmed, she slipped inside the car and waited for him to round the hood. When he tried to get inside, she understood why he'd sounded hesitant about her car. He shoved his seat back all the way, then folded his body in. His legs were still crammed uncomfortably, and his head was suspiciously close to the roof.

She bit her cheek to control her laugh. It wasn't nice to laugh at him. But he did look funny. "I'm sorry, I didn't think of how small this might be for you."

"No worries." He shifted, and his elbow bumped hers.

She pulled it back, but not because she didn't like it. Oh no, she liked it a little too much. She imagined her mom frowning at her, and that helped kill some of her liking.

"Where are we going?" he asked.

"I know a restaurant that's really quiet and tucked away."

He put his seat belt on. "How quiet? Everyone has a phone on them nowadays."

And he was a hot property, as they'd discovered. She gave him a mischievous smile. For all the stress and upset she'd been under for the last week, it was nice to feel vaguely relaxed. "Don't worry about it."

They lapsed into a companionable silence as they drove

to the place, interrupted occasionally by Dev asking her about things they passed. When they got to the restaurant, a small, inconspicuous spot on a quiet side street in Highland Park, she pulled around back instead of parking at one of the meters.

He trailed behind her as she went to the back kitchen door and knocked lightly. The door opened and a young man with a thick mustache stuck his head out. "There you are, Jia!"

"Hey, Antony." She walked inside and gestured to Dev. "This is my friend, um . . . Bob."

Antony winked. He wore a standard white chef's jacket, pristine despite the sweat that had plastered his hair to his head, declaring a busy dinner service. "Bob, eh?" He shook Dev's hand. "Pleasure. Come on, let's get you guys a seat. The crowd's died down, I had them clear out the back corner for you. No one will bother you." Antony led them through the kitchen to a private booth. True to his word, no one was there. "Menus are on the table, waiter will be with you soon. I suggest the gnocchi tonight, but everything's good, of course."

"Thanks, Antony."

The chef left and Dev raised an eyebrow. "You must be a regular here."

"I did a series about six months ago about mom-and-pop restaurants in different parts of L.A. It took off pretty nicely, though I'm not exactly a food blogger. This was one of the restaurants I went to and they got a nice little lift in business." She wrinkled her nose. "He tried to repay me in free food, but I don't feel comfortable being one of those kinds of influencers. I'm willing to accept his gratitude in this manner, though." She gestured to the almost completely private dining.

"It's not bad. I used to pay top dollar for this kind of privacy in Mumbai."

"I imagine it was hard to get around at all there."

"Yes. Here I have some level of privacy. The public in Mumbai felt like my grandparents were theirs. By extension so were we. My brother and cousin—" He cut himself off.

Jia tried to control the automatic lurch in her stomach. "It's okay, you can mention them." Since Dev hadn't said anything more about his relatives, she assumed he'd been unlucky in getting ahold of his cousin to wring more information out.

She was okay not knowing anything more, to be honest. Especially if she had to hear more about how she was collateral damage in some family feud.

She was the star, damn it! Not a side character.

"It's just that they simply didn't mind as much as I did." He pulled out his phone and scanned the bar code on the table, waiting for the menu to pop up on his screen.

The waiter materialized and poured them water. "Can I get you two anything else to drink?"

"Iced tea?" Dev asked her, and she nodded. He ordered for them, getting himself a glass of red wine. "You don't mind if I drink around you, do you?" he asked after the waiter left.

"Nope." She perused the menu. "It's a personal choice for

me, I'm not judgy about others. One of my sisters is actually a bartender."

"Not the twin."

"Nope. There're five of us. Noor, Zara, Sadia, Ayesha, me," she said with the practice of someone who had listed the names in descending order for a while.

"What do they do?"

"The bartender, of course, bartends. Otherwise they're doctors."

He raised an eyebrow. "All of them?"

"Noor and Zara are, and Ayesha is in her residency. I would have been, too, but I escaped med school."

"You went to medical school?"

She took a sip of her water. "I know, I don't come off as smart enough for that. But yeah, I went for a couple years before I decided to go full-time on the beauty stuff."

"Who said you're not smart? I think you're quite clever."

"You do?"

"Yes. You'd have to be to come up with fresh content as often as you do. You're not only an actress. You're a writer, director, and producer as well. Requires quite a few brain cells."

She stared at him, and a slow smile split over her face. "You've watched my videos?"

Was it her imagination, or were his cheeks dark red? "A few. Here and there."

"Thank you." She winked. "Hope you let the ads play."

"So you're the proper youngest then."

Dev was changing the subject, but she'd allow it. She

didn't want to tell him how many episodes of his soap she'd watched when she became infatuated with him. Not that he was infatuated with her, of course.

Yeesh. Now she was going to blush. "I am." Jia smiled fondly and put down her phone. "Sometimes I feel like Ayesha and I have two extra moms and a cool aunt."

"Speaking as a responsible oldest child, I can assure you they probably mean well."

"I tell myself that a lot." She paused. "I'm sorry about your brother, by the way." It felt weird that she'd talked to Rohan shortly before he died. She was glad they'd only conversed a little before it had petered out.

"Thank you."

"And your grandfather as well."

He nodded. Their drinks arrived. "Are you ready to order?" their waiter asked.

"Yes, I'll have the crab cakes," she said.

Dev ordered a pasta dish, using flawless Italian pronunciation. Jia sipped on her iced tea when the waiter left. "Your Italian's good."

"I spent a few months there a couple years ago. Languages are a family skill. My niece is more facile than I am."

"Can you tell me about your niece?" For fake dating scam purposes, not because she was interested. Like she'd brought him to a romantic Italian restaurant for the scam.

Dev's shoulders relaxed, and a warm smile crossed his face, transforming it. He tapped on his phone, spinning it around to show her. "That's her. Luna. I've had custody of her since my brother passed."

The photo had been taken on the Santa Monica pier, so it must be recent. The girl in the photo wore a pair of black jeans and a dark gray tank top. She was lanky and pretty, her hair curling cutely around her round face. "I didn't know your brother had a child." She hadn't done a deep dive on Dev's family, but she had cursory knowledge.

"He kept her well shielded from the press."

"That's thoughtful."

"Yes." He sounded mildly bemused and shook his head when she glanced up. "My brother wasn't the most thoughtful man in the world. But he had her young, and her mother disappeared, so I give him some credit for not just shipping her off to some boarding school. Or ignoring her altogether."

"She looks sweet. How is she adjusting to America?"

Dev tucked the phone back into his pocket. "Very well. She had her first day of school today. I was worried, but she seems to be pretty excited about it."

"Why were you worried?"

"She's never been to a real school before. Only tutors."

"I hated school. But it's probably good for her to have the experience, at least."

He nodded. "That's what she said."

Jia softened. It sounded like Dev was an especially attentive guardian. "Does she know . . . what we're doing?"

"No. She's had so much upheaval in her life, I thought . . ." He shrugged.

"Totally right call. It would be pretty difficult to explain anyway." Out of the corner of her eye, she caught a flash of light, and jumped, but there was nothing there.

He brought her attention right back to him by lightly resting his hand close to hers, close enough that his pinky brushed against her thumb. "Are you okay?"

She looked down at his hand. It was long and elegant, the knuckles prominent. He had artist's hands. She wanted to . . .

Do nothing! She slipped her hand to the safety of her lap. "Yup. I thought I saw something, but it's cool."

They were quiet as their food came. He picked up his fork. "Should we get our story straight on how we met?"

She cut into her crab cake and tried not to look at the pasta he was twirling on his fork. Her food envy would always rear its head, no matter how delicious her own meal was. "I was thinking we could stick close to the truth and say we became friends online."

"Is that a bit odd?"

"Sliding into DMs isn't too different from a dating app."

He took another bite of the pasta, and a drop of red sauce touched the corner of his lip. "Have you spoken to many people in your DMs?"

"Nope. You were the first. But that doesn't mean others will find it weird." She gestured to the corner of his mouth. If he didn't clean it up, she feared she might, and she definitely didn't need to know what his lips felt like, even under a napkin. "You have a little . . ."

He dabbed it. "Thank you."

"No problem. So, yeah, we say we met online, became friends, and now we're meeting up in real life."

"Got it. You'll have to show me how direct messages work at some point."

Jia squinted at him. "You're not on social media much, I guess."

"I am not." Dev pulled his bread plate closer to his pasta dish and twirled off a generous portion. "Here, try this. It's good."

She accepted the small plate, touched. Had he noticed her side-eyeing his food? "Have some of mine." She placed one of her crab cakes on her bread plate and slid it over.

"Thank you," he said politely. They ate for a few moments in silence, and then he stirred. "Can you tell me about your high school experience here? I'd like to know what Luna might be facing."

She smiled. "Sure." They spoke for a while about their respective teenage years. There were differences in their educations, which she expected, given their different countries, but there were a lot of similarities, too, given that they'd both stood out at their respective schools.

"I stopped going to traditional school after my parents passed," he explained. "Which was for the best. In India, my last name would have made learning almost impossible."

There was such darkness in his eyes when he spoke about his parents' deaths that Jia wanted to reach out and hug him, but she reminded herself again that she didn't know him well enough for that. Instead, she tried to do what she did best: bring the light. "I know exactly what you mean. The burden of a last name! Imagine every teacher you have thinking you'll be a carbon copy of your four smart, popular sisters, and then letting them down."

The lines around his eyes crinkled. "You got into medical school, so I imagine you didn't let them down too much."

"There's hundreds of ways to let someone down." *Jia, stop talking. Jia, you're too loud. Jia, focus.* Sure, she'd learned to mask, but it hadn't been easy.

He shook his head, and took the last bite of food on his plate. She'd already polished off hers. The other side effect of being the runt of the litter: eating extremely fast, lest someone else grab the last serving. "This was a very productive getting to know each other meal, I think," he said.

"Yup. I think we covered a lot of ground today." Despite how nervous and stiff she'd felt when the night started.

"We did, yes. I—" He frowned and reached into his pocket. "I'm sorry, someone keeps calling me."

"That's fine."

He glanced at the number and picked it up. "Hello? Oh." He listened quietly for a moment, then nodded, his frown deepening.

"I'll be right there." Dev hung up. "I'm so sorry. My niece is sick. A headache. She doesn't normally get sick."

With anyone else, Jia might think this was a ploy to get out of a boring date, but this wasn't a date and Dev wasn't that type of guy and he looked genuinely concerned. "I used to always get sick on the first day of school." She signaled for the waiter and made a signing motion. "Let's get the check. I can drive you home."

"I'm sorry—"

"Don't apologize. If she's sick, you should get home to her." Jia dared to edge her hand closer to his. "I'm sure it's a cold."

"Right." He smiled, but it was more like a baring of teeth. "A couple of weeks into living in a new country, of course she's not well. New germs for her to get used to."

"Exactly."

Dev quickly paid the check when it arrived. Once they'd hurried outside, she cleared her throat. "Um, you know, since this"—she gestured between them—"is mostly for my benefit, I can pay for our meals and stuff."

He moved closer to her as they walked, and she inhaled whatever spicy cologne he was wearing. For a second, she recalled what he'd smelled like when she was almost plastered up against him outside that bar, and then she round-house kicked that memory out of her nostrils.

"No, it's fine."

"Doesn't feel quite right," she fretted. "How about I pay for any dates that are my idea?"

He huffed out a laugh. "I can't believe I'm debating whether I get to pay for you."

"Trust me, if you'd asked me when I was really pissed at you, I wouldn't have thought I'd be conflicted about this at all." She got into her car, waiting patiently while Dev contorted his long body into her vehicle. She asked for his address and keyed it into the GPS.

"Does that mean you're not mad anymore?"

Jia kept her eyes on the road. "It's complicated."

"I understand."

Him being so agreeable was one of the reasons it was complicated. "I'm mad at your cousin. It's hard to hang out with you and not be a little confused. It's, like, dissociative to feel like I know you, except . . . I don't know you."

He hmmed.

"But I don't want to slap you anymore, no," she finished.

"Good." He leaned toward her a little, which in the cramped confines of the car meant that he was leaning toward her a lot. "I'll do my best to make up for what my family did. I promise."

She shouldn't put so much stock in his words, and maybe it was that he'd been nothing but kind to her, or how sweetly he talked about his niece, but Jia softened and nodded. "Okay."

They drove the rest of the way in relative quiet. Dev's condo building was a high-rise with big windows that she was sure gave good views of the beach.

"Thanks for the ride. I'm sorry dinner was interrupted," he said again.

"It's no problem."

"Why don't you text me when you're free next?"

A little thrill ran through her. "I will do that."

He opened the door and got out, then leaned down to peer at her. "I'm enjoying learning about you."

And even though she knew it had been a faux date for a fauxmance, she still fell into his famous brown eyes. "I hope your niece is okay."

"I'm sure she is. Text me when you get home."

She nodded. It was a phrase she'd heard ten million times, from every overprotective person in her life, but it hit different when he said it. It actually made her feel like butterflies were exploding inside her? So weird.

He tapped his knuckles on the roof of her car. "Good night, Jia."

"Good night." She said his name after he closed the door. "Dev." She watched him walk into the building. He had such broad shoulders. Broad and wide, and then they narrowed down to that—

She wasn't looking at him there!

She grabbed her phone and toggled through her recorded messages until she found the one she needed. "Hi, Jia," came her own cheerful voice. "I guess you had a good night and you're battling some physical attraction to this man. So I'm going to say this as nicely as I can: make like a fourteen-year-old, and get home and get in a cold shower."

Jia took a deep breath. Yes. Very good advice from her to her.

"What are you waiting for? Girl, go. Go!"

She threw her car into drive and went.

Chapter Eleven

"Kaka, I'm *fine*."

Dev removed his hand from his niece's forehead and tried not to give in to the urge to roll her in bubble wrap and place her in her bed.

When he'd come home on Friday, she'd been bundled under her covers, moaning from a stomach ache and burning up. Dev didn't have much experience with illness. He'd shoved his panic down and helped her sit up and drink liquids. After she'd fallen asleep, he'd sat outside her door and dozed.

She'd seemed better the next morning, her usual quiet self, but he'd taken her to a doctor anyway over her protests, and the woman had assured him Luna was fine. Though his niece had made it through the weekend pink cheeked and healthy, he didn't love the thought of her going to school today.

"Let me check your temperature one more time." He opened the kitchen drawer next to the fridge and pulled out their first-aid kit.

Luna rolled her eyes. "Do you keep one of those in every room?"

Since she'd come to live with him, yes. Never had Dev felt the sting of mortality so keenly as he did now that he had to care for a young child. "Come here."

Dutifully, she lifted her face. He scanned her forehead and nodded at the temperature readout. "Very well. You don't feel any symptoms of a cold or flu?"

"Nope."

"You could stay home for one day—"

"Please, no. I'll be that weird girl who started school and then left right away."

She was responding to his English in Hindi, which eased his concern a little. If she was well enough to mentally translate languages, hopefully her illness truly had been a quick bug. "Are you hungry?"

"Where's Adil Uncle?"

"I heard him late last night, binging a new season of some makeover show. I imagine he's sleeping in today."

Her smile was faint. "I'm not hungry."

"How about a smoothie?" Starve a fever, feed a cold, right? Or was it the other way around? His mother used to stuff them with food no matter what they felt like. Food and turmeric milk.

"A smoothie would be nice. What are you eating?"

"I already ate." His trainer had recommended disgusting protein shakes for breakfast, but Dev didn't want to tell Luna that or drink them in front of her. He might be beholden to the industry, but the last thing he wanted to do was impose the world's body image conventions on her.

He quickly pulled out the frozen fruit before she changed her mind. The chair squeaked on the tile as she settled at the counter.

"Don't you have to film today?" she asked.

"No, I'm not needed on set. I'll drop you off at school and then get some work done." His agent had sent over a few more scripts. He was tied to this production for a season, but if it or he didn't get renewed, he needed a plan B.

"Do you like it?"

"Like what?" He added a little water to the blender and set it in place.

She waited until the blending had stopped to continue. "The role?"

He glanced at her. "It's okay."

"It feels like you hate it."

"That's not true." He was excited about . . .

About . . .

Uh.

There must be something about this show that excited him? He'd been excited to get the role, right?

Or you'd just been excited about getting a fresh start. No, it had been more than that. Being a crossover star was something anyone would want. "I haven't been in this role long enough to love it or hate it," he finished. "I played Raj Kumar for eleven years. It was different." And exciting. There had always been some wacky twist, some grand adventure, some epic love story.

This show was muted, but that was what received awards

and got attention, especially in America. Realistic, relatable drama.

He set the drink in front of her. "See how it is."

Luna took a sip and made a face. "It needs more sugar."

Dev was trying to limit their added sugar, but he wanted her to drink something before she went to school, so he pulled the honey out and drizzled some in, giving it another good blend. "There you go."

She pulled it closer and took a draw. "Better."

His phone buzzed and he pulled it out. How's Luna feeling today?

"See."

He glanced up with a vague sense of inexplicable guilt. "Huh?"

"You looked more excited about that text than you did about the show."

Luna in a teasing mood was a nice thing to see, but not when she was teasing him about this. "Drink your drink. We need to leave in five minutes." He quickly typed back a response to Jia. He'd updated her the next day, but he'd been a little cautious, given his worry about Luna. Much better. It seems like it was a twenty-four-hour bug.

Phew. Glad to hear it.

He leaned against the counter. Truth be told, he'd never been very good at texting. If he could, he'd borrow from his own show and scripts as well, but he didn't know what lines Arjun and Rohan had lifted, and he couldn't very well plagiarize himself plagiarizing himself. How is your week looking?

Pretty good. Dropping some stuff off with a friend, then heading to work. Have to film some spon con today.

It took him a second to translate *spon con* into *sponsored content*. Perhaps we could try for dinner again tonight?

He held his breath, but it didn't take long for a response to come. I'm actually busy tonight.

Ah. Of course, that made sense. She was, no doubt, in high demand.

Three bubbles popped up at the bottom of the screen. That's the spon con. I have to go to an art show and take some photos. Do you want to come with me? It'll be public, but if you wear a hat or something, we should be able to skate by. Dress casual. No one will be looking for celebs there.

He quickly typed back. Yes, I would like that.

Cool, I'll pick you up at 7.

He raised a brow. Jia had dropped him off the other night, but he was unaccustomed to a woman picking him up. You'll pick me up?

I'm sure your masculinity will survive, no worries.

He bit the inside of his cheek to hide his silly smile.

"Who are you talking to?"

Dev quickly placed his phone facedown on the counter. "Nobody. Do you mind staying home with Adil Uncle tonight?" He'd have to tell his uncle, but the older man would believe him if he said he was only checking in with Jia to ensure she was okay after his cousin's meddling.

"You have work or something?"

"I'm meeting a friend."

Luna slurped the last of her smoothie. "Is it the same friend you met on Friday?"

"Yes." He hesitated. If Jia was coming here, she might run into Luna, and in that case . . . it simply didn't feel right to lie to Luna outright. "Her name is Jia Ahmed."

A blink was Luna's first response. She slowly lowered her glass. "Jia Ahmed's your friend?"

"Yes." Was *friend* the right word? Was there a right word for *acquaintance you met because your brother and cousin catfished her*? Or *woman whose YouTube videos I cannot stop consuming*?

He'd felt silly, but he'd picked up a toner and an essence on her recommendation while he was out on Saturday and carefully followed along with her when she dabbed them into her skin. He didn't think they'd done anything, but he'd give it a few more days.

"Jia Ahmed. The model."

"Do you know her?"

Luna shoved a curl out of her eyes. "Uh, yeah. I know her. Why do *you* know her? She's cool. And you're old."

He drew himself up in mock outrage. He might be a few years *older* than Jia, but that did not mean he was old. "I beg your pardon, madam. I will have you know that I am very lit."

"Oh my God, don't use that word, please." His niece glanced around, like the American police were huddled below their table.

Dev was happy there was a shadow of a smile on Luna's

lips, though. He'd never indulged his silly side with any-one else. Perhaps he should have brought it out more for his younger brother.

He shoved away the pinch of hurt. "It will be difficult, but I will try. To answer your question, we are collaborating on a project together."

"Huh." Luna placed her glass down. "Okay."

He cocked his head at the lukewarm response. If Luna thought Jia was cool—so much cooler than him—she should be more excited at the thought of her being his friend, yes? "You may get to meet her tonight."

"I can?" Luna raised her eyebrows. "I wasn't allowed to meet anyone famous Daddy knew."

"What? No actors or actresses? No singers?" Rohan had had more interesting contacts than Dev did, given his prox-imity to films instead of TV.

"No."

That was absurd. Dev had only lived in his grandparents' home for a few years, but famous people had always been parading through, paying their respects or currying some sort of favor. Granted, Rohan had lived separately, but how had he built such a bubble around his daughter? Had he been neglecting her or protecting her by keeping her out of his public life?

Perhaps if Dev hadn't tried to separate himself from ev-erything Dixit, he might know the answer to that. "I'll ask her. She's coming here first, so I'm sure it would be fine. Are you ready to head out?"

Luna glanced down at her outfit. "My new clothes haven't come yet. Do you think I look okay?"

Since she'd done him the honor of asking his opinion, he surveyed her black jeans and gray shirt with the kind of grave consideration one might give to a runway model. "I think you look lovely." The shirt dipped off her shoulder, and he did want to smooth it back into place, but he'd read an article about not policing teen women's bodies.

She rolled her eyes and drained her smoothie. "You'd say that no matter what I wore."

He busied himself with the dish towel. He was glad she thought so. It meant she was secure in his love, yes? Maybe, just maybe, he was doing a decent job fumbling through this parenting thing.

"That is true," he agreed. "But you also look lovely. Now fetch your backpack. Let's get you to school."

Do you mind meeting my niece tonight? She tells me you are much cooler and younger than me.

Jia quickly typed back. I'd love to. Also, I am.

She was so distracted by proper Dev sending her a cry laughing emoji in return that she rammed right into a big mass of a man. "Whoa there." Large hands went around her shoulders and he steadied her.

She looked up at Samson. Rhiannon's boyfriend was a former lineman and still built like one. "Hi, Samson. Sorry, I was texting and walking."

"Happens to the best of us. I was lost in my own thoughts as well." The lines next to his eyes crinkled, and he gestured to the building they were standing in front of. Crush's headquarters were in a rather unassuming place for a multimillion-dollar app. Rhiannon had chosen the Silver Lake site in lieu of the more obvious Silicon Beach locations because, in her words, *the farther we can get from the more annoying tech assholes, the better.* "You here to see Rhiannon, I'm guessing?"

She lifted the duffel bag she held. "She needed some things from the house, so I'm dropping them off for her." Rhiannon had stayed over at Samson's since the gala.

If Jia hadn't been looking right at Samson, she might have missed the way his usually pleasant face tightened. "Ah. Good." He patted her on the shoulder, and she tried not to lurch backward. He must be distracted, if he wasn't keeping his own strength in check. "I'm running late to meet my aunt for breakfast. I'll see you later."

She watched him walk to his car at a brisk clip. That was odd. Samson was usually charming and chatty to the extreme.

Jia was quickly buzzed up by the receptionist, who greeted her warmly. She made her way through the cubicles, smiling at the few people she knew. Rhiannon had recently started a more flexible work-from-home program, so there weren't nearly as many people in the office as there used to be.

She waited for Rhiannon's acknowledgment before she entered the office. "Hey there. Got your stuff."

Rhiannon glanced up from the computer. "Oh thanks. Leave it on the floor."

Jia placed it on the floor, out of the way from anyone who might enter the door. "I saw Samson when I was coming in. Did he drop you off?"

Rhi turned in her millennial pink swivel chair. The whole room was decorated in pinks, with the occasional splash of yellow. Crush colors. "Yeah. How was he?"

Jia dropped into the chair in front of her friend's desk. "Ah, fine. Why?"

Rhiannon's brow pleated. "We had a bit of a fight before he left."

Jia raised an eyebrow. In terms of couple vibes, Rhiannon and Samson didn't have the calm peacefulness of Jas and Katrina, but they didn't fight that much. "Is everything okay?"

Rhi huffed out a breath. "He wants me to move in with him."

"Oh." Jia tried not to clap her hands together, but she probably couldn't suppress all the excitement in her voice, because Rhiannon gave her a dry look. "Um, do you not want to?"

Rhiannon reclined in her chair. "I don't know. I mean, I do. I live there enough as it is. But Katrina . . ."

Ahhhhh. Jia nodded understandingly. While she didn't think she'd ever be as close to either woman as they were to each other, she absolutely understood why Rhiannon wouldn't want to leave Katrina's home. "She'll be okay. You know she's totally zen about us living our lives. I feel like she's even hinted that you should move in with Samson."

"Hmm."

"She doesn't *need* us. You know that, right?" Jia shook her head. "Katrina's panic disorder doesn't mean that she's incapable of handling her own life without chaperones. She became a millionaire before you or I started living with her."

"She likes clucking over us, though."

"Sure. But she's got Jas. She has other friends who aren't us. What's that thing she says? People come and go, you enjoy the parts in the middle? And it's not like you'd never see her again, she's your freaking business partner."

"I don't want her to be lonely. She has abandonment issues from her shitty father. What if I trigger those by telling her I want to leave?" Rhiannon played with her nails. "I don't want to hurt her."

"I think you'll hurt her more by making her think she's holding you back or something," Jia remarked.

Rhiannon sighed. "This is why it's easier to be alone."

"Easier, but not nearly as much fun. Or as delicious, given Katrina's culinary skills," Jia offered cheerfully.

"Yeah, yeah. Okay, I'll think about talking to her."

"Is Samson . . . ?"

Rhiannon waved that worry away. "I'll call him later. He's feeling a little rejected right now, but once he thinks about it, he'll understand. He's going out with Jas tonight, anyway; that'll cheer him up. Now, what's up with you? I haven't seen you in days."

Jia bit her lip. She had told Katrina the bare bones about what was going on over the past Dev-packed week. Katrina had been worried, but apparently her friend hadn't passed the message along to Rhiannon. "Um, I've seen that actor, Dev, again. And again. And again." She thought for a second. "Yes, three times."

Rhiannon's eyebrows rose so high, they were in danger of climbing off her face. "Why on earth did you do that?"

"Well, because I accidentally told my mom we were together, and my family's coming here soon and I don't want to admit to them that I was catfished and he felt bad his cousin and brother did the said catfishing so he agreed to pretend to date me."

Rhiannon steepled her hands under her chin. "I need a longer explanation."

Jia ran through as much as she'd told Katrina. When she finished, Rhiannon rubbed her forehead. "His *cousin*?"

"Yeah."

"I can't believe I missed all this. How did you get into this mess?"

"I'm not sure. Sometimes things happen to me."

Rhiannon edged her keyboard closer to her. "You know I'm going to stalk him, right?"

"I'm surprised you haven't already."

"My personal life is clearly distracting me. This is what friends do."

"I don't think friends regularly stalk people their friends are having fake relationships with."

"It's so wild, how you don't hear how silly that sentence sounds." Rhiannon twirled her pen between her fingers. "Has your family been driving you nuts?"

"No, actually. They seem to have calmed down. My mom said she's waiting to talk to Ayesha before booking their flights, but they're aiming for the end of the month. Noor and Zara have chilled out. I haven't talked to Ayesha or Sadia yet." Privately, Jia had wondered if she could have had this level of peace all along if she'd just made up a fake boyfriend that they approved of.

She could have a huge platform, do groundbreaking stuff, and no one relaxed until she had a man. Amazing. And annoying.

"Well, that's—"

A knock came at the door, and a petite woman with blond hair stuck her head in. "Rhiannon? I'm sorry, but you said it was okay to interrupt? I need a few signatures."

"Yes, Tina," Rhiannon said warmly.

She walked in and handed Rhiannon a sheaf of papers. "Here's that information you wanted, too."

"Thank you."

"I couldn't find the files on the pension plans, though."

"Hang on a second." Rhiannon tapped a button on her phone. "Lakshmi can show you."

Jia nearly groaned. Rhiannon's assistant, Lakshmi, was cool, intimidatingly cool. She was also painfully dismissive of Jia, which brought out all of Jia's worst habits, like baiting and poking.

"You know my roommate Jia, right? Jia, this is Samson's aunt's assistant. She's on-site while we iron out the details of this merger."

Jia waved at the young woman. Samson's aunt owned a rival company that was close to being a sister company. "Hi, yes, of course. We've met a few times."

Tina gave her a quick smile. It faded when the door opened and Lakshmi stuck her head inside. "Yes?" Lakshmi gave Tina a once-over, and then her attention moved to Jia. She bared her teeth. "Jia."

"Lakshmi." Jia twitched her skirt into place. Lakshmi wore a cropped tank and high-waisted jeans. The side of her head was shaved, and the rest of her hair was dyed blue. So damn cool. "Good to see you."

"Sure. Come up with any life-changing makeup hacks lately?"

The sneer in the other woman's voice turned Jia's smile syrupy. Her mother had once said that the sweeter Jia's smile, the more trouble everyone was in. "Sure. I was sent a new line of lipstick that tastes like fruit. Want to try it? It might wipe that sour expression off your face."

"Ladies."

Jia subsided at Rhiannon's chiding tone and made a mental note to work on her bitchiness—er, crankiness—again.

Rhiannon gave Lakshmi a look. "Can you help Tina find the historical paperwork on the retirement plans?"

Lakshmi refocused on Tina. "Sure. It's in the storage closet. I can show you."

Tina's lashes lowered. "Oh, you don't have to take the time. I can find it."

"Not a problem."

Jia waited a good three seconds after the coast was clear

before she muttered. "Should we lock them in that closet together so they can work stuff out or are we going to have to watch this dance for the next ten years?"

"Jia!" Rhiannon shrugged. "There's no lock on that closet, or I'd say yes."

Jia chuckled. She'd only been around Tina and Lakshmi together for a small amount of time, and their chemistry was blazingly obvious to her. She might be wary of Lakshmi, but that didn't mean she couldn't have her ships.

Rhiannon reclined in her chair. "Are you guys ever going to make peace?"

"Who, me and Lakshmi?" Jia tossed up her hands. "I'm happy to make peace. I'm extremely peaceful. She thinks I'm an airhead."

"Because you act like an airhead around her."

"If people want to assume the worst about me, why shouldn't I annoy them with it?" Jia tried to keep her tone light, though it hurt to know how many people in her life regularly dismissed her. "If they think I'm useless, then I'm not going to try to change their mind."

"I don't think Lakshmi thinks that."

Ehh, yes she did. But Jia didn't want to argue with Rhiannon over her friend.

"In any case, as someone who used to struggle with her *I'll show 'em* reflex, maybe try dialing it back a hair here or there. You don't have to be so reactive to everything."

Okay, that might be some good advice. Jia had worked hard at growing more mature over the last year or so. "I'll try."

"Good. Now, are you seeing this guy again anytime soon?"

"Yeah, tonight."

"Wow. Isn't that excessive for a fauxmance?"

"It's when we both have time. And we do have to learn about each other, or how will we fool my family?" *And I want to see him again.*

"Hmm. Yes, of course. There are no other ways to get to know each other."

"What's that supposed to mean?"

"It means I'm worried about this convoluted plan of yours," her roommate said gently.

"It's not convoluted! It's very luted."

"That's not a word."

"It'll all work out fine. I trust Dev."

"Why?"

Jia opened her mouth, then closed it again. Why did she trust Dev? It was the same question he'd asked her, and she still couldn't come up with a perfect answer. The first time she'd met him, he'd cracked her heart, and the second time he'd tried to pay her off.

"Jia?" Rhiannon prompted.

"I have a good feeling about him. It's weird, I feel like . . . like I know him."

Rhiannon's lips thinned. "But you don't."

"Oh, I know."

"Do you? Or are you getting confused because you talked to someone with his face for a couple months?" She pointed her finger. "It seems like this whole thing is an excuse to keep him around."

Jia shifted. It was nicer when Rhiannon and Katrina played her friends and not her big sisters. She had enough of those, and they made her feel foolish on a regular basis. She didn't need her friends to do the same. "I know you think I don't have very good judgment, but this catfishing incident notwithstanding, I think my instincts have served me pretty well."

Rhiannon looked immediately apologetic, which made Jia feel a little bad. "Of course. It's not that I think you have bad instincts, only that you're a little sheltered and naïve when it comes to men."

Jia nodded. "That's probably true. But I suppose the best way to learn is to try and to fail, right? It's like peach blush."

"What?"

"Peach blush. It was the it color for last summer, right? So I kept trying to make it work. Only it made me look sallow and I finally learned." Jia snapped her fingers. "But I wouldn't know peach blush was bad for me if I hadn't tried it and failed. Does that make sense?"

Rhiannon laughed. "Only you would compare men to blush palettes."

"It was a shade, not a palette," Jia corrected gently. It wouldn't do to have her roommate out there spreading misinformation.

Rhiannon's lips twitched. "Gotcha."

"Anyway, I have to head to my studio. Got some filming to

do." And she had to brainstorm some more content, maybe something she could do with perky little Harley to pull in the youths.

"It's all about the views."

Right. Which was what she was going to remember, no matter how much she trusted Dev. It was all about the views, and her future. A future that didn't include a man she barely knew, even if he made her tummy flutter when he said her name.

Chapter Twelve

Jia hadn't really registered much about Dev's home when she'd dropped him off, but now that she wasn't rushing to get him home to his sick niece, she could see it wasn't nearly as nice a place as she imagined a Bollywood dynasty member might live in. Oh, it was a good location and had decent security, but given what she knew about his family, he could probably easily afford a Malibu mansion.

She'd considered waiting downstairs or calling to let him know that she was there, but then she remembered how he'd picked her up from her door, and she parked in visitor parking. The security guard took her name and let her up with a smile and directions.

She knocked, then realized there was a doorbell. She started to reach for it when the door swung open.

The picture hadn't done Dev's niece justice. The young teen was taller than Jia, and wildly beautiful. Her hair was shorter now than it had been in the photo, and the look suited her, made her riotous curls pop. She wore black jeans and a T-shirt, both ripped and ragged looking, but in that way only expensive rips and ragged hems could look. Her skin was a deep, dark brown and glowed from health and good genes. Her lashes were naturally long, her face round and sweet.

Jia shifted when the girl continued to stare at her in silence, her mouth slightly agape. "Hi. I'm Jia. I take it you're Luna?"

The child swallowed. "Yes. You know who I am?"

"Sure thing. Your uncle showed me a picture." Jia had originally started vlogging for the twentysomethings like herself, but her demographic spanned from ages ten to eighty-three. It had been odd in the beginning, meeting people who watched the nonsense she performed in her bedroom, but now that it was more like a business, it was less weird.

Still, her hands were a little sweaty, meeting Dev's niece, though she wasn't sure why. When they continued to stand there, Jia took control. "May I come in?"

Luna shook her head. "Oh. Oh yes! Of course." She took a step back.

"Thank you." Jia slipped her shoes off without being asked to, next to the other two pairs that were right by the door.

"Luna? Did you get the door?" An older man came into view. He stopped when he saw her. "Oh."

Jia inclined her head. "Hello."

"You must be Jia." A smile split his still smooth face. "I am Dev's uncle, Adil."

Jia's shoulders immediately relaxed. There was something so kind and welcoming about Dev's uncle's manner. "Assalamu Alaikum, Uncle."

He placed his hand on his chest. "Walaikum Assalam. Come in, come in. Dev is getting dressed, but please come wait in the kitchen. Luna, why don't you go tell your kaka his friend is here?"

Luna nodded and left, casting inscrutable glances over her shoulder at Jia. Jia scoped out the place while she trailed behind Adil. She only caught a glimpse of the living room before she entered the kitchen. "You've really decorated in the little time you've been here," she remarked to Adil.

"It came furnished," he said. "I am hoping Dev finds a more permanent place soon. This kitchen is fine, but I would prefer more counter space."

Jia glanced around the kitchen. It was as generic as her staged apartment's kitchen, but here there was the delicious smell of food cooking, as well as reminders and recipes tacked up on the stainless steel fridge. It was a family kitchen. "It's nice."

"Are you hungry? Luna asked for rotis."

"No, thank you. There will be food at this event."

Adil nodded. "Please, sit down. Would you like a drink? Let me get you a glass of water."

Since he'd said it as a statement, not a question, she figured she'd get that water whether she wanted it or not. She took the seat he indicated, at the high countertop, and accepted the water. "Dev didn't mention that his uncle lived with him." She immediately wondered if that had come out wrong, but Adil only smiled cheerfully.

Adil returned to his floured work surface and rolled a section of dough into a ball. "I only came to live with him when his brother passed. My wife is gone, as well. It made sense, for two bachelors to be together. Besides, he needed help with Luna. His shooting schedule can be wild."

There was so much loss in Adil's voice. "I'm so sorry to hear about your wife. And your nephew."

Sorrow darkened Adil's eyes for a second. "We must treasure the time we have. I always felt bad I missed so much of Dev's life when he was young. I thought it might be nice to return to India for a while. Imagine my surprise when he brought me right back to America."

"You're from here?"

Adil brightened, and he rolled out the roti. "In New York. For almost thirty years."

The way he said it, the way all New York City people said it, made it clear what part of New York he'd lived in. "I'm from upstate." She was actually from western New York, not upstate, but city folk usually only differentiated between them and everyone else.

"We were neighbors! Small world, yes?"

There was something so hypnotizing about the capable way he handled the rolling pin. "Very small."

He flipped the roti to the hot pan. "I am aware of the circumstances around yours and Dev's meeting, Jia."

So much for her relaxed shoulders. "Oh."

He cast her a sympathetic glance. "I want to apologize for Rohan and his cousin. I cannot begin to guess what they were thinking. I am glad Dev is making it up to you with an outing tonight." Adil smiled. "How nice it would be if a friendship could emerge from this mess."

She busied herself by taking a sip of water. "Yes. Thank you." She hoped that was all Dev had told his uncle about tonight. Bad enough that anyone else knew about the cat-fishing; she didn't want *needs a pretend suitor* stamped on her list of flaws, too. "It is nice, I suppose."

Adil slid the roti off the pan onto a plate, buttered it, and placed it in front of her. "Here, eat. You don't know what they could be serving at this place."

Jia was too nervous to be hungry, but she didn't want to insult Dev's uncle, so she obediently took a bite.

"Jia, you're early."

Jia looked up and promptly choked on her roti. She gasped and coughed, even when Adil leaned over to wallop her on her back. She picked up her water and chugged it, then wiped away the tears that had come from her coughing fit. Thank goodness she'd worn waterproof mascara.

While she'd been sputtering, Dev had come to stand a foot or two away from her. He eyed her with concern. "Are you okay?"

She waved his thoughtfulness away. "I'm fine." Only she was *not* fine.

He was wearing jeans.

And they looked good on him. Real good. Choke on a roti good.

She'd thought he looked nice in a suit? The denim hugged

his thighs and made him even taller. His T-shirt was still a crisp white, but it was definitely more casual than she'd seen him in before, and it revealed his surprisingly muscular biceps.

Jia jerked her eyes to his. She couldn't be trusted to not look at his butt, and now apparently, she couldn't be trusted to look at his front. Neck up from now on, that was all. "Hi," she said weakly.

"Hello. I'm sorry I kept you waiting. You're early."

"I am?" Jia glanced at her phone. "Only ten minutes. Occasionally I'm early to things. Don't get used to it."

"I wouldn't dare. You've met my uncle, I see."

"I have." Jia smiled at Adil. "He was kind enough to give me a snack."

"Next time, I'll make you a proper meal," Adil promised.

Jia wasn't sure what to say to that. Was there going to be another time that Jia would be at this home to see Adil again? She settled for a polite smile, and picked up the rest of her roti to finish it off.

"What time will you be home?" Luna had slipped into the kitchen so quietly Jia had barely noticed her. She'd carefully directed her question to her uncle.

"Not too late, I don't think," Dev responded, and looked at Jia.

Jia shook her head. "Not late at all. The event should be over in a couple of hours."

Luna looked back and forth between the two of them. "Okay. I hope you two enjoy your . . ."

"Meeting," Dev said, at the same time Jia said, "Cultural event."

They both paused and looked at each other. "Uh," Jia said. "We will, thanks."

"Luna and I have at least four of our shows to catch up on," Adil said cheerfully, back to work rolling out rotis. "Take your time while you're out. We'll probably both be asleep by the time you get home."

Dev nodded. "Luna, when you're done eating, make sure you finish your homework before you join Adil Uncle for any television."

"I will. I'm not a kid."

Jia would have taken Dev for a strict parent, but the fond patience he regarded his niece with at her sharp rebuke told her that was unlikely. Patience and a little bit of flexibility was good, as far as she was concerned. She'd had strict parents, and all it had made her want to do was rebel.

He didn't kiss or hug Luna, but did lightly pat her shoulder as they passed her. "Of course not. Good night. Good night, Uncle."

"Your family's sweet," Jia said in a low voice as they walked to the door. They both put their shoes on, and Dev grabbed a jacket and a baseball cap from the hall closet. She'd barely exchanged any words with Luna, of course, but the girl had seemed quiet and well-mannered.

"They are, thank you." He put the jacket on, blessedly covering up those arms she was not looking at.

If only he could do the same with his long legs. That she was not looking at.

They left the apartment and Jia fidgeted with her purse. She was not going to be able to enjoy any part of the evening if she didn't ask. "So, your uncle mentioned that he knew about the catfishing."

Dev grimaced. "Yes. He caught me right after I found out. I promise, he would never think less of you for it."

"I didn't think he would. But . . . you didn't tell your uncle about our agreement, did you?"

He glanced at Jia as they entered the elevator. "I would never. He thinks I'm simply trying to make my family's bad behavior up to you."

"Okay." That wasn't so bad. She nodded at his hat. "Ready to disguise yourself?"

"I am, yes. Though, to be honest, I was surprised anyone wanted to photograph me here to begin with. I was never as much of a target as the others in my family. Until my grandfather and brother were gone, people were usually happy to forget I exist."

She looked all the way up at his profile. "That seems like it would be hard to do," she said without thinking.

Dev glanced down at her, and suddenly the elevator seemed a bit too small. She cleared her throat and edged away a little. "I mean, you're so big."

He stilled.

"Tall," she clarified, her cheeks heating up. "Hard to miss."

"I see," he murmured. He placed the dark cap over his

head. It obscured his face enough that they should slide by without detection. "Hopefully I can make it through this show undetected. It's an art show we are going to, correct?"

"Yes." She smiled up at him. "You'll love it."

THIS WAS THE oddest art show Dev had ever been to. There was . . . art, yes, though he wouldn't have thought to call it that. Modern art, as far as he could tell. Sculptures and paintings with blobs of paint on them, and ugly portraits that didn't look like any human he'd ever met.

There were also pancakes.

Truly, this was the oddest country. "I don't understand the significance of this," he murmured to Jia.

She looked up at him. The dim gallery lighting in the warehouse caught the shimmery thread of rose gold in her otherwise plain head scarf. It reminded him of the gold she'd worn when he'd spotted her for the first time. The pink matched the pink of her sweater and shoes and the wash of color over her eyelids. Something about how she color co-ordinated everything she wore appealed to his structured brain. "The significance of what?"

The line moved, and he automatically moved with it. He jerked his head at the table in front of them. "The pancakes?"

"Oh. It's a pancake and art show."

She said that like it was supposed to mean something, and he was still mystified. But they were at the front of the line now, so he couldn't ask her. "I'll have chocolate chip pancakes, please," she said cheerfully.

The man behind the table poured out her pancakes onto

one of the electric griddles and looked at him. Dev cleared his throat. "Yes, I shall have the same, thank you."

He accepted his stack of pancakes on a paper plate when it was finished. He hesitated at the toppings bar, but when Jia liberally doused her pancakes in syrup, he decided to do the same. Damn his carefully constructed diet for the night, he would embrace this American experience. "Is there a place to sit while we eat?"

She paused in taking a selfie of herself with the pancakes. "Oh no. Now we look at the art."

It took some doing, but he was able to cut through his pancake with his plastic fork after he observed her. He took a bite and nearly moaned at the explosion of sweetness in his mouth. It had been a long time since he'd eaten something as decadent as this. "Delicious."

"They are pretty good pancakes," Jia agreed, as they wound through the crowd. Her multi-tasking ability was impressive. She could eat and maneuver around people and use the expensive camera around her neck to film and take photos occasionally. No one glanced twice at them. Dev liked being anonymous, but it was extra nice to be anonymous with Jia.

"Are these common in America? Pancake and art shows?"

"I don't think so. I accepted the partner request from the gallery 'cause I thought it might be unique." She stopped in front of a painting with two yellow circles painted under three triangles. "I think this is very brave. Clearly, it's about how we are forced to live under the tyranny of the ruling class."

He gave her an incredulous look, and then he caught the twinkle in her eyes. He looked at the painting again, like he was seriously interpreting it. "Agreed, I feel as though it's an indictment of colonialism and the far-reaching implications of not having self-governance."

"Ah, how interesting." Jia shoved a large bite of pancake into her mouth. "What about this one?"

They moved to the left. Behind him, he heard a couple whisper, "Do you see colonialism in this?"

Dev chewed. The canvas had been painted all blue. That was it. One shade of blue. "It's a commentary on climate change."

"In favor of or against?"

"Yes."

He wasn't sure, but he was pretty sure Jia's cough was stifling a laugh. His confidence edged a little higher as they moved around the room, both of them trying to outdo the other with pretentious determinations as to the art's meaning. They got to the last painting. "Breasts," Jia said, deadpan. "I see breasts."

The unexpectedly ribald humor surprised Dev so much he snorted out a laugh. She joined him, and he cherished her giggling.

He noticed some dirty looks so he jerked his head at the door. She nodded, that impish gleam still in her eye.

Dev tossed their garbage on the way out and almost placed his hand on Jia's back to guide her before he caught himself. This had felt so much like a date that he'd forgotten himself. Not that he'd ever had a date that was this much fun, of course. "I enjoyed this, thank you for bringing me. Did you get the footage you needed?"

"Yup. I'm going to cut it in with the intro and outro I filmed today."

"It's a good partnership."

"Some influencers get trips to Aruba. Me, I get the pancakes."

"I'm sure you've been offered Aruba trips before."

She smiled and stuffed her camera away. "A few. I'm not really a travel vlogger, though, and I've never gone anywhere without my family, so I declined those."

"You're here without your family," he pointed out.

"Oh sure. I mean traveling, though, for vacation. I admire people who can go places on their own. I imagined I'd get bored without someone to share it with."

His filming schedule had been so difficult, he couldn't remember the last time he'd had a proper vacation, but he nodded. Dev had always hated being alone in hotel rooms and new cities. He was a bit of a homebody. "I understand that."

"Thanks for coming. And for, like, everything."

He didn't want Jia's gratitude, not when he was so delighted to even pretend date her. "No thanks necessary."

They walked in silence for a couple minutes. Dev didn't know where they were going, but that was okay. There were plenty of people out, and the streets were well-lit, so he didn't really mind going nowhere. He racked his brain for questions he could ask her. That was the whole purpose of this, right? To get to know her? Not simply to have fun.

Jia beat him to it. "You seem to have a really good relationship with your niece."

He shoved his hands into his pockets. He could thank Luna for inspiring him to dig out these jeans. It felt odd to wear something so casual, but for a second, when Jia had seen him, he'd hoped it had been appreciation he'd spotted in her eyes. "I hope so. We're making up for lost time."

"You weren't close to her before your brother . . ." Jia trailed off.

"No. I only saw her once or twice a year. I mostly heard about her from my grandmother." He looked down at her. It was odd, talking about anything so personal as his family with someone who was an outsider. Dixit business stayed Dixit business. "How much do you know about my family history?"

"Not much."

"I mean, did Arjun tell you anything, when you were talking to him? As me?"

"No. He was pretty vague whenever I tried to get personal. For obvious reasons, I see now. It was kind of like everything he said to me was from a script he was tailoring to fit me."

He let out a half laugh.

"What?"

"Nothing. Only . . . from what I've seen, I believe that the words they wrote you were from a script. From *Kyunki Mere Sanam Ke Liye Kuch Bhi*."

Jia stopped and faced him. "Are you serious?"

"Of course, I wouldn't know for sure unless I read the

whole exchange. You could redact your responses." Though it was her responses he really wanted to read. It was another insight into her beautiful mind.

"I don't know about that." She made a disgusted face. "Ugh, how was I so easily fooled."

"Please stop blaming yourself. I only spotted it because they were my lines. I have a rather good memory." He wouldn't tell her that he'd written those lines, and probably any other that she'd gotten. That was more personal.

She resumed walking, and he fell into step. "When I think this whole thing can't get more absurd," she muttered, then set her shoulders. "Okay. Let's get back to the Dixit family history lesson while I process this."

For once, talking about his family didn't seem impossible. "It's fairly common knowledge my grandparents virtually disowned my father when he married my mother, though I think that scandal's not as fresh for the younger generations."

"I saw something about that when I first looked you up. Because she was Muslim?"

"That was what the press believed, but their actual objection was that she was poor. You can imagine how much class mattered then, especially for the son of a couple who was so in the public eye." He tried to control his sneer, but he couldn't quite manage it, he feared. His wonderful memories of his mother were punctuated by her sadness over them not having any extended family nearby. "My father was just getting into a screenwriting career, but my parents moved to Dubai. I was raised there until I was sixteen. I never met anyone on my dad's side of the family. My folks did fine without my grandparents. Dad actually started teaching eventually, and my mother became a nurse. We were raised without cameras following us or anyone wanting anything from us. It was a good childhood." It had been a perfectly normal life, actually, away from the Dixit fame. That was probably why he didn't feel too much fear at losing his grandfather's money or not relying on the family fortune. So long as he and his little family were taken care of, he'd be fine.

"But when I was sixteen, my parents died in a car accident and my brother and I were shipped back to my grandparents' home. They took us in, because what would it look like if they didn't?" Dev shrugged. "Besides, my brother was very handsome even at thirteen; he was the spitting image of my grandfather. The world could forget who his mother was. My grandfather was less interested in me. I was still so angry about how he'd treated my parents, and I was a reminder to him about his own loss, I imagine. I only lived with them for a year or so before I left."

Jia's step faltered. "You were so young. Where did you go?"

"I tried my hand at a couple careers. Acting was the easiest paycheck. I got a flat in Mumbai, as far as I could get from them in the same city." He didn't like to think about those early years too much. He'd still been grieving the upheaval of what had been a good life, and missing his brother something fierce.

A few years later, Dev had tried to get Rohan to come live with him, but it was too late. His brother had already been sucked into the Bollywood film star machine, filled with all the debauchery and wealth that came with it. Another regret to add to his shoulders, that he hadn't taken over Rohan's guardianship when the boy was a minor.

"I'm sorry. Your family has had so many losses."

"Some people say there's a curse. My parents and uncle were young, and my brother was as well. Then my grandfather. I think that Rohan's death took too much of a toll on him." He paused. "It's quite odd to mourn your family members when a whole nation is also mourning them."

"I can't imagine," Jia murmured.

What had been in those pancakes to make him confess his darkest secrets? "Apologies, I don't know why I'm talking so much. Obviously, none of this is common knowledge. I would prefer you not share it with anyone, including your family."

She mimed locking her lips. "I have that kind of face. People tell me things."

"That must be it."

They walked quietly for a moment. "You have a nice little family now."

"Yes. I'm glad Adil Uncle could come live with us. I didn't see him much when I was growing up. I think there was some question of him taking custody of Rohan and me when we were young, but I believe my grandparents convinced him we were better off with them." More over-sharing. "It's been good to have help with Luna, too." He'd been surprised

Luna hadn't seemed overly enthused to meet or spend time with Jia earlier tonight, but he supposed that could be chalked up to shyness.

"Is Luna's mother—?"

"Out of the picture. I don't even know who she is. I think Rohan must have bought her off." He didn't know the ins and outs of what had happened when Luna was born, just that one day Rohan had been a carefree bachelor, and the next, the newspapers had proclaimed him a father. When Dev had called him, he'd refused to speak of it, merely said, *Congratulations on being a kaka, Bhai,* and hung up.

He didn't know how his grandparents had felt about Rohan's illegitimate child initially, but his grandmother at least had seemed to come around quickly. In the end, their family name had squelched the worst of the gossip.

Jia switched her purse to her other shoulder. "Luna seems to be healthy and happy, and you clearly adore her. You've made up for missed time, it appears."

"Can you make up for such a thing?"

"I think so." Her feet slowed, and he met her pace. "My roommate, Katrina, she likes to say that people come in and out of our lives, and we have to enjoy the parts in the middle. But I think it's okay to not enjoy all the parts, you know? Things change, life changes, you change. I definitely feel like my relationship with various family members has ebbed and flowed."

He filled his lungs with air. She was wise, but he already knew that from watching her deceptively simple videos. "Are your feet hurting? Those are very high heels."

Jia gave him a chiding look. "Please, I can travel up a mountain in these. It's a nice night for a walk."

"It is." They walked in silence for a moment. At some point, he'd have to walk them back to the garage they'd parked in. "Now that I have given you my family's darkest secrets, tell me something about you," he said instead.

"I'm an open book. I post my whole life online."

"Do you? I don't think you do. You're different in real life." She already knew he'd watched her videos. There was no harm in admitting that.

Her smile was faint. "I suppose my online persona is authentically real, just not all of me."

"So what are the other parts of you?"

"I don't know," she admitted. "It's a blurry line, where online ends and real life begins."

Dev nodded. "What's your favorite color?"

"Pink."

"Favorite animal?"

"Giraffes."

He straightened to his full height. *Giraffe* had been the nickname classmates had teased him with since puberty, but if she liked giraffes . . . "Favorite sibling."

She glanced around. "Did one of my sisters put you up to this? Are they going to jump out and yell at me?"

Dev chuckled. "No."

"I love all my sisters the same," Jia said loudly, then leaned in and continued in a whisper. "My twin, followed by our middle sister."

"Ayesha and . . ." He thought for a second. "Sadia."

"Wow, you do have a good memory."

Only for things he cared about, but he didn't want to spook either of them by admitting that. "It's from years of memorizing lines."

"Sadia's the one I identify the most with, probably. She's all married and happy now, but she bucked my parents to marry the guy she loved when she was like twenty."

"How did they take that?"

Jia glanced away. "They disowned her for a few years. Came around when she had my nephew and then really reconciled when her first husband passed away. But it was scary. I was only, like, thirteen, and I barely got to see her for years."

Dev's heart cracked a little. He'd seen the effects of parental estrangement in his own life. "That's terrible." For the first time, he wondered how his uncle had felt when his brother had been banished. Had the infamous playboy cried? Had he tried to see his brother? "Is that why . . . ?" He trod a little delicately. "Is that why you're so eager to please your parents?"

She came to a halt at a stoplight. He moved closer to her. He told himself it was for protection, though there wasn't much in the way of danger here. "I don't think they'd ever do that again. They regret cutting her off."

"But the fear is still there."

"Yes."

"I understand."

"I suppose you do understand rigid family members."

A car honked and Dev jolted. He'd forgotten that they

were in a public place, while he'd been spilling family secrets. "We should head back to the garage," he murmured.

"Yes, let's do that. I didn't realize it was so late."

"Time flies when you're eating pancakes, I suppose."
Their walk back to the garage was quiet. He gave her a sideways glance when they approached her car.

"I can drive you home," she blurted out.

"No, I'll take a car." It was already intimate, her coming
to his home to fetch him. Her driving him back smacked far
too much of a proper date. Especially combined with all the
soul baring they'd done this evening. "Getting into your car
is a struggle," he teased, trying to lighten the mood.

It worked; she chuckled. He opened her car door for her.
"Well, good night. I'll see you soon." He hoped he saw her
soon. He started to extend his hand to her, but Jia took another step forward, closing the distance between them.

The hug was so fleeting and quick, he might have imagined it had he not taken the split second to imprint the feel
of her whole body, from chest to thighs.

Dev didn't go around hugging women in public, and
he told himself that was the reason he stood there like a
shell-shocked buffoon until his brain kicked into gear. He
wrapped his arms around her and gave her a little squeeze.
Warmth filled him, taking up all the empty spots inside him.

He inhaled, absorbing the delicate floral scent Jia wore.
He let her go the moment her arms started to loosen. He
wanted to ask what that had been. A pity hug? A friend
hug? A business hug?

An *I'm Interested in You for Real* hug?

But he couldn't ask any of those things because he feared the answer. So he merely stepped away.

"Good night," she almost whispered and got in the car.

"Night," he repeated. He watched her drive away, wondering if that was his fate for the immediate future. Watching her drive away after she'd doled out a small crumb of affection.

He pressed his hand against his chest. He feared even if it was, he would take it.

Chapter Thirteen

Tuesday 1:25 P.M.

Jia: do you like magic?

Dev: Is this an American pickup line?

J: Ha, no.

D: Magic stresses me out. I spend all my time trying to figure out how they do it.

J: Ah

D: Why?

J: someone offered me tickets to a show

D: I'll come with you

J: No, I don't want to stress you out!

D: It's okay if you enjoy it, I will enjoy it.

J: It wouldn't work anyway. There's too
many people there. Cameras.

D: Okay, scratch that.

J: I'll come up with something more remote before then.

D: Yes, we should get to know each other
more. Before your parents come.

Thursday, 8:22 P.M.

D: What are you doing?

J: Working. What about you?

D: Also working. Night shoot downtown.

J: Cool. I love seeing shoots.

D: 📷

You will have to come sometime.
What are you working on?

J: Trying to work up some pitches for various brands.
My metrics have been slipping a lot lately.

D: I'm sorry to hear that.

Thursday, 10:45 P.M.

J: What did you do??

D: What?

J: My mentions started getting flooded, and when
I traced it back, it started with your old costar
tagging me and raving about one of my videos??

D: I simply told her my niece thinks you are cool.
It's not a lie. I did not ask her to promote you.

J: This is going to look suspicious. People
will put two and two together.

D: They won't.
People see what they want to see.

J: . . . that's true, I suppose.

D: Are you upset?

J: No. This is sweet. One tag won't get me back
to where I was, but you met my weekly goal
in about twenty minutes so thanks, haha.

D: Not a problem.

Friday Morning

Jia woke up to her phone ringing. She groped for it on the pillow next to her head, then sat straight up. Ayesha! Finally. "I've called you a million times. What have you been doing?" Jia hissed, as soon as her twin's face popped up on her phone.

"What have you been doing?" Ayesha yelped. "I go camping for a couple weeks and come back to all hell having broken loose."

"Maybe that'll teach you not to go camping." She and her twin had always been glued at the hip, but when Jia had quit med school, their paths had diverged. It was weird to see Ayesha in their old shared bedroom alone, but also a relief that she herself wasn't in that bedroom.

"Um, trust me, I'm never going camping again for other reasons." Ayesha scratched at an obvious mosquito bite on her cheek. She was dressed sedately, in monochromatic colors, a gray long-sleeved dress and a gray cotton scarf wrapped around her hair. Ayesha preferred things she could mix and match easily. She was too focused on other priorities, like her career, to care about clothes.

Jia was aware that Ayesha was about as close to a perfect Pakistani American daughter as could be, but she'd never felt any envy or anger at her twin for that. If anything, she'd tried to emulate her, as her parents had always told her to do. Unfortunately, that had always led to her eventually growing bored. A bored Jia wasn't a good thing. It led to her starting a tiny empire in her bedroom, for example. "You didn't enjoy it like you thought you would?"

"Worst rebellion against our parents ever. They were right, they didn't cross the ocean so their daughters could go sleep outside."

Jia's lips curled up. "I can teach you better ways to rebel."

"So I see." Ayesha hooked her thumb over her shoulder. "Mom's out here claiming that you're practically engaged to Dev. When did you even meet him?"

"Ugh." Jia scrubbed her face. That's right. Ayesha didn't know about the debacle of meeting Dev. "It's a long story."

"Stop touching your face," Ayesha chided, ever the young doctor.

"Right, sorry." She wanted to wail her news out to her sister. Ayesha had been the one person who had known everything: not just who Jia was talking to, but also how much she'd started to swoon over him.

Time is—

Nope, nope, she wasn't going to dwell on a single one of those fake scripted words. Dev's real words were way better. "First, make sure the hallway is clear." She wouldn't put it past Zara to be hovering out there.

Ayesha rolled her eyes, but did as she asked.

"Okay, so . . ." Jia quickly recapped the whole situation for her sister, while Ayesha's mouth opened more and more.

"Whhaaaaaat is happening?" Ayesha squealed when Jia went silent. "So Dev's *cousin* catfished you?"

"Yes." She didn't mention the brother. No need to complicate this more.

"Did he give a reason?"

"No."

"So." Ayesha stopped, then shook her head. "What's up with all these photos of you and Dev snuggling? Why is Mom planning your engagement party?"

"There was one photo, and Mom . . . she and Noor and Zara confronted me, all at once. I got overwhelmed, and well . . . I let them believe that I was dating him. It seemed to make them happy." And she so rarely made her family happy.

Ayesha made an annoyed sound. "Jia, this inability to look at long-term repercussions is a real problem."

"I know. I know."

"What are you going to do?"

"Dev agreed to play my boyfriend while Mom and Daddy are out here."

Ayesha's lips parted. "When they're *out* there?"

"Oh, they didn't tell you that? Yes, they're coming."

"They didn't tell me that, but that explains why Mom told me to give her my schedule."

Jia sat up in bed, happiness soaring through her. "Oh yay. You're coming for sure? That's wonderful."

"I suppose I am."

"Sound more excited," Jia chided. "This is fantastic. It's not going to be only me and him against the parentals, that means."

"I'll be happy to see you, Jia, but I was really hoping that at some point we would have left these wild schemes behind us. Behind you."

Jia bit her lip. "I deserve that."

"I'll talk to Mom. Of course I'll come."

"Phew."

"Let's save our phews for a minute," Ayesha said. "What's going to happen after our parents fall in love with Dev and come back home?"

"I'll tell them it didn't work out, eventually. It'll be so much easier to tell them bad news when they're back home and I don't have to see it. They'll be disappointed, but less disappointed than if they know I was catfished."

"What are you getting out of this?"

What you have. She wanted her parents to look at her, just once, the way they looked at Ayesha. Like she'd done something right, met their standards.

She knew her parents loved her. But she craved their respect, and she wouldn't have that, not from her mother at least, until she fit into the mold they had created with their first daughter.

Ayesha squinted at Jia when she didn't speak. "You're too much, you know that?"

Too much.

Oh, Jia was aware. She felt the words like a dagger in her heart, her confidence deflating. She hated those two words, though perhaps only second to *a lot. Jia is . . . a lot.* Always with that same pause between the words, the hesitation of looking for a word that could encompass superficial and silly and ditzy and foolish all in one word. Or two words, actually.

"Jia?"

She covered up her pain with a bright smile. "That's me. Too much."

SOPHIA WEPT PRETTILY on Hudson's shoulder. "I swear, I didn't mean to do it, baby."

Hudson gazed down at her with anguished tenderness.

Off to the side of the shot, Dev stifled a yawn. Devastating news in his old serial had required a cut to every single face in the scene, which meant one didn't get a break. No one was paying attention to him here, so long as he hit his cues.

Speaking of . . . Dev straightened when the two separated and slapped a smirk on. "She's lying, Chase. You know it and I know it."

"You need to back off." Hudson thrust his on-screen love behind him.

"Or what?" Seriously, or what? They needed to toss a good evil mother-in-law into this mix. Everyone on this show was relatively nice, cheating aside.

Cheating wasn't the worst thing someone should be able to do to someone on a show. No, that was a new bride washing her husband's laptop with dishwashing detergent in a misguided attempt to disinfect it.

He understood if such camp was out of place here, but it would be nice to liven this up with *something*.

Hudson took a threatening step. "Or I'll show Dominic the proof about your little side hustle."

"Cut."

Dev relaxed. Hudson walked over to him. "Good take, man. Let's hope they got it so we can finish up early today."

It was only ten, but they'd been working since three in the morning. "Let's hope. Sorry I kept screwing up on that last scene."

"You okay? You usually nail things on the first take." They walked to the shade, out of the studio lights.

Dev grabbed a bottle of water and chugged it. He did usually nail things on the first take, but then again, he was rarely so . . . what was the word? Bored? "Yes, I'm fine. The script is . . . it doesn't feel natural to me yet." Plot aside, he felt underused. He'd thought he'd be a lead in this show, but the more they filmed, the more apparent it became that his role was to act as a dark foil and prop up the golden star.

It was one thing to be sidelined for the sake of the show, but it was another to be sidelined for a boring and bland hero.

Hudson nodded sympathetically, his blond hair catching the light. "You should talk to the director. I doubt they'll rewrite, but they may take your thoughts into account. You're really killing it, though. The character feels multifaceted."

Dev didn't tell Hudson that he'd already given the writers' room some notes, and they'd shot him down. Then again, the director might be more willing to consider his concerns. "Thank you." He glanced around. Their director, Fred, was sitting under an umbrella. He looked like he was busy with the computer he held in his lap, but there was no one else currently bothering him.

"How's everything else going here?"

Dev refocused and gave a faint smile. "Well, thank you. My niece is adjusting to school." So well that Luna had a sleepover scheduled tonight with a new friend. Dev thought it was fast, but she'd been more excited than he'd ever seen her, so he'd zipped his lips.

"And you?"

Him? He was . . .

Happy. Dev blinked. It had been a while since he'd been happy. Simply texting Jia was better than dates with other women. How had it only been a couple of weeks since she'd come into his life? Perhaps it was all the extracurricular time he'd spent watching her videos, but it felt longer. Like he knew her. "I'm doing great."

Hudson clapped him on the back. "Good. Hey, listen, would you like to come over for dinner next week? My wife's a great cook. Bring a date, if you'd like. And your niece, of course; she might like my daughter."

Dev was touched. Hudson might be a bit conceited, but he was kind.

A date. Of course, there was only one woman he wanted to date. "I will, thank you."

"No problem. I'll text you the address." He jerked his chin toward Fred. "Looks like Fred's free. You might want to catch him now."

Dev nodded. They said their goodbyes, and then Dev made his way over to Fred. He felt vaguely nervous, which was odd. He'd always merely had to raise an eyebrow on any set and the director had fallen over himself to help him.

These nerves were good. If he was going to be self-sufficient, he needed to actually be self-sufficient.

"Fred?"

The smaller man blinked up at him through his thick glasses. "Dev! My man. You're killing it."

"Thanks. Sorry for all the takes today."

Fred waved his hand. "We got it finally, and that's what counts."

"Do you have a minute?"

"Sure." Fred got to his feet. "Walk with me, I gotta get something from my car. Is anything wrong?"

"It's my character."

"What about him?"

"I feel as though he's . . ." Dev hesitated, looking for the perfect English word. "One-dimensional? As a villain. All we know about him is that he's cheating. He has no identity outside his relationship with Chase."

Fred nodded. "Yup."

Dev raised an eyebrow at that ready agreement.

"You're playing the hell out of him, though."

"I . . ." This was confusing. "You want him to be a one-dimensional character?"

Fred stopped and looked up at him with sympathy. "Why are we all here, Dev?"

"On this planet, you mean?"

"Nah. On this set." Fred jerked his thumb over his shoulder. "Hudson is here to score the E for his eventual EGOT. I'm here to direct a big-budget TV tearjerker of a show that'll give me enough money that I can pick and choose future projects." He pointed at Dev. "You're here to make a splashy debut in Hollywood. Do you know how we all do that?"

"Create a fun television show that people find exciting and interesting?" Dev suggested.

"No. We do it by reinventing the wheel. Handsome square-jawed white guy with marital and friendship problems is the wheel. The rest of us are the oil that keeps that wheel running. No offense."

"None . . . taken?"

Fred patted Dev on the chest. "You deliver your lines as best you can, buddy. You probably won't get an Emmy, but we'll get enough attention that you'll get some amazing future roles. Consider it paying your dues." Fred checked his wristwatch. "Now I don't know about you, but I could really use a big lunch. You're welcome to join . . ."

"No, I'm good." Dev watched his director saunter away.

You don't seem happy.

He narrowed his eyes. He was happy in the country, yes. He was happy being away from the brunt of his family's fame. He'd even be happy paying his dues, given his latent guilt over how easy it had been to start his acting career, compared to other struggling actors.

But no, he wasn't happy with this particular show.

There was nothing he could do, though. He couldn't see them killing off their foreign villain for no reason. Not when he had some name recognition that could help them on the way to the Emmys.

Emmys for them, but not him, as Fred had so cheerfully explained to him.

So what if you're unhappy? What's the other option? There

wasn't one. When he'd spoken to his former costar yesterday, he'd been hit by a wave of homesickness, but for the show and the family he'd built there, not for the place.

Into the box go these feelings as well. You are happy and grateful to be working. All you wanted was a fresh start. You got it. Don't complain.

Dev shifted. He was simply tired from the long night. He'd go home or to his trailer and take a nap, and then everything would be fine when he woke up.

To busy himself, he checked his phone as he walked to his trailer. Jia hadn't texted him yet today, so he sent her a good morning text.

Hi. What are you up to?

He paused, the dopamine hit from her immediate reply making him dizzy. I just finished shooting. What about you?

I need to get out of the city, so I decided to take a road trip. I heard there was this place that was good for photography. I'm at the studio packing up my stuff.

His fatigue vanished. Disappearing for the day sounded like a dream. How long had it been since he'd gotten in a car and driven far away? Had he ever done that?

Only, he couldn't go on a road trip with Jia. That wouldn't be proper.

You're so boring. Live a little. What century are you stuck in, anyway? Like unmarried people don't hang out in private all the time.

Rohan's voice was too loud in his head. He supposed he was being overly conservative. He had indeed spent private time with his single female friends in the past. Jia was different.

Because you are interested in her.

He rubbed his ear. This revelation wasn't that earth-shattering. Obviously, he was interested in her. He'd bought a serum on her recommendation last night, for crying out loud, and he didn't even know what a serum was.

However, even if he did want to come, how did one invite oneself to a road trip? What was the etiquette for that?

Want to come with me?

His smile was slow. Yes.

It's like two and a half hours away. But we'll be back tonight.

That wasn't a problem. Luna wouldn't even be home till tomorrow. Sounds good.

Cool.

He thought for a second, and imagined going on a road trip in her cramped little Beetle. Can we take my car?

Chapter Fourteen

JIA HADN'T planned on hitting the road today, but Ayesha's words had so burrowed into her brain, she'd feared if she didn't leave soon, she'd pace her room for hours and then grow even more anxious when she didn't get anything done.

It was a bonus that Dev had been able to come with her. She'd felt a little shy at first, getting into his car, but he'd quickly put her at ease, telling her about his costars and Luna's first sleepover.

Between the warmth of the car and the low hum of Dev's radio, Jia dozed off at some point. She jerked awake when a phone rang.

She stirred and looked over at Dev. He'd told her he'd come straight from set, but she would have guessed as much from the eye makeup that he hadn't quite wiped off all the way. The dark liner on his waterline made his eyes pop even more than usual. "Is that you or me?"

He glanced at her. He'd reclined the seat and drove one handed, the other elegant hand resting on his thigh. The midday sun made his skin glow. "You, I believe."

Jia hunched over and dug through her purse to find her

phone. The text was short and to the point, from Harley. Hey girl! Sorry I haven't been in touch yet, but I wanted to let you know that I gave your name to Ronny from MakeOut. She was asking if I'd like to head an inspired line. That's not my thing, but I thought it might be yours! She seemed excited, she's heard of you before. Anyway, giving you a heads-up in case she emails. Good luck!

"Is everything okay?"

"Mm-hmm." Jia ruthlessly throttled back the surge of excitement. This could mean nothing. Makeup companies had approached her before, and it had always been a bad deal, one where she didn't get any creative control or they simply wanted to slap her name on a terrible product.

None of the companies had been as big as MakeOut, though. *This executive could still not even contact you.* Jia typed back a heartfelt thank-you to Harley for passing on the opportunity, and put the phone away. This was excitement or disappointment for Future Jia to deal with, not her. "How far are we?"

"We're almost there."

She scrubbed her eyes. "I am so sorry, I didn't realize I slept for so long."

"That's okay. It was a pretty scenic drive."

She swiped at her mouth with the back of her hand as surreptitiously as she could. Had she drooled? It was one thing to fall asleep in his car, it was another thing to drool. "I meant to keep you company and switch off driving, though."

"Again, no worries."

But she'd missed the view, and she didn't mean outside the car. Today was another casual day for Dev, in those drool-worthy jeans and an equally sexy gray long-sleeved ribbed Henley. He wasn't overly muscular, but the clinging knit material emphasized his lean body.

Jia tore her eyes away. She'd been thrilled he'd agreed to this trip—she had wanted to run away, but she hadn't particularly wanted to be alone—but she'd been surprised, too, given his concerns over propriety. It felt way more intimate to sit in a car with someone for hours than to sit across a table for drinks. "I'll drive on the way back."

His lips curled up. "We'll see how late it is."

"It shouldn't be too late." Jia looked out the window, some of her earlier excitement coming back to her. The scenery was flat and desolate, like they were going into no-man's-land. Which they essentially were. "I have to take a bunch of photos, record a video or three, and we can head back with the raw footage."

"Tell me about this place."

"Oh right. I forgot you hopped in your car with very little information."

He chuckled, and the low, rough sound scraped over her nerve endings. "I did. That level of impulsivity is unusual for me."

"Stick with me, kid." Oops, did that sound too much like a command? "Bombay Beach is a ghost town. Or, like, there's only two hundred people or so left living there. Artists come every spring and turn the remaining homes and signs and stuff into art installations. I think it would make a really cool feature. I figured you could wander the town while I work a bit on the beach, poke around."

"It's my pleasure. I could use a break from everything as well. So you don't need me to play cameraman?"

"I have a tripod, but if you're going to volunteer . . ."

A big brown sign came up on the right, and Dev slowed and turned his signal on. Jia snapped a quick photo as they turned onto the road. They passed a hotel and general store; both parking lots were empty. "Let's go to the water first," Jia suggested and pointed straight down the road. The place was laid out like a grid, according to the articles she'd read, about a dozen streets and cross streets filled with decrepit and decaying trailers and homes interspaced with vibrant installations.

Dev drove up the incline to the beach. "Glad we brought my car," he murmured, and she couldn't take offense at the slight to her eyelash-decorated vehicle. Her baby wouldn't have been able to make the climb.

He pulled right onto the beach. There was no sight of anybody for miles, and no other cars there. Jia was so eager, she scrambled out before he could open her door and inhaled the air. "Smell that?"

Dev got out more slowly. "It smells like . . . a small body of water."

"Yes. I love it." A thrill of excitement went through her. This wasn't her usual content, but there were only so many ways she could talk about fashion and beauty. She rounded the trunk, which Dev remote opened for her. Jia rummaged in her camera bag. "Okay. I'm going to go get some test shots. Do you want to walk around the town?" There wasn't a single car that she could see, or any sign of life. On second thought . . . "Actually, why don't you stay close." She was lucky that she'd always lived in friendly areas. She was wary of any place where she might stick out until she verified that it was safe.

Dev gave her a haughty look. "I doubt anyone would touch me."

Ah, to be so confident. "Sir, that level of protection only works when you're in a place where people recognize you or your name. I'm not sure how many of the two hundred people in this town are watching foreign soap operas."

He gave a slight dip of his head in acknowledgment. "May I stay here?"

"With me?" That gave her a thrill. He wouldn't be the first person to watch her work, but he'd be the first one she noticed while she was working. "Ummm, sure."

"I have a script I need to read, for next week's shoot." He reached into his bag in the trunk and pulled out a sheaf of papers. "This will keep me busy."

"I feel bad you came all this way to read."

"I like reading. I mostly wanted to get out of the city with you. It doesn't matter what we're doing." He met her eyes.

She was struck with a sudden wave of shyness at his blunt honesty, and she wanted to lower her gaze, but she couldn't. Instead, she cleared her throat and grabbed her tripod. "Well, in that case, enjoy your reading. I'll be right down there, closer to the water."

Jia stopped a few steps away and turned around. Dev was watching her, she was gratified to note. "I'm glad you came with me, too." And then before she could succumb to her nerves, she hustled away.

IT WAS A good thing Dev had brought the script with him. Not because he was reading it, but it was good camouflage for observing Jia.

He'd watched almost every YouTube video she had up by now—hundreds of them, thank God they were relatively short—but watching her shoot one was a whole new experience.

She'd set up her camera and sat with her legs folded on a beach blanket. Behind her was an empty doorway someone had erected on the sand, framing the water. The wind caught the tail end of her long head scarf, and it flew behind her like a flag of yellow against the deep blue sky. Her blousy shirt was the same shade of sunshine, and her shoes matched. The colors flowed over his brain, soothing any ragged neurons and synapses.

He stretched his legs long. It had been a long time since he'd sat idle somewhere, not counting work. It was calming here, with Jia not far away and the still water. There were installations in the water, too, a mailbox and a swing set.

He contemplated the swing, and the way it reflected on

the water. It made him sad, that swing. Perhaps because there was only room for one person, not two.

They'd had a swing set when he was a child. His parents had set it up in their backyard. It was weird, their house had been small, but Dev's world had felt bigger then. There had been no expectations about what careers they might enter, no press salivating over their missteps or triumphs, no one pitting brother against brother on metrics that didn't matter. He'd pushed Rohan on that swing. If he listened carefully, he could hear his little brother squealing with joy.

Was that his breathing coming harder and faster? The sudden wetness at his eyes stunned him, and he sat up straight. What was wrong with him?

"Dev?"

Pull yourself together. Men don't act like this. His father had drummed that into him. He'd been a kind father, but not one to tolerate his sons weeping over an injury that wasn't fatal.

"Dev?"

Horror ran through him, mingling with panic. No, no. The only thing worse than spiraling out was having Jia see him so weak. He opened his mouth to assure her he was fine, but nothing came out.

Her beautiful heart-shaped face came into view. Were the faint freckles across the bridge of her nose natural or makeup? He hadn't noticed them before.

Jia's small hand came to a fluttering rest on his shoulder. "It's okay," she said, confident and calm. "You're having a panic attack. I've seen this before."

He shook his head frantically. He was *not*. He'd tell her that as soon as he could speak, too.

"Match my breathing." She inhaled loudly, then exhaled.

Automatically, without conscious effort, he mimicked her, and she nodded. "Tell me something you feel."

Dev took another deep breath, then another. His hand groped for hers on his shoulder and he squeezed.

"Good," she said, like he'd spoken. "Now tell me something you see."

"You," he wheezed. Truly, it felt like there was no one else.

His breathing gradually regulated, growing calmer. His heartbeat slowed from the gallop it had taken off on. He squeezed his eyes shut, though he didn't want to stop looking at her face. As if she knew his struggle, Jia moved to sit next to him, plastering herself against his side. Dev dropped his arm around her shoulders and pulled her tight, something he would have never dared to do under normal circumstances.

When he felt more like himself, he opened his eyes, and was immediately hit with a truckload of mortification. What on earth had just happened?

He looked down at her. She was staring at the water, but glanced up. Her eyes were soft and calm. Her shirt was slightly rumpled, though he wasn't sure if it was from him or the breeze.

"Are you okay?" she asked.

"Yes. I apologize. Nothing like that has ever occurred before." He licked his lips, searching for an explanation.

"Please, there's no need to apologize. Panic attacks happen."

"Not to me." He rubbed his chest. "Never. Especially out of nowhere like that."

"Nothing triggered it?"

"No. I was simply looking at the swing and remembering the swing my family had when I was a child."

"Do you think that did it?"

The muscles in his jaw worked. "I suppose." He should move away, but he didn't want to. The warmth that had filled him when she'd hugged him had come back. He hadn't realized how cold he'd been.

"That's natural, to miss them."

"I miss my parents. I . . ." His greatest shame. "I don't think I miss my brother as much as I should. I told you we weren't close." Sometimes it felt as though strangers had mourned Rohan more than he had.

"You don't have to be close to someone to miss them. Or miss what they used to mean to you. It's part of being alive, I suppose. To miss people, or to even miss missing people. Grief is like that sometimes. Like a bubble that gets big and small."

He rubbed the bridge of his nose. Miss missing people. Yes. That was exactly how he felt about his brother, and even his grandfather, to an extent. He missed the idea of a loving grandfather. He missed the brother he'd pushed on a swing. "I blamed Rohan."

"For what?"

His words came fast, spilling over one another. "For

adapting so easily to life with our grandparents, after our parents passed. He was so happy with the attention and, later, the fame. With the industry. With our last name greasing wheels, with our grandfather's bullshit and money. Meanwhile, I would have traded all of that for our life with our parents, and I didn't think he would have. It felt like he betrayed them and me, and that's absurd."

"Why is it absurd?"

"He was a child."

"So were you."

His chest tightened. "No, I was older. At the very least, I should have mended bridges with him when I was a grown adult."

"You could have. He could have, too." She paused. "Please don't think it's my anger over the catfishing driving me to bash him or anything, but it sounds like there was some resentment on both sides. Don't take all the blame on yourself. It's okay to have complicated feelings about someone after they pass away."

He huffed out a breath. "I don't like these feelings."

"Oh, no one likes feelings." Jia rubbed his arm. "Don't you think we would all choose to be robots if we could?"

A ghost of a smile touched his lips. "You wouldn't."

"True. I do like pouring my emotions out on everyone. But I imagine those people wish I'd be a robot, sometimes."

"I would not," he said, gruffly.

She pressed slightly closer. "That's nice to hear."

Dev didn't know how long they sat there, only that he was startled by how close her face was when he looked down at her. They were real freckles, he realized, charmed. Just a couple, over her nose.

He wanted to kiss them, trace every single one.

And it was that realization, coupled with the fact that they were sitting like lovers, that made him stiffen and lean away from her. "Should we . . . ?" His voice was hoarse to the point of unintelligible. "Shall we head out?"

"You want to see the rest of the place?"

Sure. Or at least, move out of temptation's way. He would love very much to kiss her freckles, but that wasn't possible. Not only because of gentlemanly courtesy, but because this was no normal courtship. Or a courtship at all, as far as she was concerned. "Absolutely. You wanted me to play photographer, yes?" Casually, Dev separated himself from Jia and came to his feet. She shaded her eyes.

"Sure. I think the place is easy to explore by foot, but let's take the car."

"Don't want to be without transportation in case we come across those pitchfork-waving locals," he teased, eager to get them back into their previous relationship.

"It's quiet here! Freaks me out." She came to her feet and shook out the blanket.

It was quiet. Dead silent, to be exact, with barely a breeze to make a sound. "City girl."

She made a face. "I'm sorry, are you not a Mumbaikar who was raised in Dubai?"

He chuckled. It was rusty, but it felt good. "Checkmate."

The first problem came when he tried to back up the car. The second came when he tried to go forward.

He attempted it again, but the tires met resistance.

"What's wrong?"

"The car's stuck." He tried again.

"Oh no."

He got out of the SUV and bent down to look at the tires. They were sunk in the loamy sand. He muttered a curse and straightened.

"We'll need someone with a winch," she observed, standing right next to him.

Dev placed his hands on his hips and glanced around. He squinted at a sign tacked on a beam nearby. "We probably should have read that before parking here."

STUCK? CALL KIM.

"We must not be the first influencers who got stuck out here," Jia remarked. She pulled out her phone and then sighed. "Do you have reception?"

He hadn't even taken his phone out of the car. He reached in and grabbed it out of the cupholder. "No."

"What now?"

His tone instantly went to the same soothing tone he occasionally used with Luna. He was far more comfortable being the soother than the sooth-ee, that was for sure. "It's not a big deal. This place might not have a lot of residents, but it has a motel, and a grocery store. Someone will have a phone we can use to call Kim." Dev watched as Jia went to the trunk. "What are you doing?"

"Putting my camera away."

"Why would you do that?"

"Well, we have this to deal with now."

"So?" He shut his car door and hit the lock. "Doesn't mean you can't still do your work. Take photos as we walk through town. Your job doesn't need to suffer because my rental isn't as hardy as I thought it was."

She stared at him for so long he grew worried. Had he said something wrong? "Are you okay?"

"Yes. I'm not used to someone who treats my work like . . ." She shook her head and slung her camera bag across her body. "Nothing. Let's go."

It wasn't nothing. She'd become uncharacteristically subdued, and he wasn't sure why. He tried not to take it too personally. Perhaps she was worried about the car, but he'd do his best to take her mind off that. It was the least he could do for how she'd had to literally hold his hand on the beach.

Another thing to stuff into his box of feelings.

Dev had never been in a ghost town before. Hearing and seeing no one as they walked past dilapidated homes and businesses was creepy, but it was also fascinating. They met no other tourists as they sauntered down the empty street, but they did pass a "drive-in" that consisted of junked classic cars and old repurposed roller-coaster seats.

Jia looked interested when he pointed out the installment, but she didn't slow down to take photos, which surprised him. Was she feeling hesitant to work in front of him?

In case that was the issue, he stopped when they walked past an old house that had been painted with a fresh coat of bright blue paint with the word *OPERA* painted in elegant cursive above. Here, too, the artists had left their mark. "Look at that. This would look good with your yellow shirt."

"It . . . would."

He held out his hand. "Do you want to show me how to use your camera?"

"Um, okay." She gave him a quick rundown, then set it into auto mode. "Angle it—"

"Down to slim your face, up to lengthen your body." Dev smiled at Jia's raised eyebrow. "I told you, I've watched a few videos of yours. I learn quick."

Her smile was more like her normal sparkle. It emerged as he photographed her in front of the bright blue empty house. Though he wasn't the thirst trap—Rohan's words, not his—that his brother had been, Dev had to do his share of photo shoots in the past, plus he'd been around enough of them to know what was needed.

Photos. So many photos, so she could pick and choose her shots later. He tried to keep moving. She did the same between every click, but she was still a little stiff. He tried to think of how his brother had teased him the first time he'd gone to get headshots as a scrawny nineteen-year-old, to get him to loosen up. It was a good Rohan memory, and those were few and far between. "Look at you, you're a tiger," he said.

"Sorry, what?"

Oh, he'd spoken in Hindi. He switched to English. "Channel your animal side."

"My animal side?" Her lips turned up. He continued shooting as he walked around her.

"Yes. You're a tiger, you're a lion."

"And a bear, too?"

"An odd animal to wish to be, but certainly." He had the feeling he had missed some reference, but she was smiling now.

She gave an adorable "rowr" and made a claw. He kept walking around her in a semicircle. "Yes, yes, perfect. You just woke up, you saw the sun. The sun is in your eyes, shield your eyes. Now let the sun in. Squint against it a little. You're a tiger in the sun now. Now it's cloudy. Look sad that it's cloudy."

"Wait, am I still a tiger?"

"You're always a tiger." He wasn't aware he was smiling until she started laughing. He kept shooting as he walked closer, angling the camera slightly above her to catch her delight. "Perfect." He stopped and handed her the camera.

Jia quickly swiped through the photos, her face brightening. "Not bad, not bad. You make a pretty good Instagram boy—"

His heart caught, but she didn't finish. "What?" He didn't need her to clarify. He knew what she'd been about to say, and he wanted her to say it. Boyfriend.

You haven't even kissed her yet. The closest you've come to touching her was when she was comforting you during a breakdown.

It didn't matter. He didn't need their lips to meet to know that he was falling for her. Some things transcended the physical, and their connection was one of them.

Not that he didn't want the physical, of course, he corrected his brain hastily. But that would come. When it was appropriate.

Wait, will it?

Yes. A confident bubble rose up in Dev, the same confidence he imagined people like Jia and the rest of his family felt on a regular basis.

Jia was his. He'd always been a patient man. He could wait until she came to the same conclusion.

She looked up at him from under her lashes and took a step forward. Her cheeks were pink. She took another step, and Dev wondered what she was thinking. "You're—" she started, then stopped when a horn blared.

She jumped away and he whirled around, ready to both protect her and be annoyed at whoever had ruined the moment. A truck pulled up next to them, and the driver stuck his arm out the window. He was a thin man, his hair a shock of white, his skin like leather. "That car stuck on the beach belong to you two?"

Dev cleared his throat. Jia came to stand next to him, and he almost shoved her behind him again. "Yes, it does."

The driver shook his head. "Don't know when you tourists will learn not to pull onto the beach. We get one of you stuck every couple months. Bet you didn't have reception down there, did you?"

"We did not. We were going to find a phone and call someone named Kim."

"Kim's out of commission right now. He'll do it in the morning."

"We can pay him to do it sooner," Jia chimed in. "We'd really like to head back home tonight."

The local stuck a toothpick in his mouth. "Impossible. Kim's my dad. He's the firefighter and the mechanic and the auto club around here, and he's already had a few too many to be safely operating the tow truck."

This man's father was the jack-of-all-trades of this teeny town? This good Samaritan looked almost seventy. How old was his parent? "We weren't really planning on staying the night. Can you get us out?" Dev asked.

The man looked offended. "And take business from my own father? No, no one in this town's going to do that." He nodded at the opera house. "You guys look like you have stuff to do. It'll take you at least an hour or two to take photos of all the art. You'll be fine."

"But we need to—"

"Why don't you take a walk down to the bar and see if Jenny has any rooms for you for the night? I'll get my dad up early tomorrow, and he'll have the car waiting for you at the inn first thing." The man rolled up his window before Dev could keep talking, and he drove away.

"This might sound like a conspiracy theory," Jia remarked. "But what if there's no big warning sign on the beach because stranded tourists is kind of how these folks make some of their money in the off-season?"

"Is there an on-season?"

"When the artists are here. There's a festival in April."

"I bet that's a sight to see," he murmured. His brain was clicking along too fast, pondering what it would mean, he and Jia spending the night here. In this town. With perhaps nothing more than a thin wall separating them.

Luna would be fine. She wasn't going to be home until at least one tomorrow, maybe later if he knew how much his niece loved to sleep in. The problem wasn't logistics; it was an overnight trip with a woman he was interested in pursuing a romantic relationship with.

He attempted to think of how to fix this. "I can try to get a private car."

"For a rescue mission? And what will happen to your rental, who's going to come back for that?" She chuckled. "The guy's right, Dev. It's not that big a deal."

"Are you okay with this?"

"Sure." She hesitated. "Are you?"

He scratched his head. "We're not married or engaged. It's improper for us to spend the night together."

Her cheeks flushed red, and he played back his words. *Oh yikes.* What had he just said? "I mean, in such a remote place. People will think this is some kind of—" He cut himself off.

Jia gave him a wary look. "Some kind of what?"

"Something . . . improper," he repeated, because *some kind of romantic rendezvous* was stressful.

"Uh-huh. Except . . ." She glanced left, then right. "No one knows we're here together. I don't see any tabloid reporters, and I doubt there's going to be any lurking in a town where there's only one firefighter and one mechanic and they're the same person."

"I suppose that's true." These were abnormal circum-stances. She was right. No one knew about this and no one needed to know. As soon as they found service, he'd text Adil Uncle that he'd gone for a drive and had car trouble and that he'd be back as soon as possible, on the very slim chance that something came up with Luna at her sleepover. "I mean, it is true."

"Good. Now let's check out this hotel, and get a couple rooms for the night."

Chapter Fifteen

Sorry, we only have one room left."

Jia should have expected that one. One room left at the inn in a ghost town, why . . . that was exactly how her luck was shaping up.

The bar was on the first floor of the hotel. The place was only two stories, a half-dozen rooms max. It was completely empty, save for her, Dev, and the bartender slash hotel clerk. Who on earth was occupying these rooms? "One room," Dev repeated.

The woman snapped her gum. Her skin was as weathered as the mechanic's son they'd met a mile away. Jia hoped they were wearing sunscreen in this desert sun. "Pest control guy is doing routine treatments in our other rooms. We only got the one free."

Jia rubbed the bridge of her nose. Dev had gone ramrod straight next to her. His brain was probably breaking at the impropriety of them sharing a room.

But this wasn't the worst thing ever. She trusted Dev in a way she'd never trusted any other guy. He wouldn't so much as touch her. He'd accepted her body against his on the beach while he'd been having his attack, but as soon as he'd come back to himself, he'd gently rebuffed her.

It's because he doesn't want to touch you. You're fine to pal around with, but he has no romantic interest in you. You're too much.

She'd tried not to take it too personally. She'd never had a panic attack herself, but between Sadia and Katrina, she'd been around for a few of them. She understood anxiety and the pressure it could place on the human brain. Or in Dev's case, what appeared to be hugely unresolved grief.

She'd wanted to crawl into his lap and wrap herself around him like a vine until it passed. And then after, too, when he'd looked so embarrassed. Only the fact that she knew it would horrify him had kept her touch somewhat platonic.

"Are there two beds?" she said, taking initiative since Dev seemed to have lost his ability to speak.

"It's a suite. There's a queen-size bed and a foldout couch." The woman snapped her gum again. Her name tag said Jenny. Jenny seemed remarkably unbothered over whether they took a room or not, though Jia imagined it must be hard to get business out here. "It's cozy," Jenny added.

That was code for small. Jia glanced around. That would track with the rest of this place. It was dark, from the dim lighting to the dark wood. Signed dollar bills were tacked all over the walls and ceiling.

"Say, do I know you?" Jenny suddenly asked. She leaned closer, scrutinizing Dev.

Oops. Jia may have been wrong. There might be some

foreign film fans in this place after all. That would teach her not to stereotype.

"I don't think so," Dev said politely.

"Oh, you're British," Jenny said, and about twenty years seemed to melt off her as she leaned against the counter and batted her lashes. "We don't get many British people here."

"I'm not—"

There was little need for Dev to clarify, not when clarification might lead to Jenny remembering where she'd seen him. "We'll take the room." Jia rummaged in her purse to get her license and credit card, but Dev chose that second to launch into action.

He gently nudged her aside, and took out two crisp fifty-dollar bills from his wallet. Smart, not to give their names. "Will this suffice?"

"Yup." The mystery of Dev's nationality forgotten, Jenny snatched up the money. "Breakfast is served down here in the morning until ten. I recommend the patty melt."

"For breakfast?" Jia asked.

"For anything." Jenny reached under the counter and returned with a key. "Here you go. Upstairs, turn left." She jerked her chin at the stairs. "There's an ice machine and soda machine to the right. Our Wi-Fi is down, sorry."

Jia fiddled with her scarf, but she stopped when she noticed the other woman eyeing her. She might love the spotlight, but she also had a healthy wariness of negative attention based on how she looked. "There are phones in the rooms, right?"

"Nah. Everyone's got cells now, so we got rid of them."

Dev pulled out another twenty. "Do you by chance have a phone we can use? Neither of us has cell service."

Jenny didn't look surprised. She pulled out an ancient landline phone and placed it on the bar. "You can give your people this number for any emergencies."

They thanked her and Dev gestured to Jia. "Please, go ahead."

"Thanks." Jia quickly dialed Katrina, who picked up after the third ring. She turned her back on her roommate for the night, though he walked a few steps away to give her some privacy. "Hey, it's me. I had a little car trouble."

"Oh dear. Where are you? Is everything okay?"

"Yup." Jia gave her a quick rundown of what had happened. "Anyway, I wanted to let you know that I'll be back tomorrow."

"I don't like the idea of you being all alone in the middle of nowhere," Katrina fretted. "I can send Jas to get you. He'd be happy to make the drive."

Katrina's boyfriend probably would be thrilled to rescue her, even if it meant a seven-hour round trip. The former bodyguard did like to play hero. She didn't want to put anyone through that, though. "No, that's okay. I'm not alone, anyway."

Katrina paused. "Dev?"

"Yup."

"Hmm." There was a beat of silence. "Are you . . . happy about that?"

"Yes."

A hint of humor entered her roommate's voice. "Interesting."

Jia pressed the phone tighter to her ear. She glanced over her shoulder, but Dev was all the way across the room, seemingly fascinated with some of the dollar bills on the wall. He wouldn't be able to hear what Katrina was saying, surely. "Hush."

"Okay, well. Let me know if you need anything. See you tomorrow."

"Cool, thanks. Talk soon." Jia hung up. Dev made a call as well, speaking in such rapid Hindi that Jia wouldn't have been able to follow even if she did speak the language.

When he hung up, Dev turned to her. "Jia."

"It's not a big deal," she said breezily, having anticipated this conversation. "A suite is basically a luxurious L.A. apartment. We'll have plenty of space." *Your virtue is safe.*

"I merely wanted to ask if you wanted to take any photos here." Dev cocked his head, as if to encompass the room. "It's very interesting, in that deserted way."

It was so strange to have someone so supportive of her career that they actually came up with ideas for her to photograph. Even her friends or Ayesha got tired of taking hundreds of pictures of her.

That he'd bounced back so quickly from a panic attack to pivot to focusing on her made it even more amazing. "Maybe tomorrow. Let's get settled first."

They went outside and walked around the back of the building and then trudged upstairs. Jia was painfully aware

of Dev behind her on the stairs. When she opened their motel room door, Jia released the breath she was holding. This
wasn't . . . the worst.

Oh, it was no luxury hotel room, but the decor was country chic and the foldout sofa looked clean and comfortable.
She peeked into the room. The bed was heaped with pristine white pillows and a purple quilt. It was technically one
room, yes, but they'd have privacy. "It's not so bad," Jia enthused. She pointed at the red rose printed wallpaper. "Now
that would make a good background."

Dev nodded. "Why don't you settle in? I need to get something from downstairs. I'll be back."

Jia stared at the door for a moment after he left. Was he
running away? Was he so freaked out by the thought of
sharing a small room with her? She envisioned him sprint-
ing all the way back to the water and yanking his car out of
the sand with his own brute strength.

Don't worry about it.

She fumbled for her phone and scrolled through her voice
notes, but sadly, she hadn't thought to record anything for
herself in the event of a sleepover with the man she had a
crush on.

Oh no.

Oh no. No. No. No. She did not have a crush on him, she
was not developing feelings for him. She'd fallen for Dev
Dixit quickly once before; she was not doing it again.

*Are you getting confused because you talked to someone with
his face for a couple months?*

She shoved Rhiannon's voice out of her head. No. This was different. Wasn't it?

Jia's lips firmed. Yes, it was. This was real. Deep down, she'd known her text infatuation wasn't.

Her prayer alarm went off on her phone, and she gave a sigh of relief. Good, she needed some peace. She rummaged in her camera bag for a scarf.

Praying didn't take her mind completely off Dev, but it did feel good to do something as opposed to twiddling her thumbs and worrying. He knocked and entered the room just after she finished. His arms were full, which meant his biceps were prominent.

No, girl.

"Sorry, did I disturb you?"

She folded her scarf. "No, not at all."

He placed a food-laden tray on the coffee table. "I figured you might be hungry. It's getting late, and we had no lunch."

Of course he'd gone to get them sustenance. The man was annoyingly perfect, anticipating her needs. "I am hungry." Until that minute, she hadn't realized how hungry, actually. She placed her hand on her belly to still the growl.

"I stuck to the vegetarian stuff, because I wasn't sure what dietary restrictions you might have. Salads, grilled cheese, and I got extra fries. Plus I managed to hit the general store and got sodas and Twinkies. I've always wanted to try Twinkies."

She smiled, distracted by his unexpected interest in packaged desserts. "That sounds like a feast."

"It's no five-star meal, and my nutritionist might be crying somewhere, but I tried." Dev held out a package in a brown paper bag. "Here. There wasn't much of a selection, sadly."

Mystified, Jia reached into the bag, then nearly laughed. "Oh my gosh. Thank you." It was a pair of sweatpants, a T-shirt, and a hoodie emblazoned with the words *Bombay Beach* on them, all about three sizes too large for her.

She clutched the hoodie to her chest, touched. It was so thoughtful. But it also reminded her that nighttime was coming, and they'd have to figure out sleeping arrangements.

She wanted to stay with him. Even if two rooms had been available, she would have wanted to stay with him. Not so she could jump him, but so she could spend more time in his sweet company. Also so he could protect her from ghosts, this place was definitely haunted.

"Do you like games?"

Jia paused in stroking the sweatshirt. "Um, what kind of games?"

Dev pointed to the bookshelf. "Board games?"

Her eyes widened. "Oh no, that's not a good idea." Not if she actually wanted him to like her back in any way.

And she did. Another kind of peace settled over her, at that admission to herself.

"Why not?"

"Dev . . ." Jia sighed and placed the bag on the couch. "I'm the youngest of five overachieving kids. How competitive do you want to think my family made me, when it came to board games?"

His eyes smiled, even if his lips didn't. "I can handle it."

"That's what you think. And then when you're crying and I flip the table and accuse you of cheating and someone's holding another person's clump of hair, then you'll be sorry."

"Is that what life with sisters is like?"

"Oh yes." She crossed over to the table and picked up a french fry. "It actually made it really hard for me to learn how to interact with other people, having sisters. Because you can't really go from *I'm going to kill you* to *Want some ice cream?* with anyone else in your life."

His low chuckle filled the room, strumming the hairs on her arms. "I'll take your word for it. I suppose I shouldn't ask if you want to put stakes on it?"

Her competitive side clapped its hands in glee. "What kind of stakes are we talking about?"

He glanced at her from under his eyelashes. "If I win, I'd like to see the rest of your texts with my brother and cousin."

Oof. Those were high stakes. Which gave her more incentive to win. "And if I win . . ." *You take off your shirt.* "I get to go leave a dozen bad reviews on your doofus cousin's latest movie."

His lips twitched. "I'm surprised you haven't already. Is there a game that you don't take too seriously?"

She perused the shelf skeptically. "We can try Scrabble. Monopoly and Life turn me into a capitalistic fiend."

"I SWEAR, I can make this into a word." Jia perused the board carefully. She had two letters left, and she was only ten points away from beating Dev.

Turns out, she wasn't less competitive at Scrabble. Which was why she'd been staring at the game board for over fifteen minutes on her last turn. She would get those ten points, damn it. She leaned forward, dangerously close to toppling off the couch, where she sat cross-legged.

"I'm sure you can," Dev said patiently.

She placed the two letters around another. "Is that a word?"

Dev raised a thick eyebrow at her. He sat on the floor facing her, leaning back on his hands. "Is it?"

She shot him a narrow glance, trying to gauge how close he was to calling her on the word. Damn it. If he challenged her and consulted the dictionary on the shelf and she lost, she'd lose the game. She'd already lost three turns in this game by making up words. She was still pretty sore *xop* wasn't in the Scrabble dictionary. "This is my first language, and your second, damn it. How are you beating me?"

"English is one of our national languages. Besides, I went to British schools. You went to American ones." He shrugged, like that should explain things.

"Please don't assert the colonizer's supremacy here," she grumbled. "I'll make this into a word, darn it."

After another fifteen minutes of silence, Dev stirred. "You know, if you'd made this word *stick*, instead of *sticks*, you could have used the *s* over here. With what you have, that's fifteen points."

"It is," she muttered, frustrated with herself for not seeing that. She'd gone for short-term satisfaction over long-term gain! Story of her life, her sisters would chide her.

Dev sighed. Then he placed his finger on the *s* and slid it over to her. She glanced at him. "What are you doing?"

"Let's say that's what you did."

"But that's cheating!"

"It's your own letter. Please, I insist."

Jia's desire to win at all costs outweighed her reticence. "Okay." Triumphantly, she placed the letters and raised her arms in victory. "I win!"

Dev gave her an indulgent look. "Not bad."

She lowered her arms and snatched up a cold fry from the remnants of their dinner. "You knew I'd be here all night looking for a word, didn't you?"

"Very much so. I couldn't take sitting on the floor any longer. I'm too old to not have back support."

She grabbed her phone and pulled up her texts with the Liar Formerly Known as Dev and handed it to him. "Fair's fair."

He took the phone automatically, but didn't look at it. "But you won."

"We both know I didn't." She fiddled with a thread coming loose on her hem.

He gave her a long look, then stared at the phone. After a pregnant pause, he offered it back to her. "I changed my mind. I'd rather learn about you like this, in person. Delete those texts, keep them for yourself, I don't care."

Her lips parted, and she accepted his offering. How did

he have this uncanny knack to always know what to say? She stuffed another fry into her mouth, so she could have something to do.

He came to his feet and stretched.

She nearly choked on the fry, almost reliving the unfortunate roti choking of days past. She'd changed into the sweats, and she'd cinched the hoodie he'd brought her around her face. That meant she probably looked about as attractive as a child in footie pajamas.

Dev, though, still looked annoyingly good. He'd bought the same gray sweatpants for himself that he'd bought for her, and they looked different on him. When he stretched his arms up, his shirt rode up to display a one-inch slice of belly.

Jia swallowed the fry. "Is it warm in here?"

He lowered his arms. "I'm fine. I can open a window."

"No, never mind." Because then she'd be cold when she got into bed alone. Speaking of . . . "We should sleep. Our car'll be ready to go early in the morning."

"Right." Neither of them moved.

"Do you want to use the . . . ?" She gestured to the bathroom.

"Sure."

While he was gone, she pulled out the sofa bed and made it up. He stopped when he came out. "You didn't have to do that."

She fluffed the pillow and placed it on the bed. "I didn't know how many beds you've made in your life, Mr. Actor," she tried to tease, but she was mildly out of breath, because he'd turned slightly, and the curve of his butt was . . . noice.

Sexual attraction wasn't something she felt a lot of—she'd determined long ago that she needed to have a strong bond to someone first before she got all torn up about wanting to sleep with them, and her schedule hadn't lent itself to strong emotional bonds. So she figured she must be getting really bonded to Dev, because those gray sweatpants were getting sexier by the second.

It was the Scrabble, damn it.

Jia averted her eyes. She needed to stop thinking about his sweatpants because then she'd think about his shirt and then she'd think about his arms and then she'd think about the torso those arms were attached to and then his stomach and then back to his legs . . .

Jianna, control yourself.

His smile was faint. "I've made a bed or two."

Oh gosh, why did the word bed *sound so sexy?* She took a giant step away from the sofa. "Thought I'd help you out."

"I appreciate it." He walked closer. "Are you okay?"

"Yes, of course."

"You seem nervous."

"Me? Thhppt." She fiddled with the cord of her sweatshirt. She had so many cute pj's at home. Even her unicorn onesie was better than this.

"I wanted to thank you for how good-natured you've been about this. I feel bad about getting us stranded here."

Her forehead wrinkled. "Um, I'm the reason we got into this mess, 'cause I wanted to take some silly pictures."

"Silly pictures? They were for your work."

Gratitude rose up in her throat. So few understood that there was a serious, disciplined side to what she did. "Thank you."

"For what?"

"For, like, taking me seriously. Taking photos of me without getting impatient or thinking I'm vain. I don't know. Stuff like that." She was so used to having to prove herself. She hadn't had to do anything to earn this man's respect. He freely gave it to her. How weird.

"Do people not do that?"

"Some people don't, no."

"Well, perhaps it's because they haven't tried to do what you do. I couldn't do it. Anyway, I enjoy taking photos of you. It's fun. You make most things fun."

"You do, too," she breathed. "Even getting trapped in a ghost town."

He took another step closer, and she mirrored it. They were so close she could look up and count each individual eyelash of his. Jia licked her lower lip, and Dev's gaze dipped over it. What could she say? That she was growing more into him with every second, despite the short period of time they'd spent together? That she'd forgotten everything that had come before the second she'd walked up to him at a party dressed in gold? That she wanted him for more than playing her suitor with her family, that she wanted to pursue something real with him?

He released his breath in a big sigh, finishing with her name. "Jia."

That was it, only her name, said in that way that made the syllables go up and down, along with the butterflies in her stomach. She dared to edge a little bit closer. Only a breath separated them, and she inhaled it. He still smelled woodsy and dark, and she wanted nothing more than to bury her face in his neck. Jia drew in a deep breath and held it, going light-headed.

His hand came to hover over her arm, and it was like an electric shock ran through her, from innocent elbow to other not-so-innocent parts of her. They were in one room with each other, wearing their night clothes. There was a bed not so far away. The only bed in the whole place.

It had been easier to decide to wait for sex when she wasn't faced with a tall drink of water walking around with just the right amount of scruff on his face. One who let her beat him at Scrabble and then refused his rightful winnings. One who took her and her ambitions seriously.

Yes, men in the abstract were much easier to resist than this specific Man. His thumb gently brushed her elbow and she shivered. Would a kiss be the worst thing?

A tiny, disapproving Noor popped onto one shoulder. *Yes, it would. Go to bed. You're not dating this man, you're not engaged to him. Did our parents raise some girl who goes around kissing strange boys?*

Sadia popped up on her other shoulder, casually cradling her big belly. *Counterpoint: you honor yourself and your desires, honey. If that means kissing him, kiss him.*

Damn it. That was a strong counterpoint, one which justified her kissing him. If she rose up on her tiptoes . . .

He took a giant step back. "Good night, Jia." His words were rusty, like he hadn't spoken in a long time.

She licked her lips. Okay, no shoulder gallery needed, he'd made the decision for them. Cool. Cool, cool, cool, cool, cool. "Good night," she whispered. She scurried away into the bedroom and shut the door. She pressed herself back against it and touched her lips. They tasted like herself and no one else.

Oh, for crying out loud. If she'd been on the fence before, it was no longer in doubt. She'd gone and fallen hard for her fake boyfriend. The guy who let her win at Scrabble and apparently faced no epic internal struggle about kissing her. What a mess.

Chapter Sixteen

You and your friend sleep well?"

The question from behind him almost had Dev dropping the carafe of black coffee he'd picked up. "Uh." *Your friend.*

He hated that word in connection with Jia and wanted to slap it out of his own ears, but that was his problem, not Jenny's. "Very well, thank you."

Jenny walked behind the bar. "Can I get you any breakfast?"

"No, I'm good." He carefully poured a cup of coffee and placed the carafe back.

"Kim called. Your car should be delivered soon."

"Excellent." Then they could head back home. That should make him happy, but he wasn't.

You just want to go back upstairs and almost kiss her again.

Well, obviously. And that could happen, but they needed to work some stuff out first. Big-time.

"You look so familiar."

Dev glanced at Jenny warily. "Do I?"

"I actually went online last night, because I thought, gosh. That face. But I couldn't find anything. And then my friend mentioned he saw you after you got stuck and that you looked like this actor who was going to be in a new show with Hudson Rivers and Richard Reese, and that was when the lightbulb went off."

He took a sip of his coffee. She looked too certain and self-satisfied for him to feign confusion, sadly. He thought about how much cash was left in his wallet. "You got me. I'd rather people not know I was here. You understand." *Especially that he'd spent the night in one suite with this particular woman.*

Call him old-fashioned, but he knew how things worked. They could ride the line of titillation, but they couldn't flat out metaphorically French kiss in front of cameras. Getting caught seemingly sleeping together was a step too far.

"I'd rather they did!" Jenny pointed at her wall. "If you could take a photo for our wall of celebrities, that would be fantastic. Is your friend famous, too? 'Cause I have space . . ."

Dev peered at the wall in the dusky light. Sure enough, there were more than a couple of celebrities up there, though the majority appeared to be artists. If he agreed, perhaps Jenny would be satisfied. "Very well. But no, she's not."

Jenny raised her hands. "Got it."

And that was how Devanand Dixit, eldest grandson of Shweta and Vivek Dixit, left a Polaroid photo of his face on the wall of a tired hotel in the middle of the desert.

His life sure had gotten turned upside down since he'd met Jia.

Dev ventured out the front door of the inn, holding the paper cup of now lukewarm coffee. The sun kissed the horizon, sending fingers of light over the almost silent town. The temperature hadn't quite warmed up yet for the day. He'd barely slept the night before and had almost fallen out of bed when Jia's alarm had gone off for morning prayer, piercing through the thin walls of the suite.

The sleeplessness had come in handy in one respect. He'd come to a decision. He needed to tell Jia that he wanted to scrap this ridiculous arrangement of theirs. He didn't want to be her pretend boyfriend. He wanted to be her real one. Possibly more. She made him happy and made him think, and each second he was in her company felt like a second too little.

You're sounding like your scripts.

So what if he was acting out a serial? No, not a serial. A serial had foreboding moments and twists and turns. This felt more muted and warm, though it still retained an undercurrent of passion.

Dev leaned against the post at the front of the inn and thought about her possible reactions. She could say no, that despite their almost-kiss she wasn't interested in him like that. Or she could jump in his arms and declare her affections as well. Or there were about ten other scenarios that could happen between those two extremes.

The sound of a car engine came from down the road and Dev straightened as his rental came into view, towed by a truck. The truck came to a stop in front of the inn, and a stoop-shouldered elderly man got out. "This your car?"

"It is, yes."

The older man grunted, handed him a bill, and went around the truck to take the car down. A man of few words. That was fine.

Dev took out his wallet while the man unhooked his car. He really was running low on cash. He pulled out what was left and handed it to the man when he finished. The man counted it and nodded. "Thanks for paying in cash instead of asking if I take credit cards or have this app or that app."

Dev didn't have any apps for payment either. "No problem." He accepted his keys from the guy and dropped them in his pocket. He turned around and jumped to find Jia standing right behind him, silent.

She was dressed in yesterday's wilted clothes, carrying her camera and the sweats he'd bought her in the plastic bag they'd come in. This was the first time he'd ever seen her without makeup.

It was hard to look at her straight on, and not simply because she was so beautiful. He knew the names of each makeup tool she used to paint her face. There were layers of foundation and blush and highlighter and mascara and contour and eyeliner and shadow between them usually. Now, there was nothing.

His father used to tell him that he'd fallen in love with his mother within a few hours. She'd been a tailor's daughter, someone he would have never even met if Adil Uncle hadn't had a scholarship to the same private school his dad attended. They'd married within the month and had been happy together for the years they'd had.

But Dev had been skeptical of his parents' claim of instant love. Until, perhaps, now.

This could be infatuation.

No. He'd never been a man given to infatuation or fantasy. He didn't know what falling for someone felt like, but he imagined it was something like this. This calm certainty in their presence. Certainty, except for the part where he didn't know how she felt about him.

She looked like she wanted to kiss you.

That could mean anything. Kissing wasn't a declaration of love nowadays, if it had ever been.

"Good morning," she murmured.

"Good morning." He turned the car keys in a circle on his finger. "Do you want some breakfast or coffee before we leave?"

"No, I'm fine." Her gaze skittered away, which made his stomach drop.

"Jia—"

"Should we head out then?" she asked brightly.

He nodded and went to the car to open her door. She slid in, placing the bag on the floorboard, and settled her hands in her lap.

They were silent for the first fifteen minutes after they left town, and Dev finally cleared his throat. There was no way they could stand this awkwardness for two and a half hours. At some point, they needed to address that almost-kiss.

His phone beeped with a message, but he ignored it.

"Jia—" His phone started ringing, and he cursed and tapped it to silence it. "I suppose we have reception now."

A chime came from her camera bag. "I suppose so," she said, smiling ruefully.

"I think we should talk about—" Another beep, from her phone. "That is, I think of you very high—" Another beep.

"Ignore it." Jia turned toward Dev, as much as the seat belt would allow. "Continue?"

Best to do this quick. "We almost kissed last night, didn't we?"

She bit her lip, and nodded. "It's okay. I don't take it personally, that you didn't want to."

Except she'd gone rigid. He cast her an incredulous glance. "Of course I wanted to kiss you. I've wanted to do that since the minute I met you."

"You did?"

"Yes. But we were in the middle of nowhere, we hadn't had a discussion yet about our future or physical affection, there was only one bed . . ."

"Yes, yes, the one bed."

"I only thought we should talk first. Away from the bed."

"Probably a good thing you're less impulsive than me," she murmured. "I might have gone in for the kiss."

He shifted in his seat, suddenly warm. "Ah."

"I always planned on waiting for marriage to have sex, but that plan was a lot easier to stick to when there was no one I wanted to make out with." Jia scratched her head. "Is this what teens feel like? No wonder they can be volatile."

He nearly choked. "You, uh, want to . . . I see."

"Don't you?"

"Yes." Was that answer too quick? "I mean, of course. But I am fine with waiting, as well."

Jia interlinked her fingers. "So you, like, see that in our future? Marriage?"

He tightened his grip on the steering wheel. "Yes. The truth is, I like you. Very much. Romantically. I'm willing to wait as long as you like, but my end goal would be marriage. It doesn't have to be right away. We could spend more time getting to know each other, see if we suit." Dev didn't need more time. He was frighteningly ready. But he wanted Jia to have the option of time.

She opened her mouth, but her phone started chiming in rapid succession. "Argh. Hang on. Let me just turn it off . . ." She leaned over and fumbled in her bag, then pulled out the phone and stopped, half hunched over.

"Jia?"

"Oh my God," she whispered. She straightened and started scrolling through her phone. "Oh my God, oh my God, oh my God."

"Jia? What's wrong?"

"Oh my God."

The car drifted into the shoulder for a second, before he corrected it. "What?"

She turned the phone toward him. He glanced at it, but he was too careful a driver to take his eyes off the road for very long. "I can't read it. What does it say?"

"We're engaged."

Chapter Seventeen

How could you do this," Dev hissed into the phone.

Chandu was unfazed. "Dev, I had no choice."

Dev ran his hand through his hair. He'd been trying to call Chandu for hours, for the whole drive back to Jia's home in Santa Barbara.

His head ached from lack of sleep and the emotional roller coaster of the morning. While their phones continued to blow up from friends and her family, she'd read him the highlights.

Dixit's grandson is set to tie the knot with an American!

Dev's team has confirmed rumors of engagement.

Sources on set say the model has visited her fiancé during filming.

Finally, some happiness for the Dixit family; Shweta Dixit is reportedly delighted with the match and eager to welcome her new granddaughter.

Read the first texts between Dev and Jia after he slid into her DMs!

Will true love outweigh their cultural differences?

That was a fraction of the news stories. He'd stopped her from reciting the tweets aloud when her breath hitched over a particularly nasty one. *How did some nobody IG model snag him?*

Even sweet Jenny had betrayed them with amazing speed, with the photo he'd given her popping up as another story when they were a few miles from home. Jia had rushed to delete a selfie she'd posted on the beach yesterday, but some investigative soul had already put two and two together to place them in the same spot and spin a tale about a romantic rendezvous.

Nobody sleuthed better than the internet.

After that, Jia had turned her phone off and sat silently while Dev frantically hit redial. What the hell had his *team* done?

Dev turned his back on the couch, where Jia's roommates were busy consoling her. "No choice? You had no choice when you decided to announce an engagement for me?"

Chandu's voice turned frosty. "I tried to reach you all day, Dev. You didn't tell me there were these love texts between the two of you. I did what I had to do to make sure this stayed aboveboard, and I had to do it fast before it blew up and damaged both of your reputations. Especially since you're apparently staying in hotel rooms together now."

"You didn't have to say she was my fiancée."

"I didn't? Sure, the progressives would have stayed on your side. Your texts were tame compared to what the kids send nowadays. But you would have been smeared by the more conservative folks delighted to see a Dixit scandal."

"My brother brought home an illegitimate child without much of a fuss."

"People liked your brother more than you," Chandu said bluntly. "And your grandfather was alive then, and Rohan made sure he protected Luna by hiding her away. Plus, times were different. The internet was slower, tensions weren't so high."

What Chandu had said about speed wasn't wrong. How could Jenny have found a buyer for his Polaroid so fast?

"Leaking a photo where you're casually flirting with a girl, stirring up speculation, that's a lot different than texts that say *my heart beats only for you*."

Dev nearly groaned. It had only been a few texts that had leaked, thank God. Now he kind of regretted not taking Jia up on her offer to see the rest of the lines his brother and cousin had sent.

"It would have been the girl who took the brunt of that abuse, Dev," Chandu reminded him. "But if you're engaged, it doesn't matter. Now it's a love story, not a tawdry affair or a seduction."

Dev grimaced. Chandu wasn't . . . wrong. He glanced over his shoulder. Jia's face was buried in her hands. Her phone was on the coffee table in front of her. "Do you know . . . do you know how the reporters got the texts?" He hadn't thought Arjun would do something like this, but then again, he hadn't thought his own family was capable of a cruel prank like catfishing someone to begin with.

"I spoke with the tabloid who broke it." Chandu had good relationships with every tabloid in Mumbai. "They said it was leaked via a mass phone hack. If you'd told me the truth in the beginning, Dev, I would have been pre-pared. I assumed that photo of you embracing a girl was a publicity stunt."

"It's not—" He broke off as he heard a feminine voice in the background calling for Chandu, which was odd. His agent wasn't married. He was extremely dedicated to his cli-ents, which, for the last thirty years, had consisted entirely of the Dixit family.

The older man cleared his throat. "Your grandmother wishes to speak with you."

Dev pulled the phone away from his ear and stared at it for a second. "Why is my grandmother at your house?"

"I am at the compound." The gated mansion his grand-parents lived in. "We had some work to do. You know we're both night owls."

Then why hadn't Chandu picked up the phone for the last few hours, while he'd been calling?

Dear God, were his agent and his grandmother . . . no. Impossible. Also, irrelevant right now.

"Devanand," his grandmother said briskly, taking the phone from Chandu. "You lied to me."

He pinched the bridge of his nose. "Hello, Aji."

The soft murmurs went silent behind him. He glanced around to find Jia watching with a furrowed brow. She must have realized who he was talking to.

"You have your grandfather's blood in you after all, run-ning around and having affairs."

He turned away from Jia again. "That is not what is hap-pening."

"Oh? I read those texts. You are lucky Chandu thought quick and de-escalated the situation."

"He didn't de-escalate anything. I am engaged—"

"And not seducing some American sweetheart, ruining her reputation. You should thank him. I don't see why this is such an issue. If these messages are to be believed, you have feelings for this girl."

He opened his mouth, then closed it again. Damn it all. That bloody Arjun. If Dev said he hadn't sent those messages, then his grandmother—or the world—would ask who did. Then he'd have to explain about Arjun.

Shweta doted on Arjun as much as she could dote on anyone, but Dev didn't care about tanking that relationship. Oh no, he was concerned about spreading the news that Arjun had catfished Jia. He didn't think she was a fool, but she hadn't liked that he'd told Adil Uncle, he could tell. He couldn't allow anyone to make her feel bad.

He hesitated a second too long, because his grandmother hmphed. "I knew it. I will not tolerate you seducing your way through another country. We have our name to consider."

A stab of irritation hit Dev, but he shoved it down. Like their name wasn't the only thing that was constantly considered. "I never seduced my way through the first one," he pointed out.

"Which is why I'm surprised that it's you I have to be having this talk with. In any case, this is all for the best. It's time you settle down, you have the will to consider, and Chandu tells me this girl has a career, which means she is hopefully not chasing you for the money. Of course, I'll give my final approval after I meet her. If she's not acceptable, well, a broken engagement will still be better than an affair."

Oh no. "What are you talking about?"

"I am coming there. I want to see you, and you will bring this girl to me."

He stiffened. "There is no need for that, Aji."

"There is every need."

Dev's eye twitched. He dropped his voice. "This isn't seriously going to happen." He meant the engagement, but he also meant his grandmother dropping into their lives.

"You will not change my mind. I've already chartered a plane and had the servants air out the Malibu house."

He looked out toward the slice of the ocean he could see from Jia's living room. "What Malibu house?"

"The one I rented."

Dev massaged his temples. "You didn't have to do that."

"Would you rather I stay in a hotel room when I visit? Like a peasant? Expect to see me there in three days. That's as soon as I can get away. You will bring the girl, and her parents if possible. They'll know of me, of course, but they should get to know me properly."

She said that like anyone would come running to see her if he merely said her name, and she wasn't totally wrong. Jia's parents no doubt grew up on Shweta Dixit movies.

The offhand way she referred to Jia set Dev's back teeth on edge. "Her name is Jia, and I'd rather you not come—"

"Dev."

The single word silenced him. He wasn't hungry for his grandmother's approval like his brother and cousin, but his mother had drummed a strong sense of respect toward his elders into his head. It was hard to counter that programming, even when his grandmother was being objectively ridiculous.

"Unless you can give me one good reason why your own grandmother should not meet the girl her grandson is serious enough about to send her passionate love notes, I will be there soon."

He was silent. No, damn it, he couldn't give her a reason, because *it's all fake even though I wish it wasn't* wasn't a good reason. Or at least, not a reason he wanted to divulge to his grandmother.

"Goodbye," Shweta said. The phone line cut. How on earth was he going to tell Jia about this?

He turned around slowly and spread his hands in front of him. "So."

"I didn't understand the language, but going by your tone, that did not sound good." The beautiful Black woman sitting next to Jia leaned forward. This was Rhiannon, Dev had learned, and she was as sharp as Jia had described her. Katrina sat on the arm of the sofa, her fingertips touching Jia's shoulder. She'd been touching Jia in one way or another since they walked in, her face soft and empathetic. It was a shame Dev wasn't meeting Jia's friends under better conditions. Say, a triple date, not a crisis-handling meeting because he and Jia were accidentally engaged.

He quickly recapped the phone call, his voice trailing off

when he finished explaining that his grandmother was arriving in a few days and expected to meet Jia. "So it is as we suspected. The messages leaked—"

"By your idiot cousin," Katrina said.

"I can think of better words than idiot," Rhiannon remarked.

"My agent claims that the messages were part of a mass phone hack. The tabloid would have no reason to lie, so it's possible. But also very probable my cousin leaked them," he added in a rush.

"We'll have Jas secure your phone, in case it was yours that was hacked," Katrina assured Jia.

"In any case, after the messages leaked and Chandu couldn't get ahold of me, he decided to come up with a narrative that would defuse things as quickly as possible but also allow us to continue seeing each other. Because he assumed those texts were actually between Jia and me, because why would there be any other explanation." He heaved a giant sigh. "My God, Jia. I'm so sorry." The guilt and regret he'd been feeling since Arjun's actions had come to light were increasing at exponential speed.

Jia lifted her chin. Her face was pale, and she looked much younger than her almost thirty years. "Your grandma's coming here. To meet me."

Dev shifted his weight. "Yes."

"To vet me for your bride."

He sighed. "Yes."

"Because she thinks we have a romantic relationship already."

"Yes."

"Because the texts your cousin sent me became public."

With every word, Jia's roommates bristled, but he welcomed their accusatory stares. He felt guilty enough on his family's behalf to be raked over the coals. "Yes."

She dropped her face into her hands again. "My parents and sisters have called me fifty times. What am I supposed to tell them?" Her phone gave a faint vibration, and she gave a half laugh that sounded vaguely hysterical. "Fifty-one, probably."

"We can fix this," Rhiannon said soothingly. "We release a statement. We flatly deny that any part of this is real, say the texts and photos are made up or doctored."

"My parents would know I lied about Dev then," Jia pointed out.

Rhiannon recalibrated. "Then we can say it's true, but you're not engaged. It's not the 1900s. There's no scandal in two healthy consenting adults dating."

Dev shoved his hands in his pockets and he met Jia's eyes. How to explain this to people who were so far outside his culture? "Your Hollywood-famous families have no comparison to ours. My family occupies an odd space in society, where the public feels like we . . . belong to them. I was able to avoid too much public scrutiny for years, because the rest of my family was so much more high profile than me, but now I'm one of the few left."

"So they feel entitled to knowing about your life," Katrina summarized. "But that doesn't mean they get to have a say in it."

"It's not fair, but they'll have an opinion. It was one thing when no one knew who Jia was, but now that they do, they'll scrutinize and judge her."

"You see it all the time in internet fandoms, or with the British royals, where the fanbases are passionate. It doesn't help that we're so obviously different from each other," Jia said haltingly.

"I don't care about any of that." Just in case she had any doubt. He rubbed his thumb over his palm. "Chandu wasn't totally wrong. If we're engaged or married, I can protect Jia from the worst of it. I don't like the way this part of the world works, but it's reality."

"What are you saying? That you let the engagement stand?" Rhiannon drew herself up. "That's ridiculous."

Dev took a step forward, then glanced between Jia's annoyed roommates. "Rhiannon and Katrina, would you mind if I have a moment with Jia?"

"If we leave you alone, how else are you going to turn this into some soap opera?" Rhiannon asked. "Will you knock yourself on the head and get amnesia? Turn up with a secret twin?"

He deserved their ire, so he answered her sarcasm seriously. "Not at all. Please, I need to speak with Jia."

Jia lifted her head. "It's okay, guys. Dev and I have important things to discuss, like where we're registered."

He wasn't the only one relieved Jia's sense of humor was intact. Both Katrina and Rhiannon relaxed. They shot him warning looks and left them alone. He walked closer, then stopped, not eager to crowd her.

"Jia—"

"I know, you're sorry." Jia looked up at him. He was relieved to note that while her eyes were red, she wasn't crying. "Can you sit down, my neck hurts."

He'd do literally whatever she wanted right now. "Of course."

She played with a thread on her shirt, twisting it around her finger. "I screwed everything up. These texts, that selfie of me at the beach. I should have been more discreet." Her eyes grew wet, and whatever relief he'd felt quickly evaporated. "I can't do anything right. Everyone's going to know that now."

"No, no. This has nothing to do with you."

Jia continued like she hadn't heard him. "I'm backsliding in my career. I'm too tired to generate any more content." Her tears spilled over. "And now I'm engaged to the face of my catfish. I'm a complete failure."

"You're not a failure." He patted in his pocket and found the handkerchief he always carried. He handed it to her, but she didn't move to dab her tears. "Not one bit."

"My family won't see it that way." She twisted the handkerchief in her hands. "This is going to be it. Confirm that I'm the family screw-up. I'll have to move back home with nothing to show for my independence except the knowledge that everyone was right. I'm impulsive and reckless and don't think and I can't be trusted—"

"Hey." Dev pulled Jia's fists into his hands and looked deep into her watery eyes. "I don't like you talking about my fiancée like that."

She stopped for a second and stared at him, startled. Then she let out a weak half sob. It wasn't her usual deep laugh, but it would do.

He squeezed her hands. They were small and fragile in his. "Here's what I think we should do," he started, then paused. Because the answer that was so obvious to him was also possibly the most absurd one.

"What?"

"I think we should be engaged. For real."

Her mouth dropped open. "You can't be serious."

Dev hadn't known what certainty felt like until this very moment. Wasn't this what he'd basically been angling for this morning in the car? Granted, he'd wanted to spend more time together before an engagement, but in the end, what did it matter?

He'd already made up his mind. Jia was exactly what he was looking for, and she'd fallen into his lap by pure chance. "I'm serious. I wouldn't mind it," he said. "I could see it. We would suit. I . . . admire you very much. I think we could have fun together, and I think we communicate well." *Say the mushy words in your head.* No, he couldn't. These all sounded like stilted reasons, but the other ones were far too flowery.

One good thing was that her shock had gotten rid of her tears. Her expressive eyes brightened for a second, but then they quickly shuttered. "You wouldn't mind it," she repeated, without inflection.

Uh-oh. He might be dense, but even he knew he'd chosen his words poorly there. "I mean, I think we could be a good match." He breathed out a rough sigh. "Right now, our options are that we confess what actually happened, or we claim that it was all real, the texts, our relationships. We can tell your parents the truth about the engagement being made up, that's your choice, but if we don't, my grandmother and Chandu won't breathe a word." The next words were harder to force out. "And if you decide we don't suit, we can end the engagement. People will talk, but it won't be the first wedding to be called off."

"Wedding," she repeated.

He wasn't scared of the word, but he feared she might be. "Even a wedding won't be without escape," he said quietly. "If the marriage doesn't work out as you'd want it to, divorce is an option." And if they did the wedding before his birthday, she'd walk away immensely wealthier, with half his inheritance.

Dev looked down at Jia's hands and took the handkerchief. She jumped when he tore off a strip of it, then she gave a little squeak when he slid to the floor on one knee. He took her limp hand. "Jia, I'm sorry I'm not able to explain myself better. But the truth is, this morning, I was already thinking along these lines anyway. I'm sorry this happened in such a manner, but I do believe fate works in mysterious ways. Would you do me the honor?"

She licked her lips, and then gave the slightest of nods.

He gently tied the fabric around her ring finger, making a silent vow. From now on, he would do his best to make sure everything was in her control. "You call the shots," he said quietly. "What we tell anyone, whether we stay together, whether you want to meet my grandmother, everything. I'll back you up."

Her phone gave another vibration, distracting both of them. She released his hand, her fingers curling in to hold the fabric in place. "We're engaged," she announced, in a clear, firm tone that shouldn't have surprised him, given what he'd witnessed of her resilience already. "I'm going to call my family and tell them it's true, that we've been talking for a while, it got more serious than I'd let on before. I'll tell them that I don't have a ring or anything, that you were waiting to ask their permission when you met them in person. They'll love that."

He nodded. "I will keep to this story too."

Jia's phone vibrated yet again, and she came to her feet and scooped it up. "First I need to shower. I need to get clean and dressed and put on fresh makeup, and then I'll be able to think."

"I think that's a fine plan," Dev said gently. "If you don't mind, Luna will be home soon from her sleepover, and I need to break this to her before someone else does."

Jia jerked. "Oh my, of course. Luna! I completely forgot about her."

"She and I are something of a package deal. In case you wish to factor that into your decision-making." He tried to be as delicate as he could. He didn't blame her if she didn't want to take responsibility for a thirteen-year-old right away, but Luna wasn't going anywhere.

Jia gave Dev an impatient look that relieved him instantly. "Of course she's a part of this. I have no issues with having a niece right away. I'd like to spend more time getting to know her. Should we break the news to her together?"

"Let me talk to her alone for now." Best to see how his niece reacted first.

"Right. Go home and be with her. I'll text you once I'm done with my family. Here, let me show you out."

He followed behind her. She opened the front door, and he paused, awkward. How on earth did someone take leave of another after something like this?

She seemed to sense his confusion, because she gave a wry smile. "Can we hug?"

Oh thank God. "Yes, please." He opened his arms and she flowed right into them. He looked down at her upturned face and the vulnerable curve of her cheek. It was a perfect cheek to kiss. Surely, as an engaged man, he could kiss his fiancée, yes?

Lights flashed in warning.

Oh, wait, that was him. He leaned away from the light switches on the wall. "Ahem."

She disengaged from him. "What a wild road trip this was, huh?"

"I agree." His smile felt more genuine than any smile he'd had in a while. "I will talk to you soon, Jia."

Chapter Eighteen

JIA TOOK five deep breaths. Then another five.

Her hands were shaking so hard she could barely flip open her laptop. This was it, the turning point on her family's opinion of her, the moment they decided she was either past redemption or the same silly but benign Jia.

She'd responded to Ayesha's frantic warning texts first, telling her everything was handled, then sent a message to the family group chat that they could have a phone call, but she'd also messaged Sadia privately. The whole gang would be on this call, but she wanted to speak with her middle sister first.

Jia leaned back against her headboard and played with the cord on her sweatshirt as she waited. The piece of handkerchief Dev had turned into a makeshift ring lay next to her.

I wouldn't mind it.

Yes, exactly what every prospective bride wanted to hear regarding marriage to her. Yikes.

The problem was, when he'd first proposed a real proposal . . . she *really* hadn't minded it, like kind of wanted it? And that was, um, a very big problem. Because all he could say was that he *wouldn't mind it.*

He said some other stuff too.

Her brain couldn't focus on that, though. It was the equivalent of reading one negative comment and eighty positive ones. The negative one stuck with her long after the others.

The computer chimed and she straightened. Only one window popped up, her middle sister's concerned face filling the screen. Sadia's cheeks and breasts had rounded with her pregnancy, just like they had when she'd been pregnant with her first child, Kareem. Her middle sister was so pretty, with smooth brown skin and shiny hair that tumbled past her shoulders. She wore a tank top, which displayed her impressive assets. "What on earth is going on," Sadia began, and Jia gave a half wail.

"Uh-oh." Sadia leaned in close. "Baby, take a deep breath."

"I can't. I messed everything up." She blinked back her tears. She would not fall to pieces, not yet.

"You didn't. Granted, I'm just getting briefed on the whole story, but I'm on your side."

If only she had time to spill the whole sordid story to her sister.

"Do you want to be engaged to this guy? Does he want to be engaged to you?"

He *didn't mind* it. "Yes."

"Well, then, there you go." Sadia leaned back in her chair. "Sounds like the two of you are on the same page."

"It's not that easy—"

"Why not?" Sadia shook her head, her hair swishing. "Sometimes, when you take out the noise, life can be exactly that easy."

Jia picked at her nails. "I wish I could do something without drama."

"Then you wouldn't be you." Sadia gave her a soft smile. "And I think you're pretty wonderful."

Jia took the cocoon of acceptance and nestled into it. Sadia was right. Why couldn't things be simple?

Her phone buzzed again, and she sighed. Oh right. That was why. "I'm on your side," Sadia murmured. "I won't let them browbeat you."

Truly, middle daughters deserved hazard pay. "Okay. Let's patch them in."

Sadia saluted her, and three more windows popped up, full of all the women in Jia's family, plus her dad, brow furrowed, leaning over her mother's shoulder. Ayesha sat next to her mom.

Jia braced herself.

"Jia, what on earth . . . ?"

"You didn't tell us?"

"So irresponsible—"

"Everyone calm down, let her—"

"We don't know him."

"You didn't want an engagement party?"

"I had a new dress I wanted to wear."

"I'm sure there's a good explanation."

"Jianna, this is too much," her mother broke through.

"The whole family is talking. And you don't even answer our calls or our texts, so we have had to look foolish. What is this engagement? We have not even met him yet!"

"Now, now," her father said, with far more calm, though Jia caught the thread of worry in his usually soothing voice. "I am sure there's a perfectly good explanation for why the news is saying Jia and this Dixit boy are engaged."

They all quieted and looked at her with varying degrees of worry and accusation. Jia took a deep breath. Out of sight of the camera, she let her fingers creep to that piece of fabric.

He could have been fooling her. He could claim tomorrow that he didn't even know her. *I wouldn't mind it.*

"Because we've been talking about becoming engaged," she said calmly.

The call erupted again, and this time even her father spoke a little louder than usual. She raised her hand, and she was gratified that they all quickly quieted. "Look, I know this feels sudden, but as you can see, Dev and I have been talking for a while."

"Talking. You've barely been in his presence for less than a month," Noor pointed out.

"Right, well, it's not a formal engagement. His people jumped the gun a little. He was planning on asking Mom and Daddy's permission first." Dev's suggestion had been the wisest, she'd decided. She didn't want her parents to hate her fake fiancé.

Real fiancé?

"What a gentleman," Sadia broke in, rubbing her round

belly. Jia wondered if the gesture was a subtle reminder to her parents about what was at stake if they did turn their backs on her.

"He is," Jia said in a rush. "We have so much fun together. He's a really kind person and good with his niece. He's not stuck-up, and he's very self-sufficient and down to earth for someone who is as famous as he is." All true things.

And I want to kiss him.

She'd keep that one to herself.

"Speaking of famous," Sadia interjected, "I'm surprised you're mad, Mom. You cut me off when I married someone who had zero dollars to his name. Now that Jia's with a rich guy, you're mad about that, too?" Oh, Sadia was definitely reminding their parents of their past behavior.

Seeing as how her sister didn't love confrontation, Jia was grateful beyond words.

Mohammad lowered his head. Their mother drew herself up. "We were wrong to do that, but our objection to Paul wasn't that he wasn't rich, it was that your life would be hard with him, and we didn't want that for any of our girls. We don't know this Dev enough to know whether he will be good to Jia. She barely knows him."

Ayesha lifted an eyebrow. "People get married after knowing someone for far less time. I'm probably going to have an arranged marriage eventually. Mom, Daddy, you met and married in the same week. So why is this so different?"

Jia felt a rush of affection. Ayesha had every right to be concerned about this sudden news, given that she knew everything, but her twin was rolling with the shenanigans. "What Ayesha said."

"Because our families knew each other," her mother snapped back. "It is not at all the same thing."

"I'm meeting his grandmother in a few days, so that'll be taken care of," Jia said.

Zara leaned forward. "His grandma's coming there?"

"Yes."

"Shweta Dixit is coming to America?" Noor clarified, then coughed.

Jia eyed her eldest sister with concern, but nodded.

"Then we'll come there, too," Farzana said crisply. "We can move up our trip. Mohammad, call the airline."

What the . . . "Wait, wait, there's no need to do that."

"There's every need."

"We'll all come," Zara announced.

Oh no.

"Sadia and Noor cannot fly right now, and you must stay here to look after them," Mohammad said firmly. There went the hope that her father would talk some sense into her mom.

"I don't think that's necessary," Noor protested.

Oh no. "This is all unnecessary," Jia tried weakly.

"It is not in the least unnecessary," Farzana declared. "It is essential we meet his family before we agree to the match."

"What if you call in and meet his grandmother that way?"

"That's not how it's done, for a child's marriage. This is not a work meeting."

If her video wasn't on, Jia would bang her head against the

headboard. Why had she even mentioned Dev's grandma? They could have had a little more time to process this.

"Send us the details on when his family will be there," Mohammad said. He had his phone in his hand and his glasses perched on his nose. "We can figure out the logistics then."

Sadia resettled herself in her chair. "I think this is an overreaction."

"I will not have another daughter run off and elope with someone."

Sadia's face went blank at their mother's pointed reminder of her own rebellion, and a surge of sympathy ran through Jia. There was no need for her parents to slap at Sadia right now, when her sister was just trying to help her. "It's fine, you can come here." Jia forced a smile. "It'll be so much fun." So much fun, to introduce her family to a Bollywood legend who had probably read the passionate texts she had allegedly sent to her grandson. Only not that grandson, not really. The other grandson. Oh, and the third grandson, too.

So fun.

Farzana was already rising from her chair. "We have to pack. Remember, Jia, you're a potentially engaged woman, not a wife. Behave accordingly."

Jia couldn't help herself. "What does that mean, Mom?"

"You know very well," Farzana huffed.

The little devil that lived perpetually on Jia's shoulder egged her on. "I don't. What can a wife do that a fiancée can't?"

"Jia, stop teasing your mother." But there was a suppressed thread of laughter in her father's directive.

"Fine. I promise, Mom, I will be as saintly as possible." *For me*, she thought to herself. Her parents and Ayesha left the call.

Noor and Zara gave her disappointed looks and disconnected as well. Sadia fiddled with the ends of her hair. It had grown quickly while she'd been pregnant, and now it hung down her back. "You okay?"

No, she was not. "Yup. What could possibly be wrong?"

Her older sister didn't look convinced, but she nodded. "Call me if you need anything. Love you."

"Love you, too." Jia picked up the fabric ring and twisted it around her fingers. Should she send Dev the rings she'd bookmarked on her wish board, so he could buy her a real one? Would that be tacky?

Her brow furrowed. It was a problem if she didn't even know if he would find that tacky, right? If she was going to marry him?

Be engaged to him. She didn't have to marry him right away. She had plenty of time to figure out his tackiness boundaries.

You're too much, you know that?

Jia launched herself off the bed, trying to shake her twin's words out of her head, but it was impossible. How did normal regular people go through their lives without getting into weird situations? Seriously, how?

She stumbled downstairs, and just as she was about to ask Sienna where her roommates were, she caught a flash of color outside the big doors that led to the backyard. She flung them open and strode outside, coming to a halt when she saw who was in the comfy white chaise overlooking the ocean.

Aw, no. It was not her day.

Lakshmi glanced up, which made it impossible for Jia to slink back inside without detection. Rhiannon's assistant was dressed in a flowing crimson caftan paired with black boots, and her hair was clipped up in an elaborate updo.

So damn *cool.* Jia shuffled her feet, feeling especially small and plain. "Hey. I was looking for Rhiannon and Katrina. Sorry, didn't know you were here."

"I'm not sure where Katrina is, but Rhiannon will be right out. We're working on something." Lakshmi closed the laptop. "I hear congratulations are in order. My grandma's going to want an autograph from your new husband."

Jia wasn't sure who was more surprised by her bursting into tears, her or Lakshmi. But it was definitely Jia who was shocked when Lakshmi appeared by her side. "Hey," the other woman said, and patted her twice, awkwardly, on the head. "Heterosexual marriage isn't *that* bad. Or so I've heard."

That only made her cry harder. Lakshmi patted her again, harder. "There, there. Please don't cry. I'm not good with tears."

"Stop hitting me," Jia sobbed.

Lakshmi paused mid-swat. "Stop crying, then! I'm trying to comfort you."

"You're terrible at it." Each word was punctuated by a gasp. It was like all the pent-up drama and worry and lies had come flooding out of her eyes at once.

Lakshmi gave a muttered curse and grabbed her by the

arm to march Jia over to the chaise opposite the one she'd been sitting on. She shoved Jia down, and Jia was too worked up to protest being manhandled. "I bet you never cry," she whispered. Lakshmi probably absorbed her own tears and used them for fuel.

"I cry sometimes."

That startled Jia enough that she subsided to sniffles. "You do?"

Lakshmi grimaced. "No, I'm trying to make you feel better. But I do have emotions." She handed Jia a napkin. "I'm guessing your love life isn't as rosy as the media made it out to be?"

"No." Jia blew her nose. "It's not." And then, because it seemed like everyone in this house might as well know, she ran through the highlights of her and Dev's relationship, catfishing included.

"Hmm," Lakshmi said, when she was done. "Interesting."

"Interesting?"

"Yes. More interesting than I thought you could be. No offense, but you always struck me as kinda shiny and smooth and soft. No depth, you know?"

Jia clutched her snotty napkin. "How am I supposed to not be offended by that?"

"It's not as if you like me much either," Lakshmi said matter-of-factly.

"I didn't dislike you! I pretended to not like you because I didn't want you to think I cared that you didn't like me!"

"Huh." Lakshmi squinted. "Why did you care?"

"Everyone wants people to like them."

"No, they don't." Realization dawned in the other woman's dark eyes. "Oh, you're one of those."

"One of those what?"

"One of those kids who was raised with weaponized disappointment, so you're super insecure and crave external validation and when you perceive the slightest rejection you convince yourself you're a failure, all while pretending you're a tough cookie who doesn't give a fuck what anyone thinks about you."

Jia's mouth dropped open. "Oh, shit."

"Uh-huh."

"Oh, *shit.*"

Lakshmi gave a sympathetic nod. "Yeah."

"Oh, shit."

Lakshmi handed Jia her coffee mug and Jia took a deep drink, coughing slightly. It was bitter but the black brew washed the uncharacteristic swears out of her mouth. "How did you know that?"

Lakshmi lifted her chin and draped her arm over her knee, her dress flowing around her. The silver studs on her boots gleamed in the sunlight. "I am good. Also, hello Kettle. I am the Pot. Or, former Pot."

Jia let out a shaky breath. It was like Lakshmi had peered into her soul and ripped out her deepest secret. "How did you do it? Stop caring what people thought?"

"Oh, years of therapy. Here is the secret." She leaned closer, and so did Jia. "I stopped."

"Wow," Jia deadpanned. "Amazing."

"No, really." Lakshmi lifted a shoulder. "I decided I had

two options: I could be miserable and live my life as others wanted me to, or I could be happy and do what I wanted. Boiled down to that, the choice was easy."

"But *how* do I stop?"

"Be confident. Twist what others tell you are your weaknesses into strengths. What did I call you? Soft? You're kind."

Jia played with the napkin. "Flighty."

"A dreamer."

"Frivolous."

"Lighthearted."

"Impulsive."

"Good at thinking on your feet."

Jia swallowed. "Too much."

Lakshmi waved her hand. "That's not an insult. Would you rather be too little?"

Jia sat back, the gears in her brain turning. It couldn't be that easy. It wouldn't be that easy. It would take, as Lakshmi noted, years to unpack all her anxiety about others', especially her family's, opinions.

Yet, this could be a way to start?

"Put aside everyone else's feelings. Do you want to get engaged to this guy?"

"Yes." She didn't even hesitate, which made her chest swell. Yes. She could be confident about this, and she'd stick to it. No matter what anyone else thought about them.

She wasn't lonely right now, as she'd been when Arjun had found her. She wanted Dev in her life, she didn't need him in her life, and that made all the difference. They might have taken a twisty road, but she liked the destination.

Lakshmi opened her laptop. "Then I guess we need to do some preliminary research on Shweta Dixit and come up with a plan."

"We?"

"Sure." Lakshmi's smile was the first genuine one the woman had given to her. "I owe it to you. I judged you too quick, and I try not to do that. We probably have more in common than we don't."

"I didn't make it easy on you," Jia said magnanimously.

"You definitely did not. But I'm usually better at seeing through a tough act. So. Plan?"

"I'm not good at sticking to plans."

"No one is. Remember that thing about being quick at thinking on your feet? Let's make a couple of general plans, and you can twist those as you see fit."

Her brisk no-nonsense approach calmed Jia. "I should text Dev."

Lakshmi was already typing. "Go ahead."

Told my family that we're engaged. They're coming in a few days to meet your grandma. The game is afoot, I repeat, the game is afoot.

Jia hit send and turned to her new friend. "Okay. Let's make a plan."

DEV ENTERED HIS apartment and dropped his keys on the table in the foyer. The noise of the metal hitting the wood punctuated the clatter of a pot in the kitchen. Dev followed the sound and winced when he found his uncle standing behind the stove. Every burner was on full blast, and the stove was on. The kitchen wasn't small, but it was warm from the heat. Competing scents warred with one another, adding to the chaos.

Though he hadn't lived with his uncle for long, Dev was quite aware that this cooking frenzy probably wasn't a great sign.

Adil whirled around. "There you are. Young man, where have you been?"

Dev shifted from one foot to the other. He'd never had to deal with an elder catching him sneaking into the house, but he imagined it felt like this. "I told you, I got stuck a few hours east of here."

"With your fiancée?" Adil Uncle drew himself up to his whole five feet and five inches and glared at Dev. "Imagine my surprise to find out you are engaged. You didn't respond to my texts. I had no idea what to say to everyone calling me for information."

Fuck. "I'm sorry, I had so many messages, I missed yours. I should have informed you what was going on."

"What is going on, exactly, Dev? You told me you were simply meeting with her to atone for your brother and cousin's behavior, as a friend."

Dev rested his hands on the counter for support. "I know. Uncle, you must have seen the messages that were leaked. Those were the texts between Jia and Arjun. Chandu did the first thing he could to kill the gossip, and said we were engaged."

Adil Uncle narrowed his gaze. "But . . . in that case, you could say your people made an error."

"That'll hurt Jia."

His uncle waved the spatula he was holding. Something red spattered on the stove. "You can't get married to save a reputation, Dev. This isn't the twentieth century."

"I'm getting married to her because I admire her greatly," he said simply. "And I cannot imagine a better partner and coparent to Luna."

Adil Uncle scrutinized Dev for a long moment, and slowly, he lowered his utensil. "You *want* this."

"I do." Dev controlled the quiver of his lips. Under the panic and the worry was pure excitement at the prospect of actually being married to Jia at some vague point in the future.

"You're a romantic like your parents, I see. The rest of your father's family couldn't stifle that out of you."

His cheeks grew warm. "I don't know about romantic."

"I do." Adil dropped his spatula in the pot and stirred with vigor. "Well, now. This is a different story. I have been praying for you to find a good woman, and here she is. It calls for a celebration. We will invite her and her family over, and I will cook."

"Actually . . ." He hesitated. "Aji has told me she is coming here to meet Jia."

Adil's head came up. "I see."

Dev flinched at his uncle's carefully neutral tone. Adil had never met his sister's husband's parents, and had only spoken with them on the phone when Dev and Rohan's parents had died.

While his grandfather had sneered at any mention of his

mother, Adil Uncle had been careful to never malign Dev's father or his paternal family in his presence. Dev would never permit his uncle to feel left out of important family decisions. "Of course, you will be there as well. Jia has already met you, you will be a friendly face. You live with us, it is even more important you get along."

Adil cleared his throat and dashed his arm over his eyes. "Yes, yes. I would like that very much. By the way, you should speak to Luna."

Dev stilled. Oh no. That did not sound promising. "Did you tell her?"

"I didn't have to. Her friends have been texting her all morning. She was deeply unhappy when I picked her up from her sleepover."

He hadn't gotten to Luna soon enough. "Unhappy how?"

"She wouldn't talk to me or look me in the eye, only asked if it was true. I couldn't tell her if it was or wasn't."

"I'll talk to her."

"Do that. And then we can discuss what you know of Jia's favorite sweets. I must make her something when we come together."

Dev didn't think his uncle meant pancakes, so he made a mental note to ask Jia if there were any Desi sweets she liked or was interested in. "Yes, of course." Dev patted Adil on the shoulder as he walked past him.

Dev knocked on Luna's door. There was no answer, so he knocked again.

"What?"

He raised an eyebrow at the sullen tone. "Luna, it's me. May I come in?"

There was such a long pause, Dev shifted, wondering if she'd deny him. "Fine."

He opened the door slowly. "Hey, beti."

Luna didn't look up from her phone. "What do you want?"

"I heard you learned some gossip about me."

She stiffened. "Is it gossip or is it true?"

Dev came to sit on the edge of her bed. "Can you please put your phone down?"

"No."

He raked his hand through his hair, taken aback by her blatant defiance. This must have been what Adil Uncle had experienced with the great Bagel Bites War. "Please?"

He was relieved that she tossed the phone to the side, because he wasn't sure what to do with open and obvious mutiny. He was also relieved she was speaking in Hindi and not a language he didn't understand.

The hurt in her eyes made him cringe. He sat on the side of the bed. "The rumors are true."

"You said you were just friends with her. My friends sent me messages this morning asking if you'd really been talking to her for months."

"We started as just friends." He hoped she didn't notice that he was sidestepping the thing about him talking to her for months. He felt like he had. Did that count? "You're upset, and you're right to be," he said gently. "I should have told you earlier."

"Why would you? My dad barely told me what was going on in his life, either. You're like him. I'm nothing to you."

Oh no. Dev slowly gathered her hands up, giving her time to pull away if she wanted to. "I know I wasn't around much before your father passed, but it sounds like he tried to protect you as best he could."

Luna blinked rapidly, and he waited for her to cry, but she kept the tears at bay. He'd rather she cry. A good sob never hurt a teenager, as far as he was concerned.

"He wanted to hide me," she said.

His rejection of that claim was immediate. "No."

"Yes. You weren't there." Her chest rose and fell. "The other stars' kids, they got paraded around town. He didn't even want anyone to take photos of me."

"I wouldn't want anyone to take photos of you, either."

"Because you love me. He didn't." Dev didn't have a second to be happy that Luna was so conscious and secure of his love, because she continued. "I was too ugly. Ajoba said it was a shame I took after my mother, because I'd never be a great actress, and Baba agreed with him. I didn't look like a Dixit."

No. Surely his grandfather and Rohan wouldn't be so insensitive to say such a thing to a tween girl.

Wait, who was he thinking of? Of course they would. Still, he tried one more attempt. "Chandu Uncle said he kept you isolated for your protection."

She stared at him like he had grown two heads. "He only kept me because Aji made him. She bribed him."

The air grew very tight in his lungs. "No."

"Yes. Aji made him take me when he found out I was his and then paid his gambling debts whenever he wanted so he wouldn't send me off to the boarding schools. All the servants knew. They told me from the time I was little."

He needed to have a long talk with his grandmother when she arrived, clearly. He couldn't quite picture his stoic, distant grandmother doing such a thing purely out of emotion, but it had also been out of character for Rohan to take on the responsibility of a young daughter when he didn't have to. Did Dev truly know anyone in his family?

Her lips wobbled. "I know I'm not supposed to hate him, but I do."

Dev thought back to yesterday and that swing set. *Things change, life changes, you change.* "It is quite acceptable to have conflicting feelings about someone."

Luna looked away. "I'm starting to be happy. And now you're getting married to someone who might hate me."

"No," he said forcefully. "Jia would never hate you, or treat you poorly."

"You don't know that. She's barely met me. She's so cool and cute, and look at me." Luna gestured to herself, and the ratty shorts and T-shirt she must have slept in. "When she doesn't like me, you'll send me away. Baba talked about sending me away to school in England. I don't want to go to England! It's cold."

"No one is sending you to England," he said, as soothing as he could.

She sniffled. "There's a boarding school in the south of France that's not bad. Madrid, too. It's why I learned both languages, so I could convince him to send me to one of those instead."

Oh for crying out . . .

Dev might have unresolved grief for his brother, but right now, if Rohan had been in front of him, he would have punched him in his smug, pretty face. "The only time you will need to use your French or Spanish is when we go to one of those places on holiday," he said firmly. "May I hug you?" He let his arms rest open, unwilling to pressure his niece.

She surprised him with a nod, and then shocked him by crawling right into his lap. She was almost too big for this, but he had plenty of room for her. He enclosed his arms around her and rocked her. She smelled like lavender and his heart hitched to finally embrace her. Those absent icy places in his chest were getting overfilled. "You have followed Jia online?"

Her curls tickled his nose when she nodded.

"Tell me, does she strike you as the type of person who would be cruel to someone? Or belittle their appearance?"

"No."

"No. The opposite, I would say." Jia's platform was radically positive when it came to acceptance and kindness.

"People can be different offline than they are online."

Wise girl. "That is true, but Jia is authentic. I wouldn't think of marrying someone who wouldn't be a good aunt to you, and I will listen to you if you have concerns after you meet her."

"You will?"

"Of course." He brushed his lips over her forehead. "And

as you mentioned, she is younger and cooler than me. You might enjoy having someone around who isn't ancient."

That got a tiny smile from her. "When's the wedding?"

"I don't know. When Aji comes, we will probably discuss that."

Luna sat up straight. Dev had wondered about the connection between Luna and her great-grandmother. If Aji really had given Rohan money to keep his daughter . . . well, their attachment made more sense. "She's coming here?" Luna looked around and grimaced. "She's not going to like this place, Kaka. It's small, for her."

"I'm aware. She's rented a place in Malibu. We'll go stay with her there for a few days."

"Malibu!" Luna brightened. "But I didn't order any bikinis. I won't have time to get any before that. All the girls here wear two piece suits."

"Bikinis?" He cleared his throat to hide his instant horror. He hoped Jia had more insight than his various self-help books on parenting young women. "I mean, oh no. I suppose what you have will do." His phone buzzed, reminding him that he had a message. He pulled it out of his pocket while Luna scrambled off the bed and dragged out her suitcase.

His dismay as he read Jia's text must have been apparent, because Luna paused in rummaging around in her drawers. "Are you okay?"

"Yes," he wheezed. No, he was not okay.

He had to meet Jia's parents? His grandmother was going to meet Jia's parents?

"Kaka, are you sure?"

He forced a smile. "Everything's going to be great," he told Luna. It would be. He was good with older adults, even skeptical ones. Dev may not have his brother's or cousin's breezy charm, but he had his own skills.

He texted her back. No problem.

How did Luna take it?

Luna appeared less heartbroken now, at the prospect of seeing her grandmother, but her trauma ran deeper than he'd imagined. She's a little upset. She fears you won't want her around.

Aw. ☹ I could never! Perhaps I could spend some time with her over the weekend to get to know her a little better.

That would be nice. Are you okay?

Yes.

"Luna?"

She gave him a questioning glance as she folded her swimsuit.

He thought about his grandfather and Rohan. About his father, fighting his parents and throwing the comfortable life he'd known away for love. "We decide what a Dixit looks like. You and I. No one else. Understand?"

She froze, and gave a single nod. "Yes, Kaka."

He felt comfortable giving her a hug as he passed her, and exulted when she hugged him back. Between her and his uncle and Jia, soon he'd have no empty spaces left in his heart. No boxes to stuff his feelings into.

He couldn't wait.

Chapter Nineteen

Dev drove down the winding road of the Pacific Coast Highway, the sun shining bright on the ocean on his left. It glittered like a gem, a scene out of a movie, and he couldn't enjoy it because he was too stressed out about the next couple days.

Thankfully, he was off work until next week, so that was one less thing to worry about. He and Jia hadn't had much time to talk, though they'd texted quite a bit. Her family was arriving tomorrow; his grandmother was already settled into her new Malibu home. He'd tried to reassure Jia a few more times that she wasn't in too deep, she could call this off if she wished, but she'd told him that she was committed to the plan. He liked her calling it a plan; that gave the whole scheme a sense of structure it was badly lacking.

The GPS alerted him to a turn, and he pulled off the main highway. "Wow," Luna whispered, when they finally came to a stop in front of a home.

Dev peered up at the beach house. *Wow* was right. The beach house wasn't as big as his grandmother's estate in

Mumbai, but it was built on a prime piece of land towering over the ocean. No peekaboo views here.

"Can we come live here?" Luna asked from the back seat.

"I would also like to live here." Adil Uncle craned his neck.

"No. We have a perfectly fine home."

"But this is so much nicer. I bet a lot of Hollywood actors live out here."

Dev cast his niece a quelling look, but he didn't really mean it. She'd alternated between perfectly normal and silent and moody for the last few days, and he was happy to see her so chatty. Not happy enough to buy her a Malibu beach house, though. "Please do not create a PowerPoint on this topic. The commute to the set would be far too long. Besides, I'm not a proper Hollywood star yet."

"You could be, if you wined and dined producers here! And I could get a horse. I'd like to ride a horse on the beach."

Dev twisted in his seat. "If we move here, you'll have to switch schools. What about all those friends you've made? The orchestra you're auditioning for?"

He felt bad when Luna visibly deflated, and he hurried to make it up. "We can look into horse riding lessons, though, if you like."

She perked up. "I saw a flier at school."

"Something tells me she was only after horse lessons all along," Adil murmured, as she scrambled out of the car.

Dev had the vague suspicion his uncle was right. Luna was a businesswoman in the making, for sure. "Come. We will get our luggage later."

Or someone would get it for them. A butler opened the front door before they could reach it. Dev inclined his head at the man and bid him a pleasant good morning, but the servant only held out his hand, silent. Most of Shweta's servants were quiet.

It was enough to rake across every democratic nerve he had. Dev reached into his pocket, pulled out his wallet, wrapped a twenty around his car keys, and handed it to the man. The older man's eyes widened, and he quickly pocketed the cash. There was almost a smile around his lips when he nodded at Dev and skipped down the stairs.

Another woman arrived. Pinky, one of his grandmother's longtime housekeepers. She did smile at them, and Luna whooped. "Pinky!" His niece ran to the woman to give her a hug. The round maternal maid gave her a fierce hug back. "Hello, beti. Hello, Dev."

Pinky had been around when Dev and Rohan had come to live at the compound, and if they'd had any soft maternal presence in their lives after their mother had died, it was her. Dev stooped to give Pinky a hug. "You look lovely, Pinky."

Pinky tittered. "What a nice compliment, coming from such a handsome man." She smiled at his uncle politely.

"Pinky, this is my uncle, Adil."

"Hello, sir."

His uncle shifted. "No need for sirs," he said gruffly. "Hello. Dev and Luna have spoken of you fondly."

Pinky's smile turned genuine. "Your grandmother is in the kitchen, children. Come, I'll show you."

"The kitchen?" As far as Dev knew, his grandmother didn't even know where the kitchen in her home was.

"Oh yes. She's started taking cooking lessons."

Dev raised an eyebrow. That was . . . out of character. Shweta had been retired for a while, but she filled her days with leisurely activities, not labor.

Things had changed. They found Shweta at the stove, and Dev did a double take. His grandmother's long hair was disheveled and loose down her back, instead of in its neat bun or braid. She wore loose linen capris and a T-shirt advertising a mobile company.

He didn't think he'd seen her in anything but a sari. Ever. How bizarre.

"Aji," Luna cheered and broke away from them.

Their grandmother turned, and pure delight filled her eyes at Luna's approach. She pulled her great-granddaughter in for a hug, resting her hand over the girl's head. "Look how big you've gotten," she crooned, in a tone he'd never heard before. Her gaze was a little more guarded when she turned her attention to him. "Dev. How good to see you. It's been months."

Had it? He supposed it had. They hadn't been in America long, but he'd only seen his grandma sporadically while he'd been busy settling Rohan's estate and wrapping things up in Mumbai. He'd assumed she'd been busy doing the same with his grandfather's estate. It hadn't occurred to him that Shweta might want to see him. Or at least Luna, or that Luna might have been missing her.

It had taken his niece a year to hug him like she hugged the older woman. He didn't want to feel bad about that, but it did smart a little. Dev inclined his head. "Aji. Nice to see you, too."

"What are you cooking, Aji?" Luna leaned back, but she kept her arms around their grandmother's waist.

Shweta touched her nose. "I know how much you like prawns. I learned how to make a curry for you."

"You've been taking cooking lessons?" Dev probed.

"Yes. I always wanted to, but your grandfather didn't allow me to go into the kitchen. It was high time I learned."

How odd. He'd never heard Shweta so much as subtly criticize her late husband. "I see."

Luna twisted around her to sniff at the stove. "Can I have some?"

"In an hour or so, let's let it simmer a little. Why are you speaking in English?"

"Oh, Kaka says I can speak whatever I want."

Shweta frowned at Dev. "She speaks fine English, she must not lose her Hindi. Or she will become like these NRIs who come home and butcher our language."

Dev tucked his hands in his pockets. He knew exactly what his grandmother wasn't saying. She probably envisioned Luna as the next reigning Bollywood starlet, and nonresident Indians did have a tougher time of it there.

If that was what his niece wanted, fine, but Dev wasn't about to push her to think acting was her only option. "Luna speaks five languages," he said mildly. "This is a good age to pick them up and stay fluent. There's no danger of her losing any of them." He changed the subject. His uncle had hung back. He placed his hand on the older man's shoulder and tugged him forward. "This is Adil Uncle."

His uncle cleared his throat and straightened. "Madam. It is an honor."

Shweta looked down her elegant nose, and Dev tensed, in case she said something cutting and rude.

What had it been like, before he was born, when his father had brought his mother home that one and only time before they'd run away? Had his grandmother screamed at the couple, or stayed silent?

She did neither now, and she didn't avoid the specter of Dev's mother, either, which surprised him. "You look like your sister."

"I know."

"You may call me Aai," she announced. "Or Auntie."

Adil blinked. "Ah. Yes."

"You are a chef?"

"Oh no." His uncle shook his head so hard, his whisps of hair trembled. "I was a taxi driver."

"Adil Uncle is the best chef," Luna broke in.

Dev wondered if his niece was still trying to make up for the Bagel Bites War, but she wasn't wrong. "Agreed. He is being modest. He is the reason we have not starved on our own."

His grandmother nodded decisively. "Excellent. You can teach me. I do not want to backslide in my class."

Adil Uncle's eyes widened so much, the whites showed

all around his pupils. "I—I would be honored to teach you, Auntie, but—"

"Good, it is settled."

"I can't believe you're here," Luna said happily.

"I couldn't possibly not come when I heard your uncle met someone."

Luna's face turned inscrutable. She gave her grandmother a squeeze and stepped back, simultaneously sidestepping the mention of Jia. "Can we see the rest of the house? Can we go on the beach? Can we get a horse and ride on the beach?"

Shweta raised a groomed eyebrow. "You want a horse? I will buy one right—"

"We've already made arrangements for horse riding," Dev exaggerated. He had to have a talk with his niece about asking for things from her great-grandmother. It took Shweta seconds to snap her fingers and buy something extravagant.

Thankfully, Shweta conceded. "A walk is good enough for now. Pinky, will you watch the stove? And have Arjun show Dev and Adil to their rooms."

Dev froze mid-step. "Arjun is here?" he demanded.

There was probably a little too much aggression in his tone, judging by Luna's sideways glance, but Shweta only shrugged. "Yes, I insisted he come with me. Why?"

"No reason. Do you know where my cousin is, Pinky?"

"Upstairs, fourth door on the left."

"Perfect." Dev was probably showing too many teeth for a plain old smile. "I'll go say hello to him."

"I should come with you," his uncle said, his forehead creased in worry.

Oh no. He didn't want any witnesses. "Nonsense, I know you'll want a nice cup of chai first, won't you?"

His grandmother straightened. "Of course, I cannot believe I did not offer you one. Pinky?"

Adil gave Dev a subtle glare at the neat trap. His uncle wouldn't dream of insulting his host by declining the drink now.

Dev took the stairs two at a time. *Don't hit Arjun until you find out whether he's guilty. Or he'll be too bloody to talk.*

He shoved the bedroom door open. His cousin whirled around from the mirror he was primping in front of. He was a handsome man, a more refined and elegant version of Rohan, but dressed far more garishly than his brother would have ever dared, in a blindingly hideous orange and green plaid shirt and green pants. Arjun held up his hand, which was, Dev was happy to note, shaking. "Hello, Bhai."

"I'm not your brother," Dev said flatly, and Arjun's face fell.

Still, he rallied. "It's so good to see you."

"Is it?" Dev shut the door.

"I know you're mad."

"You have no idea what mad is." He stalked Rohan, until his younger cousin was cornered. "I am beyond mad. I left mad behind a long time ago. Explain yourself."

Arjun frowned. "I—"

Dev grabbed him and put him in a headlock before he

could get another word out. Arjun flailed as Dev dragged him over to the open window and shoved him out of it. "What are you doing?" Arjun yelled.

"Did you catfish that poor girl with my account and then release those texts?" Dev demanded. "I want a clear yes or no." This wasn't what he'd intended by making sure his cousin was guilty, but it was effective. At least this room didn't face the beach, so Luna wasn't likely to see one of her uncles about to throw the other one out the window.

"I don't know what you're— Ah! Okay. Yes. Yes. Yes to the catfishing, but no to the texts! My phone really was hacked, along with a bazillion other celebrities! Didn't you see the nudes of me?"

Dev evaluated the words, paying attention to the nuances of his cousin's voice. It sounded like he was uttering the truth. "If I saw nudes of you, I'd be blind." He yanked Arjun back inside.

Arjun straightened his shirt while glaring at Dev. "You rude son of— Oof." He flinched when Dev punched him in the stomach. "Why," he gasped. "I already told you."

"Because you did a tremendously hideous thing," Dev said calmly. "And you will apologize to me, and if she wishes to see your ugly face, Jia as well. Both for the catfishing and the texts."

Arjun came to his full height, with some difficulty. "I told you, it was a hack."

"It wouldn't have been hacked if you hadn't had the messages in the first place."

Arjun licked his lips. "I know. Trust me, I know."

Dev flung his arms wide. "What the fuck were you thinking, doing something like this?"

Arjun rubbed his arms and pouted. "It was Rohan's idea," he muttered.

Dev pointed at the bed. "Sit down." He was already taller than his cousin, but he'd like to really intimidate him.

Arjun sat.

"I require a better explanation than that."

"Rohan wanted to prank you, so he sent a few messages to random women."

Dev slapped his forehead, his hurt at his brother's perpetual dislike of him subsumed by panic. "There are *more* women?"

"No! No. The others didn't answer."

"And you were in on this joke. Using my old scripts for lines to feed her."

"I helped him splice them up," Arjun confessed. "Rohan said you wrote most of them. You're not a bad writer, by the way."

Oh, that one hurt. Arjun liking anything wasn't a good endorsement as far as he was concerned right now. "And after he died?"

Arjun hung his head. "I don't know. Rohan was my buddy. I missed him, and Luna, too. I wasn't thinking straight, so when Jia started texting again a couple months ago . . ."

"You thought you'd prank boring old me as well."

"No! I thought to help you."

"Help me!"

"Yeah, because of the will. You need to find a wife, so I thought maybe . . ." He trailed off. "I didn't think far enough about her meeting you or anything. But it seems like you did fall in love with her! So it worked."

Dear Lord. Adil Uncle hadn't been that far off base with his matchmaking theory. "It . . . worked?" Dev growled. "It has turned my life upside down."

"In a bad way?"

"Could there be a good way?"

"Sure." Arjun squinted at him. "You're right, you were boring. Got up, went to work, always on time, hit all your marks, went home, slept. No way you would have even talked to a girl like that without someone forcing you into it."

"What do you mean a girl like that?"

"I mean a talented, popular, outgoing one. And look! According to Aji, you're marrying her soon."

Dev opened his mouth and closed it, wishing he could dispute anything his cousin was saying. "What you did was horrible, despite the result."

Arjun sobered. "I know. I realized as soon as Jia started pushing to meet me. I mean, you. I'm sorry about that. I don't know what I was thinking."

Dev leaned away. He hadn't expected a sincere apology from his selfish, foolish cousin. "I don't know either."

"Have you told Aji?"

"No."

Arjun looked up at him from under his lashes. "Are you going to?"

"Worried about your own inheritance now?" Dev's lip curled. "No, I'm not going to."

His cousin released a giant sigh of relief. "Thank you."

"I literally can't, not without exposing what happened. I won't do that to Jia. She feels embarrassed, though I've assured her the embarrassment belongs to you and you only." He narrowed his eyes at Arjun. "And you won't tell Aji either, will you?"

"Trust me, that's the last thing I want. I'll beg Jia's forgiveness, and then we can never discuss this again."

"If Jia wants you to stay out of her sight, you'll do that, too."

"But I've never been to Malibu. Plus, what will I tell Aji when I hole up in my room?" Arjun whined.

"Tell her whatever you want."

"But there's a surfboard in the garage." A pout started to form on his cousin's annoyingly symmetrical face, but it dissolved like sugar in the rain when Dev took a step toward him. "Fine, fine."

"I'm going to go settle my uncle into his room. I mean it, Arjun, no more shenanigans."

Arjun was silent until Dev reached the door. "I was trying to help."

Dev rubbed his eyes. The sad, plaintive note in Arjun's voice made him sound much younger than his thirty years.

He's acting.

Only, Dev didn't think he was. He was, in fact, pretty sure Arjun had just been more honest in the last few minutes than he had in a while.

He turned around and looked his cousin up and down with new eyes. "Do me a favor and never try to help me again." He tried not to feel bad when Arjun visibly deflated. The man had done something awful and cruel, and it was only by pure luck that Jia and Dev might actually have a chance together, and that she hadn't been irreparably traumatized, her ability to trust demolished.

And yet . . .

Dev was tired of being wary of family members. It was a slap in the face to know his little brother had disliked him enough to play such a cruel joke on him. Arjun's earnest desire to help, however misguided that help had been, well, it didn't make up for his strained relationship with his brother, but it wasn't the worst consolation prize. Rohan's part in this may have been motivated by cruelty, but Arjun hadn't seemed to come from a place of malice.

People change. "At the very least, don't help me again without asking first," he clarified, and Arjun brightened.

"Will do. Want to go surfing with me? I brought new swim trunks. Shorter inseams are very in right now."

Dev held up his hand, palm out. "We're not there yet, brother."

Arjun nodded amicably, his grin slow, but real. "Fair enough, Bhai."

Chapter Twenty

THE FLIGHT was exhausting. Jia, you could not move to New York City? You had to come to Los Angeles? It would have been a closer trip for us."

Jia glanced in the rearview mirror. "What would I be doing in New York City?"

"You work from home. You could be doing the same things you do here."

Jia didn't bother to explain to her mother that the connections she was making in entertainment were quite different in L.A. Her mom knew that already. Farzana liked to complain about things she knew no one could possibly change. Had Jia moved to New York, her mom would have complained about the noise and weather. "Not quite."

Despite her mother's crankiness, and the fact that her family was here under bizarre circumstances, joy had filled Jia when they'd walked out of LAX. That happiness had been reflected in their faces, and when her parents and twin had hugged her, they'd given her a little piece of her old home, enough to ground her in her new home.

It was almost enough to make her forget that they were

now driving straight from the airport to Dev's grandmother's Malibu home for their weekend trip. Where his cousin also was. His terrible, no-good cousin.

She'd kind of moved on, she'd thought, from being catfished, but seeing Arjun's name had slammed all that mortification back at her, knocking her out of the careful plans she'd made. But then she'd recalibrated. She'd declined an apology, mostly because she preferred to never see Arjun's face if she could help it. Dev had promised to keep him out of view.

It was probably unrealistic to assume that was an actual possibility when he was in the same house and Dev's only cousin, but she'd keep her fingers crossed.

"If you couldn't live closer, at least you found a boy who seems nice. Mo, InshAllah, soon we'll only have one daughter left to get married off. Remember when your mother said five girls would be a burden and a headache? I wish she was here to see this."

Jia's grandmother was in Pakistan, not dead, but her mom rarely made a distinction between the two when it came to her mother-in-law. Her father only grunted, too busy taking in the scenery to listen to his wife.

Ayesha cleared her throat. Her sister sat in the passenger seat. Jia hadn't been able to hug her hard enough. Her sister raised her eyebrow a millimeter, and as womb mates, Jia got the message immediately.

This is a bad idea. Jia shifted. "Engaged is different than married, Mom."

"Yes, of course. But you are on the right track."

Her dad readjusted his legs in the cramped back seat. She'd borrowed Jas's car to transport everyone, but her dad was tall. Tall and skinny, and no matter how well he got his clothes tailored, they always hung off his lanky frame. Today's athletic shirt and pants were no different. "Don't pressure her, Farzana."

The way he said it made Jia believe he'd had to repeat those words a lot over the five-and-a-half-hour flight.

"I'm not pressuring her."

"And don't pressure the boy when we meet him, either," Mohammad warned.

"I will not," Farzana huffed. "You act like I am new to marrying my daughters off. I know how to trap a good man."

Jia turned her signal on. "That sounds ethical."

"I hope we have time to freshen up before we meet his grandmother," her mom fretted. "You packed appropriate things to wear for the weekend, didn't you, Jia? It wouldn't do to meet Shweta Dixit looking cheap."

She had two closets and a storage unit full of really nice clothes. What did her mom think she did online? "Oops, I packed crop tops and miniskirts."

Her mom pretended not to hear her, which was standard. "Traditional wear, of course. Modest, light colors, and you must not put on any flashy makeup or jewelry. I do not want her to get the wrong idea about us."

That was the antithesis of Jia's whole aesthetic, but she agreed this one time. She'd opted to pack more conservative outfits, unsure of where Shweta Dixit fell on style. "Yes, Mom. No flashy stuff, got it."

"I mean modest in the traditional sense, not the modern sense," Farzana insisted.

Jia was well aware that the things she wore and considered modest would have been haram when her mother was her age. Times changed. "Got it. I have packed a light pink potato sack."

"I'm wearing a light pink sack, pick another color, please," Ayesha said primly, laughter dancing in her eyes.

Farzana's cascade of sniffs caught her and her sister off guard. "You okay, Mom?" Ayesha twisted in her seat.

Mohammad turned to his wife. "What's wrong?"

Jia caught her mother wiping her tears in the rearview mirror. "It's nice to hear you two together again. I've missed this banter between my baby girls."

Jia softened into a pile of goo. Her mother drove her crazy sometimes, but she also loved her daughters. "You can join my and Ayesha's video chats whenever you want. Moving across the country just means the banter happens in different mediums," Jia said.

"Exactly right," Ayesha agreed. "Distance doesn't make any difference whatsoever." She faced forward, head high, but she also snaked her hand over the console to touch her fingertips to Jia's leg. Jia released the wheel to grasp her twin's hand.

"Do you know what the population of Malibu is, Jia?" Mohammad asked.

Jia squeezed her sister's fingers. "I don't. Why don't you look it up, Dad?"

"Hmm. I shall. Farzana, look at those boats out there . . ."

"It's gorgeous." Farzana tapped her window. "See the red one?"

Her father dutifully leaned over his wife. "Can't wait to catch up with you properly," Ayesha murmured to Jia.

Jia wished she could talk to her sister about what was going to go down, but she couldn't. Her mother had the ears of a bat. Ayesha had lodged her complaint against the ruse via text, and that would have to do until they were alone. "Can't wait to catch up either," she responded, also sotto voce.

"What are you two whispering about up there?" their mother asked.

"Nothing." Jia came to a stop in front of the beach house they were spending a couple of nights at. Nerves started to tremble in her belly, too many to appreciate the beautiful home.

"Are you okay?" Ayesha whispered.

Jia nodded without looking at her sister and circled the car to help her dad get their bags. Her parents pulled ahead, leaving her and Ayesha to walk slowly behind them toward the imposing home. "I'm fine. Why wouldn't I be?" She smiled at her sister. It was probably a tight smile.

"Um, I don't think you need me to list all the reasons you ought to be freaking out right now."

Ayesha was right. She didn't need the list.

They came to a stop outside the door, and Farzana turned

to face them. She fixed her collar. "Do I look okay?" Her whisper was fierce. "I don't want to risk meeting Shweta looking too rumpled."

Jia raised an eyebrow. If she didn't know better, she'd think her unflappable mother was a little starstruck. "You look pretty, MashAllah."

Mohammad cleared his throat and bared his teeth. "I don't have any stuck lettuce, do I? I knew I shouldn't have had a salad for lunch."

Was her dad starstruck too? "You're fine, Dad."

Their mother considered her husband's teeth with more care. "Yes, you're good." Farzana straightened her shoulders. "Best behavior, girls."

She and Ayesha exchanged a glance. "Um, can someone press that doorbell?" Jia suggested.

Farzana jumped. "Yes, I shall."

Jia shoved her hands into the pockets of her dress to keep from picking at her nails. Her dress was modest enough for their mom, but it was also a bright sunshine yellow. The color gave her courage, and she needed it for this, meeting her fake fiancé's world-famous grandmother.

The door opened, and they were greeted by a smiling woman in plain clothes. "Hello."

"Hi," Mohammad's voice went up and he cleared his throat. "I am Dr. Ahmed."

The woman inclined her head and stepped aside. "Come," she said, and they followed her into the home. "I will—"

"Ahmed family. Welcome."

The deep, throaty voice made them all jump. They looked

up the stairway, and Jia did a double take. She wasn't sure what she'd expected from a Bollywood legend, but the woman with salt-and-pepper hair, dressed in leggings and an oversize tunic, all of which was smudged with dirt, wasn't it.

Jia's father was the first one to break the spell. "Mrs. Dixit," he said, and the reverence in his tone startled Jia. She'd never heard her father speak like that to anyone. "You need no introduction. I am Mohammad Ahmed, this is my wife, Farzana, and our daughters, Jia and Ayesha."

Shweta's gaze moved over each of them. "You may call me Shweta," she said in Hindi, and unfortunately, that exhausted most of what Jia knew in Hindi.

"Our daughters only speak English, unfortunately," Farzana said regretfully, like it was her greatest shame in life that she hadn't raised bilingual children.

Shweta raised one eyebrow. Damn. Jia only hoped her eyebrows remained that perfect when she got to Shweta's age. "Not even Urdu?"

"No."

"Hmm." Shweta came down the stairs with an old world grace. "Did you have a good drive?"

"Lovely. We took the long way and drove all along the coast." Mohammad's voice was hoarse.

"How nice. Apologies for my appearance. I was repotting the plants on my balcony when I saw you arrive."

"Please, we came off a long flight," Farzana said. "We are the ones who are rumpled."

Shweta looked between Jia and Ayesha. "Which one of you is Jia?"

Jia took a step forward. "I am."

Shweta looked her up and down, and Jia felt stripped naked in that pause. "Hmm," Shweta said again. "I like your dress. I wore that exact color to an award show last year. Bright colors are appropriate for a pretty girl like you."

Jia blinked at the compliment. So much for her mom always trying to shove her into pastels. "Thank you."

"Is your grandson not here to greet us?" Farzana's forehead started to crease.

"I am afraid he went to the store. He expected you later. He'll be here shortly. Why don't we all go freshen up in the meantime?"

"Yes, that would be perfect." Farzana nearly curtseyed.

Shweta turned to her employee. "Pinky, can you show the Ahmed family to their rooms please?"

Pinky inclined her head and they followed her up the stairs. When they got upstairs and looked out the huge windows, Mohammad let out a little hum, and Farzana and Ayesha gasped at the pure blue ocean in the backyard. Jia didn't make a noise, but she was moved by the sight too. Oh, to wake up to that water every day.

Someday. When she owned her own makeup company, she'd buy a place like this. She'd give a lot to charity, she tacked on in her own head, and then she'd buy a place like this.

Their parents were shown to one room, and she and

Ayesha were put right next door. Her sister didn't even give Jia a chance to appreciate the view before she whirled on her. "I hate this."

"So you've said."

"No, I really, really hate this. This is a terrible idea, Jia." Ayesha wrung her hands. "I can't believe you're going along with this engagement."

"What's the alternative? I tell everyone those texts aren't between me and Dev?" Jia flipped open her suitcase and pulled out the dresses she'd bought to wear over the next couple of days. She hoped Shweta approved of the red shalwar kameez she'd chosen for dinner.

Ayesha stomped over to her own bag. "You could say you're not engaged, at least. I'm worried about you, you doofus. I can totally see you getting married because you're stubborn and don't want to tell Mom that you screwed up."

"Lower your voice," Jia hissed. "You know she has, like, a sonar when it comes to us talking about her."

Ayesha pulled out her clothes. "You know I'm right."

"You're not right. For the record, both Dev and I know we can pull out at any time before marriage. Or even after." She almost tacked on a ribald joke, but Ayesha wasn't in the mood. "And secondly, I'm not doing this to please Mom or anyone else." She was past that. She was evolved now, thank you very much.

Pleasing herself caused way less stress than trying to please everyone else. It was like she'd taken a dial and turned down all the noise in her brain. She could finally hear herself think.

"I cannot believe you're actually considering marrying him."

Jia shrugged. "It wouldn't be so bad. I could do a lot worse."

"That's not a ringing endorsement, that he's not the worst you can do."

"Okay, he's probably the best I could do, is that better?"

Ayesha crossed her arms over her chest. "Yeah? What's so great about him?"

"He's perfect."

"No man is perfect." Her sister said the words with such world weariness, she sounded like Rhiannon. When this was all over, Jia hoped she could introduce her family to her second family.

"He is. He's kind and has this really dry sense of humor." She paused. "He cracks me up, actually. He seems all stern at first glance, but underneath that seriousness, he's a sweet pussycat. He let me win at Scrabble." Jia shook her head. "And did it in such a charming way, it didn't hurt my pride one bit."

"Hmm. What else?"

Jia stretched to hang her clothes in the closet. "Oh, he's great with his niece. She lives with him, and he is so patient. He takes her to school every day and helps her with her homework at night."

"How does he feel about your work?"

"He loves it. He even takes photos for me. He treats me like I'm actually a serious businesswoman and not a—" She caught Ayesha's look. "What?"

"Wait a darn second. You like him."

"That's what I've been trying to tell you."

Ayesha clasped her hands over her mouth. "No. You liiiiiiiiiike him."

Jia glared at her sister and shushed her. It wouldn't do for their mom to hear she liiiiiiiiked her fiancé! "Very mature."

"Oh my goodness." Ayesha rested her arm on the bureau. "This is going to make a great storytime someday for you. Talk about content."

Jia growled. "Quit it." *Quit telling the truth.*

"What's wrong? I think it's sweet that you're falling for the man you got maneuvered into a fake relationship with." Ayesha squinted. "Weird, but sweet. Why didn't you tell me this before? If you'd said, *Ayesha, I'm madly in love with this man and can't wait to make out with him,* then I wouldn't have worried. Of course I'll help you close this deal now."

Jia groaned. *Sisters.* "You stink. Why don't you shower first?"

Ayesha's mood had undergone a 180. She walked to the bathroom, whistling a jaunty tune. "Jia and Dev, sittin' in a tree . . ." She ducked without turning around, and the pillow Jia had thrown smacked right into the wall. "Stop damaging your future in-law's house," Ayesha chided her.

"I'm gonna damage some*body*. Hurry up."

"Why, you want to see your fiancé?" Ayesha made kissing noises and crossed her arms over her chest until they wrapped around her.

Jia picked up another pillow, but Ayesha kicked the bathroom door closed on her laugh.

DEV HAD WANTED to be at the house to greet Jia and her family, but his uncle had insisted he go to the market to pick up some items for the dinner he'd seized control of cooking. Since Adil had been uncharacteristically quiet over the past twenty-four hours, Dev hadn't wanted to deny him his fresh spinach. He'd rushed home as soon as he'd gotten the texts that she'd arrived earlier than planned.

He made a quick stop to drop the groceries off in the kitchen. Adil Uncle greeted him when he entered with a grumbled, "About time."

Dev didn't take offense. The older man had cooking stains on his apron and a general frazzled air about him. His uncle might be more nervous than he was, though he wasn't sure why. "I came as quickly as I could. Is Luna with Aji?"

"Yes." Adil Uncle peered into the bag of groceries, and gave a satisfied grunt. "Yes, good, you got what I needed."

"And Jia? Did you meet her and her family?"

"Not yet, though I believe your grandmother did."

Damn. He'd wished to be here to facilitate that meeting. He hoped his grandmother had checked her imposing nature for a minute. "It would have been better for you to greet her, since you've already met," he murmured.

"I don't know about that." Adil Uncle busied himself emptying the bags. "In any case, I believe Pinky showed them to their rooms. I think I saw Jia leave the house a few minutes ago. She was headed for the beach."

Dev glanced out the window and caught a flash of pink. Protocol dictated he greet her parents immediately, but these were unusual circumstances, and he'd like to see her first.

He'd gotten more nervous as the day went on. He tried to tell himself that her parents were normal people, who did normal people things, but he was still worried. "Thank you."

Dev pushed his shirt sleeves up as he went outside. He'd dithered over what to wear. He'd gradually relaxed his wardrobe around Jia, but this wasn't just Jia he was meeting, now was it? So he'd donned slacks and a button-down shirt, despite how warm it was today.

He slowed as he approached Jia. She wore a pink shalwar kameez and matching hijab. Her feet were buried in the sand. "Jia," he said, but she didn't turn around.

Perhaps she couldn't hear him over the sound of the ocean. "Jia," he said, louder now, and placed his hand lightly on her shoulder.

She stiffened and dropped her hand over his. Dev couldn't tell the sequence of events of what happened next, except that he flew through the air and landed facedown, the wind knocked out of him. He rolled onto his back, coughing sand out of his mouth.

"Oh my God." The woman who had sent him airborne crouched down next to him, and now that her face was visible, he could see this was not Jia, but a very good facsimile of her. Ayesha.

She pulled a headphone out of her ear. "Dev? I'm so sorry. I didn't mean to—"

"What on earth is going on?" Jia's strong voice carried over the beach. He turned his head slightly. She wore a blood-red dress adorned with embroidered flowers.

Since they weren't alone and since he couldn't talk yet, he tried to convey comfort and reassurance through his look, though he wasn't sure if he accomplished that goal. Hard to accomplish anything when one's lungs had been squeezed flat.

"He startled me," Ayesha explained.

He placed his hand on his chest and wheezed. "Apologies, I didn't mean to. I thought you were Jia. I said your name. Uh, Jia's name."

Ayesha grimaced. "I was blasting my music kind of loud."

Dev came to a seated position. The sand was firmer than it looked. "That was an impressive throw."

"Fun fact, Ayesha's a black belt." Jia's smile was small and apologetic. "It's a bad idea to startle her."

"What is happening down here?" An older couple came into view and Dev mentally groaned. So not only had he startled Jia's sister bad enough that she'd karate tossed him, now he had to meet her parents sprawled on the ground with his clothes all sandy.

Dev came to his feet and dusted off his pants. "You must be Dr. and Dr. Ahmed. I'm Dev Dixit. I apologize for not being here when you arrived."

"Hmmm." Her father regarded him with a disapproving frown. "You came home and decided to come play in the sand instead of greeting us?"

"He wasn't playing in the sand. I accidentally tripped him," Ayesha said in a rush.

Their mother's eyes widened. "Ayesha. How could you do that?"

Mischief danced in Jia's eyes. "Yeah, Ayesha. How could you do that?"

"I startled—" Dev started to explain, but Ayesha cut him off.

"I am very clumsy."

Mohammad shook his head. His clothes were similar to Dev's, slacks and a button-down shirt, sans sand. "Apologies on behalf of our daughter, Dev."

"It was my fault," he assured them hastily, extending his hand. Then he saw it had sand on it, so he pulled it back and tried to wipe it surreptitiously on his thigh.

"What a gentleman you are," Farzana crooned as she looked him up and down. He'd been on the receiving end of that calculating look from aunties before, so it didn't faze him too much. This time, actually, he welcomed it. Her parents liking him would make this all easier on Jia.

"Shall we go inside?" he suggested. "We can relax in the living room until dinner."

"That would be nice."

They walked to the house, Jia at his side. So much for talking to her first. He let his pinkie brush against hers, hoping to convey some comfort.

"I understand you parent your niece, Dev," Mohammad said, and Dev tucked his hand close to his side guiltily. "We would love to meet her and your uncle, as well."

"I do, yes." They entered the back door, which led directly into the spacious living room. He gestured to the seats. "Please make yourselves at home. I'll go fetch them."

"I'll come with you," Jia said, her tone bright.

Her mother frowned and opened her mouth, presumably to stop the two of them from going off alone, but Ayesha spoke up. "Mom, is that a Picasso?"

"Where?"

Ayesha winked at Jia and led their parents to the wall, and Dev smiled. He'd forgive his future sister-in-law for tossing him into the sand if she could keep running interference like this.

Chapter Twenty-One

Jia released the breath of anxiety she'd been holding as she walked next to Dev. When she'd first come across him lying on the sand at Ayesha's feet, she'd met his dark gaze for one pregnant moment. She'd never been able to speak with someone in a look like she did with Ayesha, but it was so easy with him.

Are you okay? his look asked, though he was the one vanquished on the ground.

As well as can be.

Don't worry.

I'll try.

She stopped walking, and he turned to look at her. She stared at him for a long moment, then launched herself into his arms and buried her face in his neck and inhaled. Dev's hands smoothed down her back, so his fingertips rested on the curve of her butt.

She wanted him to go lower, and just the fact that that thought popped into her head was enough to have her pulling back. They stared at each other, and Dev finally smiled. "Hi."

"Hi."

He pressed his forehead against hers. "I missed you."

"I missed you, too." Oof . . . this was getting sappy, and she loved every second of it.

"How are you holding up?"

"Remarkably well." This was stressful, but it had become ten times less so when he showed up.

"Good." He held out his hand. It was an odd thrill to hold his hand, one she hadn't really experienced with another man. She felt secure and happy, having him in her grip.

"Come, let's find Adil Uncle, and then we can track down Luna. It would be good for you to see her one-on-one before she meets everyone."

Because she was going to parent the girl when they got married. Phew.

If you get married.

Jia snuck a look at Dev's elegant profile. It was weird how their marriage had become far more certain in her head as time went on.

They entered the gourmet kitchen to find both members of Dev's household. Adil was tossing gummy bears at Luna, who was catching them with her mouth.

Jia straightened, trying to calm her sudden renewed nerves. In one sense, it was easier to face a Bollywood legend over the man and child who lived with her new fiancé. It seemed the stakes were higher with these two, as far as them liking her went.

"How many times have I told you two not to play this game? You could choke," Dev said, in greeting.

"I'm not going to choke," Luna said to Dev, but then she caught sight of Jia, and her eyes widened. "Uh, hi."

Jia gave her brightest smile. *She's nervous, too.* She'd raised hundreds of thousands of young women via the internet. Surely, she could win this one over. "Hello, Luna. It's good to see you again. And you, Uncle."

Dev's uncle gave her a bright smile. He was dressed in a stained apron, which surprised her a little. She'd assumed Shweta Dixit would travel with a gourmet chef to tend to her, but except for Pinky and a silent man who had moved their car for them, Jia hadn't seen any servants. "Hello, Jia. I am glad we could meet again, especially under such good circumstances. You look lovely, MashAllah."

Dev shifted. "Jia's family is in the living room. Come, why don't we all go sit with them." Dev's suggestion was more of a command than an invitation, but neither of his family members moved.

Luna cleared her throat. "If you'll notice, I'm covered in dirt. I was gardening with Aji."

"And I have been cooking all day. I still have some things to finish." Adil Uncle gestured to a cheese tray on the counter. "Why don't you take that in to them in the meantime?"

Jia might have been insulted that neither of them wanted to meet her family, if she wasn't quite familiar with the taste of anxiety and the fear of a poor reception. She placed her hand lightly on Dev's arm. She almost got distracted by said arm, but caught herself in time. "I understand you might want to clean up, but it would be nice if you could come quickly. I've never done anything like this before and I'd like to have some friendly familiar faces from Dev's side of the family in the room."

Luna gave a fake yawn. "I'm kind of tired."

Yes, she'd have to put in a bit of work to win the teen over.

Adil Uncle rubbed his neck. "I'm sure your parents are mostly here to meet Dev's grandmother."

Ah. Knowing what she knew about Dev's parents and the contention between the two sides of his family, she wondered if Adil was a little insecure about his place. "They are here to meet all of Dev's close family. You're his elder. And frankly, they'll have more in common with you. Your presence would probably put them at ease."

"What Jia said," Dev agreed gruffly. "Can you please go get dressed quickly?"

Adil opened his mouth, but whatever he was going to say was cut off by the back door banging open. A dark-haired man walked in. He looked like a lighter-skinned version of Dev's late brother. He was dressed in bright orange swim trunks and a purple tank top.

Jia didn't need an introduction. *Arjun.* The infamous, annoying Arjun.

Her hand curled into a fist at her side.

He appeared as startled to see them as they were to see him. His surprise flipped quickly to alarm when Dev took a step forward. "I was just getting my dinner and going upstairs!"

Adil cleared his throat and launched into motion. "Come, Luna. Let us get ready."

"But I don't—"

"No. We must be quick, your uncle and aunt are correct. Come on." Adil helped her down and shuffled her out.

With no witnesses in the room, Dev took a step toward his cousin and growled. Straight up growled.

Oh damn, that was sexy. She hadn't known he could growl.

Dev said something in Hindi, and Arjun's face fell. Though she knew he was an actor and probably a manipulative asshole, given what he'd done to her, she couldn't help but feel a beat of compassion for him.

Jia gave a mental sigh. As far as logistics went, she couldn't avoid Dev's family member, not if they were going to be together. She took a step toward Arjun. "I presume you're the cousin."

The man shuffled his feet and put his head down. At least he had the grace to look shamefaced. "I am."

"I changed my mind. I'd like an apology."

He took a deep breath. "I am extremely sorry. I didn't mean to hurt you."

"Why did you do it?"

Arjun looked at Dev, as if to confirm that he could speak, and Jia snapped her fingers. "Look at me, please."

He turned his gaze back to her. He really was a handsome guy, with his floofy hair and perfectly sculpted smooth face. She preferred Dev's stern bearded look any day.

"It started off as a prank, with Rohan. And then, afterward, I think I thought I was helping Dev get a girl, because he needs to marry—"

"Enough," Dev said quietly.

Arjun hung his head. "Anyway, there's no excuse. I'm so sorry."

Jia regarded him with frustration and annoyance. He sounded sincere, and matchmaking for Dev was a weirdly noble, if terribly misguided, act. When—if—she and Dev married, it wouldn't make sense to hate his cousin. She had to somehow make peace with the guy, but she was still so angry with remembered mortification.

What would her sisters do? Her twin would forgive and forget. Noor and Zara would spend the next forty years passive aggressively poking at the guy. Sadia would quietly poison him and bury him in the ocean.

Jia had her own style, though, and she was learning how to embrace it. "Can I throw something at you?" Jia asked politely.

"I'm sorry?"

"I think I'd feel much better if I could throw something at you."

Arjun looked at Dev askance, and Dev shrugged. If she hadn't been standing so close to her fiancé, she might have missed the flash of impish glee in his eyes. Perhaps he also wanted someone to throw something at his handsome cousin. "I think that's the least you owe her."

"Fine," he said. "But not the fac— Ugh."

Jia put Luna's now empty glass of milk back on the counter. "Sorry, did you say not the face?"

Arjun wiped the milk out of his eyes. "Yes. It's okay, though."

"Thank you, that was quite nice." She paused. "I'd prefer it if you could stay away from dinner tonight while my family's here, but I am willing to accept your presence in passing otherwise. But you need to be on your best behavior. Are we clear?"

"Yes, ma'am."

"And you are never, ever to do something like this to another woman."

"I promise, I will not."

She waved her hand at him, as regal as any queen. "You may leave."

Dev waited for Arjun to slink out of the room. "That was beautiful," he said with great admiration.

Jia preened. "Thank you."

"You're going to make an excellent bhabi."

Jia faltered. She hadn't thought about that, that she'd be Arjun's sister-in-law. "I hope so."

"I know so." He squeezed her. "Come, let's get back to our families."

Dev's grandparents' house parties had been legendary events, still talked about decades later. Tigers and magicians and elephants and world-famous musical acts had been the bare minimum for Shweta and Vivek Dixit.

This was a far more muted affair, just his and Jia's families, but his grandmother was firmly in her charismatic element. She sat at the head of the table like it was a throne. Her silver-shot hair was pulled back in a bun, her red sari vivid and hand embroidered, and a shade brighter than Jia's.

She'd been beautiful as a young woman, but Shweta was still stunning in her seventies. Her big dark eyes were lined with a touch of kohl, and a subtle blush colored her cheeks. Someone had mastered the no-makeup makeup look, clearly.

And you have watched far too many of Jia's videos, Dev thought. Then, *No such thing as too much.*

He'd worried for no reason. Luna had been quiet, but had tolerated the elder Ahmeds fawning over and complimenting her. Adil Uncle had been warm and welcoming. And Shweta had Farzana and Mohammad eating out of the palm of her hand since the second she'd swanned into the room. "Mrs. Dixit," Farzana began, and Shweta immediately interrupted her.

"Call me Shweta. Mrs. Dixit was my mother-in-law, and Dev can tell you, she was terrible."

Dev had never met his great-grandparents, but his grandma often bent the truth for a good one-liner.

"Shweta," Farzana breathed now. "I wasn't permitted to watch many Bollywood movies as a child, but I always snuck yours. It is an honor to be sitting here."

"Yes," Mohammad agreed. Jia's father was a man of few words, but his distracted air hid a sharp gaze.

Shweta resettled her body. "Thank you both. And thank you for coming. I was dying to meet you . . . and Jia, of course." Her dark gaze settled on Jia. "I've heard much about you, my dear. I have so many questions for you."

"I'm an open book," Jia said.

"Your parents and sisters are all physicians. An admirable middle-class profession. Why did you not go this route?"

Dev pressed his lips together, hoping the Ahmeds were fine with being classed as the bourgeoisie. Everything was middle class to his grandmother, he supposed.

Jia took a bite of her potatoes. "I wanted a career in entertainment."

"In making ten-minute videos, generally about your face or body."

Dev tensed, ready to intervene if his grandmother got snarky or cruel.

Jia looked amused rather than insulted, like she was quite accustomed to someone mocking her work. "Yes."

"I have watched some videos on there. One where you show how to wing an eyeliner with a, I believe it was a . . . bobby pin."

"I went viral for that one," Jia said good-naturedly.

Shweta raised a thin eyebrow. "And you prefer this to saving lives like your sister?"

Dev opened his mouth to put a stop to the line of questioning, but it was Jia's mother who jumped in. "We are very proud of all our daughters." Farzana smiled sweetly. "Are you not also in entertainment? Jia merely forged her career in a new medium."

"Excellent point. There is something to be said for reaching the public directly. I would have liked to bypass the casting agents and producers when I was young." Shweta's mouth twisted.

"You were quite the trailblazer," Jia said softly.

"Being a trailblazer is hardly fun. You would know that, of course."

Jia's eyes widened. "I would?"

"Of course."

Farzana took a bite of her food. "Adil Bhai, this curry is amazing."

His uncle looked up from his plate and gave a soft smile. "Thank you, but, uh, Auntie made this one."

"With Adil's final approval. He kindly volunteered to make everything else. Jia, do you cook?"

"I'm afraid not."

"Then you are lucky to have Dev's uncle living with him. He is a fine chef." Shweta took a naan from the basket on the center of the table.

Jia smiled warmly at Adil. "Yes, I can't wait to sample more of his food."

"We are, indeed, lucky." Dev regarded his grandmother. She was being so kind. It wasn't that she was normally un-kind, but he'd never seen her go this far out of her way to be nice. That it was to the brother of the woman her son had run away with made it even more peculiar.

Adil's shoulders relaxed and his smile grew stronger. "Thank you."

"Dev, you're not eating." Shweta smiled at him. "Is some-thing wrong?"

He shook his head and ripped his roti in half. "No."

"It's a shame Arjun couldn't join us," Farzana said to Shweta.

"Yes, he said he wasn't feeling well. You will meet him tomorrow. He is a very good boy. He took time off from his movie to come travel here with me."

Dev hoped his snort of disbelief didn't reach his grandmother's ears.

"He's very talented, as well. He takes after his grandfather," Shweta added. "He will be cast as a movie hero for many years to come." Dev didn't think his grandmother had meant that as a dig on his television career, but he couldn't be sure.

"This one, on the other hand," Shweta waved at Dev. "He's come to America to do more television."

Oh okay. He was sure now.

"I like television, and some actors in our country would kill to be a crossover star," Dev said. He ripped his flatbread in half.

"We both know you went into television to be different from the rest of us. And *star* is the key word. You're a villain, not the hero."

He wasn't surprised at all Shweta knew what his role in *Hope Street* was. She had influence everywhere.

"Villains are admired in this country," Mohammad pointed out. "He could be quite the lovable bad guy."

Not with my one-note story, I can't. "We shall see. Aji, why don't you tell us about any new projects you have going on?"

Mohammad's eyes lit up. "Are you acting?"

Shweta shook her head. "No, no, I retired long ago. I'm executive producing three films and a serial now."

A serial? "Since when are you doing television?" Dev placed the same intonation on the last word that Shweta had.

"Since I realized there was money to be made there."

"Which serial is it? I keep up on quite a few of them," Farzana confessed.

"A new one." Shweta launched into an enthusiastic description, just as Dev had hoped she would.

He let the conversation flow around him for a bit. The elder Ahmeds kept it going, for which he was grateful.

When the plates were cleared, and a cake brought to the table, Shweta finally addressed the younger generation. "Ayesha, your mother tells me you're considering an arranged marriage. What a good daughter. Congratulations. This is how marriages should be done. None of these love matches."

"Three of my daughters had love matches. I am glad Ayesha's sensible." Farzana gave her second-youngest daughter an approving look, which Ayesha returned with a slightly annoyed shake of her head. This clearly wasn't meant to be dinnertime conversation.

Jia spoke up. "Ayesha isn't doing it to be a good daughter. It's what she actually wants."

He'd quickly picked up on the dynamic between the twins, and as someone who had mostly been an estranged elder child, Dev was fascinated by the way they were interconnected. Jia stood up for Ayesha, often working as her mouthpiece or the distraction. Ayesha sweetly and quietly took the attention off her sister when things got too negative for her.

Farzana waved off Jia's explanation. "It doesn't matter why. It is good. We will start meeting boys soon."

Shweta stroked the stem of her wineglass. "Make sure you look past pretty faces, yes? Because I can assure you, my dear, that fades quickly."

Ayesha flushed. "Of course."

Shweta nodded in approval. "Good. Take the physical out of things completely. That is another thing the children these days rush, their physical needs."

Dev choked on his drink of water. "Aji." He tipped his head at Luna, who had stopped playing with her food instantly at the word *physical.* "Luna, are you finished eating? Why don't you go to your room?"

His niece pushed back from the table. "Can I see if Arjun Kaka wants to play video games?"

Mentally, he sighed. He'd be annoyed at his cousin for a while, but Luna did like her uncle. "Yes."

Shweta looked between him and Jia consideringly as Luna left. "You may have a fourth love marriage on your hands, eh, Farzana?"

Farzana's laugh was coy. "Oh, if I did, it would be fine. Dev is an accomplished young man."

"We weren't thrilled with being caught off guard with the engagement news, but meeting you and Dev has been a relief," Mohammad added. "We'll have to start thinking of wedding dates."

Jia straightened. "We haven't gotten that far," she said hastily.

Shweta picked at her cake. "I don't see why not. That's your generation's problem. You date until all the mystery is gone, until you hate each other. Ridiculous. If you meet someone you like, you should marry them and be done with it. Then if you have problems, you have to deal with them and can't go anywhere."

"What a lovely description of marriage," Dev said. "Not prisonlike at all."

"One of the new movies I am producing is set in a college. Kids these days, younger than these two, they are going around, sleeping together, never seeing each other again after. There is no permanency anymore."

Farzana gasped. "Jia! Is this right?"

"No!" Jia grimaced. "Uh, we are not . . . we haven't . . ."

"That's enough, Aji," he said softly.

"Apologies, Jia. Of course you and my grandson would never be so wild." Her smirk was more than a little disbelieving. "I am merely saying, best to have the marriage quickly. You two do like each other, yes?"

Dev was caught off guard by how quickly Jia said, "Of course we do."

He met her eyes. "Very much so." More than he should. More than he'd planned to.

"Then you should just get married now."

Jia let out a little laugh. "You mean a trip to Vegas?"

"No need for Las Vegas." Shweta looked around the home. "We can do it right here. Tomorrow."

Farzana laughed, then quieted when she saw Shweta was straight-faced. "You can't be serious."

"She's not," Dev said sharply. What on earth was his grandmother thinking?

"I very much am." Shweta pressed her hand to her chest. Her dark eyes welled up with tears. "You see, if we don't do it now, I may never get to see the ceremony." She paused dramatically, but not long enough for Dev to prepare himself for her next words. "I do not have long to live."

The indrawn gasp was collective among those at the table, and Shweta nodded, satisfied with that reaction. "Yes."

Dev was the only one who didn't outwardly react. Bullshit. If she was really sick, she would have told him immediately upon his arrival.

Farzana was the first to speak. "My God. I am so sorry."

Shweta inclined her head. "Thank you. I trust you won't speak of this to anyone."

Because it's a lie.

"Of course not."

"Do you know how long . . . ?" Mohammad asked delicately.

"I don't know."

Dev shifted, surprised to find a trace of panic strumming through his veins. His grandmother wasn't actually dying. He could tell when she was acting, what her tells were. So why was his upper lip sweating? "Aji," he said sharply.

Pressure squeezed his thigh. Jia squeezed again, looking

up into his face worriedly. He gave a small nod, trying to tell her he was okay. Only he wasn't sure he was.

"Please let me know if there's anything I can do. Perhaps you can visit our home while you're in America," Mohammad suggested. "I work at a large teaching center."

"I don't think any experimental treatments can help me now. But thank you." Shweta looked back at Dev and Jia. "Anyway. That's why it would be nice to see at least one of my grandchildren taken care of before I go."

"I absolutely understand that," Farzana said. "But I do not think Dev and Jia are quite at the point where they can get married so quickly. Like you want the best for your grandson, I want the best for my daughter."

Adil cleared his throat. "Perhaps we should think of a more realistic timeline for a wedding."

Bless his uncle, who knew the circumstances of their convoluted path to engagement.

Shweta leaned back in her chair. Her sharp gaze reassessed the table, and he could tell the exact second she made a tactical change. "There is another reason for haste. You see, my husband, he was very stubborn, and he tied up Dev's inheritance with a requirement he marry."

"Aji!" He half stood, though the cat was already out of the bag. The last thing he wanted was to air this particular laundry in front of Jia and her family. Or anyone, really.

Shweta continued as if he'd said nothing. "The condition expires in a couple months."

Farzana stiffened. "So unless he marries . . ."

"Immediately, yes, he will be left without a single dime of our family's fortune. I could give him money, of course, but he's frighteningly stubborn and won't accept it. Even though he depleted most of his own savings paying his late brother's debts. Rohan had a thing for horse racing, sadly."

He tossed his napkin over his uneaten cake. "Aji, I think we need to stop—"

"Dev and I will think about it."

Chapter Twenty-Two

W HAT WERE you thinking?"

That was a question Jia had gotten a lot in her life, but this was the first time Dev had directed it at her. He delivered it with gentle curiosity, like she hadn't just agreed that they should get married tomorrow in front of both their families.

He closed the door to the dining room, where her parents and Shweta were politely arguing the pros and cons of their immediate marriage, with Adil Uncle and Ayesha watching aghast.

There was no point in pretending she didn't know what he was talking about. "It seemed like a decent idea. I was being honest."

He gave her a long steady look. The sun was dying outside, and it streamed through the windows, warming his brown skin. "I don't think your parents agree with you."

"Yeah, actually, I was surprised they don't."

He glanced away. "Is that why you said it? You wanted to please them some more?"

"Nope."

"Then why?"

"Your grandma's sick, Dev. If she genuinely doesn't have much time, then we should do it now rather than later."

"I'm not convinced she's sick."

Jia raised an eyebrow. "Way harsh, Dev. That would be taking the meddling auntie shtick a little far, wouldn't it? No one cares that much."

"She does. If I lose the inheritance, the money will revert to my grandfather's sister—whom my grandmother hates."

"Is this will even legal?"

"Maybe not in America." He shrugged. "It doesn't matter. I don't want the money. She taught me how to act, I can spot her tells. That was a manipulation tactic, nothing more. What's your motivation, is the bigger question."

"I genuinely think it would be a good idea. It's what my gut is telling me." *Also, now you're getting something tangible out of it.*

Another woman might worry that a man had a literal fortune to gain upon their wedding, might think he was marrying her for wealth, but given Dev's resistance to getting hitched before the deadline, Jia wasn't too worried about that. The truth was, despite how much Lakshmi had empowered her, she couldn't banish all her insecurities in a matter of days, and Dev having something to gain from marrying her other than herself actually put her at ease.

This was a curveball to their plan, but she was going to react to it and adjust and be flexible. This was what she was good at.

"Has your gut never led you astray?"

"Not yet, not when I feel like this."

He was silent for a beat and her heart sped up, so fast it was like a jackrabbit in her chest. This was a weird, bizarre way to tell someone she had feelings for them, she supposed.

"You want to . . . marry me?"

Her heart froze. She stiffened. "You don't have to say it like that, like it's absurd. We already said we'd give the engagement a shot."

"An engagement is different. An engagement has an out."

"I mean, technically, like you said, marriage has an out. Not that I'm going into this expecting a divorce. We can have a prenup. I don't want your money."

"There'll be no prenup." Dev hesitated. "I feel like I went from convincing you to you convincing me."

"You didn't have to work too hard to convince me before. I was on board from jump. You're kind and practical and handsome and generous. The longer we wait, the more rumors there'll be, the more we'll have to finagle our families. I'm sick of the drama, let's just do it."

Dev shook his head. "I don't know if any good marriage started with *let's just do it.*"

She wrinkled her nose. "I mean, our engagement started with you saying *I wouldn't mind it.*"

"That bothered you?"

She pursed her lips. There was no need for him to find out how annoying her insecurities were before they got married, yet she couldn't lie. "Yeah, it bothered the hell out of me."

"I'm sorry. I tried to clarify, it was more than that."

"And this is more than that. There's other reasons to get married tomorrow."

"Like what?"

"Like . . ."

Tell him.

The words bubbled up in her throat, and she tried to beat them back. The same spontaneity that he said he liked about her—that had been what had forced her to make that declaration at the dinner table, even though she'd known it would complicate everything. "I like you more than a lot. And . . . what I've learned over time is that we don't have *much* time. If we want to get married, we should do it now. Even if we didn't have all these zany factors pushing us together, I'd still say we do it now."

The silence dragged on for so long, she almost threw up. She would have, if he hadn't reached out to hold her hand. Dev moved closer. "I watched all your videos, you know. I couldn't stop. Perhaps that's why I feel as though I know you so well."

She gave a breathless laugh, flattered. He'd watched *all* her content? The highest of compliments. "I wish I had a cheat sheet like that for you."

Dev stroked his finger over her cheek, the most intimately he'd touched her yet. She stilled, out of fear he would stop. "You knew me before you met me. You read my words."

What? She wrinkled her nose. "Oh, you mean your dialogue."

"Yes. But I wrote it. I did a lot of the writing for my own character on *Kyunki Mere Sanam Ke Liye Kuch Bhi*. I wrote some in English. Rohan and Arjun translated the rest from Hindi. Poorly, I might add."

"So . . . I was talking to you?"

"So to speak."

It was like a hundred butterflies exploded in her chest. "Dev. You should have told me. Also, I want to throw more milk in Arjun's face. But this is very romantic."

His chuckle was wry. "In a certain light, I suppose."

"You're a good writer! And you're a romantic. Those were some mushy lines."

He ducked his head. "Only on paper, I fear."

"You can be mushy in real life, too. That Scrabble win made my heart flutter."

Dev lifted her hand to his lips. "Thank you."

"You're welcome." Her whole hand tingled. What would it feel like when they kissed for real?

His thumb played over her knuckles, like he knew. "Jia?"

"Yes."

"We can't get married right now."

His words were a splash of cold water, halting all tingling. "What?" She pressed her hands against his chest, and he backed up. "You're going to say all those beautiful things and then reject me?"

"I'm not rejecting you." His chest rose and fell. "I realized what's been bothering me."

"What?"

He grimaced. "This feels like blackmail. Like you have no choice but to be engaged to me or marry me, because you don't want your family to find out about everything that's gone on. I don't want that, not for either of us."

She struggled to speak. "So that's your objection? Your only hesitation."

"Yes. Are you annoyed? You sound annoyed."

"Oh, I'm annoyed, that you think I don't know my own mind. I wouldn't tie myself to somebody for life, just to please my parents."

"I've known many people who would do exactly that."

She pursed her lips and tried to think. *Be fair.* He didn't know that this was the new and improved Jia, one who was focused on her own happiness. "So if that concern was gone, if you knew I wasn't doing this to keep my parents from finding out about the catfishing, we could get married tomorrow?"

"Yes, but—"

"Yes or no."

"Yes."

She nodded, still annoyed. "Cool. Move aside." Jia stalked past him and jerked open the door.

Everyone in the room stopped talking when she walked in. *The heroine stands in the spotlight, about to make her grand gesture for her fiancé.* This went against everything she'd wanted her whole life. Her family would never respect her after this.

But she wasn't about to have Dev thinking he was blackmailing her into marriage. Some things were more important than her parent's approval. "Everyone, I have to confess something. I was cat—"

"Burgled," Dev said loudly, stepping in front of her. She tried to move around him, and he nudged her back.

Her dad shook his head. "What?"

"Someone . . . stole Jia's earrings from her, and she was worried about telling you, that it would make her look irresponsible."

Farzana scratched her cheek. "Which earrings?"

What. A. Weirdo.

A positively endearing weirdo. Jia raised an eyebrow at him. "Do you remember which earrings, Dev, because I don't."

Her fiancé swallowed. For all that he was an actor, he was terrible at improv. "The diamond ones."

"Jia, the ones Noor gave you?"

She tossed up her hands. "Sure."

Farzana tsked. "Well, that's terrible, but it's not your fault. And I'm not sure why you're bringing it up now."

"Me neither," she muttered.

Farzana turned to Shweta. "We were just telling your grandmother, Dev, that while we appreciate her situation, we don't want Jia to feel pressured—"

"And I was explaining to Jia's parents that elders should be present at a wedding to give their blessings, and I'm not sure I will be healthy enough to travel to America again over the next couple months."

Farzana gritted her teeth. "And I was explaining back that I empathize. Were it me, I would want to know that my children were taken care of. But we want a big wedding for our daughter, and this isn't something to rush."

Funny how *taken care of* and *married* were one and the same in both women's playbooks but Jia couldn't afford to be distracted. "I appreciate you wanting to protect me, but I want to marry Dev."

"And I wish to marry her," Dev said quietly. "At the time of her choosing, whether it's tomorrow or six months from now."

"Well." Adil gave them a kind, encouraging smile, and Jia automatically smiled back. She was looking forward to getting a loving live-in uncle. "It sounds like you both have made up your minds."

"Unmake them up." Farzana raised her fingers and counted off. "We don't know you well enough, Dev. We have no proper clothes, no time to plan a party, and your other sisters aren't even here, Jia."

Jia bit her lip. Her older sisters missing this was painful, but . . . "Only Noor and Zara had big fancy weddings, it's not like it's family tradition. I have a huge closet and my roommates can bring clothes for Ayesha and me, and Daddy has his suit. Sadia, Noor, and Zara can call in."

"It would only be a civil ceremony?" Her mother spat out the words like they left a bad taste in her mouth.

"Sadia's had two of those by now," she reminded her mother. Zara's husband was Christian, and they'd had a small mixed wedding as well. This wasn't breaking any new ground in her family, in that sense.

Dev shifted. "I would be fine with a religious ceremony, if Jia would prefer that."

Farzana tossed up her hands. "And where on earth would we get someone to perform that on such short notice?"

Shweta took a sip of her wine. "I apologize for my presumptuousness, but I did look into that and have spoken to the local imam. He is happy to assist. I also took care of some of the more boring paperwork."

Jia imagined Shweta had only had to think of what she wanted for people to fall all over themselves to accommodate her. Did she have a Hindu priest and a civil servant on standby, too? "Lots of people do the nikah low-key. We can have a big fancy party later."

"Such a practical girl you are, Jia. Yes, I promise, we will have the biggest and fanciest wedding at a later date, in a leisurely manner," Shweta said with approval. "We will invite thousands. Have one here, and another in India, so all our contacts can come."

Adil cleared his throat. "If it is in India, Jia's whole family may not be able to attend," he reminded Shweta. "A neutral place may be preferable."

She shrugged. "Dubai, then."

Farzana paused, and Jia could see the stars forming in her eyes. "Thousands?"

"Thousands," Mohammad repeated, weaker, probably thinking of the cost.

"Everybody who is anybody will come for my first grandson's wedding. Of course, I will pay for it all." Shweta waved that worry away.

"See?" Jia raised her hands. "All set."

"Not all set." Farzana took a deep breath and pulled out her trump card. "What will people say?"

The words landed in the quiet room with the gravity of a thousand aunties whispering the same thing. Jia's smile was slow. Freedom ran through her veins, and independence made her heart sing.

I had two options: I could be miserable and live my life as others wanted me to, or I could be happy and do what I wanted.

"I don't care," she said crisply, and her mother reared back like she'd been stabbed.

"Exactly that," Shweta said. "Dixits create our own narrative. We will say it is a love match, and Dev wished for his poor grandmother to witness the union. No one will question this."

Her mother gritted her teeth. "Ayesha. Talk some sense into your sister."

Ayesha leaned forward, her eyes big. "Jia, are you sure?"

"Very."

Ayesha sat back. "Okay."

"That's all you can say?" Farzana asked her daughter.

Jia tensed. *Jia is too much. Jia is a lot.*

"She's being sensible." Ayesha took a sip of her water. "She's got a gut feeling if she's this certain. Her gut is always right."

Warmth spread through Jia. She hadn't really thought her sister would betray her in front of their parents, but this was nice confirmation.

Farzana pressed her lips together and crossed her arms over her chest, momentarily outnumbered. "Humph."

Shweta rubbed her hands together briskly. "Now, let's start getting plans together for a celebration tomorrow, eh? Adil, we will have to come up with the perfect menu."

Chapter Twenty-Three

Dev found Shweta in her small office, and he entered without waiting for permission. He sat across from the desk and gazed at the top of his grandmother's head. There was a slight bald patch forming at the crown there that he'd never noticed. She lifted her head and peered at him over her glasses. "Stop," she barked.

"Stop what?"

"Staring at me."

"I'm merely trying to figure out what your game is. First of all, are you really sick?"

"I have some blockages in my arteries, the doctor says."

Another jolt of that worry and unease, at the thought of his indomitable grandmother being ill. He had complicated feelings about his brother's and grandfather's deaths. They'd be multiplied tenfold for Aji. "What does that mean? Are you actually dying?"

She played with her pen, then set it down. "Not exactly. It's manageable with medicine and diet." She pouted. "They want me to go vegetarian, can you imagine?"

Dev heaved a sigh of relief and made a mental note to talk

to Adil about tasty vegetarian meals for her. "You can't lie about this stuff. You made it sound like you were expiring on the spot."

Shweta made an unbothered noise. "I do what I need to do."

"Can I ask you something? Why are you so determined to see me married before the deadline? I told you I don't care about the money—"

"I care." Her soft words cut him off quicker than a shout would have. "I have tried to break that will, and I cannot. And if you don't get money, Luna doesn't get any money, and I won't have that. I can leave you what's mine, but you deserve *his* money as well." Shweta shook her head, and he was shocked to see tears shining in her eyes. "He kept my son and you and Rohan from me all those years. I won't let him rob you of your birthright."

"You . . ." Dev leaned forward in his chair. "Wait, did you say *he* did? Like you had no part in disowning my parents?" He regretted the words as soon as he said them. One of the silent understandings of their relationship was that they didn't talk about the past. "Never mind."

She blinked rapidly. "No. No, let me clear something up. What say did you think I had in that house? Your grandfather sent my baby boy away, and kept my grandsons from me as well, and then your parents died there, far from me. You were so grown-up and distant when you came back. I had a chance with Rohan so I gave him as much money as I could, trying to make up for everything. And even that was wrong, because all it did was spoil him, like it spoiled . . ."

She took a deep breath and looked back at her computer. It was a credit to her years of acting that she was able to recover her composure so quickly. She typed something on her keyboard and then closed her laptop. "The lawyers will have the prenup ready by morning."

Were they done talking about the past? Because for once, he wanted to pry into that box. "No prenup."

"Yes, prenup. Or she could take you for half your wealth a week after marriage."

"I don't care if she does. That money isn't mine." If anything, it was a relief that she'd get something out of this if he wasn't a perfect husband. Dev braced his hands on the arms of the chair. "Go back to what you were saying."

She made a dismissive noise. "There's no need to dwell on the past. There are, of course, things I wish I'd done differently in life. Things I wish I'd said. But those things can't be done or said now."

"Why not? We have time. Say them. Do them."

Shweta looked away, blinking, then shook her head. "No. I don't think so."

She sounded final, so he dug out another box. "Luna told me you paid Rohan to keep her. Is that true?"

Shweta pressed her hand to her chest. "How on earth did she find that out?"

"Is it true?"

Shweta's lips thinned. "Luna is family. I couldn't tolerate the thought of family being raised somewhere else, like you were. Rohan was a good boy, just selfish. He needed some urging, and I gave it."

"Did he keep her tucked away for her own protection or because he was ashamed of her? Because she didn't fit the perfect Dixit mold?"

Her face dropped, and for a second, she wasn't a Bollywood legend, but a tired older woman. She'd shrunk, he realized, in the past year, her shoulders growing more stooped. "I think you know the answer to that."

Dev's grip tightened on the arms of his chair. He did know, and he hated it. "I miss him, but I also didn't like him very much."

Her smile was wry. "Welcome to being a part of a family. We don't choose every member, unfortunately."

People come in and out of our lives, and we have to enjoy the parts in the middle. But I think it's okay to not enjoy all the parts. "You're so close with Luna. She hasn't hugged me the way she hugs you."

Shweta feigned interest in her nails. "I do miss her."

"Why didn't you fight me on custody?"

"I fought your uncle once for custody of you because I was selfish. I didn't encourage him to see you. I regret that. Adil is a good man and would have raised you and Rohan to be good men." His grandmother gave a tired shrug. "I love Luna like she's the daughter I never had. But I knew she'd be better off with you. I knew you would give her the best home you possibly could, and you'd protect her."

Dev frowned, disquieted. He didn't like that his distant relationship with his grandmother had blinded him. He'd taken Luna across the world from the one person who had shown her unconditional love.

"Speaking of Luna, perhaps you should go tell her about the wedding? She'll be excited."

Dev didn't know about that. She'd reacted so poorly to the news of the engagement. And given what Aji had confirmed about Rohan, he didn't blame her. Still, it was his responsibility to tell her. "You're correct. Are you going to bed?"

His grandmother got a faraway look in her eyes. "No. I sleep late. I'll go listen to the ocean. It sounds different here, no?"

"Very different. Different isn't bad."

"No, it's not."

Dev hesitated, but there were so many more things he wished to say to his grandmother, he didn't know where to start. So he ended up only wishing her good night.

The house was big enough that he didn't come across any Ahmeds on the way to Luna's bedroom. The door was slightly ajar, and Luna and Arjun sat on the end of the bed, controllers in their hands, both of them intent on the racing game on the television. "You're still playing," he said.

Arjun raised a finger. "Hang on, I'm about to— shit!"

"Language," Dev reminded his cousin, but it was drowned out by Luna's whoop of victory.

His niece held out her hand. "Pay up."

"No gambling." Dev sat in an armchair close to the bed. God, he *was* boring, but he didn't know any other way to be.

"Don't worry, we're playing for candy." Arjun pulled a wrapped sweet from his pocket. "I'd be broke if we were playing for money. Did you have a good dinner?" There was no animosity in his voice for not being invited.

Was *good* the right word for going from a rushed engagement to a rushed wedding? "Yes, we did." He paused. "Arjun, can you excuse us? I need to speak with Luna."

"Sure." Arjun tousled their niece's hair affectionately. His face was softer than Dev had ever seen it. "See you later, beti."

Dev smiled at Luna once his cousin was gone. "You had fun with Arjun Kaka?"

"Oh yes. When Baba was around, he came by once a week, at least, and always played with me."

She'd seen Arjun more than she'd seen him. Had Luna and Arjun also been close? Had he taken her away from two people who had loved her? "Do you ever wish we'd stayed in India?"

Luna tossed her controller to the bed and curled her legs under her. "Sometimes. Mostly I miss Aji and Arjun Kaka. It's nice that they could visit."

Do you wish you could have lived with them instead of me? Only that was far too heavy a question to lay on his niece right now, before he'd talked to her therapist. "I have something I need to tell you. Jia and I decided that we'd like to hold the wedding tomorrow."

She froze. "Your wedding?"

"Yes."

"Your and Jia's wedding?"

"Yes."

The famous Dixit muscle ticked in her small jaw. "Why? You said there would be time."

"I know. And there will be, but we thought . . . it's convenient, to do it now, while your grandmother is here. This will purely be to make things legal. We'll have a big reception later down the road."

Her face darkened. "She's going to live with us right away?"

Luna was jumping ahead of them with logistics. He didn't know what was going to happen after the wedding. Was Jia planning on moving in? Her home was big, but she had roommates, and they couldn't all move in with her. Did she want some time to herself? She'd never even lived on her own. Perhaps she needed a taste of independence before she launched into wedded life.

Later. He'd deal with that later. "Do you honestly see her as a wicked stepmother?"

"You don't know what someone's like right away!"

"I would never bring anyone into our home who would hurt you," Dev said simply. "You're my number one priority, Luna. I'll put you first. Do you trust me?"

The naked longing in her gaze broke his heart. He got up and came to sit next to her, pulling her close to him. "I don't want to lose this." Her voice was muffled.

There was no way he would let her lose her stability. "You're not losing anything. You're gaining someone who is going to do their best to love you and care about you as much as I do."

Her answer was a skeptical hmm, and he squeezed her. "Give her a chance? Please?"

Luna's sigh was long, but there was acceptance in it. "Fine. No promises, though."

Jia had tried to sleep, but after talking some more with her parents and then calling her older sisters and navigating their surprise and dismay—though Noor had been pretty pumped about that inheritance—she'd been too wound up to settle down. Plus, one of Dev's texts had worried her. Can you please include Luna tomorrow?

It was too much to hope the child would welcome her with open arms. Of course she'd include Luna when they were getting ready. Hopefully, she'd warm up quickly.

Around midnight, Jia crept downstairs. She quietly opened the back door and slipped outside, taking a deep bracing breath of the chilly night air. She stopped at who was seated at the patio table.

"Auntie," she said, surprised. "I'm sorry, I didn't expect anyone to be out here." She pulled her sweatshirt tighter.

"I actually feared you and Dev might be out here together in a tryst. Truly, he's nothing like the other men in his family," Shweta said dryly.

Jia tried to resist the urge to smooth her clothes. She and Dev hadn't done anything yet, so there was no need to get embarrassed in front of his grandmother. Except for the parade of thoughts that ran through her mind about Dev's arms and legs and back and everything every time she saw him. "I came out for some air. If you'll—"

"Have a seat." Shweta nodded at the chair next to hers.

There was no way to avoid a direct order from an elder, so Jia walked over and sat down. Shweta produced a pack of cigarettes and a lighter from her flowing nightgown. "Do you smoke?" she asked Jia and lit up.

"No." *Not your place, not your place . . .* "Should you be smoking?"

Shweta took a long drag. "You should have asked me that question thirty years ago. A little late now, hmm? Might as well enjoy a cigarette now and then before I go."

Jia bit her lip. "I'm sorry you're sick."

"I'm sorry, too. Of course, Dev told you I may have exaggerated my condition for your parents?"

"He did, yes." Jia had been relieved for Dev's sake. Who faked a medical illness to get their own way?

She thought Shweta might apologize, but instead, the older woman stared out at the sea. "Is Burbank far from here?"

"An hour, maybe?"

"Ah. I slept with a dashing producer at his home there thirty-five years ago or so." She cast a glance at Jia's face and chuckled. "Don't look so shocked. You should have seen me then."

"I'm more shocked that you're telling me you did it, not about the act. And I saw you then. You were stunning."

"I was. I thought I wasn't. At that age, I was playing the mother of men who were older than me, while my husband was still playing the hero with nineteen-year-old actresses." Shweta shook her head in disgust. "He played the hero with them offscreen too."

"I'm sorry," Jia said, though she wasn't sure if she was supposed to say anything at all.

"I fear Arjun, Arjun's father, and Rohan followed in Vivek's footsteps. Philanderers. I told myself boys will be boys, but I should have done a better job with them."

Jia shifted. This was getting into deeply personal territory, and she didn't think she was supposed to be listening to it.

"You know Rohan's the reason Dev left Mumbai, don't you? After Rohan died, you could see how guilty he felt for not grieving him more. I don't blame him for running away. I often dreamed of starting fresh somewhere, but I didn't have the courage. That's the man you're marrying, Jia. Resourceful and clever and brave. He takes after his father." Sadness darkened Shweta's eyes. "Possibly his mother, too, though I didn't know her well."

"You care for him deeply."

"He's the best of us," she admitted softly. "Him and Luna. I want him to be happy. I apologize for pushing the two of you this evening, but I have spent a lot of time lately thinking of the things I regret. Ensuring his future is set will give me ease."

"I understand. My parents want the best for me and my sisters too. But you can't push someone into doing what you think is the best for them. You have to kind of hope that they just find the best."

Shweta's gaze was unwavering. "Are you saying you're not the best?"

Jia scoffed. "I'd never say that."

"I wouldn't either. In spite of your background and inability to speak our language, I believe I will be getting a decent granddaughter in you."

"You'll get someone who won't tolerate you speaking that

way about her." Jia lifted her chin. "I'll try to learn your language, but all of me is more than decent."

Shweta laughed, the dry bark turning into a cough. She shook her head when Jia almost came to her feet. "I'm okay," she wheezed.

Jia drummed her fingers on her leg. "You won't be staying in California for long?"

"Oh no." Shweta looked out at the ocean again. "I don't belong here. I only came to see my grandson taken care of."

Anticipation and nerves fluttered in Jia's belly. "I'll take care of him."

Shweta smiled faintly. "I believe you will. I've watched your videos, you know. If you wished it, you could go into acting. You have a very expressive face."

That was high praise, coming from Shweta. "Acting's not a part of my plan."

"What is?"

"I want to have my own line of makeup, especially focused on girls of color."

"Then why don't you?"

Jia shook her head. "Not yet."

Shweta nodded. "Be careful how many times in your life you say not yet, beti. You'd be surprised how quickly time flies." Her long fingers stubbed out her cigarette in the ashtray on the table. "I suppose I shall go rest now. I won't be able to stand it if I have puffy eyes tomorrow."

"I know a great trick for that."

"I'm sure you do."

Chapter Twenty-Four

Are you sure you want to do this?"

Jia paused in curling her hair. Her mother stood behind her. Her hands had probably gone numb from all the wringing she was doing.

Jia was anxious, too, but for other reasons. They'd decided to hold the ceremony around sunset to capitalize on golden hour lighting—her insistence—and though that was hours away, she had a ton of things to do before then.

She'd called Rhiannon and Katrina in the morning to break the news to them. They'd been shocked, but rallied quickly to support her decision and take down her instructions on what clothes to pull from her closet.

She'd texted Lakshmi, too, after a brief hesitation, and invited her to the ceremony. They weren't besties yet, but she hoped soon she'd be able to count the other woman a vital member of her girl group. Unfortunately, Lakshmi was out of town, but had conveyed her congrats. She hadn't seemed surprised at all.

"Jia?"

Jia tried to focus on her mother. "Yup. Hand me the pins from over there?"

"You sound calm," Ayesha remarked and fetched the pins.

"Too calm," Farzana said grimly.

"I thought you've always wanted me to be calm." Jia placed the curling iron down and used her fingers to loosen up the waves. She twisted the tamed strands into a bun and pinned them into place.

"I didn't want you to be calm about having a shotgun wedding."

Ayesha covered her mouth when she yawned and plopped down on the bed. Her hair was still wet from her shower. "I think for it to be a shotgun wedding, she'd have to be pregnant."

"Don't even joke about such things. Jia, we can work through this, figure out what to say to put off Shweta without insulting her. I haven't had practice dealing with many pushy potential in-laws, but I watched my mother manipulate the mothers of every suitor who came to my door. I shall leave the window open for a future marriage between you and Dev while still ensuring that it doesn't happen now."

"I want it now."

Her mother's smile slipped. "Dear, be reasonable."

Ugh. Yet another phrase Jia had heard a lot in her life. "I am being reasonable."

Farzana started pacing, like she hadn't even heard Jia. "I will still not sacrifice my daughter's happiness. You are my priority, just as her grandson is hers." Farzana shook her head. "Of course, the inheritance complicates things, but he has the capacity to earn money. You'll be taken care of one way or another. Your father and I have discussed this. It is unacceptable to shove you into a marriage with a man you barely know."

"I can take care of myself." Still, Jia was touched. She'd misjudged her mother and how much she wanted rich husbands for her daughters due to her own leftover immigrant trauma of arriving in a new country broke and hungry. This level of ferocious mama bear protection was so heartwarming.

Too bad it was coming at the wrong time. There was a certain amusing irony in the fact that her mother was dead set against Jia marrying the man she'd originally fake dated to impress her. Later, when she had time and didn't have to think about which eyeshadow palettes she needed, she'd laugh at this. "I know him. Don't worry about it."

Farzana released a deep sigh and leaned back against the poster of the bed. "I swear to God, child, I will never understand you."

Jia grimaced. "I know. I wish you could. I'm sorry I'm disappointing you. Again." She was sorry, and yet, the panic she might normally feel at disappointing her parents was nowhere to be found. Did she not need anyone's approval anymore?

The heroine swans offstage to do whatever the hell she wants, Teflon courses through her veins.

Okay, that might be a bit of an exaggeration, but not much. Bless Lakshmi.

Farzana's chest rose, and her next words surprised Jia. "I

learned many years ago that any disappointment I feel with any of my daughters is my issue to deal with, not yours." She walked over to the vanity and touched Jia's face. "I love you. I want you to be happy. Your heart is so kind and precious. I suppose that's why we're all so protective of you. We never want to see you hurt."

Jia curled her hand around her mother's, holding it to her cheek. "I always thought you were hovering over me because you thought I was a goofball who couldn't tie my own shoes without help," she said lightly, though she wasn't joking. Her chest had gone all tight.

"No. You can do anything you put your mind to." Farzana dropped a kiss on her head. "We've known that from the time you were a baby. You dream so big, but dreams don't always come true."

"I don't see much point in putting dreams away on the off chance they won't come true." She noticed Ayesha freeze in the mirror. "Right, Ayesha?"

Her twin cleared her throat. She busied herself folding a shirt. "Right."

Her mother inhaled. "I don't want to see you hurt."

"I don't think I will be. But if I am, it's how I'll learn and grow."

Her mother nodded. "You know my feelings, but I will support you, if you truly want to do this. InshAllah, you will be happy."

This wasn't the woman who had screamed at Sadia all those years ago for marrying an unsuitable man. Jia wasn't the only one who had grown. "Thank you, Mom."

A knock came at the door, and Luna peeked in, her face wary and concerned. "Hi. My uncle told me you were looking for me."

"We were, yes." Jia motioned her in. "I thought you might like to get ready with us."

Luna came fully into the room. "Okay." She stopped when she noticed Ayesha and her mother in the room as well.

If there was one thing their mother knew, though, it was young girls. She took charge, placing her arm around Luna. "Hello, dear. We didn't get a chance to get acquainted yesterday. You may call me Auntie Farzana. Come, let's see what dress you've chosen to wear today." She took the garment bag from Luna's arms.

"Aji brought me clothes from India, so I picked one of those."

Jia smiled. "Excellent. Why don't you get dressed, Luna, and then we can discuss what you'd like to do with your hair and makeup."

Luna looked moderately interested. "Are you going to do it?"

Jia picked up a makeup brush and swished it in the air. "Do you honestly think I'd let anyone else do it? Come here, I have something for you, too."

Luna accepted the wrapped present Jia handed her. "Should I open it now?"

"Yes, you'll need it for the day."

Luna's chuckle when she opened the gift was small, but authentic. "Did Kaka tell you I spend too much time on my phone?"

"He did, indeed. Now you can make sure it has style."

Luna turned the crystal-encrusted phone case over in her hands, and the fake diamonds winked. When she pressed a button on the side, the border of the case lit up, like a built-in ring light. Jia gave a moment of thanks for her goody bag stash. There was no way she would have had time to get a teen-friendly present amidst this chaos.

"He got me a boring old black case. This'll match my dress today. Thanks." There was wary interest in Luna's gaze when she looked up.

Jia wasn't naïve enough to think the girl would be won over with one present, but it couldn't hurt. "Not a problem."

Another knock came on the door, and Rhiannon and Katrina walked in. Rhiannon held up dry cleaning bags and a bottle of sparkling grape juice. "Hello all! Looking for the bridal suite."

Farzana beamed at Rhiannon. "Rhiannon, how are you? Your mother says hello, and told me to tell you to call her."

Rhiannon nodded and hugged Jia's mother. "Sounds about right."

After everyone greeted everyone else, Rhiannon threw her arm around Jia's shoulder. Her friend looked at her with concern, not condemnation. "Are you sure you want to do this?"

"Yes." She braced herself for the arguments, the reasons against it, but Rhiannon's lips curled.

"He's no peach blush, eh?"

"Not in the slightest."

"Then let's get you married."

DEV FOUND MOHAMMAD sitting on the deck of the house, overlooking the beach. He approached slowly, more than a little worried. Had this been a normal state of events, he would have already spent a great deal of time with his soon-to-be father-in-law. As it was, he only had time to get the man's blessing before the ceremony in a couple hours.

Jia's father glanced up as he approached and gave him a kind smile. He was dressed in a slightly baggy suit. "Dev."

"Dr. Ahmed."

"Please, no need to revert to formalities. Mohammad is fine."

"Okay." He took a deep breath, bracing himself. "I know this is all a little unorthodox."

Mohammad laughed. "A little. I understand family dynamics, especially when there's an elder who may or may not be sick, Dev. But I fear your family is using my daughter."

Dev paused. "Is that what Jia said? That she feels like she is being used?" He hadn't seen her since last night. Had she changed her mind?

"Not at all. She is ready and willing to marry you immediately. I know what you're here for, for my blessing. I thank you for seeking it, but I am hesitant to give it." Mohammad raised his hand and counted off each point. "You two barely know each other. We barely know you. I do not appreciate one of my daughters being pressured into a commitment, especially into a family that is so different from our own, one that has such a wildly different way of life. This inheritance business alone is strange."

"I am well aware of that. My grandfather was a strange man." He spread his hands. "I don't care about the money, at all, by the way."

"Then why rush? We take marriage seriously. It is not something I want one of my children to enter into lightly." There was a finality to Mohammad's words that struck fear into Dev's heart. It was scarier than if the man had yelled his opposition to this match.

"It's not something I enter into lightly," Dev said quietly. "And I think it matters how Jia feels. She wants this wedding now, and I want what she wants."

"Jia has a history of jumping into situations with both feet, without looking."

"And she always lands on her feet, does she not? The decisions she makes are good for her."

Mohammad's eyes narrowed, and Dev finally caught the upset the man had been hiding behind his easygoing facade. "Just because she gets lucky—"

"It's not lucky. You only think she's lucky because she makes things look easy. Have you watched her videos? I've watched every single one. She makes shadows appear on her face where there are none! She excels at making difficult things look flawless when in fact she is putting one hundred percent of herself into everything she does. She's smart. She's not flighty."

"That may be—"

"No maybe about it, it is." Dev shook his head, frustrated. "She craves your and her mother's approval, but she can't change who she is. And who she is is someone who propels herself into life without spending eons weighing all the pros and cons. I admire that about her."

Mohammad studied him. "You've watched all her videos?"

"Yes." Dev clasped his hands together. He didn't know if he'd ever spoken so passionately in his life, off a stage.

Mohammad looked out over the ocean. "She is set on this impulsive wedding," he said quietly.

Dev knew that, but his heart still soared. "Good," he managed. "So am I."

"Very well. I can't stop you, and I'm not about to repeat history by opposing another daughter's choice in a mate." Mohammad's chest rose. "I suppose once you are married, we will have plenty of time to get to know each other."

The relief was overwhelming. "We will."

"And this is only the formality. We want her to have a proper celebration as soon as possible."

"That's what I want as well."

"I will want to spend some time with this imam your grandmother found, to make sure we approve."

"Of course."

Jia's father sighed. "Then I believe we should discuss the marriage contract, yes?"

Elation soared through Dev. "Yes."

The older man reached into his pocket and pulled out his phone. "First things first, however. Her sisters wanted to meet you before the ceremony. Do you mind if I call them?"

He would agree to walk on hot coals at this point. "Not at all."

Mohammad handed Dev the phone, stood, and clapped him on the shoulder. "Survive this"—he nodded at the phone—"and I'll give you my blessing."

What? He didn't have time to clarify what the older man meant, though, because the call connected.

"Hello?"

"Hello?"

"Well, well, well. Look who it is."

Dev focused on the small phone screen. He could identify them based on Jia's descriptions alone. The woman with the hijab and the oxygen tank, that was Noor. The polished one, that was Zara. The pregnant woman, Sadia. "Hello," he said and waved. "Um, I'm Dev. It's a pleasure to meet you."

Noor squinted at him. "You're not that handsome in real life."

His lips parted.

"Are you still tall at least?"

"Yes," he managed.

"Good. We could use some more tall genes in this family."

"It's a pleasure to meet you," Sadia said warmly. The peacemaker of the family, but also the one who had rebelled to marry the man she loved. "This wedding has come as a shock to us. We're sorry we can't be there."

"Still not quite sure why it has to be today." Zara's eyes narrowed. "What's your game, what's the rush?"

"Ah—"

"Besides your grandmother," Noor interjected. "So sorry about that."

"And this ridiculous will," Zara added. "Which I'm still skeptical of. I'd like a copy, please."

Dev would have whiplash if they were here. "I'm sorry you can't be here as well. As for the rush, well, Jia and I simply . . . we wish to be together, as quickly as possible."

Sadia visibly softened, but the eldest sisters didn't so much as bat an eye. "Jia told us you were willing to wait, despite your grandma and the money, so that's a point for you," Noor said.

Thank God. He imagined he'd need many points.

"Are you rushing just for sex?" Zara demanded.

"Oh God, no." He looked around, fearing someone might hear. "I'd never . . . for that."

"He's blushing," Sadia said. "That's cute."

"Listen, Dev. We love our sister very much."

He met Noor's eyes. Her worried eyes. "I understand. I know what it's like to protect family."

"Good. Then you know that if you hurt her, there is nowhere on this planet you could go where we would not destroy you."

"We don't care how much money you have or how much power your family wields. We will kill you and make it look like an accident. We're physicians. We know exactly how to do that." Zara's teeth flashed, and her bright smile was made scarier by her fierce words.

Sadia stroked her belly. "Shoot, I'm just a bartender, but I'll happily stab an ice pick through your eye."

So much for the peacemaker.

He didn't mind, though. He wished he could have had a sibling relationship like this. He was happy Jia had it. Maybe eventually, her siblings could become his. "Understood," Dev repeated. "I won't hurt her, I promise."

"Sweet." Noor's smile was chilling as well, but contained a trace of friendliness. "Now, let's get this wedding on the road, eh?"

Chapter Twenty-Five

Dᴇᴠ ʜᴀᴅɴ'ᴛ played the center of attention at a party in . . . well, ever. Tonight, though, he was smack-dab, literally, in the center of the room, seated with Jia on the low couch. He'd opted for what he had easiest access to and donned a western suit. She wore an icy white shalwar kameez with delicate silver beading and a silver hijab to match. As usual, everything was perfectly color coordinated, from her shoes to her jewelry. He'd used his niece as a small spy and had matched Jia with a white rose boutonniere, tied with a silver ribbon.

The imam was a kind man who had seemed only mildly star struck over Shweta, but had quickly gotten down to business to speak with their elders and go over the marriage contract and impart some words of wisdom to Dev and Jia before the event. Dev had tried to pay attention to every second of the ceremony so he could commit it to memory, but he was so distracted by Jia's elegant profile and all the warmth inside of him that he could barely focus.

This was what happiness felt like. No, wait, even more specifically: this was what a family felt like. Was that all he'd been missing, all those empty aching spots inside him? It hadn't been a lack of love in him. It had been people to give his affection to. Who could have known.

As the ceremony wrapped up, Dev stiffened. Oh shoot. A ring. They hadn't discussed whether they'd exchange rings, but he'd wanted to get one for Jia.

Like she'd read his mind, his grandmother nudged him, a blue box in her hand.

He accepted it, grateful. "Thank you."

She held on to the box a little longer than necessary. "It was your father's, inherited from your great-grandparents," she said quietly. "So consider it a gift from him, not me."

He nodded, touched. "Thank you again, then." He flipped open the box and nearly choked at what was inside. By Jia's gasp, he could tell she was shocked too.

"Holy moly, is that rock for my finger or for a mountain?"

"Jia," her mother hissed and poked her from behind. While Farzana clearly had her reservations about their marriage, she'd gotten into the spirit of things. Her makeup was flawless, and her light blue outfit set off the sapphire earrings in her ears and the bangles on her wrist.

Jia cleared her throat. "Sorry."

"An understandable reaction," Dev said. The ring was set in platinum and boasted a clear yellow diamond, surrounded by a dozen smaller diamonds. It was heavy and gaudy, and when he slipped it on Jia's small finger, it nearly toppled over from its own weight.

"It's . . . nice," she said weakly.

He clasped her cold fingers between his. "We'll buy you

something else next week," he murmured. He'd already planned on a proper engagement ring to make up for the piece of fabric he'd used to propose to her. He'd buy a matched set, as well as a band for him.

There was something about others knowing that he belonged to Jia that quite pleased him.

"Oh, but you gave this to me tonight."

"It's a perfectly nice ring," Noor chimed in, her voice fuzzy from the tablet Farzana was holding.

"We can put this ring on a chain for you to wear and get you something more to your taste." He readjusted the top-heavy ring. "Deal?"

Jia smiled up at him. "Deal."

He wanted to drop a kiss on her upturned nose, but married or not, he couldn't imagine kissing her in front of both their families. He returned her grin, instead.

It was the last second they had to look into each other's eyes before their families toasted them and they posed for photos. His grandmother oozed satisfaction, and Dev was so happy, he couldn't even be annoyed that her manipulations had worked. Adil Uncle was still a little muted around his grandmother, but he beamed with pride. Dev had hired a caterer to do the heavy lifting for their celebratory dinner, so his uncle could relax and enjoy his time. He and Mohammad had a love of tennis in common, so they'd quickly become friends.

Arjun, Dev was happy to note, was on his best behavior, charming the elder Ahmeds with stories of Bollywood scandals. When he started in on charming Ayesha, though, Dev intervened, pulling him aside. "Watch it," he murmured to his cousin.

Arjun opened his eyes wide. "I'm just talking to her!"

"Best that be all you do."

Arjun grumbled. "I wouldn't dare. Besides, she's not my type. Do you know if Jia's friends . . . ?"

"Both in relationships."

Arjun pouted. "You could have invited someone for me, Bhai."

"You're lucky to be here at all."

A rare flash of sobriety cleared Arjun's face. "I agree. Thank you, both of you, for giving me a second chance. I don't deserve it. But I do wish you many wonderful years together."

Dev dropped his hand on his cousin's shoulder for a second and squeezed. "Thank you."

Their grandmother joined them. "Arjun, you will be next, of course."

The younger man took a step back, and then kept walking. "I'm sorry, you're breaking up. I am going through a tunnel."

Shweta shook her head indulgently, then turned to him. "Marriage looks good on you, Dev."

"It feels good, so far."

She adjusted her sari, though its sharp pleats needed no adjustment. "I was thinking I could stay for an extra week. Luna and Adil could remain here. It would give you and your new wife some alone time."

Dev took a sip of his sparkling water. Luna had warmed

to the excitement of the event, or at least, warmed to being dressed up and the only child in attendance, and thus, fawned over by everyone. Jia's sister had particularly bonded with his niece, and the girl was following Ayesha around like a duckling, asking for gruesome medical stories. "I think Luna would like that very much." So would his grandmother. Her eyes held a hint of yearning, more vulnerability than he'd seen from her outside of a movie screen. One week out of school wouldn't hurt his smart niece.

She raised her hand and beckoned Adil over. "I told Dev our plan," she explained to his uncle.

"Yes, it's a good idea." Adil Uncle smiled at him. "Newlyweds should have some time to themselves."

Dev tried not to think of what he and Jia could do with all that privacy. "I'll drive home tonight and get Luna's belongings."

"There's no need to do such a thing on your wedding night," his grandmother protested.

Adil agreed. "I will go."

The wedding night he wouldn't be able to actually spend with Jia? She was rooming with her sister, and his room had a full bed that barely fit him. Plus, if he couldn't kiss her in front of her parents, he didn't think he could sleep in the same bed with her while they were under the same roof, even if they didn't do anything. This was too new. "Jia will understand. Uncle, you have trouble driving at night."

"I'll buy Luna whatever she needs for the week."

Oh boy. This, he had to curb now. "No. Aji, try to refrain

from any lavish gifts, please. I can tell you this: I would have killed for affection in lieu of presents when we first came to live with you."

Something flickered in his grandmother's eyes. "Very well. I will spoil Luna with affection over the next week. And perhaps some small trinkets here and there."

"That's fine."

His grandmother patted him on the arm. "You've become a good man. I'll go tell Luna the news."

Adil rocked back on his heels. "She's right. You've become a very good man."

Dev turned his gaze to the floor, vaguely embarrassed by the praise. "You've helped with that, over the past year. I can't thank you enough."

"No thanks are necessary. We are family. You are the son I never had."

They both found it necessary to look away from each other after that. "Do you have any marriage advice for me?" Everyone had some advice for him, he'd found.

"Go slow. These are strange circumstances. You know, it would not even hurt for you to live apart for a time, while you learn about each other. Your aunt and I, we did not live together for a year after our nikah." His smile was nostalgic. "And then we had thirty perfect years together. There is value in patience."

Dev nodded, all that making sense to him. He wanted thirty, forty, fifty years with Jia. If that meant he had to go slow and steady in the beginning, that would be fine.

"I believe your bride is calling you."

His *bride*. A month ago, he wouldn't have thought such a word was even applicable to him. Dev made his way over to the table she stood next to, Luna at her side. *His family*.

"Time to cut the cake." She reached up, and he stilled, but she was only brushing something off his shoulder. Nonetheless, the wifely gesture pleased him.

He looked down at his niece. "Luna, I'm not sure I told you how pretty you look tonight."

Luna preened. She was beautiful, in a pale yellow dress Aji had brought for her. "Thank you. Jia taught me how to bring out my curls and minimize frizz."

It was thanks to his hundreds of hours of watching Jia's channel that Dev even knew what that meant. "Ah. Interesting."

His niece edged closer to him. "Did Aji speak to you?"

"Yes." He turned to his wife—wife! "Luna and Adil Uncle will be staying here for the week."

"Oh. Nice."

"I was thinking I'd go get their clothes from the house tonight and come back. You don't mind, do you? I'll be back late, so we can see each other in the morning."

Jia's brow furrowed for a second. "Um, sure. That's great."

"Good." He lowered his voice as Luna wandered away. "Are you happy?"

Her frown cleared. "Very."

"HE SEEMS CUTE."

"Cute? He's hot."

"Can you get me Arjun's autograph? It's not for me, it's for a friend."

Jia smiled at the screen of her tablet. She'd come into the bedroom to plug it in and say goodbye to her sisters. Though it had been her idea, she was sad that they hadn't been able to be here. "Thank you guys for staying up so late." They'd dressed up, too, though they were all the way across the country in their own homes.

"We wouldn't miss it for the world," Noor said warmly, and then yawned. "But I do have to get to bed."

"Me too," Zara said.

She said her goodbyes to the two of them and their screens winked off. Sadia took a sip of her lemonade and studied Jia. "Um, do we need to have a talk tonight?"

"A talk about what?"

Sadia cleared her throat. "You know. Birds and bees."

Jia's eyes widened. "For crying out loud. I was in medical school, Sadia. And I've had internet access forever. I know about the birds and bees."

Sadia fiddled with her shirt. "But you've never . . ."

"I've never wanted to," Jia pointed out. "Don't worry. I'm looking forward to this and know what to expect."

"Okay, but . . . if it's not that great the first time, that's okay. Sometimes it takes practice to get in the groove of things. And if he's not that good, but eager to please, you can work with that, as well. There's toys! And lots of material about—"

Jia nearly threw her tablet away. "Can we stop, please?"

"You're happy with this, right?"

Jia smiled softly. Everyone was asking her that tonight. "I know it's sudden, but yes. I'm happy."

"I'm not worried about it being sudden for you. You always did make faster decisions than anyone. I used to worry about it, but I don't any longer. You know what you're doing." Sadia gave her a warm grin. "Good night. Sneak away and kiss your handsome husband at least once tonight when Mom and Daddy aren't looking."

Her handsome husband was going to leave soon to go get Luna's things, and Jia probably wouldn't see him until tomorrow. Actually, she probably wouldn't have a private meeting with him until tomorrow night, after her parents left for the airport. Which was disappointing as heck.

She wasn't sure what she'd envisioned for her wedding night, but certainly, she'd hoped for at least a kiss. And more.

But that was far too much to explain to Sadia now. "I'll try," Jia said cheekily.

She put her tablet away. It was a little bizarre, actually, how little anxiety she felt. She pulled out her phone and navigated to the voice note she'd recorded during a small window of privacy earlier in the day. "Hi Jia," came her own voice. "Do you regret anything?"

"Nope," she said.

"Good. That's what confidence feels like. Memorize this feeling." The recording ended.

Are you sure you're confident? He seemed totally fine about running away from you right after the wedding.

She slammed the lid on that box of insecurities. He was a practical man, and Luna needed her stuff. Sure, could he have taken Jia with him? Could they have had a romantic night drive along the PCH, and at least smooched a little here and there, giddy on being young and married?

Sure. Sure. But again, he was practical. He wasn't too much, like her. He wasn't too little, either. He was just right.

Chapter Twenty-Six

JIA GLANCED in her rearview mirror at her mother. "Are you crying?"

"No," Farzana sobbed. Mohammad put his arm around his wife.

"She is having a delayed reaction to yesterday," her father said. "She'll be fine once she's on the plane."

Farzana wailed. "Soon all my daughters will be gone."

"Are we dying or getting married?" Jia whispered to her sister and got a poke in return.

Ayesha twisted in her seat. "Mom, please. You can't cry all the way through LAX."

Farzana sniffled. "We should have accepted Shweta's offer to charter a plane for us."

"She just became family," Jia said dryly. "Let's not go taking advantage of the Dixit fortune right away, hmm?"

Farzana glared at Jia, which was better than crying in her back seat. "What a tacky thing to suggest. I would never."

Jia inched along in the LAX roundabout. The traffic was, as usual, horrendous, but luckily her family was flying out of the first terminal. "Sorry, Mom."

"You will bring Dev to our home next month, for at least a full week. That way we can all get to know him, and you can spend time with your sisters and we can plan your real wedding," Mohammad said. There was no arguing with the stern tone in his voice, and Jia didn't want to. As far as her father was concerned, yesterday's ceremony had merely been paperwork.

"Of course."

"Good."

They pulled up in front of the terminal and said goodbye in a flurry of hugs and kisses. Jia's mood depressed a little as she left her family and got back in her car.

She placed her hands on the steering wheel, then frowned. Where was she supposed to go? She hadn't discussed this with Dev before leaving. The house had been so busy, what with her family packing up and saying their goodbyes. She'd only waved at him.

She called Dev as she worked her way out of the airport's congestion.

He answered on the first ring. "Hello?"

"I dropped them off. I'm leaving LAX now." She wiped her palms on her pant legs.

"I'm home. Would you . . . would you like to come to my home for dinner? I mean. Our home? The flat?"

Her heart sped up. There was no need to get too excited. She'd been to his home before, and they'd had dinner together.

Never as a married couple, though.

"Sure."

"Great. See you soon."

She hung up and made sure she drove as sedately as possible, though she wanted to speed demon all the way there. She'd be so annoyed if she got delayed by a ticket, though.

Dev opened the door before Jia could knock and then looked sheepish. "The guard rang me that you were coming up."

"Oh, how nice." She took a step in and gazed up at him.

She wasn't sure who moved first, but their mouths fused together. Slowly, his arms came around her waist, pulling her tight to him.

For all the suddenness, it was relatively chaste. No tongue, just softly parted lips brushing against each other. Still, this sweet, soft kiss made her feel like the Fourth of July had taken up residence in her belly. Forget butterflies, she had fireworks.

His hand smoothed up and down her back. She wound her arms around his neck and rose up on her tiptoes, but it was still hard to get the right angle, him being so much taller than her.

He made a rough noise against her lips and lifted her abruptly off her feet. The wall came up against her back for support, and he pressed himself against her front, keeping her suspended there. She felt shameless as she wrapped her wobbly legs around his waist for stability.

How could she have wondered if her attraction to Dev was based on anything other than him in real life? This desire ran bone-deep, and it wasn't for any photo on her phone, but for the flesh-and-blood man.

Dear diary, this is how you kiss a woman.

Everything was new and clumsy, but neither of them cared. His tongue brushed against hers, and the sensation was so delightful she sought it out, chasing his warmth. His hands grew more sure on her waist as they kissed for long minutes, warm, drugging kisses that shoved every other thought out of her head.

He was so warm and strong, and she wanted to crawl inside him and steal some of that warmth for herself. She plastered herself against him tighter.

He ripped his mouth away and she moaned. "We don't have to do this right now," he said.

What? Her brain was a bunch of fried synapses that were never going to fire again.

"Would you rather wait? Or have dinner? It doesn't have to be tonight, even."

Being a gentleman was all cute, but not now. "Are you trying to kill me?" she wheezed.

His smile was slow. "I take that as a no."

"I'm tired of waiting. I'm certain. Are you?"

"More certain than I've ever been of anything." He paused. "I regret to inform you of one thing, though."

"What's that?"

"There's only one bed."

Her laughter trailed behind them as he carried her to the bedroom. She wrapped her arms and legs around him like a spider monkey and kissed his neck and cheeks, the stubble there making her lips tingle.

Her legs were wobbly when he lowered her to her feet

next to the bed, but she steadied herself against the night-stand. The curtains in the room were closed, the midday sun peeking around them, their own sexy cocoon.

His fingers were economical and quick as he unbuttoned his shirt, but her mind provided a bass beat for her first private striptease. Each motion revealed a new, tantalizing slice of skin and muscle. His flat brown nipples were fascinating. She wanted to touch them, and then she remembered she could do exactly that.

He stood patiently for her while she took her time exploring his torso. Over the pebbled skin of his nipples, down the subtly ridged lean belly, around the perfect circle of his navel. She stroked her forefinger along his smooth flank and slowly moved around him in a full circle, trailing that finger over his back, along his other side, back to his belly button.

She faced him. "Pretty good view, sir."

His face cracked a smile, but his gaze was hot. Still, he stood there, his body vibrating but leashed.

"I suppose I should be taking things off, too."

His nostrils flared, but he neither agreed nor disagreed.

He was leaving everything up to her, she realized. Oh, fun. She quickly undid her head scarf. She wished she could have brushed out her hair—it didn't fall out in a cascade of curls, but in a limp bun. Scarf head, her nemesis.

He didn't seem to mind, though. "Do you need help taking the pins out?"

She could do her hair in her sleep, but she nodded and turned around. His forearm grazed her shoulder as he removed the pins from her bun, one by one. She counted them as he unraveled her.

Her hair fell down her back, and his long, elegant fingers combed through it. Her eyes slit in pleasure as he rubbed her head gently, taking away the pressure of her hairstyle.

She turned around and pulled off her shirt and pants, until she was standing in front of him in only a lacy bra and panties. "You're overdressed," she pointed out, and she'd had no idea she could sound so throaty and sexy.

His smile was slow and he stripped off his pants, and his boxer briefs, too. Her husband fisted his erection and stroked it, bringing a flush to her cheeks. No, her whole body. "What are you thinking?" he asked.

She answered without thinking. "That I hope we both like this."

Dev's chuckle was low and more confident than she'd ever heard from him. "Consider that my mission." He crossed the distance between them and placed a kiss on her shoulder. Then along her neck. She tilted her head back to give him more access.

Her bra sagged as he unhooked it. Her panties fell on the floor, and then he was walking her backward, until the backs of her knees hit the bed. She sat down and he sat next to her, gently pushing her back to a reclining position.

She closed her eyes as his lips moved over her whole body. It was nice when he touched her nipples, but she gasped when he licked her belly. He paused, then did it again. He was plucking open nerve endings she hadn't known existed.

When his fingers found her clitoris, she nearly jackknifed

up, but he pressed her back down again firmly. He slipped off the bed to kneel on the floor. "Wait," she blurted out.

Dev stilled immediately. "Yes?"

She hadn't thought they'd get to oral sex right away. Jia rose up on her elbows and stared down at her husband's face. His hair was tousled, his breathing fast. "Nothing, I wanted you to know I've really been looking forward to this act, but no pressure, I'm sure you'll do great."

He nodded. "Thank you." He lowered his head and licked her, and she fell back.

Dev alternated his touch between soft and hard, quick and slow. This kind of kissing was new and a little clumsy, too, but he was a quick learner and totally attuned to her every sigh. She squeezed her eyes shut tight, until starbursts exploded.

Oh wait. Those starbursts were from him, and the orgasm he was giving her. She opened her eyes. If she'd had the energy, she would have pumped her arms and given a whoop of joy, but all she could do was give his head a single pat. His hair was coarse yet silky, and she stayed to pet it. "Nice," she muttered.

He pushed himself up on his arms and moved, gently rearranging her limp body farther up the bed. Dev kissed her mouth, and then her cheek. "Condom," she managed to say.

He nibbled her ear, making her shudder. "Already on. Don't worry."

When! But that was okay. He was right, Jia didn't have to worry with Dev. There was no doubt he had her best interests at heart.

She embraced him while he slid inside her. It was a strange sensation. Tight and too intrusive. "Okay?" he asked.

Jia shifted, seeking some kind of relief from that over-filled feeling. "It's not bad."

His lips twitched. "I'd like it to be more than that." He lowered his head and kissed her. While she focused on that, his hand slipped between them, finding the bundle of nerves he'd already skillfully finessed.

Her legs relaxed around his hips, and the fit grew easier. His body moved slowly, giving her plenty of time to adjust. She didn't feel the urge to have an orgasm now, and while pleasurable, this wasn't as good as what he'd done to her before. Still, she gained happiness in his facial expressions, the nerves he was stroking, the way his sweat dripped off his body onto hers.

When he came inside her, she stroked his sweaty shoulders and breathed as fast as him. Dev lifted his head and looked down at her. "Holy . . ." He shook his head. "That was amazing."

"Yeah. Much better than not bad. Pretty great, actually."

His chuckle was weak. He reached between them and slid out of her, and then staggered to the bathroom.

A stray thought whispered through her brain when he came back and she sat up straight as he got under the covers. "I'm supposed to pee."

Dev looked vaguely confused, but he nodded, and she swung her legs off the bed. She pondered wrapping the comforter around herself, but that was foolish. He'd been inside of her. He was her husband. He was naked, too.

She was supremely conscious of his gaze on her bare back as she walked to the bathroom, but this kind of attention was nice, too. If she hadn't been so blissed out, she would have watched him coming and going.

She glanced over her shoulder before she shut the door, and his eyes darted up from her butt. He gave a good-natured shrug. "Don't mind me, just watching."

She chuckled. She did her business quickly, eager to get back to bed. It was as she was washing her hands that she noticed the bottles next to the sink.

She picked up the familiar cleansers, and then the essence. There was a serum she loved, too, and a snail mucin she was rather fond of. Had Dev stocked her favorite skin care supplies for her?

She shook a bottle. They'd been used, though.

Jia left the bathroom, a quizzical smile on her face, and her husband's attention snapped right back to her. "I have to ask you something." She came to a stop next to the bed and nudged him over. This was her side.

He moved to the other side without protest, and opened his arms. She flowed right into them and twined her legs with his hairier ones. "What?" His chest rumbled.

She stuck her thumb over her shoulder. "What's the deal with the skin care stuff? It's too much of a coincidence that we like the same exact products, right?"

The room was dim, but it couldn't hide his ruddy cheeks. "Ah. I bought whatever you recommended online. It got to be a habit."

Jia rolled her lips in tight. It wouldn't do for him to think she was laughing at him. "That's adorable."

"It is?" His shoulders lowered. "Oh good. I just realized it might seem a little stalker like."

"Oh, if you weren't so handsome and talented and married to me, it might be. Context really is everything." She snuggled deeper in his arms, sleepily smiling when he kissed her forehead. "Hope you used my affiliate links."

He pulled her close, spooning her tight. They lay in silence for a little bit, and though Jia wasn't a huge fan of silence, it felt rather right here.

"Any regrets?" Dev asked.

"About the sex?"

"About anything."

"Nope."

He stroked her arm. "Can you stay the night?"

She paused. Boy, they really hadn't talked about important stuff. Here they were married, and he was asking if they could have a sleepover. But instead of delving into things like their future living situation, she kept it light. "I'd like that."

He rolled her over. "Good. We'll order dinner in ten minutes."

It turned into an hour, but she didn't mind.

Chapter Twenty-Seven

Until he'd lived with Luna and his uncle, Dev had never really been eager to get home. Home had just been a place to sleep. After only a couple of days married to Jia, though, Dev found himself counting the minutes until he could leave the set.

While he waited for production to wrap he scrolled through the photos of the house his real estate agent had sent him. The flat was fine for now, but they needed more room. He was loath to touch his grandfather's money, but he had enough saved on his own that he could manage a decent house.

"Hey, man, congratulations."

Dev lowered his phone and smiled at Hudson. He'd been fielding congratulations all day. Paparazzi had been camped outside his building since the news of his wedding had "leaked," but he and Jia had managed to dodge them.

The surprise wedding had caused a small stir, but not nearly of the same magnitude as the engagement. Unless Jia's waistline started expanding soon, the media would eventually lose interest. It would be nice to settle into marriage with some degree of normalcy.

"Thank you."

Hudson dropped into the seat next to him. "You should have said something. Can't believe we found out about your marriage from the gossip sites."

Chandu had released a statement, along with one of their wedding photos. In it, he'd been looking down at Jia while she gazed bashfully at the floor. He'd wanted to choose one of the photos where they'd been smiling and laughing, but his agent had assured him the one they'd run would get better press.

Whatever. He was more concerned about the fact that Jia still hadn't moved in. He'd brought up a potential living arrangement and she'd vaguely said something about not being in a hurry. He didn't want her to think he was in a hurry! So he'd dropped the topic like a hot potato. She could keep ferrying clothes back and forth from her home, and they could decide at a later date what they'd do long-term. In the meantime, he'd keep looking for houses that would suit them. "Apologies, it was a sudden decision, and a private affair."

"I understand, totally. The engagement sounded sudden, too." Hudson paused, like he thought Dev might give him some dirt. When he remained quiet, the other man tossed his blond hair. "I had no idea what a big deal you were until that story broke, by the way. I thought you were a big fish in a little pond, but there you were, on supermarket tabloids, no less."

Dev raised an eyebrow at the edge in his costar's tone. "Are you saying India—the country—is a little pond?"

"You know what I mean."

"Not really. There's literally billions of us." He gestured at the set, and Kalpana the makeup artist, who wasn't far away. "And that's not counting the entire diaspora." He downplayed his fame out of humility and to distance himself from his family, but this golden child's condescension was annoying. "I was the lead of the top ranked serial for a decade. I am a big fish in a massive pond."

Hudson's face went tight, though Dev had kept his tone mild. Hudson waved the script he was holding. "No offense, dude. I came over here to offer my congrats and make sure you saw the rewrites. Looks like you get some time off to swim, big fish."

"What?" Dev accepted the sheaf of papers and thumbed through it, his alarm growing with every page. He'd essentially been cut out of the next episode, his role reduced to a few lines.

Hudson made a sympathetic noise. "I know, man, bummer. It happens to the best of us. Don't complain next time, or they get kinda cranky."

But Hudson had told him to . . . Dev nearly slapped himself. Of course Hudson had sabotaged him. The man's role had expanded to fill Dev's space, and he was chasing that shiny Emmy. "Thanks," he said, through gritted teeth, and came to his feet.

Hudson's smile was sweet. "No problem."

Dev texted Jia as he walked away from the asshole. Where are you?

Home.

On my way.

How do you feel about Chinese? she asked.

Sounds good. He hesitated, but put his phone away. Talking about his feelings instead of shoving them down in a box was hard enough in person. He didn't need to do it over text.

Jia was already unpacking the Chinese food when he got there. She gave him a bright smile when he walked in, and he responded. She was dressed in dark skinny jeans and a loose hot pink blouse. Her feet were bare, her toes painted a matching pink. She'd taken her hijab off but hadn't combed her hair, and a clump of it stuck out on top of her head. Beautiful.

"Hey there, handsome."

He smiled, some of the emotional weight leaving him. "Hello." He pressed a kiss on her cheek, though she turned her face so it would land on her lips. She was so sweet. Simply being in her presence eased him. "Smells good," he remarked, and went to the sink to wash his hands.

"Thank you, I've been toiling away all day to make it." She dumped lo mein in a bowl and handed him a pair of chopsticks.

They ate at the small breakfast table. "How was your day?" he asked.

"Great." She swung her legs, and that was when he noticed the vibrating energy running through her.

He stopped with a piece of broccoli halfway to his mouth. "Did something happen?"

"Yeah. I mean, it may not be a big deal. I got a call from this woman at MakeOut. She wants to have a meeting with me to discuss a makeup line."

The barely suppressed glee in her voice told him this was a potentially very big thing. "Congratulations!"

"Thank you." She nibbled on a snow pea. "I don't want to get too excited. I've been in talks for stuff like this before, and it's fallen through."

"If you get the line, will you move away from social media?"

"Not totally. But it would be a good stepping-stone to my eventual goal." Her eyes darkened. "Of course, it could bomb, and that could make my goal even harder to get to."

"Or it could do well." He thought of what his niece had said about his job, and how right she'd been. "I don't believe you're happy, doing what you're doing now."

"I'm not." She wrinkled her nose, and gave a startled laugh. "I haven't admitted that out loud yet, but I really don't think I can do it anymore. I'm burned out. I was burned out before I got sick, but now I really feel like I'm frantically chasing likes. I want to do something different for a change."

"So do it. If this MakeOut deal falls through, find something else. Don't be stuck in something you hate."

"It's not bad advice." She swallowed a bite of food. "What about you, how was your day?"

"Ah . . ." Since she'd just delivered good news, he hated

to bring down the mood, but he needed to share this with her. "Actually, not great. They seem to have reduced my role a little."

Her brow creased. "What? Why?"

"I don't know."

"Well, how do you feel?"

He thought about that for a second, pushed past his bruised pride. "I'm annoyed but not devastated. Luna is right, this show isn't for me."

"Do you miss your old job?"

"I do," he confessed. "I thought a drama here would offer me the same things." It didn't. *Hope Street* had no passion, no excitement. If he was bored, how would viewers feel? He longed for his old show, missed the wild storylines, the over-the-top characters, the dramatic close-ups.

"Oh no, Desi soaps are their own breed. There's nothing quite comparable to them here."

"I needed the move, though. I like it here. So it's not like I'll be able to return to my old job, even if the show hadn't ended."

She made a sympathetic noise. "You wrote for the show. It's clear you had a passion for it." She reached across the table and put her hand over his. "Maybe you should restart the soap here."

He chuckled. "They killed me off in the finale."

"How many identical twins did you have over its run? There's no such thing as dead in a soap opera."

"This is true." Dev turned his hand over and held hers. "Don't worry, I'll find a place for myself here."

"I have no doubt of it." She cocked her head. "Isn't it interesting that we both kind of hate our jobs? Like we're at a crossroads at the exact same time."

"I imagine we'll face many more crossroads over the years." He liked this part, talking them through with her. His problems seemed less intense when he had someone to share the burden with.

He wanted to accelerate this domesticity. A house. Once he had a proper home for them, and once Adil Uncle and Luna came back, he'd have more of that family feel. He didn't know yet how he'd balance that with the whole not rushing her thing, but he would. He'd vowed things would proceed at her pace, and he'd stick to it.

Her eyes smiled. "I imagine we will."

They may have only enjoyed a couple of days of wedded bliss, but he recognized the tone in her voice. Dev came to his feet and walked around the table to tug Jia up.

"Excuse me, I'm not done eating," she teased.

"We'll eat later." He kissed her, and she responded instantly, rising on her tiptoes. With their height difference, the logistics of intimacy were a little difficult, but not impossible. He hoisted her up and deposited her on the table, unsnapping the button on her jeans.

"Here?" She breathed.

"Unless you have an objection." He kissed her again.

Her head was shaking, but she gave him a verbal confirmation as soon as their mouths separated. "Nope, zero objections."

They were getting good at taking their clothes off fast,

though they only stripped off the bare minimum now. He actually liked this, when they were in too much of a rush to take everything off.

The best part of sex was her, and he paid attention to her cues. She liked his hands and his mouth, so he gave her both generously. It didn't take long for her, with his fingertips slicking over her clit and his lips on hers.

She gasped when she climaxed, her head tipping back. He pressed hot, open-mouthed kisses all over her neck and fell into her arms when he shuddered out his own release.

"I like this," she whispered into the silence of the room.

He let out a laugh. "Me too."

"It's going well so far, right?"

There was an odd note in her voice and he straightened up, pulling away from her. "Yes, I think so. Don't you?"

"Yup." Her smile was bright. "I like how we're going really slow, you know? Getting to know each other. Not rushing."

He feared his smile was too tight. It was good he hadn't demanded she move in properly, then. She needed time.

However, it wouldn't do for Luna to return next week and see Jia coming back and forth to the apartment, married or not, so he'd have to figure something out soon to give her the independence she wanted while still giving this marriage and them a chance.

It was a problem, but he'd always been good at solving those.

Chapter Twenty-Eight

"WHERE ARE you?"

Jia glanced up from her computer and refocused on her phone, where Ayesha's face was displayed. "What?"

"It's not home and it's not your studio." Ayesha gasped, and she leaned forward, delighted scandal on her face. "Jia! Are you living with Dev?"

"Be mature. He's my husband." She paused. Besides, she wasn't sure she could call the past week living together. She'd fetched a suitcase of clothes, and he'd only gotten around to clearing out a drawer for her yesterday. The most presence she had in this place was in the office, where he'd carved out a corner for her, and the bathroom, where they used the same skin products. "How is it going talking everyone out of a huge wedding reception?"

"Only Daddy is firmly on your side." Ayesha lowered her voice to mimic their father. "'We can't allow the groom's side to pay for everything, but five daughters isn't cheap, I should get a break on one of them by now.'"

Jia chuckled. "Sadia saved him money!" The first time because she eloped, and the second because her husband was wealthy and insisted on paying for everything.

"The elders didn't."

"Well, I will." Jia had felt obligated to post a couple wedding shots on her socials, but she still wanted glamorous photos of her and Dev, big Bollywood sweeping pictures. She even had locations in mind.

But social media and reality were two different things, and she wasn't about to waste oodles of money and time on a fancy reception, even if her new grandmother-in-law was going to pay for it. She had more important stuff to focus on, like the contracts MakeOut had sent over this morning. They were only nondisclosure agreements so they could talk further, but she'd enjoyed speaking with the executives there so far. She had all her fingers crossed.

"Jia?" Dev's voice came from the hallway.

"You sound busy," Ayesha said, again in a singsong voice.

Jia rolled her eyes. "We're not going to have a sex romp, Ayesha. It's the middle of the day."

"Oh. I can't believe I have to tell you this, old married lady, but I'm pretty sure sex isn't limited to after the sun goes down."

Jia ended the call on Ayesha's laughter and glanced up when Dev appeared in the doorway. Her heart melted a little, just as it did whenever she saw him. His face was bright.

He rarely looked stern anymore, and when he did, it was easy to tease him into a smile. She rose to her feet. "What's up?"

"Are you busy?"

"Not too busy."

"I have a surprise for you. Can you come with me?"

"Sure." Jia eyed Dev as she neared him. He was practically jumping in eagerness. "What's up with you?"

"Come. Hurry."

He refused to tell her what was up, even as they left his apartment building and went to the garage. She got in his car when he held her door open for her, moving her skirt when it might otherwise get caught in the door.

"Where are we going?" she asked as they left the garage.

He casually picked up her hand. This one-handed driving had made her nervous in the beginning, but now she liked the self-assured way he drove, and the way he couldn't seem to keep his hands away from her. "You'll see."

How strange. She could tell she wasn't going to get any more information out of him, so she relaxed back into the seat. They drove through a couple of neighborhoods, then up through the twisting hills, through residential neighborhoods.

"I was thinking, the flat might get too small for us, once Luna and Adil Uncle are back."

"Oh?" Her heart picked up speed. Okay, good. They were going to discuss what their lives were going to look like, long-term. It would be nice to not live out of a suitcase any longer.

"I'd like for us to have our own place. A proper fresh start, a more permanent one."

Her smile was slow. "I'd like that."

"Good. Because I've put an offer in on a place."

Her smile stopped. "You . . . bought a place? Already?"

"I know, it's not like me. Your impulsivity is rubbing off." He glanced at her. "I wanted to surprise you."

"Surprise," she said weakly. He'd bought their home without even showing it to her?

It's okay. Don't rain on his parade. He's clearly superexcited and proud of this. "I'd like to see it." That was the understatement of the century. "Is that where we're going?"

"Yes."

Anticipation replaced some of her unease when they pulled up in front of an unassuming white house. It was no mansion, and it also wasn't small. The home was well-kept, the lawn green and the flowers beautiful. Jia stopped outside the gate to the walkway and waited for Dev to open it for her. "It's cute," she enthused. Okay, so he should have consulted her first, but this was nice so far.

Her optimism grew when they got inside the vacant house and he showed her each room. There was a large master bedroom with a bathroom attached and two other en suite rooms. Plenty of space for Adil Uncle and Luna, and a guest room to boot for his or her family. The kitchen was charming instead of state of the art, and that suited her fine. In her mind, she began redecorating each room as she walked through, imagining it on social media. She could even document the renovations as they went! Talk about content. "Oh, it's adorable."

"You think so? Good." He cocked his head. "And I haven't shown you the best part. Come outside."

Jia followed Dev to the back and breathed in deep at the view. Perched as they were on the hill, they had a clear view of the valley. "Gorgeous."

"Oh yes, the view. I'm talking about this." He gestured.

She followed him to a small house and squealed. "A little house?"

"Yes." He smiled at her excitement and unlocked the door. Inside was a surprisingly spacious one-bedroom, one-bath home.

"I love it." She brushed her fingers over the white-and-black-checkered countertop.

"I thought it could be yours," he said quietly.

Like, as her studio? Her fake home for social media? She opened her mouth, to tell him that was perfect, but then he continued, "I thought, instead of bringing a suitcase like you're doing now, in the beginning at least, you could have your privacy here."

Jia blinked at him, uncertain if Dev was saying what she thought he was saying. "You want me to live in here? Even though we're married?"

"For a little while, sure. You could have your independence, and we can slowly get accustomed to living together."

She squinted at him. *What on* . . . "So you would live in the main house, and I would live here."

"Temporarily." He paced to the window and looked out. "I think this place has a better view than the house, to be honest."

She didn't care about the view. Had he lost all his marbles? *He's sane. He doesn't want to be with you.* Jia closed her eyes.

The confidence she'd so carefully cultivated since before her wedding deflated like a sad balloon. She was too much, and he didn't want to even live in the same house as her after their marriage. She'd annoyed him or frustrated him or she was too needy.

"Jia?"

She opened her eyes. "Hmm."

"Is everything okay?"

What could she say? No, it wasn't okay, but there was nothing she could do about that. She couldn't make him want to spend time with her. "Hmm."

She wasn't sure what she said to him after that, only that they drove back to Santa Monica in silence. She stirred when they pulled into the garage. "I have to go to my place," she said quietly.

"Do you need more clothes?"

Sure. "Yeah. And I need to see Katrina and Rhiannon." Hopefully they'd be home.

"Jia . . ." Dev held her arm when she would have gotten out. "You don't seem . . . right. Are you sure everything's okay?"

"Everything's fine." *You bought me a house and told me you don't want to live with me in it. After not even being married to me for a week.* The honeymoon was most definitely over. "I'll see you in a little while." And because she'd somehow fallen for her dense husband, she kissed him on the cheek.

Chapter Twenty-Nine

JIA HADN'T expected a party when she got home but when she opened the door to Katrina's house, that was what it sounded like was happening. She followed the noise to the kitchen, where she found Katrina, Rhiannon, and Lakshmi gathered around the kitchen table. They wore comfortable clothes and had fruity drinks spread out in front of them, and the music piping through the speakers was loud. Prince, if Jia wasn't mistaken.

They looked up when she walked in. "Well, well, well, look who decided to leave her man for a few—" Rhiannon started, then broke off. "What's wrong?"

"Nothing," Jia said.

"You're crying," Lakshmi pointed out, with a trace of panic in her voice, and came to her feet. "Again."

Jia brushed her fingers over her cheeks. "Oh, am I?" She wished she'd thought to tape some affirmations for herself, but she'd had none to play while she drove up. Of course she'd cried.

The other women all glanced at one another. Katrina

pasted a determined smile over her face. "Jia, come sit down."

It was too much work to pretend nothing was wrong, so Jia did just that, dropping down into a seat at the table. "Are you hungry?" Katrina continued, but she didn't wait or seem deterred by Jia's anemic no. She whirled away to the fridge, and Jia didn't bother to protest. If the world was ending, Katrina would pause while they were all running from zombies to make sure everyone was stuffed. That was how she rolled.

Rhiannon scooched her chair closer to Jia. "What happened? Did that inspirational body builder comment something passive-aggressive on one of your posts?" Her words were light but her eyes were serious.

Jia shook her head, wishing the water would stop leaking from her eyes. "No."

Lakshmi returned with a roll of paper towels and tore off a handful for Jia. "Is it your husband?"

Rhiannon gave a low growl in her throat when Jia buried her face in the towels. "Do we need to kill him, Jia?"

"We don't kill anyone," Lakshmi chided her boss. "Sienna, turn off."

The pleasant female robot voice came from the speakers. "Sienna is turning off."

Lakshmi waited a beat, then leaned forward. "You want us to kill him?"

Jia choked out a laugh. Katrina placed a sandwich in front of her, and she picked up a triangle to give her hands something to do. "No. There's no need for violence. It's dumb. He did something that was objectively thoughtful, and I got my feelings hurt." She nibbled at the sandwich.

"What did he do?"

"He bought us a house."

"Well, that is nice," Katrina said as she sat down. She picked up her daiquiri and took a sip. "But that can't be the only thing he did. Did you disagree on what house to buy?"

"No, because I didn't know what house he was going to buy. He just bought it. Like, done deal."

Lakshmi drew in a sharp breath. "Oh no. I would hate that."

"I did, at first, and then I saw the house, and it's exactly what I would have wanted. So I kinda lost my annoyance over that."

"Then why did you come here crying?" Rhiannon asked slowly.

"Because the place has a little house in the back, and he said I could stay there," Jia wailed.

The women exchanged a look. "Wait. Like, by yourself?" Rhiannon asked.

Jia nodded and swiped the rough towel over her nose.

"Did you ever discuss living separately before?"

"No," Jia said.

Lakshmi picked up her drink. "I know you don't drink, honey, but you sure you don't want a shot?"

Jia might have snatched the bottle of tequila if she didn't know even a sip would leave her ill tomorrow.

Rhiannon drummed her fingers on the table. "I don't understand. He doesn't want to live with you?"

Self-pity settled into Jia's bones. "I guess not."

"That doesn't sound right," Katrina said slowly. "You've been telling us every thoughtful thing this guy has been doing for weeks. Why would he suddenly run cold like this?"

Jia dashed at her eyes with the backs of her hands. "Because he realized he doesn't like me, only we're married now, and he can't back out."

"Eh." Lakshmi shook her head. "There's ways out. That doesn't hold water. There's no need to banish you to the basement."

"Then maybe he didn't want it in the first place. Maybe he got pressured into everything and he's making the best of a bad situation. Maybe he just wanted the money from his inheritance."

"In that case, fuck him." Rhiannon wrapped her arm around Jia's shoulders, and she leaned into her friend's side. "Tomorrow, we'll go get your stuff from his place."

Something broke in Jia at the thought of never seeing Dev again. Oof, that would hurt way more than any catfishing could.

Lakshmi cracked her knuckles. "We can still kill him, if you like. Make it look like an accident."

"Wait, wait, wait." Katrina reached across the table and grasped Jia's hands. "Let's all take a second. Jia, did you ask him why he did this?"

"No."

"Because as someone who has been with someone for a minute now who doesn't like talking or explaining themselves but is selfless almost to a fault, I can tell you that occasionally you have to directly ask them why they're doing what they do. You might be surprised by the answer. No one tells you that this is a big part of relationships. Sometimes it's not all about big misunderstandings." Katrina's eyes were warm and kind. "Sometimes it's about learning how to talk to each other. We all have insecurities, and we have to help each other navigate around them."

"Ugh." Jia scrubbed her eyes. "It's so much work."

"Yeah, I know. I'd like to say it's always worth it. For some people, it isn't. I think for you, it could be."

Lakshmi handed her another paper towel, and Jia dabbed at her eyes. "What if he gives me a terrible answer? How will I recover?"

"With us, silly," Katrina said matter-of-factly. "With your sisters. Ain't no man in the world who is impossible to recover from. You only need the right support to do it."

Jia sighed. "Loving people is so annoying."

"It is," Rhiannon agreed. "I also have good feelings about you and Dev, though." She rose to her feet. "Just in case . . . Sienna, turn back on and tell us what the maximum murder sentence is in the state of California."

Jia's watery chuckle fell over Sienna's robotic confusion. "I'm tired."

"Then you'll sleep here," Katrina said. She nudged Jia's

plate toward her, and Jia reluctantly picked up the rest of the sandwich. "Tomorrow, you'll confront your husband and ask him what the hell he was thinking. And then you see what he says. He'll either give you a good answer, or an answer that will result in us preventing Lakshmi from putting a hit on him."

Lakshmi nodded, mouth turned down. "I am on board with this, though I really hate how little you all utilize my dark web skills."

"So much for all my newfound confidence and not caring what people think of me," Jia said glumly to Lakshmi.

"One, it's your husband. You can care what he thinks of you. Two, did you miss the part where I told you it took me years of therapy to get that kind of confidence? I gave you this magical tool like two minutes ago. Have a little patience."

Jia's spirits rose a little. "That's true."

Rhiannon looked between them. "What are you two talking about? Are you friends now?"

"We're getting there." Lakshmi winked at Jia. "Which is good. Trying to pass the Bechdel test with only you two is tough."

Jia glanced around the group. "Has someone else been having man problems?"

"We were trying to explain to Katrina that Jas most definitely intended her ring as an engagement ring, but for someone who loves communication, she doesn't want to clarify things with her boo," Lakshmi explained.

Katrina waved her hand. The diamond on it glinted. "It's a promise ring!"

Lakshmi snorted. "Get engaged already and put that man out of his misery."

"If you got engaged, Rhiannon probably won't feel as bad about moving into Samson's place," Jia said, without thinking, then winced. "Oops. Sorry, Rhiannon."

Katrina turned to face her best friend. "What is she talking about? You want to move in with Samson?"

Rhiannon's lips thinned, but she sighed. "We've been talking about it."

"You should do it. Are you not doing it because of me?" Katrina's face tightened. "Rhiannon, you're gone more often than not right now anyway. Put *your* man out of his misery."

"I didn't want you to think I was abandoning you!"

"Neither of you is abandoning me. We're not going to stop being friends, are we?" Katrina gestured at the table. "This group is staying intact, even if we all live under separate roofs. Don't insult me by suggesting otherwise."

"So Rhiannon is moving in with her man, and Katrina and Jia are going to learn to communicate with theirs." Lakshmi drained her glass. "And some day, we shall pass that elusive Bechdel."

An imp of mischief worked its way to Jia's shoulder, and she welcomed it after her recent misery. "If we talk about your love life, Lakshmi, do we pass it?"

"There's no love life, so sure."

"None?" Jia took a larger bite of her sandwich. "It doesn't

take long to move from friend zone to end zone, I'm just saying."

Lakshmi gave a mock growl. Jia welcomed the chuckles, as well as the paper towel roll Lakshmi tossed at her. She wasn't looking forward to asking Dev what he was thinking tomorrow, but at least for tonight, she'd be with the people who would help her if things went sour. She was a lucky girl, with or without a ring on her finger.

Chapter Thirty

DEV HAD never been an anxious person, but then again, he'd never had his new wife entirely shut down and suddenly run away. He'd texted Jia twice since she'd gone home, ostensibly to get more clothes, and her responses had been short and sweet, and delayed, like she didn't have her phone perpetually in her hand. He hadn't liked sleeping without her in their bed last night. When it had become their bed, he wasn't sure.

"Something is wrong."

He returned his attention back to his phone and his grandmother. She'd called from the beach to give him an update on Luna. "No, nothing. Let me speak to Luna." He smiled at his niece. She was covered in sand, and dressed in a bright green two-piece swimsuit his grandmother had surely bought for her. "Hello, beti. Are you having fun and wearing sunscreen?"

"Hi, Kaka. Yes. How are you and Jia, I mean, Auntie, settling in?"

"Well," he lied.

Luna's eyes flickered away, clearly distracted. "Good.

Okay, I'm going to go. Adil Uncle found a Frisbee. Love you!"

He paused. Had she ever told him she loved him before? He wanted her to say it again, in every language she knew, but she was already gone, his grandmother back. "She's having fun," he said, instead. Her skin had glowed with health and affection.

"She is. Now, tell me what's wrong."

His grandmother looked far too determined to put off, so he quickly told her about his problems at work, which were a problem, just not *the* problem.

She made a dismissive gesture when he was finished. "Good riddance. Who cares. Make your own show."

"I can't just make my own show. That's not how things work."

"You can when you're a Dixit. You miss your old show? Make it again, set it in America, for the American market. Done."

He stopped. It was almost exactly what Jia had suggested. "I can't do that."

"You shaped a number of the arcs on your old show, so you can do it creatively. You're about to receive a large sum of money, so you can do it financially. What is stopping you?"

Nothing. He could do exactly what he loved, tell the stories he wanted to tell, in the location he wanted to be in. He could cast unknown talent, the actors Hollywood ignored. He could use his grandfather's money for something good, to lift up people who weren't lucky enough to be born Dixits, and entertain all classes of people. Oh, the old man would *hate* that. "It's something to think about."

"Now, what's really bothering you?"

He didn't want to tell his grandmother about Jia, but then he looked around his quiet flat again. "Jia went to her house yesterday and hasn't come back."

"Why?"

"I don't know. I showed her the home I bought us, and she seemed to like it, but then she became upset and left."

"You didn't seek her input in buying her own house?" Aji muttered a brief curse. "I did not teach any of you boys anything. A woman wants a say in where she is going to live, Devanand."

Oh. She had a point. Dev had never thought Jia might want to go through the tedious chore of finding a house and negotiating and closing. He rubbed his hands over his face. "I didn't think of that."

His grandmother's tone turned lecturing. "Here is what you're going to do. When she gets over her anger and comes back, you will be nice to her, you will say sorry, and you will cook her a good meal. Understand?"

"Yes, Aji."

"Do not screw this up. You got a sweet girl. A miracle you found her, really, when you're such a house chicken."

His lips twitched. "Yes, Aji."

She sniffed. "It is good I am here to give you advice."

Dev cradled his phone. "It is good. Have you considered extending your trip?"

"For how long?"

"Indefinitely."

Shweta gave an incredulous laugh. "I don't belong here."

"Says who? Don't you like it?"

"Of course I like it."

Dev fiddled with a pen. "I think Luna is happier when we're both regularly in her life. She'll probably adjust better to Jia if she could visit you whenever she wished it."

Aji looked toward the ocean. A lock of silver hair fell over her forehead. "I do miss her."

His heart swelled at the gruff admission. "She misses you. I do not like thinking I took her away from you. If you came here for extended visits, even, it would be good."

"There is more freedom here, is there not? No one standing outside the gates, no one paying attention to me when I go to the market."

"There is."

"I like attention, but not having it sometimes has its perks," Aji mused. "I will consider it."

"Good."

"Chandu would come with me, though." There was a gleam in his grandmother's eye that Dev had not expected to ever see. "We are enjoying each other's company, if you know what I mean."

Ew. That is, he was happy for his grandmother. But it was his *grandmother.* And his *agent.*

Ew.

The front door opened and closed, and Dev straightened, relieved on every possible axis. "Jia's here. I must go."

Shweta's laugh was throaty. "Good luck."

Dev hung up and placed his phone on the island as Jia appeared in the kitchen. "Hello," he said, stilted. He gestured at his phone. "I was talking to my family."

Her eyes were shadowed. Were they bloodshot? Had she been crying? "How is everyone?"

"Good."

She drifted into the kitchen, pulled out a stool next to where he sat, and clasped her hands on the granite counter. They were both silent for a moment, and then both spoke at once. "I'm sorry—"

"I need to ask—"

They stopped, and Dev gestured. "Sorry, go ahead."

"No, you go ahead. What are you sorry for?"

This felt vaguely like a trap, but Dev forged ahead. "I'm sorry I bought a house without consulting you at all."

Jia's mouth turned down. "Asking me first would have been nice."

"I'm used to doing this stuff, is all. The boring chores. I thought it would be a nice surprise, and if it was a done deal, you wouldn't have to worry about anything."

Jia nodded slowly. "Okay. That makes sense."

"We can still back out. We can go look at houses together, find one we both like and want to live in."

"I'll be honest, I didn't hate the house. Yeah, I was annoyed at first, but then I saw the place, and you did a really good job. It's probably exactly the place I would have picked. Like, consult me next time, but this once, it turned out okay."

Relief washed over him, followed immediately by confusion. "But wait, then why were you upset? You seemed mad."

"Because you got me my own place." Her voice was so tiny, he had to lean forward to listen.

Then he wondered if he'd misheard her. "You got upset because I said the back house could be yours?"

"You said I could live there. Away from you and Luna." The hurt in her gaze hurt him. "How did you think that would make me feel? Like you didn't want me around. Like maybe you found me annoying or too much or . . ."

He closed his hands over hers, and she stopped. "Jia . . . no. I want to be with you all the time. There is nothing I love more than spending time with you." He struggled to express himself. "When I'm with you, it's like . . . like I'm covered in a blanket of peace. Peace that makes me laugh."

He was rewarded with a choked chuckle. "What a terrible analogy."

"I know. I'm better at flowery analogies in Hindi." He rubbed his thumb over the back of her hand. "You staying in that house . . . it was a suggestion, because I wanted to give you options. You lived with your family, then Ayesha, then Katrina and Rhiannon. I wanted to give you some independence before you lived with me. Adil Uncle and my aunt did that. Did the nikah to make things legal, and then lived separately until a year later."

"Well, I don't want that."

"I don't either. I want you to be happy. I was merely giving you options so you could be happy."

"We both need to be happy. If you tell me I should live alone, I'm going to assume that's what would make *you* happy."

"It wouldn't. I would tolerate it."

She picked at her cuticles. "Then you have to say that. The back house can be for Adil Uncle or guests or a studio. I live with you. In your bed, in your house."

Dev's lips slowly turned up. "I would be okay with that."

She slipped off the stool to wrap her arms around his neck. He buried his face in her neck and breathed in her floral scent, relief filling him.

She kissed his neck, then kissed up to his ear. "Guess what," she whispered.

He turned his head, so their lips were close to each other. "What?"

"I love you."

His smile came from deep inside of him, and he got off the stool to pick her up and hug her close. Her body was soft and got softer as he carried her to their bedroom. "I love you, too. Are you sure you like that house?"

"Yes. But I get to renovate it. You may have opinions," she added graciously, as she slipped out of his hold and began unbuttoning her shirt. "But don't you dare think you're fixing it up without me."

He couldn't resist kissing her on her pursed lips. When they were naked and tangled together, and he was driving inside her, he wondered how he'd gotten so lucky.

The pleasure came upon him quickly, but the greatest

pleasure was afterward, when she curled up in his arms happily. "I'm lucky," she said, her voice muffled.

He hadn't realized he'd spoken out loud. "We both are. Fate certainly took a twisted road to get us here. A comedy of errors." How many variables had brought them to this place? His family's name, his cousin's foolishness, his old words, perfectly placed paparazzi.

Jia rolled over onto him and stretched. "What is it called when it's not mistakes that get you to the end? A comedy of perfection?"

Dev chuckled. "Or of love. A comedy of love?"

"I'll take it," she announced, kissing him.

He'd take it, too.

Jɪᴀ ᴡᴏᴋᴇ ᴜᴘ to Dev saying something in Hindi against her ear. Her eyes were bleary, the room dark. She was a little sweaty from being wrapped up in his big spoon, but that was a small price to pay.

She had no illusions that everything would be perfect now. This was real life. They had families and friends and lives they had to figure out how to mesh together. She was confident in their chances, though. They'd talk and communicate and laugh and push and challenge each other. What more could she possibly ask for?

Her stomach chose that moment to growl. They'd made love for a long time, forgoing all sustenance. A girl needed to eat.

He whispered something again, which reminded her that

she needed to download a language app soon. She turned her head to look over her shoulder. "What did you say?" It was probably about his arm being numb. She had been sleeping on it for a while. The trials of the big spoon.

Dev kissed her neck. His hand skated up her belly and she shivered. "I said, that line from my show was true. I did search the universe for you."

The heroine rests securely in her lover's arms while the spotlight dims.

She interlaced her fingers with his and pulled him in close. Food could wait. This was sustenance, too. "I'm so glad that search led to this."

About the author

About the book

Insights,
Interviews
& More . . .

Meet Alisha Rai

M. Ladrigan

ALISHA RAI pens award-winning contemporary romances and is the first author to have an indie-published book appear on the *Washington Post*'s annual Best Books list. Her books have also been recognized as Best Books of the Year by NPR, Vulture, *Entertainment Weekly*, Amazon, *Kirkus*, Bustle, and *Cosmopolitan*. She spends most of her time daydreaming, traveling, and tweeting.

To find out more about her books or to sign up for her newsletter, visit www.alisharai.com. ✍

Dear Readers

Dear Readers,

When I titled this series Modern Love, I did so with a wink. One of the things I find beautiful and frustrating about contemporary novels is that they're a snapshot of reality at the time they're written. The world can and does change rapidly. Not much can actually stay "modern" indefinitely.

Love, though? Love is always fresh and new and cutting-edge. In a hundred years, when people have progressed to swiping holograms instead of pictures, and the technology in these books belongs in museums, I hope one of my great-grandnieces pauses in her self-driving hovercraft to identify with the love in Modern Love.

I wrote *First Comes Like* during a globally difficult snapshot of time, one filled with loss and isolation and stress for me and everyone I know. I have always been an optimistic person, and I write optimistic books, but finding optimism during such a massive crisis is a challenge even for us professional romantics.

In order to keep going, I sought out every tiny pocket of happiness I could find. Sometimes that meant marveling at how technology could keep my far-flung friends and family ▶

Dear Readers *(continued)*

connected. Sometimes it meant driving out to an almost deserted ghost town so I could gaze at art crafted by long-gone artists.* Sometimes it just meant cheering when a plant I thought I killed sprouted a tiny new leaf.

But many times, most times, it meant sitting on my couch with a good book written by a favorite author.

I hope this book and this series is a pocket of happiness for you, whether you're reading it on release day or having it scanned into your brain via a chip in a hundred years. Thank you for taking this road trip with me.

All my love,
Alisha

*Like Rhiannon, Katrina, and Jia, I'm a California transplant, and exploring this state has been a great joy. I've taken significant liberties fictionalizing Bombay Beach in this book, but the art installations are all real and worth a visit. If you do go play influencer, please remember to support the local economy however you can!

Reading Group Guide

1. Jia is furious and mortified when she discovers she's been catfished. Can you imagine ever being in a similar situation? How would you react?

2. Do you think Jia is right to eventually, even grudgingly, forgive Arjun?

3. What does being a social media influencer mean to you? Do you see it as a "real" job?

4. Jia hates being described as "too much" or "a lot." Do you understand why that upsets her?

5. Dev thought both his grandparents didn't approve of his mother because she was of a lower class and different religion. His grandmother seems to welcome Jia, despite their differences. Do you believe Shweta when she says her husband didn't permit her to have a say back then? Or is she simply extremely eager for Dev to get married?

6. Jia's relationship with her eldest sisters can be contentious. Are they too hard on her? Is she too defensive with them? ▶

7. Do you think Jia and Luna will eventually get along? Do you think she will treat Luna like a daughter/niece or more like a sister?

8. Lakshmi makes Jia realize that most of her insecurities stem from a fear of disappointing people. Can you empathize with that fear? How could she overcome it?

9. Do you think Chandu misled the press to believe Jia and Dev were engaged purely out of practical reasons? Or do you think he had an ulterior motive?

10. Jia notes that she and Dev are both at a crossroads in their professional lives, even as their personal lives seem settled. Where do you see the couple in five years? ∾

MORE FROM ALISHA RAI

GIRL GONE VIRAL

"*Girl Gone Viral* is a fun, sexy rom-com
that's impossible to resist."

— PopSugar

THE RIGHT SWIPE

"Alisha Rai delivers compelling emotion,
fascinating characters, and edgy romance in a razor-sharp,
thoroughly modern voice that readers will adore. I sure did!"

— Jayne Ann Krentz

HURTS TO LOVE YOU

"True to Rai's style, family secrets and surprises add complexity
to this strong story about how wealth and privilege can do as
much to destroy happiness as to facilitate it."

— *Publishers Weekly*

WRONG TO NEED YOU

"Rai has crafted a series as deliciously soapy as a CW drama . . .
some of the best romance writing of the year here."

— *Entertainment Weekly*

HATE TO WANT YOU

"Alisha Rai blends emotional characters with passionate sensuality
in some of the best examples of erotic romance available."

— Sarah MacLean for *The Washington Post*